NEW TOEIC 新制多益

聽力 5 回

附音檔
QRcode

全真模擬試題 ＋ 詳盡解析

LC

笛藤出版

NEW 新制多益
TOEIC
聽力 5 回

附音檔 QRcode
全真模擬試題 ＋ 詳盡解析

NEW TOEIC新制多益：聽力五回 全真模擬試題＋詳盡解析 /
Michael A. Putlack等合著；陳怡臻譯.
-- 初版. -- 臺北市：笛藤, 2020.03
　　面；　公分
ISBN 978-957-710-780-0（平裝）
1.多益測驗
805.1895　　　　　　　　　　　　　　　　109002105

2022年4月27日　初版第2刷　定價 380 元

作者	Michael A. Putlack、Stephen Poirier
	Tony Covello、多樂院多益研究所
譯者	陳怡臻
編輯	江品萱
封面設計	王舒玗
總編輯	賴巧凌
發行所	笛藤出版圖書有限公司
發行人	林建仲
地址	台北市中山區長安東路二段171號3樓3室
電話	(02) 2777-3682
傳真	(02) 2777-3672
總經銷	聯合發行股份有限公司
地址	新北市新店區寶橋路235巷6弄6號2樓
電話	(02)2917-8022・(02)2917-8042
製版廠	造極彩色印刷製版股份有限公司
地址	新北市中和區中山路2段340巷36號
電話	(02)2240-0333・(02)2248-3904
印刷廠	皇甫彩藝印刷股份有限公司
地址	新北市中和區中正路988巷10號
電話	(02) 3234-5871
郵撥帳戶	八方出版股份有限公司
郵撥帳號	19809050

前言

　　多益在全世界中是公認具權威的英語考試之一。也因為如此，在學校或是職場上判斷一個人的英語實力時，多以多益分數作為標準，但是想要得到期望的分數卻不容易。

　　若是想在多益考試中取得理想成績，首先必須要有基本英語實力作為基礎，但即使已經具備基本實力，卻無法瞭解考試的特點或是對考試沒有充分準備的話，在考場上是絕對無法發揮出自己真正的實力。

　　〈用500個問題完成的多益實戰〉系列是透過針對不同的領域分成的五次模擬考試幫助考生能夠在實際考試中充分地發揮出自己的實力。在這本書中收錄的所有試題都反映出了多益的最新方向，其試題難度也與實際試題難度相同。因此，透過本系列學習的考生們能夠在較短的時間內培養出對於實際面對考試的適應能力。

　　我們多樂院多益研究所肩負著驕傲及使命感開發了和實際多益試題最為接近的模擬試題，而本系列就是其成果之一。真心地希望透過此書讓所有考生們都能得到自己期望的多益分數。

多樂院多益研究所

目錄

請搭配音檔進行 https://reurl.cc/vnygxo

多益是什麼

多益(TOEIC)是Test of English for International Communication的縮寫，這是用來測試非英語系國家的人在國際環境中生活或執行業務時所需要的實用英語能力考試。目前不只是韓國和日本，全世界約有60個國家每年會有400萬名以上的考生報考多益，而其考試結果也會在招聘及晉升、海外派遣工作人員的選拔等多種領域上作為選擇的依據之一。

● 考試題型

類別	PART	題型內容		題數	作答時間	配分
Listening Comprehension	1	照片描述		6	45分	495分
	2	應答問題		25		
	3	簡短對話		39		
	4	簡短文章		30		
Reading Comprehension	5	句子填空		30	75分	495分
	6	段落填空		16		
	7	閱讀理解	多篇閱讀	29		
			單篇閱讀	28		
TOTAL				200	120分	990分

● 出題內容

多益考試的目的是為了測試日常生活和執行業務所需要的英語能力，所以出題內容也不會脫離這個範圍。即使是在涉及商務相關主題的情況下，也不會要求具備有專門知識，並且也不會要求瞭解特定國家或文化。具體的出題內容如下。

一般商務（General Business）	契約、協商、行銷、營業、策劃、會議相關
辦公室（Office）	公司內部規定、辦公室流程、辦公室器材及傢俱相關
人事（Personal）	求職、招聘、晉升、退休、工資、獎勵相關
財務（Finance and Budgeting）	投資、稅務、會計、銀行業務相關
製造（Manufacturing）	製造、全套整組設備經營、品質管理相關
開發（Corporate Development）	研究、調查、實驗、新產品研發相關
採購（Purchasing）	購物、訂貨、裝貨、結算相關
外食（Dining Out）	午餐、晚餐、聚餐、招待會相關
保健（Health）	醫院預約、看醫生、醫療保險業務相關
旅遊（Travel）	交通方式、住宿、機票預訂及取消相關
娛樂（Entertainment）	觀看電影及戲劇、欣賞演出、參觀展示會相關
房屋／公司地產（Housing / Corporate Property）	不動產買賣及租賃、電力及瓦斯服務相關

● 考試當天流程

應考生需攜帶身分證（或有個人大頭照之有效證件）及文具(2B鉛筆、橡皮擦)，於考前三十分鐘抵達考場，並依工作人員指示進入考場就座。

時間	行程
9:20 - 9:40	**考場就座** 依准考證號碼依序入座，非考試相關物品須放置於工作人員指定位置。
9:40 - 9:50	**注意事項說明** 在答案卡上寫好姓名、准考證號碼等，並回答有關職業或是應考次數等相關問券調查。
9:50	**測驗時間開始，禁止進入考場** 測驗開始時便禁止出入，遲到者便視同放棄考試資格。
9:50 - 10:05	**核對身分證** 在聽力測驗開始之前，監考人員會核對身分並在答案卡上簽名。 閱讀測驗時，監考人員會再次進行核對並簽名。
10:08 - 10:10	**破損檢查** 確認拿到的試題本有無破損，確認後在試題本上填寫准考證號碼，在答案卡上填寫試題本編號。即使發現試題本有破損，若考試開始的話則不會給予更換試題本，此時重要的是應當要迅速地再檢查過一遍。
10:10 - 10:55	**聽力測驗作答** 45分鐘的時間作答聽力測驗的問題。
10:55 - 12:10	**閱讀測驗作答** 75分鐘的時間作答閱讀測驗的問題。

● 成績查詢

可從台灣區多益官方網站（http://www.toeic.com.tw）查詢成績。
成績單發放則是依照應試者報考時選擇的方式選擇郵寄或是網路發放。

模擬考試分數計算方法

多益分數是以5分為一單位來計分，每領域的滿分都為495分。總分(Total Score)則是會落在10分到990分之間，兩領域都獲得滿分的話則會拿到990分，但是實際成績是根據多益特有的統計處理方式計算，因此不能單純地以正確答案個數或是錯誤答案個數來計算多益成績。但模擬考試通常可以透過下列兩種方法來估算自己的分數。

● **單純利用換算法的情況：以每題5分來計算**

   聽力測驗答對75題，閱讀測驗答對69題的情況→(375)+(345)=720分

● **利用分數換算表的情況**

Listening Comprehension		Reading Comprehension	
答對題數	換算分數	答對題數	換算分數
96-100	475-495	96-100	460-495
91-95	435-495	91-95	425-490
86-90	405-475	86-90	395-465
81-85	370-450	81-85	370-440
76-80	345-420	76-80	335-415
71-75	320-390	71-75	310-390
66-70	290-360	66-70	280-365
61-65	265-335	61-65	250-335
56-60	235-310	56-60	220-305
51-55	210-280	51-55	195-270
46-50	180-255	46-50	165-240
41-45	155-230	41-45	140-215
36-40	125-205	36-40	115-180
31-35	105-175	31-35	95-145
26-30	85-145	26-30	75-120
21-25	60-115	21-25	60-95
16-20	30-90	16-20	45-75
11-15	5-70	11-15	30-55
6-10	5-60	6-10	10-40
1-5	5-50	1-5	5-30
0	5-35	0	5-15

   聽力測驗答對90題，閱讀測驗答對76題的情況→(405～475)+(335～415)=740～890分

Actual Test 實戰測驗

1

LISTENING TEST

In the Listening test, you will be asked to demonstrate how well you understand spoken English. The entire Listening test will last approximately 45 minutes. There are four parts, and directions are given for each part. You must mark your answers on the separate answer sheet. Do not write your answers in your test book.

PART 1

Directions: For each question in this part, you will hear four statements about a picture in your test book. When you hear the statements, you must select the one statement that best describes what you see in the picture. Then find the number of the question on your answer sheet and mark your answer. The statements will not be printed in your test book and will be spoken only one time.

Statement (D), "The man is holding his hands together," is the best description of the picture, so you should select answer (D) and mark it on your answer sheet.

1.

2.

GO ON TO THE NEXT PAGE

3.

4.

5.

6.

GO ON TO THE NEXT PAGE ➤

13

PART 2

Directions: You will hear a question or statement and three responses spoken in English. They will not be printed in your test book and will be spoken only one time. Select the best response to the question or statement and mark the letter (A), (B), or (C) on your answer sheet.

7. Mark your answer on your answer sheet.

8. Mark your answer on your answer sheet.

9. Mark your answer on your answer sheet.

10. Mark your answer on your answer sheet.

11. Mark your answer on your answer sheet.

12. Mark your answer on your answer sheet.

13. Mark your answer on your answer sheet.

14. Mark your answer on your answer sheet.

15. Mark your answer on your answer sheet.

16. Mark your answer on your answer sheet.

17. Mark your answer on your answer sheet.

18. Mark your answer on your answer sheet.

19. Mark your answer on your answer sheet.

20. Mark your answer on your answer sheet.

21. Mark your answer on your answer sheet.

22. Mark your answer on your answer sheet.

23. Mark your answer on your answer sheet.

24. Mark your answer on your answer sheet.

25. Mark your answer on your answer sheet.

26. Mark your answer on your answer sheet.

27. Mark your answer on your answer sheet.

28. Mark your answer on your answer sheet.

29. Mark your answer on your answer sheet.

30. Mark your answer on your answer sheet.

31. Mark your answer on your answer sheet.

PART 3

Directions: You will hear some conversations between two or more people. You will be asked to answer three questions about what the speakers say in each conversation. Select the best response to each question and mark the letter (A), (B), (C), or (D) on your answer sheet. The conversations will not be printed in your test book and will be spoken only one time.

32. Why did the woman call the man?

(A) To ask for advice
(B) To demand an apology
(C) To request repairs
(D) To make a suggestion

33. What is suggested about the woman?

(A) She called the man earlier.
(B) She is a customer service representative.
(C) She is leaving the office soon.
(D) She is upset with the man.

34. What does the man tell the woman to do?

(A) Wait for him to visit her office
(B) Borrow a coworker's machine
(C) Consider purchasing some equipment
(D) Request more funding for the budget

35. Who most likely is the man?

(A) A real estate agent
(B) A banker
(C) An architect
(D) A financial advisor

36. What does the woman ask about?

(A) How much she needs to spend
(B) When a contract will be signed
(C) Where she should meet the man
(D) Why her offer was rejected

37. What will the woman probably do next?

(A) Schedule a meeting with a bank
(B) Ask about a price
(C) Give the man some information
(D) Offer to negotiate

38. In which department does the man work?

(A) Accounting
(B) Shipping
(C) Sales
(D) Personnel

39. What is the problem?

(A) The man has rejected the woman's claim.
(B) The woman did not complete her application.
(C) Insurance will not cover the woman's operation.
(D) Some information on a form is not accurate.

40. What will the woman most likely do next?

(A) Contact her insurance company
(B) Schedule a meeting with the man
(C) Finish a work assignment
(D) Sign some documents

41. What are the speakers mainly discussing?

(A) An investment made in their company
(B) A decline in their market share
(C) An opportunity to acquire a competitor
(D) A product available on the market

42. How does the woman suggest raising funds?

(A) By getting a bank loan
(B) By raising money themselves
(C) By finding investors
(D) By selling some of their assets

43. What does the man say he will do?

(A) Talk with some lawyers
(B) Call the owner of Deerfield Manufacturing
(C) Make a bid on some items
(D) Invest his personal funds

GO ON TO THE NEXT PAGE

44. What does the woman say about Samantha?

(A) She did not complete an assignment on time.
(B) She forgot to attend a conference.
(C) She used some incorrect material.
(D) She photocopied the wrong papers.

45. Why is the woman concerned?

(A) She is late for a meeting.
(B) She is unprepared for a presentation.
(C) She has not made any sales yet.
(D) She cannot log on to her computer.

46. What does the man offer to do?

(A) Print a report
(B) Speak with a sales representative
(C) Give a speech
(D) Rewrite a document

47. According to the woman, what happened last week?

(A) A special dinner was held.
(B) New employees were hired.
(C) A sales record was set.
(D) Awards were given out.

48. Why is the man pleased?

(A) He will get some extra money.
(B) His transfer application was accepted.
(C) He signed a new client to a contract.
(D) He met the CEO of the company.

49. What does the woman imply when she says, "You don't want to do that"?

(A) The man had better apply for a promotion.
(B) The man needs to finish his report.
(C) The man should cancel his meeting.
(D) The man ought to apologize at once.

50. What is the conversation mainly about?

(A) A seminar
(B) A conference
(C) A workshop
(D) A job fair

51. Where will the man post an announcement?

(A) In a newspaper
(B) On the Internet
(C) On the bulletin board
(D) In the employee lounge

52. What does the woman say she will do?

(A) Discuss an event with some colleagues
(B) Apply to teach a training program
(C) Arrange a meeting with her supervisor
(D) Take the day off tomorrow

53. What are the speakers mainly discussing?

(A) An upcoming interview
(B) The location of a business
(C) A meeting with Mr. Briggs
(D) A work assignment

54. How will the man go to Jenkins Consulting?

(A) By subway
(B) By bus
(C) By car
(D) By taxi

55. What does Mary offer to do?

(A) Show the man where a place is
(B) Complete the man's report
(C) Talk to Mr. Briggs
(D) Call someone at Jenkins Consulting

56. What is the conversation mostly about?

(A) Changing jobs
(B) Moving to a new home
(C) Getting managerial experience
(D) Asking for a pay raise

57. What does the woman mean when she says, "Definitely"?

(A) She is excited about working in Montgomery.
(B) The open position is better than her current job.
(C) She will apply to transfer to another branch.
(D) Her career is something she considers important.

58. What does the man suggest the woman do?

(A) Take classes at a college
(B) Buy a better car
(C) Move to another city
(D) Get some more experience

59. Who most likely is the man?

(A) A cashier
(B) A customer
(C) A supervisor
(D) A store owner

60. What is the problem?

(A) The wrong date was printed.
(B) An item has expired.
(C) Some products are out of stock.
(D) The customer lost her credit card.

61. What does Denice tell the man to do?

(A) Read the local newspaper
(B) Apologize to the woman
(C) Process a return
(D) Give a customer a discount

Summer Lecture Series

Speaker	Date
Harold Grace	June 11
Angela Steele	June 28
Marcia White	July 16
Orlando Watson	August 2

62. Look at the graphic. Which date is a replacement speaker needed on?

(A) June 11
(B) June 28
(C) July 16
(D) August 2

63. What does the man say about Derrick Stone?

(A) He is an employee at the library.
(B) His schedule is full this summer.
(C) He no longer lives in the area.
(D) He was considered as a speaker last year.

64. What will the man probably do next?

(A) Contact Derrick Stone
(B) Reschedule a lecture
(C) Send funds to a speaker
(D) Print a flyer for an event

GO ON TO THE NEXT PAGE ➔

Department	Floor
Sales / Shipping	First
Accounting / HR	Second
R&D	Third
Marketing	Fourth

		2	1	Main Office
Elevator				
		3	Employee Lounge	4

65. What is the man's problem?

(A) He is late for a meeting.
(B) He forgot to bring some papers.
(C) He cannot find an office.
(D) He does not have his ID card.

66. Look at the graphic. Which floor will the speakers go to?

(A) The first floor
(B) The second floor
(C) The third floor
(D) The fourth floor

67. What is indicated about the speakers?

(A) They worked together at a different company.
(B) They both live in Scofield.
(C) They will collaborate on a project soon.
(D) They have a meeting scheduled for today.

68. What is suggested about the man?

(A) He has not met the woman before.
(B) He drove to the woman's office.
(C) He hopes to sign the woman as a client.
(D) He is only meeting the woman.

69. Look at the graphic. Where is the conference room?

(A) Room 1
(B) Room 2
(C) Room 3
(D) Room 4

70. What does the man request?

(A) Some refreshments
(B) Some visual equipment
(C) Photocopies
(D) A pen and a notepad

PART 4

Directions: You will hear some talks given by a single speaker. You will be asked to answer three questions about what the speaker says in each talk. Select the best response to each question and mark the letter (A), (B), (C), or (D) on your answer sheet. The talks will not be printed in your test book and will be spoken only one time.

71. What is the speaker mainly discussing?
(A) Plans to acquire a competitor
(B) The company's yearly profit
(C) The auto insurance industry
(D) Recent insurance pricing issues

72. What does the speaker want to do?
(A) Set up a meeting
(B) Change positions
(C) Purchase some insurance
(D) Analyze a rival company

73. What will most likely happen next?
(A) A budget will be explained.
(B) Another person will speak.
(C) A survey will be conducted.
(D) Some slides will be shown.

74. What does the speaker imply when she says, "That's not ideal for me"?
(A) She cannot conduct a telephone interview.
(B) She is not willing to leave her office.
(C) She believes an offer is very low.
(D) She cannot meet on Wednesday.

75. Why does the speaker suggest going by subway?
(A) She expects traffic to be heavy.
(B) Her building has no parking lot.
(C) Driving downtown is too difficult.
(D) Her office is next to the subway station.

76. What does the speaker request the listener do?
(A) Give a product demonstration
(B) Send a confirmation e-mail
(C) Bring some documents
(D) Give her a phone call

77. What does the speaker mean when he says, "That has never happened before"?
(A) The company has never matched its production goals.
(B) The company has never made a profit.
(C) The company has never rewarded its employees.
(D) The company has never opened international branches.

78. What will all of the employees receive?
(A) Cash
(B) Stock options
(C) Extra time off
(D) Various presents

79. What will the speaker do next week?
(A) Tour individual departments
(B) Name some winners
(C) Sign a new contract
(D) Introduce the current quarter's plan

80. What kind of business most likely is Castor?
(A) A textile company
(B) An electronics firm
(C) A cosmetics manufacturer
(D) A hair salon

81. What will happen on December 15?
(A) A sale will begin.
(B) A new product will become available.
(C) Some retail outlets will open.
(D) A production demonstration will take place.

82. Why would a person visit a place where Castor products are sold?
(A) To sign up to win a prize
(B) To apply for a job
(C) To place an order
(D) To receive a free sample

GO ON TO THE NEXT PAGE

83. According to the speaker, what is a possible benefit of building a new stadium?

    (A) A professional sports team will play there.
    (B) It will increase employment.
    (C) Many concerts will be held there.
    (D) It will provide entertainment for residents.

84. Why does the speaker say, "That likely won't remain the same though"?

    (A) To claim the stadium will take years to build
    (B) To indicate that a price will change
    (C) To predict that taxes will increase
    (D) To say the stadium will be made bigger

85. What will listeners probably hear next?

    (A) Some ads
    (B) A sports update
    (C) A weather report
    (D) Some music

86. Who most likely are the listeners?

    (A) Business owners
    (B) Jobseekers
    (C) Recruiters
    (D) Marketing students

87. According to the speaker, what disadvantage do small companies have?

    (A) A lack of resources
    (B) Little local influence
    (C) Poor marketing skills
    (D) Few quality employees

88. What does the speaker tell the listeners to do?

    (A) Do a role-playing activity
    (B) Take notes on her comments
    (C) Find a person to work with
    (D) Describe their personal situations

89. Where does the talk most likely take place?

    (A) At a convention
    (B) At a trade show
    (C) At a staff meeting
    (D) At an awards ceremony

90. How does the speaker hope to make money for the company?

    (A) By eliminating several franchises
    (B) By purchasing cheaper ingredients
    (C) By spending more on marketing
    (D) By changing the company's image

91. What does the speaker say about some desserts?

    (A) They will no longer be served.
    (B) They are low-fat options.
    (C) Their prices have been lowered.
    (D) Their serving sizes are large.

92. Why is the message being played?

    (A) The bank is not open now.
    (B) There is a holiday.
    (C) The operators are all busy.
    (D) There is a technical problem.

93. How can a person find out how much money is owed on a credit card?

    (A) By pressing 1
    (B) By pressing 2
    (C) By dialing another number
    (D) By leaving a voice message

94. What is mentioned about the bank's services?

    (A) They are being upgraded.
    (B) They can be accessed online.
    (C) They are no longer available online.
    (D) They are used by people worldwide.

Contact Person	Phone Number
Robert Spartan	874-8547
Jessica Davis	874-9038
Marcia West	874-1294
Allen Barksdale	874-7594

Training Schedule		
Mon.	9:00 A.M. – 12:00 P.M.	Sales Dept.
Mon.	1:00 P.M. – 4:00 P.M.	Personnel Dept.
Tues.	9:00 A.M. – 12:00 P.M.	Publicity Dept.
Tues.	1:00 P.M. – 4:00 P.M.	Accounting Dept.

95. What does the speaker mention about Canada?

(A) Some new branches recently opened there.

(B) It is the company's most profitable area.

(C) The revenues there have not been reported yet.

(D) Sales are equal to those in Asia.

96. According to the speaker, what do some listeners need to do?

(A) Apply for a benefit

(B) Work overtime

(C) Submit their data reports

(D) Sign up for a seminar

97. Look at the graphic. What number will the listeners call?

(A) 874-8547

(B) 874-9038

(C) 874-1294

(D) 874-7594

98. Look at the graphic. Which department do the listeners work in?

(A) The Sales Department

(B) The Personnel Department

(C) The Publicity Department

(D) The Accounting Department

99. What does the speaker say about the training session?

(A) Everyone must take part in it.

(B) It will last for two hours.

(C) It concerns some new equipment.

(D) The listeners will do it in a lab.

100. What does the speaker tell John to do?

(A) Pay for his own training

(B) Cancel his business trip

(C) Get training on a different day

(D) Make a flight reservation

This is the end of the Listening test.

Actual Test 實戰測驗

2

LISTENING TEST

In the Listening test, you will be asked to demonstrate how well you understand spoken English. The entire Listening test will last approximately 45 minutes. There are four parts, and directions are given for each part. You must mark your answers on the separate answer sheet. Do not write your answers in your test book.

PART 1

Directions: For each question in this part, you will hear four statements about a picture in your test book. When you hear the statements, you must select the one statement that best describes what you see in the picture. Then find the number of the question on your answer sheet and mark your answer. The statements will not be printed in your test book and will be spoken only one time.

Statement (D), "The man is holding his hands together," is the best description of the picture, so you should select answer (D) and mark it on your answer sheet.

1.

2.

GO ON TO THE NEXT PAGE ➤

25

3.

4.

5.

6.

GO ON TO THE NEXT PAGE ➤

PART 2

Directions: You will hear a question or statement and three responses spoken in English. They will not be printed in your test book and will be spoken only one time. Select the best response to the question or statement and mark the letter (A), (B), or (C) on your answer sheet.

7. Mark your answer on your answer sheet.

8. Mark your answer on your answer sheet.

9. Mark your answer on your answer sheet.

10. Mark your answer on your answer sheet.

11. Mark your answer on your answer sheet.

12. Mark your answer on your answer sheet.

13. Mark your answer on your answer sheet.

14. Mark your answer on your answer sheet.

15. Mark your answer on your answer sheet.

16. Mark your answer on your answer sheet.

17. Mark your answer on your answer sheet.

18. Mark your answer on your answer sheet.

19. Mark your answer on your answer sheet.

20. Mark your answer on your answer sheet.

21. Mark your answer on your answer sheet.

22. Mark your answer on your answer sheet.

23. Mark your answer on your answer sheet.

24. Mark your answer on your answer sheet.

25. Mark your answer on your answer sheet.

26. Mark your answer on your answer sheet.

27. Mark your answer on your answer sheet.

28. Mark your answer on your answer sheet.

29. Mark your answer on your answer sheet.

30. Mark your answer on your answer sheet.

31. Mark your answer on your answer sheet.

PART 3

Directions: You will hear some conversations between two or more people. You will be asked to answer three questions about what the speakers say in each conversation. Select the best response to each question and mark the letter (A), (B), (C), or (D) on your answer sheet. The conversations will not be printed in your test book and will be spoken only one time.

32. What are the speakers mainly discussing?
    (A) A writing seminar
    (B) The woman's presentation
    (C) The man's report
    (D) An upcoming meeting

33. What does the woman dislike about the man's work?
    (A) Some of the writing is not clear.
    (B) He did not include his analysis.
    (C) It contains a few mistakes.
    (D) There are no graphs or charts in it.

34. By when should the man complete the assignment?
    (A) Before the woman's meeting ends
    (B) Before lunch finishes
    (C) Before the end of the day
    (D) Before this Friday

35. Who most likely is the woman?
    (A) A trainer
    (B) An interviewer
    (C) A client
    (D) A computer programmer

36. What does the woman indicate about the new employees?
    (A) They come from places around the country.
    (B) They are not able to understand the information.
    (C) They know more than previous new hires.
    (D) They went on a tour of a facility today.

37. What does the woman suggest will happen tomorrow?
    (A) A program for employees will finish.
    (B) Some job applicants will be interviewed.
    (C) New employees will be sent on a trip.
    (D) A training session will start.

38. Why did the woman call the man?
    (A) To find out his location
    (B) To have him give her car a tune up
    (C) To inquire about her vehicle
    (D) To learn how much she owes for a service

39. Why does the woman say, "I don't believe so"?
    (A) She cannot wait for an hour and a half.
    (B) She does not want to get the oil changed.
    (C) She is unable to come tomorrow morning.
    (D) She does not think a service is necessary.

40. What does the man recommend the woman do?
    (A) Rent a car for the next two days
    (B) Consider buying a new vehicle
    (C) Complete the work on her car
    (D) Speak with Greg before she leaves

41. What does the woman say about Mr. Sanders?
    (A) He is currently out of the country.
    (B) He was unable to meet her today.
    (C) He is applying for a job at her firm.
    (D) He congratulated her on her performance.

42. What does the woman imply when she says, "Would you mind getting together for a bit"?
    (A) She needs some of the man's files.
    (B) She does not have any new clients.
    (C) She wants to talk about Mr. Sanders.
    (D) She would like to talk about a transfer.

43. What will the speakers do tomorrow?
    (A) Have a meal together
    (B) Meet in the woman's office
    (C) Prepare for a presentation
    (D) Travel to PLL, Inc.

GO ON TO THE NEXT PAGE

44. What are the speakers discussing?

(A) A new employee
(B) An awards ceremony
(C) A gift for a colleague
(D) A donation to a charity

45. What is suggested about the woman?

(A) She is in the same department as the men.
(B) She will be away from her workplace this afternoon.
(C) She is collecting money from some employees.
(D) She is good friends with Justine Hamilton.

46. What does Richard tell the man to do?

(A) Help organize an event
(B) Make a suggestion
(C) Buy a present
(D) Give money to Darlene

47. What are the speakers talking about?

(A) A marketing seminar
(B) A product demonstration
(C) A stockholders' meeting
(D) A speech by the CEO

48. According to the man, what has he been doing today?

(A) Meeting members of the press
(B) Designing a product
(C) Visiting local stores
(D) Practicing his speech

49. What does the man suggest the woman do?

(A) Contact Matthew
(B) Set up some items
(C) Repair an item
(D) Prepare her presentation

50. What will the clients do on Thursday night?

(A) See a sporting event
(B) Watch a movie
(C) Have dinner at a restaurant
(D) Attend a concert

51. What is suggested about the clients?

(A) They will arrive in the afternoon.
(B) They are driving from their office.
(C) They are staying for one week.
(D) They have visited the area before.

52. What does the woman say about Cynthia?

(A) She drives a van.
(B) She speaks a foreign language.
(C) She works in the Berlin office.
(D) She is flying to the city tomorrow.

53. What does Craig say about the flyers?

(A) They cost too much to print.
(B) He approved the design.
(C) They were made by the Graphics Department.
(D) He dislikes their appearance.

54. What did Jason do?

(A) He registered for a conference.
(B) He made a new design.
(C) He visited the printer.
(D) He spoke with the woman.

55. What does the woman imply when she says, "I had totally forgotten about that"?

(A) A price cannot be reduced.
(B) No new individuals can be hired.
(C) The budget was recently changed.
(D) An order needs to be canceled.

56. Where does the conversation most likely take place?

(A) In an office
(B) At a factory
(C) At a conference center
(D) In a dentist's office

57. What will happen at 2:00?

(A) A dental appointment will begin.
(B) A shipment will be sent out.
(C) A telephone call will be made.
(D) A meeting with the CEO will start.

58. What does the man say about the clients?

(A) They are visiting from England.
(B) Their orders are not arriving on time.
(C) They need demonstrations of some products.
(D) They canceled a recent purchase.

59. What are the speakers mainly discussing?

(A) A lack of volunteers
(B) Job advertisements
(C) A charity event
(D) Sponsors of a fair

60. What does the man suggest about the previous year's county fair?

(A) It set a record for attendance.
(B) It did not have enough workers.
(C) It was canceled due to the weather.
(D) It lasted for one week.

61. What will the woman do after lunch?

(A) Interview job applicants
(B) Make a new schedule
(C) Talk to some sponsors
(D) Visit another company

This coupon is valid at all
Roth Clothing Stores

Present this coupon to get the
following discount:

Wednesday 10%
Thursday 15%
Friday 20%
Saturday 25%

62. Look at the graphic. When is the man making his purchase?

(A) On Wednesday
(B) On Thursday
(C) On Friday
(D) On Saturday

63. Why does the man need a suit?

(A) For an awards ceremony
(B) For an interview
(C) For a graduation ceremony
(D) For a wedding

64. What is suggested about the man?

(A) He will have his suit fitted at the store.
(B) He will get an extra $10 discount.
(C) He will make his purchase on another day.
(D) He is a frequent shopper at the store.

GO ON TO THE NEXT PAGE

Room	Maximum Number of People
Silver Room	80
Gold Room	100
Platinum Room	120
Diamond Room	150

65. What type of event will the man's company hold?

(A) A stockholders' meeting
(B) A company orientation
(C) An awards ceremony
(D) A retirement party

66. Look at the graphic. Which room is the most appropriate for the man's company?

(A) Silver Room
(B) Gold Room
(C) Platinum Room
(D) Diamond Room

67. What does the woman suggest doing?

(A) Paying the deposit this week
(B) Getting together for a meeting
(C) Confirming a reservation online
(D) Selecting the food to be served

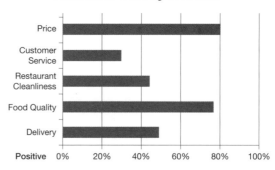

Customer Survey Results

68. What does the woman say about the restaurants in Surrey?

(A) Some of them closed due to a lack of business.
(B) They conducted surveys one week ago.
(C) They hired several new employees.
(D) They brought in more money than before.

69. What does the man say about the restaurants?

(A) They frequently offer special prices.
(B) They changed their menus recently.
(C) They use food produced in nearby areas.
(D) They train employees to be polite.

70. Look at the graphic. What will the woman discuss next?

(A) Customer Service
(B) Restaurant Cleanliness
(C) Food Quality
(D) Delivery

PART 4

Directions: You will hear some talks given by a single speaker. You will be asked to answer three questions about what the speaker says in each talk. Select the best response to each question and mark the letter (A), (B), (C), or (D) on your answer sheet. The talks will not be printed in your test book and will be spoken only one time.

71. Where does the announcement most likely take place?

(A) At a bus terminal
(B) In a train station
(C) In a subway station
(D) At an airport

72. Why is there a problem?

(A) A machine stopped working.
(B) Too many seats were sold.
(C) The computer system failed.
(D) Some passengers are late.

73. What does the speaker say that volunteers will be given?

(A) Extra mileage
(B) Five hundred euros
(C) A seat in business class
(D) A free first-class ticket

74. What type of store do the listeners work at?

(A) An appliance store
(B) A clothing store
(C) A supermarket
(D) An electronics store

75. What does the speaker mean when he says, "That's not good enough"?

(A) Prices must be lowered.
(B) Employees have to work harder.
(C) The company should make more money.
(D) A service needs to improve.

76. What does the speaker tell Larry to do?

(A) Place an advertisement
(B) Contact some customers
(C) Apply for a transfer
(D) Interview some job candidates

77. Why is the store having a sale?

(A) It is celebrating its grand opening.
(B) It needs to get rid of some items.
(C) It is going out of business soon.
(D) It is holding its annual sale.

78. How much is the discount on fruit?

(A) 20%
(B) 30%
(C) 40%
(D) 50%

79. What does the speaker say about parking?

(A) It is free for thirty minutes.
(B) There are a limited number of spaces.
(C) It can be done behind the store.
(D) A parking lot is across the street.

80. What problem does the speaker mention?

(A) Some items were damaged.
(B) An order was sent to the wrong address.
(C) Incorrect items were mailed.
(D) A bill was too high.

81. What will happen in three days?

(A) A restaurant will open.
(B) A sale will end.
(C) A contract will be signed.
(D) An order will be shipped.

82. Why does the speaker say, "It's imperative that you do this"?

(A) He wants a full refund.
(B) He expects an apology.
(C) He needs replacement items quickly.
(D) He requires free installation.

GO ON TO THE NEXT PAGE

83. Where most likely does the speech take place?

(A) At a retirement party
(B) At a farewell party
(C) At an awards ceremony
(D) At a signing ceremony

84. Who is the speaker?

(A) An author
(B) An editor
(C) A proofreader
(D) An agent

85. What does the speaker suggest about Peter Welling?

(A) He has known her for many years.
(B) He is a member of her family.
(C) He signed her to her first contract.
(D) He helped motivate her to work.

86. Why does the speaker thank Mr. Hancock?

(A) He was a popular speaker at an event.
(B) His firm successfully marketed a seminar.
(C) He helped the firm earn record profits.
(D) He signed contracts with several companies.

87. What will happen in February?

(A) A proposal will be sent.
(B) An international visit will be made.
(C) An event will take place.
(D) A company will be founded.

88. What will the speaker's assistant do?

(A) Mail a contract
(B) Provide some information
(C) Pick up a client at the airport
(D) Sign some documents

89. Who most likely are the listeners?

(A) Ticket collectors
(B) Volunteers
(C) Vendors
(D) Festival attendees

90. What does the speaker tell the listeners to wear?

(A) Sunglasses
(B) T-shirts
(C) Gloves
(D) Hats

91. What most likely will happen next?

(A) People will visit the hospital.
(B) People will be allowed into the festival.
(C) A concert will begin.
(D) Tickets will be sold.

92. How much vitamin B does the speaker need?

(A) A two-month supply
(B) A three-month supply
(C) A six-month supply
(D) A twelve-month supply

93. What does the speaker mean when he says, "I was unable to do so"?

(A) He could not order more of something.
(B) He could not pay for an order.
(C) He could not provide his address.
(D) He could not alter the delivery date.

94. What does the speaker request?

(A) A reduced price
(B) A phone call
(C) A confirmation e-mail
(D) A free sample

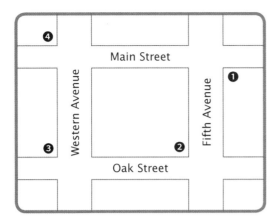

95. Why was the bridge closed?

   (A) A ship collided with it.
   (B) The lanes were being painted.
   (C) It was being fixed.
   (D) An extension was added to it.

96. Look at the graphic. Where is Faraday Towers?

   (A) Site 1
   (B) Site 2
   (C) Site 3
   (D) Site 4

97. What will listeners hear next?

   (A) An advertisement
   (B) A weather broadcast
   (C) Economic news
   (D) Some music

E-Mail Inbox	
Sender	**Subject**
Greg Towson	Sales Figures for March
Andrea Sparks	Denver Trip Itinerary
Nicholas Wentz	Openings at Other Branches
Melissa Martinez	Employee Complaints

98. Look at the graphic. Who sent the e-mail the speaker mentions?

   (A) Greg Towson
   (B) Andrea Sparks
   (C) Nicholas Wentz
   (D) Melissa Martinez

99. According to the speaker, what happened on Monday?

   (A) A new advertisement was released.
   (B) Sales data was submitted.
   (C) A sale at a store began.
   (D) Some new workers were hired.

100. Why will the listeners most likely be pleased next week?

   (A) Everyone will receive a bonus.
   (B) Sales numbers will be positive.
   (C) Employees' hours will be reduced.
   (D) Some awards will be presented.

This is the end of the Listening test.

Actual Test 實戰測驗

3

LISTENING TEST

In the Listening test, you will be asked to demonstrate how well you understand spoken English. The entire Listening test will last approximately 45 minutes. There are four parts, and directions are given for each part. You must mark your answers on the separate answer sheet. Do not write your answers in your test book.

PART 1

Directions: For each question in this part, you will hear four statements about a picture in your test book. When you hear the statements, you must select the one statement that best describes what you see in the picture. Then find the number of the question on your answer sheet and mark your answer. The statements will not be printed in your test book and will be spoken only one time.

Statement (D), "The man is holding his hands together," is the best description of the picture, so you should select answer (D) and mark it on your answer sheet.

1.

2.

GO ON TO THE NEXT PAGE

ACTUAL TEST **3**

3.

4.

5.

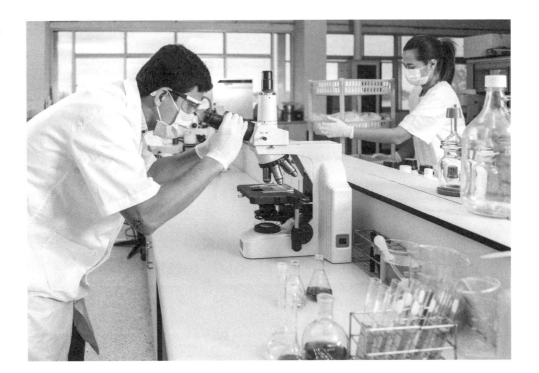

6.

GO ON TO THE NEXT PAGE

ACTUAL TEST **3**

PART 2

Directions: You will hear a question or statement and three responses spoken in English. They will not be printed in your test book and will be spoken only one time. Select the best response to the question or statement and mark the letter (A), (B), or (C) on your answer sheet.

7. Mark your answer on your answer sheet.

8. Mark your answer on your answer sheet.

9. Mark your answer on your answer sheet.

10. Mark your answer on your answer sheet.

11. Mark your answer on your answer sheet.

12. Mark your answer on your answer sheet.

13. Mark your answer on your answer sheet.

14. Mark your answer on your answer sheet.

15. Mark your answer on your answer sheet.

16. Mark your answer on your answer sheet.

17. Mark your answer on your answer sheet.

18. Mark your answer on your answer sheet.

19. Mark your answer on your answer sheet.

20. Mark your answer on your answer sheet.

21. Mark your answer on your answer sheet.

22. Mark your answer on your answer sheet.

23. Mark your answer on your answer sheet.

24. Mark your answer on your answer sheet.

25. Mark your answer on your answer sheet.

26. Mark your answer on your answer sheet.

27. Mark your answer on your answer sheet.

28. Mark your answer on your answer sheet.

29. Mark your answer on your answer sheet.

30. Mark your answer on your answer sheet.

31. Mark your answer on your answer sheet.

PART 3

Directions: You will hear some conversations between two or more people. You will be asked to answer three questions about what the speakers say in each conversation. Select the best response to each question and mark the letter (A), (B), (C), or (D) on your answer sheet. The conversations will not be printed in your test book and will be spoken only one time.

32. What is the woman doing?
    (A) Interviewing for a position
    (B) Requesting a transfer
    (C) Discussing a new project
    (D) Talking about moving

33. Why does the man mention his boss?
    (A) To repeat his boss's offer
    (B) To say he will meet his boss soon
    (C) To suggest the woman meet with his boss
    (D) To provide his boss's contact information

34. What is suggested about the woman?
    (A) She is willing to begin work in February.
    (B) She agrees to work at Trinity Chemicals.
    (C) She currently lives in Brownsville.
    (D) She does not have much prior experience.

35. What does the man suggest about the woman?
    (A) She will get transferred soon.
    (B) She is a part-time employee.
    (C) She recently moved to the city.
    (D) She lives far from the office.

36. What did the woman do yesterday?
    (A) She bought a new car.
    (B) She interviewed for a position.
    (C) She had a request rejected.
    (D) She tried to visit an office.

37. What does the man offer to do?
    (A) Give a tour of the facility
    (B) Assist with an application process
    (C) Submit a benefits form
    (D) Provide directions to a branch office

38. What does the man imply when he says, "You should thank Roger"?
    (A) Roger ran a successful campaign.
    (B) Roger worked on an advertisement.
    (C) Roger solved the woman's problem.
    (D) Roger sold the most items last month.

39. What is suggested about the woman?
    (A) She needs the services of a graphic designer.
    (B) She works in the Sales Department.
    (C) She is the man's supervisor.
    (D) She shares an office with the man.

40. What will the man give the woman?
    (A) A flyer
    (B) An invoice
    (C) An application form
    (D) A telephone number

41. Why did the woman visit the man?
    (A) She needs him to unlock her office door.
    (B) She discovered a problem with some paperwork.
    (C) Her company ID is not functioning right.
    (D) Her computer log in was not processed right.

42. What does the man want the woman to do?
    (A) Complete some forms
    (B) Attend an orientation session
    (C) Have her picture taken
    (D) Answer a questionnaire

43. How much time does the man say the woman needs?
    (A) Five minutes
    (B) Ten minutes
    (C) Fifteen minutes
    (D) Thirty minutes

GO ON TO THE NEXT PAGE

44. What is indicated about the company?

    (A) It is in the manufacturing industry.
    (B) It has lost money for more than a year.
    (C) It has offices in several countries.
    (D) It recently hired several new employees.

45. How does the woman propose firing employees?

    (A) By how long ago they were hired
    (B) By how they are performing
    (C) By how much they are paid
    (D) By how close to retirement they are

46. What does the man want the woman to do?

    (A) Research the recent sales data
    (B) Decide which employees to fire
    (C) Speak with some supervisors
    (D) Schedule a meeting for tomorrow

47. What is the problem?

    (A) A meeting was canceled.
    (B) Some items need to be delivered.
    (C) A price was increased.
    (D) An order has not yet arrived.

48. What does the man say he will do?

    (A) Meet with a coworker
    (B) Attend a seminar
    (C) Register for a marketing conference
    (D) Have lunch in his office

49. What does Kelly suggest doing?

    (A) Visiting 209 Westinghouse Road
    (B) Consulting with Mr. Andrews
    (C) Speaking with Jessica
    (D) Visiting the Marketing Department

50. Why did the man call the woman?

    (A) To find out her location
    (B) To confirm her recent order
    (C) To ask for her address
    (D) To say he can pick up her package

51. Why does the man say, "I'm really sorry"?

    (A) To apologize for a mistake
    (B) To reject the woman's request
    (C) To ask the woman to repeat herself
    (D) To say that an item is not available

52. What will the woman have to do for the man?

    (A) Provide photographic identification
    (B) Complete some paperwork
    (C) Pay cash for some items
    (D) Have a meeting with his assistant

53. What are the speakers mainly discussing?

    (A) A computer program
    (B) A problem with the Internet
    (C) The woman's e-mail
    (D) A staff meeting

54. What does Matt say about the memo?

    (A) He forgot to read it.
    (B) It was sent out this morning.
    (C) He wrote it for his colleagues.
    (D) It referred to a budget meeting.

55. Who most likely is Mr. Rogers?

    (A) The woman's client
    (B) The speakers' supervisor
    (C) A computer programmer
    (D) A maintenance worker

56. Where does the conversation most likely take place?

(A) At a newspaper
(B) At a supermarket
(C) At a restaurant
(D) At a bakery

57. What does the man propose doing?

(A) Calling an editor to complain
(B) Training employees better
(C) Canceling newspaper subscription
(D) Offering items at a discount

58. What is the woman concerned about?

(A) The cost of rent for the building
(B) The space that is available
(C) The prices that are charged
(D) The quality of the service

59. Where does the conversation most likely take place?

(A) At an amusement park
(B) At a museum
(C) At a theater
(D) At a gift shop

60. What does the man ask about?

(A) The availability of a bus
(B) The price of a ticket
(C) The time of a tour
(D) The location of a store

61. According to the woman, how can the man get a discount?

(A) By spending at least $15
(B) By making an online purchase
(C) By downloading a coupon
(D) By becoming a member

Thank you for shopping at Marcy's

Item Number	Item	Price
KP895	Screwdriver	$5.99
RY564	Power Drill	$28.99
XJ292	Saw	$12.99
MK646	Hammer	$6.99

62. What is indicated about the store?

(A) It had a sale on the weekend.
(B) It has extended its hours of operation.
(C) It is located in a shopping center.
(D) It had its grand opening last week.

63. Look at the receipt. Which item should the man get a discount on?

(A) The screwdriver
(B) The power drill
(C) The saw
(D) The hammer

64. What will the man most likely do next?

(A) Give the woman his credit card
(B) Speak with a customer service agent
(C) Receive a coupon from the woman
(D) Show the woman the items he bought

GO ON TO THE NEXT PAGE

Section	Price per Ticket
Section A	$15
Section B	$25
Section C	$40
Section D	$60

65. What does the man say about tonight's performance?

(A) It is sold out.
(B) It has been postponed.
(C) It is the show's opening night.
(D) It will start at 7:00 P.M.

66. Look at the graphic. How much will the woman pay for each ticket?

(A) $15
(B) $25
(C) $40
(D) $60

67. What will the woman probably do next?

(A) Provide some personal information
(B) Choose which seats she wants
(C) Confirm her address
(D) Spell her name for the man again

Orientation Schedule		
Time	Speaker	Topic
9:00 A.M. – 9:15 A.M.	Tristan Roberts	Welcome Speech
9:15 A.M. – 9:45 A.M.	Eric Mueller	Job Duties and Responsibilities
9:45 A.M. – 10:00 A.M.	Marcus Wembley	Insurance Paperwork
10:00 A.M. – 10:30 A.M.	Porter Stroman	Company Facilities

68. Look at the graphic. Who is the man?

(A) Tristan Roberts
(B) Eric Mueller
(C) Marcus Wembley
(D) Porter Stroman

69. What is the woman doing this afternoon?

(A) Taking some personal time off
(B) Flying to another city
(C) Attending a conference
(D) Speaking at an orientation session

70. How will the woman discuss the matter with the man?

(A) By e-mail
(B) Over the phone
(C) By text message
(D) In person

PART 4

Directions: You will hear some talks given by a single speaker. You will be asked to answer three questions about what the speaker says in each talk. Select the best response to each question and mark the letter (A), (B), (C), or (D) on your answer sheet. The talks will not be printed in your test book and will be spoken only one time.

71. How long will the next part of the workshop last?

(A) Thirty minutes
(B) Sixty minutes
(C) Ninety minutes
(D) One hundred twenty minutes

72. What does the speaker imply when she says, "I know that can be hard at times"?

(A) Banks rarely lend money to new businesses.
(B) Few people successfully start businesses.
(C) Paying taxes can cost a lot of money.
(D) Getting a business license is not easy.

73. What will the listeners probably do next?

(A) Answer some questions
(B) Look at a graphic
(C) Fill out a questionnaire
(D) Take a break

74. What is being advertised?

(A) A lower price
(B) A special offer
(C) A new menu
(D) An internship opportunity

75. What is indicated about the coffee beans used?

(A) They come from the same place.
(B) They are imported from Indonesia.
(C) They are roasted two times.
(D) They come from local farmers.

76. What is suggested about Coffee Time?

(A) It is lowering its prices soon.
(B) More employees are needed there.
(C) Its owner will open a second branch.
(D) Many of its customers are students.

77. Why did the speaker make the phone call?

(A) To ask if an item is in stock
(B) To confirm a price
(C) To make a change to an order
(D) To alter his payment date

78. What does the speaker mean when he says, "The timing is absolutely crucial"?

(A) He must call some customers soon.
(B) He needs some items by Saturday.
(C) He can pay by this afternoon.
(D) He wants his order delivered today.

79. What does the speaker request?

(A) Installation instructions
(B) An e-mailed response
(C) A new bill
(D) A full refund

80. What is the news report mainly about?

(A) National news
(B) Economic conditions
(C) A technological breakthrough
(D) The state budget

81. What does the speaker say about housing prices?

(A) They have remained steady.
(B) They are declining severely.
(C) They are moving up slowly.
(D) They are increasing rapidly.

82. What will listeners hear next?

(A) A traffic update
(B) A sports report
(C) Some music
(D) A weather report

GO ON TO THE NEXT PAGE

83. What problem does the speaker mention?

(A) Cashiers do not do their jobs well.
(B) Customers are complaining about prices.
(C) Transactions are taking too long.
(D) Cash registers are not working properly.

84. What does the man suggest doing?

(A) Putting up a sign for customers
(B) Asking cashiers to help with bagging
(C) Charging customers for the bags they use
(D) Having bags be close to customers

85. What does the man request by next week?

(A) Pictures of the cashiers
(B) A report on a change
(C) The hiring of new employees
(D) Training for employees

86. What is the talk mainly about?

(A) Some branches in Europe that will open
(B) The company's revenues around the world
(C) The situations at other company locations
(D) A manager who was recently hired

87. What does the speaker imply when she says, "I think Claire Putnam deserves some congratulations"?

(A) Ms. Putnam manages the Paris branch.
(B) Ms. Putnam will be an excellent CEO.
(C) Ms. Putnam is the employee of the year.
(D) Ms. Putnam made her managers work harder.

88. What will happen in April?

(A) Managers will go on business trips.
(B) A manager will give a speech.
(C) The company will publish some reports.
(D) New branches will open in Europe.

89. What did Greg Sullivan do?

(A) Signed a new contract
(B) Quit his job
(C) Moved to another state
(D) Asked for a raise

90. Where does the speaker say that Jessica must go?

(A) To a lunch meeting
(B) To Murphy International
(C) To her office
(D) To another country

91. What does the speaker suggest about Greg Sullivan?

(A) He was able to speak a foreign language.
(B) He had a client at RWT International.
(C) He wrote detailed reports on his work.
(D) He got along well with his colleagues.

92. Who most likely is the speaker?

(A) A government employee
(B) A lawyer
(C) An accountant
(D) A consultant

93. What does the speaker indicate about his talk?

(A) It will last for less than an hour.
(B) It will explain how to follow the law.
(C) It will require the listeners to answer questions.
(D) It will involve showing a video.

94. What does the speaker ask the listeners to do?

(A) Look at some printed material
(B) Raise their hands when they have questions
(C) Sign some documents
(D) Submit forms to his assistant

Departure Time	Destination
11:00 A.M.	Glendale
11:30 A.M.	Portsmouth
12:45 P.M.	Haverford
1:00 P.M.	Glendale
2:15 P.M.	Springfield
3:30 P.M.	Portsmouth

95. In which industry does the speaker most likely work?

(A) The manufacturing industry
(B) The shipping industry
(C) The computer industry
(D) The textile industry

96. Look at the graphic. Where will the meeting be?

(A) Glendale
(B) Portsmouth
(C) Haverford
(D) Springfield

97. What does the speaker suggest doing after arriving?

(A) Purchasing supplies
(B) Finding accommodations
(C) Getting some food
(D) Renting a vehicle

Floor	Exhibit
First	Art and Architecture
Second	Native American Relics
Third	American History
Fourth	Pop Culture

98. Look at the graphic. On which floor is an exhibit closing soon?

(A) The first floor
(B) The second floor
(C) The third floor
(D) The fourth floor

99. Why would a listener go to the first floor?

(A) To return a borrowed item
(B) To sign up for a tour
(C) To watch a movie
(D) To purchase souvenirs

100. Where does the speaker tell listeners to go?

(A) To the ticket booth
(B) To a temporary exhibit
(C) To the gift shop
(D) To the café

This is the end of the Listening test.

Actual Test 實戰測驗

LC

4

LISTENING TEST

In the Listening test, you will be asked to demonstrate how well you understand spoken English. The entire Listening test will last approximately 45 minutes. There are four parts, and directions are given for each part. You must mark your answers on the separate answer sheet. Do not write your answers in your test book.

PART 1

Directions: For each question in this part, you will hear four statements about a picture in your test book. When you hear the statements, you must select the one statement that best describes what you see in the picture. Then find the number of the question on your answer sheet and mark your answer. The statements will not be printed in your test book and will be spoken only one time.

Statement (D), "The man is holding his hands together," is the best description of the picture, so you should select answer (D) and mark it on your answer sheet.

1.

2.

GO ON TO THE NEXT PAGE

3.

4.

5.

6.

GO ON TO THE NEXT PAGE ➤

PART 2

Directions: You will hear a question or statement and three responses spoken in English. They will not be printed in your test book and will be spoken only one time. Select the best response to the question or statement and mark the letter (A), (B), or (C) on your answer sheet.

7. Mark your answer on your answer sheet.

8. Mark your answer on your answer sheet.

9. Mark your answer on your answer sheet.

10. Mark your answer on your answer sheet.

11. Mark your answer on your answer sheet.

12. Mark your answer on your answer sheet.

13. Mark your answer on your answer sheet.

14. Mark your answer on your answer sheet.

15. Mark your answer on your answer sheet.

16. Mark your answer on your answer sheet.

17. Mark your answer on your answer sheet.

18. Mark your answer on your answer sheet.

19. Mark your answer on your answer sheet.

20. Mark your answer on your answer sheet.

21. Mark your answer on your answer sheet.

22. Mark your answer on your answer sheet.

23. Mark your answer on your answer sheet.

24. Mark your answer on your answer sheet.

25. Mark your answer on your answer sheet.

26. Mark your answer on your answer sheet.

27. Mark your answer on your answer sheet.

28. Mark your answer on your answer sheet.

29. Mark your answer on your answer sheet.

30. Mark your answer on your answer sheet.

31. Mark your answer on your answer sheet.

PART 3

Directions: You will hear some conversations between two or more people. You will be asked to answer three questions about what the speakers say in each conversation. Select the best response to each question and mark the letter (A), (B), (C), or (D) on your answer sheet. The conversations will not be printed in your test book and will be spoken only one time.

32. Where does the conversation take place?

(A) At a shopping center
(B) In an office
(C) At a restaurant
(D) In an apartment building

33. What does the woman suggest the man do?

(A) Apply for another job
(B) Have a dinner party at his home
(C) Get to know his neighbors
(D) Get his place renovated

34. What will the man do on Friday night?

(A) Go to a work-related event
(B) Stay at his home
(C) Watch a sporting event
(D) Attend a cookout

35. Why did the woman call the man?

(A) She was charged too much money.
(B) Her electricity is not working.
(C) She needs the gas disconnected.
(D) Her home suffered some damage.

36. What does the man ask the woman for?

(A) Her phone number
(B) Her name
(C) Her address
(D) Her account number

37. What will the man send the woman?

(A) A refund
(B) A bill
(C) A letter of apology
(D) A coupon

38. Where does the conversation most likely take place?

(A) At a newspaper
(B) At a bank
(C) At a utility company
(D) At a post office

39. What does the woman mean when she says, "Not at all"?

(A) She is satisfied with the service she gets.
(B) She does not want to answer the question.
(C) She does not have much time to talk.
(D) She is interested in what the man is saying.

40. What does the man suggest the woman do?

(A) Purchase an app
(B) Visit another branch
(C) Talk to his supervisor
(D) Pay for a new service

41. Who most likely is the woman?

(A) A salesperson
(B) A cashier
(C) A bank teller
(D) A store owner

42. What does the man indicate about himself?

(A) He has spoken with the woman before.
(B) He moved to the area last week.
(C) He graduated from college recently.
(D) He was recently hired for a job.

43. What does the man ask about?

(A) The changing rooms
(B) The return policy
(C) The customer service desk
(D) The types of styles available

GO ON TO THE NEXT PAGE

44. What is the problem?

    (A) An order has been delayed.
    (B) Some machines are not working.
    (C) A customer did not send a payment.
    (D) Some equipment parts are missing.

45. What does the woman imply when she says, "The second one looks more serious"?

    (A) Repairs will not be completed today.
    (B) A replacement cost will be very high.
    (C) More workers need to be hired.
    (D) The CEO ought to be contacted.

46. Where does the man tell the woman to go?

    (A) To the branch in Europe
    (B) To Midland
    (C) To her office
    (D) To the company doing the repairs

47. What is Bob looking for?

    (A) Some toner cartridges
    (B) A stapler
    (C) Some paperclips
    (D) Some copy paper

48. According to the woman, what will happen on Thursday?

    (A) A repairman will arrive.
    (B) A document will be signed.
    (C) Some supplies will be delivered.
    (D) Some papers will be mailed.

49. What does George tell Bob to do?

    (A) Ask to be reimbursed
    (B) Visit another department
    (C) Speak with his boss
    (D) Go to a store across the street

50. What does the woman request the man do?

    (A) Give her a ride somewhere
    (B) Help her with an assignment
    (C) Let her know his address
    (D) Make a suggestion for her

51. What does the woman need fixed?

    (A) Her briefcase
    (B) Her phone
    (C) Her laptop
    (D) Her printer

52. What will the woman most likely do next?

    (A) Look for a bus that she can take
    (B) Find out the location of a store
    (C) Ask another colleague for assistance
    (D) Make a phone call to a friend

53. Why most likely is the woman visiting Duncan Associates?

    (A) To make a presentation
    (B) To sign a contract
    (C) To interview for a position
    (D) To discuss an offer

54. How does the man tell the woman to visit Duncan Associates?

    (A) By car
    (B) By bus
    (C) By taxi
    (D) By subway

55. Why does the man say, "I made that mistake as well"?

    (A) To indicate he took a bus and was late for a meeting
    (B) To mention that he wrote down the address incorrectly
    (C) To tell the woman to be cautious around Ms. Voss
    (D) To state he did not prepare well for a meeting once

56. What are the speakers mainly discussing?

   (A) A contract that was signed
   (B) An opportunity to be promoted
   (C) A meeting that was announced
   (D) An emergency that must be solved

57. How does the man feel about working overtime?

   (A) He is pleased to make more money.
   (B) He is not interested in doing it.
   (C) He wishes he could do it more often.
   (D) He dislikes staying late after work.

58. What does the woman recommend doing?

   (A) Completing their budget report
   (B) Going to a meeting room
   (C) Applying for a transfer
   (D) Speaking with Mr. Miller

59. Why does Lucy want to change shifts?

   (A) She has a doctor's appointment.
   (B) She wants to go to her hometown.
   (C) She will be interviewing for another job.
   (D) She has to meet a family member.

60. What is Tina doing tomorrow?

   (A) Watching a movie
   (B) Attending a job fair
   (C) Meeting a client
   (D) Going out for dinner

61. Why does the man offer to help Lucy?

   (A) He does not want to work tomorrow.
   (B) He wants to work more hours.
   (C) He would like to get more experience.
   (D) He has no plans for the weekend.

City	Distance To
Watertown	5km
New Weston City	19km
Providence	46km
Belmont	83km

62. Look at the graphic. How far do the speakers have to drive before they stop for the first time?

   (A) 5 kilometers
   (B) 19 kilometers
   (C) 46 kilometers
   (D) 83 kilometers

63. What does the woman say she will do?

   (A) Look for a place to park
   (B) Call her supervisor
   (C) Get directions to their final destination
   (D) Find a place to eat online

64. What are the speakers doing this afternoon?

   (A) Attending a meeting
   (B) Giving a demonstration
   (C) Going to a seminar
   (D) Leading a training session

ACTUAL TEST 4

GO ON TO THE NEXT PAGE ➡

Black and White Copies (Brochure)	$2/page
Color Copies (Brochure)	$4/page
Black and White Copies (Poster)	$3/page
Color Copies (Poster)	$5/page

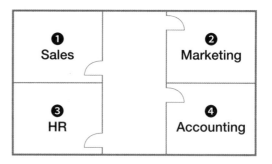

65. Why is the man in a hurry?

(A) He will hand out items at a conference tomorrow.

(B) An event has been rescheduled to start earlier.

(C) Some last-minute changes caused a big delay.

(D) His boss needs the items by the end of the day.

66. Look at the graphic. What is the basic rate the man will pay?

(A) $2 per page

(B) $3 per page

(C) $4 per page

(D) $5 per page

67. How does the woman want to get the information from the man?

(A) In person

(B) By fax

(C) By phone

(D) By e-mail

68. What is the woman looking for?

(A) A company card

(B) A presentation folder

(C) Some snack food

(D) Her clients

69. What does the man offer to do?

(A) Provide directions

(B) Make a purchase

(C) Spend his own money

(D) Pour some coffee

70. Look at the graphic. Where will the man most likely go next?

(A) Office 1

(B) Office 2

(C) Office 3

(D) Office 4

PART 4

Directions: You will hear some talks given by a single speaker. You will be asked to answer three questions about what the speaker says in each talk. Select the best response to each question and mark the letter (A), (B), (C), or (D) on your answer sheet. The talks will not be printed in your test book and will be spoken only one time.

71. Why did the speaker call Ms. Hardy?

(A) To ask to meet her today
(B) To postpone their conference
(C) To invite her to a seminar
(D) To have her e-mail him some files

72. What does the speaker say about his boss?

(A) He asked the speaker to go on a trip.
(B) He canceled a planned meeting.
(C) He is currently out of the office.
(D) He plans to accompany the speaker.

73. What does the speaker suggest about Ms. Hardy?

(A) Her office is next to his.
(B) She is ready to sign a contract.
(C) Her manager wants to meet her.
(D) He wants her to contact him.

74. What happened five years ago?

(A) Approval was granted.
(B) Funds were requested.
(C) Plans were made.
(D) A city was founded.

75. Where will the tunnel be built?

(A) Under a river
(B) Beneath a bay
(C) Through a mountain
(D) Through a hill

76. What does the speaker imply when she says, "This should no longer be the case"?

(A) The population will stop declining.
(B) More industries will arrive.
(C) Unemployment will get better.
(D) Traffic will improve.

77. What problem does the speaker mention?

(A) Sales have declined.
(B) Customers have complained.
(C) Prices have increased.
(D) Quality has gotten bad.

78. What kind of event will be held?

(A) A sale
(B) A free giveaway
(C) A fundraiser
(D) A raffle

79. When will the event end?

(A) Tomorrow
(B) This weekend
(C) This month
(D) Next month

80. Who are the listeners?

(A) Interns
(B) Job applicants
(C) Researchers
(D) Assistants

81. What does the speaker tell the listeners to do?

(A) Take some papers with them
(B) Fill out some forms
(C) Respond to an e-mail
(D) Go on a short tour

82. How can the listeners get assistance?

(A) By contacting the speaker
(B) By asking the speaker's helper
(C) By consulting a manual
(D) By looking at a Web site

GO ON TO THE NEXT PAGE

83. What industry does the speaker work in?

(A) Construction
(B) Textiles
(C) Manufacturing
(D) Travel

84. Why does the speaker say, "We're quite pleased about that"?

(A) A client approved an idea.
(B) A project will finish ahead of schedule.
(C) No accidents have occurred lately.
(D) There is still money left in the budget.

85. What does the speaker tell the listeners to do?

(A) Speak with some employees
(B) Introduce themselves to one another
(C) Look at some plans
(D) Put on some safety gear

86. Where does the announcement take place?

(A) On an airplane
(B) On a bus
(C) On a subway
(D) On a train

87. What does the speaker mean when she says, "Please have them available if they are requested"?

(A) The listeners will be asked for their passports.
(B) The listeners may have to show their tickets.
(C) The listeners might have to change seats.
(D) The listeners need to have their receipts.

88. What does the speaker say is available?

(A) Refreshments
(B) Reading material
(C) Wireless Internet
(D) Blankets and pillows

89. What is the speaker mainly discussing?

(A) Summer vacation
(B) Employee benefits
(C) Office renovations
(D) A business trip

90. What will happen tomorrow?

(A) New computers will be delivered.
(B) A list will be provided.
(C) Desks will be purchased.
(D) Employees will be hired.

91. What does the speaker tell the listeners to do?

(A) Box up the necessary equipment
(B) Clean up their workspaces
(C) Sign up for a work event
(D) Move some of their computer files

92. How has the Delmont Ski Resort changed?

(A) It has new places for skiers.
(B) It has larger rooms.
(C) It has been renovated.
(D) It has hired a new chef.

93. What special is being offered to visitors?

(A) Reduced room prices
(B) Free skiing lessons
(C) Half price on skiing equipment
(D) A complimentary daily breakfast

94. What is Montross?

(A) A nearby city
(B) A mountain
(C) A restaurant
(D) A café

Lecturer	Time	Topic
Leslie Davidson	10:00 A.M. – 11:00 A.M.	Imports and Exports
Marcus Wild	11:10 A.M. – 12:00 P.M.	International Law
Jeremy Sparks	1:00 P.M. – 1:50 P.M.	Effective Logistics
Allison Booth	2:00 P.M. – 3:20 P.M.	Computer Technology

Date	Event
June 27	Fundraiser
July 15	A Midsummer Night's Dream
July 25	Fundraiser
August 3	Romeo and Juliet
August 11	Fundraiser

95. Why did the speaker make the call?

(A) To request a brochure for a seminar
(B) To inquire about prices
(C) To confirm the time of a lecture
(D) To book tickets for a conference

96. When will the event take place?

(A) This weekend
(B) Next weekend
(C) This month
(D) Next month

97. Look at the graphic. Which lecturer does the speaker want to hear?

(A) Leslie Davidson
(B) Marcus Wild
(C) Jeremy Sparks
(D) Allison Booth

98. Who most likely are the listeners?

(A) Audience members
(B) Performers
(C) Volunteers
(D) Theater critics

99. What will the speaker give each listener?

(A) A bonus
(B) Paid vacation
(C) Free tickets
(D) A role in a play

100. Look at the graphic. When does the speech take place?

(A) June 27
(B) July 25
(C) August 3
(D) August 11

This is the end of the Listening test.

Actual Test 實戰測驗

5

LISTENING TEST

In the Listening test, you will be asked to demonstrate how well you understand spoken English. The entire Listening test will last approximately 45 minutes. There are four parts, and directions are given for each part. You must mark your answers on the separate answer sheet. Do not write your answers in your test book.

PART 1

Directions: For each question in this part, you will hear four statements about a picture in your test book. When you hear the statements, you must select the one statement that best describes what you see in the picture. Then find the number of the question on your answer sheet and mark your answer. The statements will not be printed in your test book and will be spoken only one time.

Statement (D), "The man is holding his hands together," is the best description of the picture, so you should select answer (D) and mark it on your answer sheet.

1.

2.

GO ON TO THE NEXT PAGE

ACTUAL TEST **5**

3.

4.

5.

6.

GO ON TO THE NEXT PAGE ➤

PART 2

Directions: You will hear a question or statement and three responses spoken in English. They will not be printed in your test book and will be spoken only one time. Select the best response to the question or statement and mark the letter (A), (B), or (C) on your answer sheet.

7. Mark your answer on your answer sheet.

8. Mark your answer on your answer sheet.

9. Mark your answer on your answer sheet.

10. Mark your answer on your answer sheet.

11. Mark your answer on your answer sheet.

12. Mark your answer on your answer sheet.

13. Mark your answer on your answer sheet.

14. Mark your answer on your answer sheet.

15. Mark your answer on your answer sheet.

16. Mark your answer on your answer sheet.

17. Mark your answer on your answer sheet.

18. Mark your answer on your answer sheet.

19. Mark your answer on your answer sheet.

20. Mark your answer on your answer sheet.

21. Mark your answer on your answer sheet.

22. Mark your answer on your answer sheet.

23. Mark your answer on your answer sheet.

24. Mark your answer on your answer sheet.

25. Mark your answer on your answer sheet.

26. Mark your answer on your answer sheet.

27. Mark your answer on your answer sheet.

28. Mark your answer on your answer sheet.

29. Mark your answer on your answer sheet.

30. Mark your answer on your answer sheet.

31. Mark your answer on your answer sheet.

PART 3

Directions: You will hear some conversations between two or more people. You will be asked to answer three questions about what the speakers say in each conversation. Select the best response to each question and mark the letter (A), (B), (C), or (D) on your answer sheet. The conversations will not be printed in your test book and will be spoken only one time.

32. Why did the man visit the store?

(A) To get a present for his wife
(B) To have an item repaired
(C) To find out what is on sale
(D) To pick up an item he ordered

33. What does the woman say about the earrings?

(A) They are made of gold.
(B) They are being discounted.
(C) They are handmade.
(D) They are her favorite style.

34. What does the man ask the woman for?

(A) A necklace
(B) A ring
(C) A bracelet
(D) A watch

35. What are the speakers mainly discussing?

(A) The woman's work hours
(B) An item that the man wants
(C) The magazines the man reads
(D) The hours of the bookstore

36. Why does the woman mention the backroom?

(A) To tell the man she will go there
(B) To indicate where her manager is
(C) To say where an item might be
(D) To point out that she just came from there

37. What is suggested about the man?

(A) He needs to return to his workplace soon.
(B) He wants to purchase a new bicycle.
(C) He has never visited the store before.
(D) He subscribes to several magazines.

38. Where does the conversation most likely take place?

(A) At a café
(B) At a restaurant
(C) At a catering company
(D) At a deli

39. Why does the woman have to leave soon?

(A) She is late for work.
(B) She has to complete a project.
(C) She needs to catch a train.
(D) She has a meeting to attend.

40. What will the man bring the woman?

(A) A menu
(B) A beverage
(C) A piece of cheesecake
(D) A napkin

41. What is the man's problem?

(A) He received data with mistakes in it.
(B) He forgot to print a document for the woman.
(C) He did not make any sales this week.
(D) He has not completed some assigned work.

42. Why does the woman say, "You should have handled that a long time ago"?

(A) To ask for an apology
(B) To insist on getting the budget report
(C) To reject the man's request
(D) To advise the man to try a different solution

43. What is suggested about the Sales Department?

(A) Its employees have taken the day off.
(B) It does not have any working phones now.
(C) It is on higher floor than the man's office.
(D) It is supervised by the woman.

GO ON TO THE NEXT PAGE

44. What are the speakers mainly discussing?

(A) The branch office in Louisville
(B) The need to conduct interviews
(C) A project that is starting soon
(D) Some newly hired employees

45. What does the man suggest doing?

(A) Having a meal together
(B) Assigning him a different project
(C) Introducing him to Henry
(D) Interviewing more people

46. What will the woman do tomorrow?

(A) Take part in an orientation session
(B) Eat lunch with a client
(C) Spend time at another office
(D) Give a tour to some visitors

47. Where most likely does the conversation take place?

(A) At a furniture store
(B) At a construction company
(C) At a home improvement store
(D) At an electronics store

48. What does the man say about products by Whitman?

(A) They are very expensive.
(B) They are not good.
(C) They do not have enough colors.
(D) They do not last long enough.

49. What is suggested about the man?

(A) He will ask the women for advice.
(B) He would like to receive a free sample.
(C) He plans to visit another store.
(D) He will make a purchase tomorrow.

50. Where does the woman work?

(A) At a clothing store
(B) At a dental clinic
(C) At a gym
(D) At a childcare facility

51. What does the man want to do?

(A) Get a second opinion
(B) Speak with another person
(C) Pay with cash
(D) Change his appointment

52. What is suggested about the Wakefield Shopping Center?

(A) It has several different floors.
(B) It is close to the woman's location.
(C) It recently opened for the day.
(D) It is having a sale at all of its stores.

53. What is the man's problem?

(A) He forgot to buy a bus pass.
(B) He cannot drive for a few days.
(C) He got lost on his way to work.
(D) He often gets caught in morning traffic.

54. What does the woman imply when she says, "Don't you live in the Silver Springs neighborhood"?

(A) She is unfamiliar with the city.
(B) She cannot drive the man to his home.
(C) She thinks she cannot help the man.
(D) She does not remember the exact location.

55. What does the woman tell the man to do?

(A) Wait outside her home in the morning
(B) Give her a call when he wants to leave
(C) Let her know what his address is
(D) Send her a reminder before work ends

56. What is the problem?

    (A) A consulting company was fired.
    (B) A campaign was delayed.
    (C) An ad has not been finished.
    (D) Sales have declined.

57. According to the woman, what has she been doing?

    (A) Attending meetings
    (B) Reading a report
    (C) Working with a focus group
    (D) Writing an ad

58. What does the woman tell the man to do?

    (A) Focus harder on his assignment
    (B) Speak with someone in Marketing
    (C) Ask other people what they think
    (D) Compile more data on sales

59. Where does the conversation most likely take place?

    (A) At a clothing store
    (B) At a grocery store
    (C) At an appliance store
    (D) At a stationery store

60. What does the woman want to do?

    (A) Pay with a credit card
    (B) Order something online
    (C) Exchange some items
    (D) Get a refund

61. What does Mr. Davenport indicate about Ms. Cormack?

    (A) She owns the store.
    (B) She has met him before.
    (C) She belongs to the shoppers' club.
    (D) She bought the items from him last night.

Item	Quantity	Price
Copy Paper (5,000 Sheets)	4	$12.99
Ballpoint Pens (Box of 20)	2	$10.99
Stapler	2	$5.99
Paperclips (1,000)	1	$8.99

62. When did the man make the order?

    (A) Last week
    (B) Two days ago
    (C) Yesterday
    (D) This morning

63. Look at the graphic. What is the unit price of the item the man wants more of?

    (A) $5.99
    (B) $8.99
    (C) $10.99
    (D) $12.99

64. What will Ms. Muller do?

    (A) Call the store later
    (B) Receive an order
    (C) Submit an online payment
    (D) Arrange for shipping

GO ON TO THE NEXT PAGE

June 19	June 20	June 21	June 22	June 23
		Annual Parade		

65. What does the woman say about the parade?

(A) It is being held for the first time.

(B) It will be on the weekend.

(C) It is a popular event in the city.

(D) It causes traffic to be bad.

66. Look at the graphic. When will the product demonstration be held?

(A) On June 19

(B) On June 20

(C) On June 22

(D) On June 23

67. What will the woman send the man?

(A) The names of some reporters

(B) A copy of a press release

(C) A script to proofread

(D) An advertisement for the parade

Davis Clothes

★ **Special Sale** ★

When August 15-25

What All clothes at the store

How Much 20% discount

Why End-of-summer sale

68. Look at the graphic. Which section has a mistake?

(A) When

(B) What

(C) How Much

(D) Why

69. What does the man ask the woman to do?

(A) Talk to the employees

(B) Call the newspaper

(C) Place a new advertisement

(D) Apologize to a customer

70. What does the man say about posters?

(A) They should be in color.

(B) The woman should make them by hand.

(C) They will probably be effective.

(D) The woman needs to hang them in the windows.

PART 4

Directions: You will hear some talks given by a single speaker. You will be asked to answer three questions about what the speaker says in each talk. Select the best response to each question and mark the letter (A), (B), (C), or (D) on your answer sheet. The talks will not be printed in your test book and will be spoken only one time.

71. What will happen today?

    (A) A store will have its grand opening.
    (B) Some training will take place.
    (C) Customer complaints will be solved.
    (D) A sale will be held.

72. Why are some of the listeners nervous?

    (A) They are worried about being late.
    (B) They do not like angry customers.
    (C) They have to speak in public.
    (D) They have no relevant experience.

73. What does the speaker tell the listeners to do?

    (A) Be polite to customers
    (B) Work overtime
    (C) Complete some forms
    (D) Ask their bosses for help

74. What is the problem?

    (A) Some software has a virus.
    (B) A machine has broken.
    (C) A person has not arrived.
    (D) Some parts are missing.

75. When will the demonstration begin?

    (A) In a few minutes
    (B) In an hour
    (C) Tomorrow
    (D) Next week

76. What will probably happen next?

    (A) An apology will be made.
    (B) Another person will speak.
    (C) An item will be repaired.
    (D) A lab will be opened.

77. What is suggested about the speaker?

    (A) He has met the listener in person.
    (B) He is an employee at Darwin Construction.
    (C) He will visit the listener tomorrow.
    (D) He works in the R&D Department.

78. How does the speaker change the order?

    (A) By canceling it
    (B) By ordering many different items
    (C) By having the shipping expedited
    (D) By purchasing a cheaper item

79. Why does the speaker say, "She's new here"?

    (A) To explain why a person made a mistake
    (B) To ask about introducing someone
    (C) To insist a person be given a tour
    (D) To say way some paperwork should be submitted

80. Where does the talk most likely take place?

    (A) At a bakery
    (B) At a cafeteria
    (C) At a restaurant
    (D) At a café

81. What does the speaker imply when she says, "You should give it some serious thought"?

    (A) The listeners should come back later.
    (B) The pork chop tastes good.
    (C) There are no seats available.
    (D) The dessert is recommended.

82. What does the speaker tell the listeners to do?

    (A) Look at the menu
    (B) Pay a bill
    (C) Make their orders
    (D) Change tables

GO ON TO THE NEXT PAGE

83. According to the speaker, what happened at last month's meeting?

(A) Sales data was discussed.
(B) An idea was suggested.
(C) A new product was introduced.
(D) Some promotions were announced.

84. What does the speaker say about complaints about customer service?

(A) They have been reduced recently.
(B) They are making sales decline.
(C) They have increased by 45%.
(D) They no longer occur.

85. What is suggested about Henry?

(A) He is the departmental manager.
(B) He works in the Marketing Department.
(C) He is a new employee.
(D) He is attending the meeting.

86. Why does the speaker apologize?

(A) He lost track of time.
(B) He missed his flight.
(C) He made a mistake.
(D) He arrived late.

87. Who most likely is the speaker?

(A) A curator
(B) A sculptor
(C) A painter
(D) A designer

88. What will the speaker do later?

(A) Sell some products
(B) Lead a tour
(C) Give a demonstration
(D) Sign autographs

89. What is the purpose of the message?

(A) To provide an e-mail address
(B) To give some instructions
(C) To ask the listener to call again
(D) To reschedule an appointment

90. Where is Greg Anderson?

(A) On vacation
(B) Out of the country
(C) At a doctor's appointment
(D) At a relative's home

91. What does the speaker suggest about Ruth Duncan?

(A) She is his colleague.
(B) She is an intern.
(C) She is at a factory.
(D) She handles his personal business.

92. What does the speaker say about Leslie Haynes?

(A) She resigned her position.
(B) She is currently sick.
(C) She will give a report soon.
(D) She will attend the parade.

93. What will the weather be like on the day of the parade?

(A) It will be cloudy.
(B) It will be sunny.
(C) It will be rainy.
(D) It will be windy.

94. What does the speaker mean when he says, "That's all for now"?

(A) A commercial will come on next.
(B) Some music will be played.
(C) His report is done.
(D) The news broadcast is going to end.

Speaker	Topic	Time
Glenn Harper	Business Regulations	1:00 – 1:50 P.M.
Tanya Radcliffe	Role-Playing Activities	2:00 – 2:50 P.M.
Maria Wills	International Laws	3:00 – 3:50 P.M.
Jessica Dane	Q&A Session	4:00 – 4:50 P.M.
Teresa Jone	Team-Building Activities	5:00 – 5:50 P.M.

Mr. Martindale's Afternoon Deliveries

Customer	Address
Henry Voss	584 Cloverdale Lane
Judith Smith	90 Anderson Drive
Karen Winkler	291 State Street
Peter Duncan	73 Washington Avenue

95. Look at the graphic. Who is the speaker?

(A) Tanya Radcliffe
(B) Maria Willa
(C) Jessica Dane
(D) Teresa Jones

96. What will the listeners do during the session?

(A) Read from a book
(B) Give feedback to one another
(C) Make oral presentations
(D) Watch a short video

97. What does the speaker tell the listeners to do?

(A) Take good notes
(B) Fill out some documents
(C) Introduce themselves
(D) Get into groups

98. Look at the graphic. Where is the speaker now?

(A) 584 Cloverdale Lane
(B) 90 Anderson Drive
(C) 291 State Street
(D) 73 Washington Avenue

99. How did the speaker try to contact the customer?

(A) By phone
(B) By text message
(C) By fax
(D) By e-mail

100. What does the speaker request?

(A) A receipt
(B) A cash payment
(C) Help with installation
(D) Verbal instructions

This is the end of the Listening test.

裁切線

確認

准考證號碼

姓名

ANSWER SHEET

TOEIC TOEIC實戰測試

READING COMPREHENSION (Part 5-7)

No.	ANSWER	No.	ANSWER	No.	ANSWER	No.	ANSWER
101	Ⓐ Ⓑ Ⓒ Ⓓ	121	Ⓐ Ⓑ Ⓒ Ⓓ	141	Ⓐ Ⓑ Ⓒ Ⓓ	161	Ⓐ Ⓑ Ⓒ Ⓓ	181	Ⓐ Ⓑ Ⓒ Ⓓ
102	Ⓐ Ⓑ Ⓒ Ⓓ	122	Ⓐ Ⓑ Ⓒ Ⓓ	142	Ⓐ Ⓑ Ⓒ Ⓓ	162	Ⓐ Ⓑ Ⓒ Ⓓ	182	Ⓐ Ⓑ Ⓒ Ⓓ
103	Ⓐ Ⓑ Ⓒ Ⓓ	123	Ⓐ Ⓑ Ⓒ Ⓓ	143	Ⓐ Ⓑ Ⓒ Ⓓ	163	Ⓐ Ⓑ Ⓒ Ⓓ	183	Ⓐ Ⓑ Ⓒ Ⓓ
104	Ⓐ Ⓑ Ⓒ Ⓓ	124	Ⓐ Ⓑ Ⓒ Ⓓ	144	Ⓐ Ⓑ Ⓒ Ⓓ	164	Ⓐ Ⓑ Ⓒ Ⓓ	184	Ⓐ Ⓑ Ⓒ Ⓓ
105	Ⓐ Ⓑ Ⓒ Ⓓ	125	Ⓐ Ⓑ Ⓒ Ⓓ	145	Ⓐ Ⓑ Ⓒ Ⓓ	165	Ⓐ Ⓑ Ⓒ Ⓓ	185	Ⓐ Ⓑ Ⓒ Ⓓ
106	Ⓐ Ⓑ Ⓒ Ⓓ	126	Ⓐ Ⓑ Ⓒ Ⓓ	146	Ⓐ Ⓑ Ⓒ Ⓓ	166	Ⓐ Ⓑ Ⓒ Ⓓ	186	Ⓐ Ⓑ Ⓒ Ⓓ
107	Ⓐ Ⓑ Ⓒ Ⓓ	127	Ⓐ Ⓑ Ⓒ Ⓓ	147	Ⓐ Ⓑ Ⓒ Ⓓ	167	Ⓐ Ⓑ Ⓒ Ⓓ	187	Ⓐ Ⓑ Ⓒ Ⓓ
108	Ⓐ Ⓑ Ⓒ Ⓓ	128	Ⓐ Ⓑ Ⓒ Ⓓ	148	Ⓐ Ⓑ Ⓒ Ⓓ	168	Ⓐ Ⓑ Ⓒ Ⓓ	188	Ⓐ Ⓑ Ⓒ Ⓓ
109	Ⓐ Ⓑ Ⓒ Ⓓ	129	Ⓐ Ⓑ Ⓒ Ⓓ	149	Ⓐ Ⓑ Ⓒ Ⓓ	169	Ⓐ Ⓑ Ⓒ Ⓓ	189	Ⓐ Ⓑ Ⓒ Ⓓ
110	Ⓐ Ⓑ Ⓒ Ⓓ	130	Ⓐ Ⓑ Ⓒ Ⓓ	150	Ⓐ Ⓑ Ⓒ Ⓓ	170	Ⓐ Ⓑ Ⓒ Ⓓ	190	Ⓐ Ⓑ Ⓒ Ⓓ
111	Ⓐ Ⓑ Ⓒ Ⓓ	131	Ⓐ Ⓑ Ⓒ Ⓓ	151	Ⓐ Ⓑ Ⓒ Ⓓ	171	Ⓐ Ⓑ Ⓒ Ⓓ	191	Ⓐ Ⓑ Ⓒ Ⓓ
112	Ⓐ Ⓑ Ⓒ Ⓓ	132	Ⓐ Ⓑ Ⓒ Ⓓ	152	Ⓐ Ⓑ Ⓒ Ⓓ	172	Ⓐ Ⓑ Ⓒ Ⓓ	192	Ⓐ Ⓑ Ⓒ Ⓓ
113	Ⓐ Ⓑ Ⓒ Ⓓ	133	Ⓐ Ⓑ Ⓒ Ⓓ	153	Ⓐ Ⓑ Ⓒ Ⓓ	173	Ⓐ Ⓑ Ⓒ Ⓓ	193	Ⓐ Ⓑ Ⓒ Ⓓ
114	Ⓐ Ⓑ Ⓒ Ⓓ	134	Ⓐ Ⓑ Ⓒ Ⓓ	154	Ⓐ Ⓑ Ⓒ Ⓓ	174	Ⓐ Ⓑ Ⓒ Ⓓ	194	Ⓐ Ⓑ Ⓒ Ⓓ
115	Ⓐ Ⓑ Ⓒ Ⓓ	135	Ⓐ Ⓑ Ⓒ Ⓓ	155	Ⓐ Ⓑ Ⓒ Ⓓ	175	Ⓐ Ⓑ Ⓒ Ⓓ	195	Ⓐ Ⓑ Ⓒ Ⓓ
116	Ⓐ Ⓑ Ⓒ Ⓓ	136	Ⓐ Ⓑ Ⓒ Ⓓ	156	Ⓐ Ⓑ Ⓒ Ⓓ	176	Ⓐ Ⓑ Ⓒ Ⓓ	196	Ⓐ Ⓑ Ⓒ Ⓓ
117	Ⓐ Ⓑ Ⓒ Ⓓ	137	Ⓐ Ⓑ Ⓒ Ⓓ	157	Ⓐ Ⓑ Ⓒ Ⓓ	177	Ⓐ Ⓑ Ⓒ Ⓓ	197	Ⓐ Ⓑ Ⓒ Ⓓ
118	Ⓐ Ⓑ Ⓒ Ⓓ	138	Ⓐ Ⓑ Ⓒ Ⓓ	158	Ⓐ Ⓑ Ⓒ Ⓓ	178	Ⓐ Ⓑ Ⓒ Ⓓ	198	Ⓐ Ⓑ Ⓒ Ⓓ
119	Ⓐ Ⓑ Ⓒ Ⓓ	139	Ⓐ Ⓑ Ⓒ Ⓓ	159	Ⓐ Ⓑ Ⓒ Ⓓ	179	Ⓐ Ⓑ Ⓒ Ⓓ	199	Ⓐ Ⓑ Ⓒ Ⓓ
120	Ⓐ Ⓑ Ⓒ Ⓓ	140	Ⓐ Ⓑ Ⓒ Ⓓ	160	Ⓐ Ⓑ Ⓒ Ⓓ	180	Ⓐ Ⓑ Ⓒ Ⓓ	200	Ⓐ Ⓑ Ⓒ Ⓓ

LISTENING COMPREHENSION (Part 1-4)

No.	ANSWER	No.	ANSWER	No.	ANSWER	No.	ANSWER
1	Ⓐ Ⓑ Ⓒ Ⓓ	21	Ⓐ Ⓑ Ⓒ	41	Ⓐ Ⓑ Ⓒ Ⓓ	61	Ⓐ Ⓑ Ⓒ Ⓓ	81	Ⓐ Ⓑ Ⓒ Ⓓ
2	Ⓐ Ⓑ Ⓒ Ⓓ	22	Ⓐ Ⓑ Ⓒ	42	Ⓐ Ⓑ Ⓒ Ⓓ	62	Ⓐ Ⓑ Ⓒ Ⓓ	82	Ⓐ Ⓑ Ⓒ Ⓓ
3	Ⓐ Ⓑ Ⓒ Ⓓ	23	Ⓐ Ⓑ Ⓒ	43	Ⓐ Ⓑ Ⓒ Ⓓ	63	Ⓐ Ⓑ Ⓒ Ⓓ	83	Ⓐ Ⓑ Ⓒ Ⓓ
4	Ⓐ Ⓑ Ⓒ Ⓓ	24	Ⓐ Ⓑ Ⓒ	44	Ⓐ Ⓑ Ⓒ Ⓓ	64	Ⓐ Ⓑ Ⓒ Ⓓ	84	Ⓐ Ⓑ Ⓒ Ⓓ
5	Ⓐ Ⓑ Ⓒ Ⓓ	25	Ⓐ Ⓑ Ⓒ	45	Ⓐ Ⓑ Ⓒ Ⓓ	65	Ⓐ Ⓑ Ⓒ Ⓓ	85	Ⓐ Ⓑ Ⓒ Ⓓ
6	Ⓐ Ⓑ Ⓒ Ⓓ	26	Ⓐ Ⓑ Ⓒ	46	Ⓐ Ⓑ Ⓒ Ⓓ	66	Ⓐ Ⓑ Ⓒ Ⓓ	86	Ⓐ Ⓑ Ⓒ Ⓓ
7	Ⓐ Ⓑ Ⓒ	27	Ⓐ Ⓑ Ⓒ	47	Ⓐ Ⓑ Ⓒ Ⓓ	67	Ⓐ Ⓑ Ⓒ Ⓓ	87	Ⓐ Ⓑ Ⓒ Ⓓ
8	Ⓐ Ⓑ Ⓒ	28	Ⓐ Ⓑ Ⓒ	48	Ⓐ Ⓑ Ⓒ Ⓓ	68	Ⓐ Ⓑ Ⓒ Ⓓ	88	Ⓐ Ⓑ Ⓒ Ⓓ
9	Ⓐ Ⓑ Ⓒ	29	Ⓐ Ⓑ Ⓒ	49	Ⓐ Ⓑ Ⓒ Ⓓ	69	Ⓐ Ⓑ Ⓒ Ⓓ	89	Ⓐ Ⓑ Ⓒ Ⓓ
10	Ⓐ Ⓑ Ⓒ	30	Ⓐ Ⓑ Ⓒ	50	Ⓐ Ⓑ Ⓒ Ⓓ	70	Ⓐ Ⓑ Ⓒ Ⓓ	90	Ⓐ Ⓑ Ⓒ Ⓓ
11	Ⓐ Ⓑ Ⓒ	31	Ⓐ Ⓑ Ⓒ	51	Ⓐ Ⓑ Ⓒ Ⓓ	71	Ⓐ Ⓑ Ⓒ Ⓓ	91	Ⓐ Ⓑ Ⓒ Ⓓ
12	Ⓐ Ⓑ Ⓒ	32	Ⓐ Ⓑ Ⓒ	52	Ⓐ Ⓑ Ⓒ Ⓓ	72	Ⓐ Ⓑ Ⓒ Ⓓ	92	Ⓐ Ⓑ Ⓒ Ⓓ
13	Ⓐ Ⓑ Ⓒ	33	Ⓐ Ⓑ Ⓒ	53	Ⓐ Ⓑ Ⓒ Ⓓ	73	Ⓐ Ⓑ Ⓒ Ⓓ	93	Ⓐ Ⓑ Ⓒ Ⓓ
14	Ⓐ Ⓑ Ⓒ	34	Ⓐ Ⓑ Ⓒ	54	Ⓐ Ⓑ Ⓒ Ⓓ	74	Ⓐ Ⓑ Ⓒ Ⓓ	94	Ⓐ Ⓑ Ⓒ Ⓓ
15	Ⓐ Ⓑ Ⓒ	35	Ⓐ Ⓑ Ⓒ	55	Ⓐ Ⓑ Ⓒ Ⓓ	75	Ⓐ Ⓑ Ⓒ Ⓓ	95	Ⓐ Ⓑ Ⓒ Ⓓ
16	Ⓐ Ⓑ Ⓒ	36	Ⓐ Ⓑ Ⓒ	56	Ⓐ Ⓑ Ⓒ Ⓓ	76	Ⓐ Ⓑ Ⓒ Ⓓ	96	Ⓐ Ⓑ Ⓒ Ⓓ
17	Ⓐ Ⓑ Ⓒ	37	Ⓐ Ⓑ Ⓒ	57	Ⓐ Ⓑ Ⓒ Ⓓ	77	Ⓐ Ⓑ Ⓒ Ⓓ	97	Ⓐ Ⓑ Ⓒ Ⓓ
18	Ⓐ Ⓑ Ⓒ	38	Ⓐ Ⓑ Ⓒ	58	Ⓐ Ⓑ Ⓒ Ⓓ	78	Ⓐ Ⓑ Ⓒ Ⓓ	98	Ⓐ Ⓑ Ⓒ Ⓓ
19	Ⓐ Ⓑ Ⓒ	39	Ⓐ Ⓑ Ⓒ	59	Ⓐ Ⓑ Ⓒ Ⓓ	79	Ⓐ Ⓑ Ⓒ Ⓓ	99	Ⓐ Ⓑ Ⓒ Ⓓ
20	Ⓐ Ⓑ Ⓒ	40	Ⓐ Ⓑ Ⓒ	60	Ⓐ Ⓑ Ⓒ Ⓓ	80	Ⓐ Ⓑ Ⓒ Ⓓ	100	Ⓐ Ⓑ Ⓒ Ⓓ

ANSWER SHEET

TOEIC TOEIC實戰測試

准考證號碼

姓名

確認

LISTENING COMPREHENSION (Part 1-4)

No.	ANSWER	No.	ANSWER	No.	ANSWER	No.	ANSWER	No.	ANSWER
1	Ⓐ Ⓑ Ⓒ	21	Ⓐ Ⓑ Ⓒ Ⓓ	41	Ⓐ Ⓑ Ⓒ Ⓓ	61	Ⓐ Ⓑ Ⓒ Ⓓ	81	Ⓐ Ⓑ Ⓒ Ⓓ
2	Ⓐ Ⓑ Ⓒ	22	Ⓐ Ⓑ Ⓒ Ⓓ	42	Ⓐ Ⓑ Ⓒ Ⓓ	62	Ⓐ Ⓑ Ⓒ Ⓓ	82	Ⓐ Ⓑ Ⓒ Ⓓ
3	Ⓐ Ⓑ Ⓒ Ⓓ	23	Ⓐ Ⓑ Ⓒ Ⓓ	43	Ⓐ Ⓑ Ⓒ Ⓓ	63	Ⓐ Ⓑ Ⓒ Ⓓ	83	Ⓐ Ⓑ Ⓒ Ⓓ
4	Ⓐ Ⓑ Ⓒ Ⓓ	24	Ⓐ Ⓑ Ⓒ Ⓓ	44	Ⓐ Ⓑ Ⓒ Ⓓ	64	Ⓐ Ⓑ Ⓒ Ⓓ	84	Ⓐ Ⓑ Ⓒ Ⓓ
5	Ⓐ Ⓑ Ⓒ	25	Ⓐ Ⓑ Ⓒ Ⓓ	45	Ⓐ Ⓑ Ⓒ Ⓓ	65	Ⓐ Ⓑ Ⓒ Ⓓ	85	Ⓐ Ⓑ Ⓒ Ⓓ
6	Ⓐ Ⓑ Ⓒ Ⓓ	26	Ⓐ Ⓑ Ⓒ Ⓓ	46	Ⓐ Ⓑ Ⓒ Ⓓ	66	Ⓐ Ⓑ Ⓒ Ⓓ	86	Ⓐ Ⓑ Ⓒ Ⓓ
7	Ⓐ Ⓑ Ⓒ	27	Ⓐ Ⓑ Ⓒ	47	Ⓐ Ⓑ Ⓒ Ⓓ	67	Ⓐ Ⓑ Ⓒ Ⓓ	87	Ⓐ Ⓑ Ⓒ Ⓓ
8	Ⓐ Ⓑ Ⓒ	28	Ⓐ Ⓑ Ⓒ	48	Ⓐ Ⓑ Ⓒ Ⓓ	68	Ⓐ Ⓑ Ⓒ Ⓓ	88	Ⓐ Ⓑ Ⓒ Ⓓ
9	Ⓐ Ⓑ Ⓒ	29	Ⓐ Ⓑ Ⓒ	49	Ⓐ Ⓑ Ⓒ Ⓓ	69	Ⓐ Ⓑ Ⓒ Ⓓ	89	Ⓐ Ⓑ Ⓒ Ⓓ
10	Ⓐ Ⓑ Ⓒ	30	Ⓐ Ⓑ Ⓒ Ⓓ	50	Ⓐ Ⓑ Ⓒ Ⓓ	70	Ⓐ Ⓑ Ⓒ Ⓓ	90	Ⓐ Ⓑ Ⓒ Ⓓ
11	Ⓐ Ⓑ Ⓒ	31	Ⓐ Ⓑ Ⓒ Ⓓ	51	Ⓐ Ⓑ Ⓒ Ⓓ	71	Ⓐ Ⓑ Ⓒ Ⓓ	91	Ⓐ Ⓑ Ⓒ Ⓓ
12	Ⓐ Ⓑ Ⓒ	32	Ⓐ Ⓑ Ⓒ Ⓓ	52	Ⓐ Ⓑ Ⓒ Ⓓ	72	Ⓐ Ⓑ Ⓒ Ⓓ	92	Ⓐ Ⓑ Ⓒ Ⓓ
13	Ⓐ Ⓑ Ⓒ	33	Ⓐ Ⓑ Ⓒ Ⓓ	53	Ⓐ Ⓑ Ⓒ Ⓓ	73	Ⓐ Ⓑ Ⓒ Ⓓ	93	Ⓐ Ⓑ Ⓒ Ⓓ
14	Ⓐ Ⓑ Ⓒ	34	Ⓐ Ⓑ Ⓒ Ⓓ	54	Ⓐ Ⓑ Ⓒ Ⓓ	74	Ⓐ Ⓑ Ⓒ Ⓓ	94	Ⓐ Ⓑ Ⓒ Ⓓ
15	Ⓐ Ⓑ Ⓒ	35	Ⓐ Ⓑ Ⓒ Ⓓ	55	Ⓐ Ⓑ Ⓒ Ⓓ	75	Ⓐ Ⓑ Ⓒ Ⓓ	95	Ⓐ Ⓑ Ⓒ Ⓓ
16	Ⓐ Ⓑ Ⓒ	36	Ⓐ Ⓑ Ⓒ Ⓓ	56	Ⓐ Ⓑ Ⓒ Ⓓ	76	Ⓐ Ⓑ Ⓒ Ⓓ	96	Ⓐ Ⓑ Ⓒ Ⓓ
17	Ⓐ Ⓑ Ⓒ	37	Ⓐ Ⓑ Ⓒ Ⓓ	57	Ⓐ Ⓑ Ⓒ Ⓓ	77	Ⓐ Ⓑ Ⓒ Ⓓ	97	Ⓐ Ⓑ Ⓒ Ⓓ
18	Ⓐ Ⓑ Ⓒ	38	Ⓐ Ⓑ Ⓒ Ⓓ	58	Ⓐ Ⓑ Ⓒ Ⓓ	78	Ⓐ Ⓑ Ⓒ Ⓓ	98	Ⓐ Ⓑ Ⓒ Ⓓ
19	Ⓐ Ⓑ Ⓒ	39	Ⓐ Ⓑ Ⓒ Ⓓ	59	Ⓐ Ⓑ Ⓒ Ⓓ	79	Ⓐ Ⓑ Ⓒ Ⓓ	99	Ⓐ Ⓑ Ⓒ Ⓓ
20	Ⓐ Ⓑ Ⓒ	40	Ⓐ Ⓑ Ⓒ Ⓓ	60	Ⓐ Ⓑ Ⓒ Ⓓ	80	Ⓐ Ⓑ Ⓒ Ⓓ	100	Ⓐ Ⓑ Ⓒ Ⓓ

READING COMPREHENSION (Part 5-7)

No.	ANSWER	No.	ANSWER	No.	ANSWER	No.	ANSWER	No.	ANSWER
101	Ⓐ Ⓑ Ⓒ Ⓓ	121	Ⓐ Ⓑ Ⓒ Ⓓ	141	Ⓐ Ⓑ Ⓒ Ⓓ	161	Ⓐ Ⓑ Ⓒ Ⓓ	181	Ⓐ Ⓑ Ⓒ Ⓓ
102	Ⓐ Ⓑ Ⓒ Ⓓ	122	Ⓐ Ⓑ Ⓒ Ⓓ	142	Ⓐ Ⓑ Ⓒ Ⓓ	162	Ⓐ Ⓑ Ⓒ Ⓓ	182	Ⓐ Ⓑ Ⓒ Ⓓ
103	Ⓐ Ⓑ Ⓒ Ⓓ	123	Ⓐ Ⓑ Ⓒ Ⓓ	143	Ⓐ Ⓑ Ⓒ Ⓓ	163	Ⓐ Ⓑ Ⓒ Ⓓ	183	Ⓐ Ⓑ Ⓒ Ⓓ
104	Ⓐ Ⓑ Ⓒ Ⓓ	124	Ⓐ Ⓑ Ⓒ Ⓓ	144	Ⓐ Ⓑ Ⓒ Ⓓ	164	Ⓐ Ⓑ Ⓒ Ⓓ	184	Ⓐ Ⓑ Ⓒ Ⓓ
105	Ⓐ Ⓑ Ⓒ Ⓓ	125	Ⓐ Ⓑ Ⓒ Ⓓ	145	Ⓐ Ⓑ Ⓒ Ⓓ	165	Ⓐ Ⓑ Ⓒ Ⓓ	185	Ⓐ Ⓑ Ⓒ Ⓓ
106	Ⓐ Ⓑ Ⓒ Ⓓ	126	Ⓐ Ⓑ Ⓒ Ⓓ	146	Ⓐ Ⓑ Ⓒ Ⓓ	166	Ⓐ Ⓑ Ⓒ Ⓓ	186	Ⓐ Ⓑ Ⓒ Ⓓ
107	Ⓐ Ⓑ Ⓒ Ⓓ	127	Ⓐ Ⓑ Ⓒ Ⓓ	147	Ⓐ Ⓑ Ⓒ Ⓓ	167	Ⓐ Ⓑ Ⓒ Ⓓ	187	Ⓐ Ⓑ Ⓒ Ⓓ
108	Ⓐ Ⓑ Ⓒ Ⓓ	128	Ⓐ Ⓑ Ⓒ Ⓓ	148	Ⓐ Ⓑ Ⓒ Ⓓ	168	Ⓐ Ⓑ Ⓒ Ⓓ	188	Ⓐ Ⓑ Ⓒ Ⓓ
109	Ⓐ Ⓑ Ⓒ Ⓓ	129	Ⓐ Ⓑ Ⓒ Ⓓ	149	Ⓐ Ⓑ Ⓒ Ⓓ	169	Ⓐ Ⓑ Ⓒ Ⓓ	189	Ⓐ Ⓑ Ⓒ Ⓓ
110	Ⓐ Ⓑ Ⓒ Ⓓ	130	Ⓐ Ⓑ Ⓒ Ⓓ	150	Ⓐ Ⓑ Ⓒ Ⓓ	170	Ⓐ Ⓑ Ⓒ Ⓓ	190	Ⓐ Ⓑ Ⓒ Ⓓ
111	Ⓐ Ⓑ Ⓒ Ⓓ	131	Ⓐ Ⓑ Ⓒ Ⓓ	151	Ⓐ Ⓑ Ⓒ Ⓓ	171	Ⓐ Ⓑ Ⓒ Ⓓ	191	Ⓐ Ⓑ Ⓒ Ⓓ
112	Ⓐ Ⓑ Ⓒ Ⓓ	132	Ⓐ Ⓑ Ⓒ Ⓓ	152	Ⓐ Ⓑ Ⓒ Ⓓ	172	Ⓐ Ⓑ Ⓒ Ⓓ	192	Ⓐ Ⓑ Ⓒ Ⓓ
113	Ⓐ Ⓑ Ⓒ Ⓓ	133	Ⓐ Ⓑ Ⓒ Ⓓ	153	Ⓐ Ⓑ Ⓒ Ⓓ	173	Ⓐ Ⓑ Ⓒ Ⓓ	193	Ⓐ Ⓑ Ⓒ Ⓓ
114	Ⓐ Ⓑ Ⓒ Ⓓ	134	Ⓐ Ⓑ Ⓒ Ⓓ	154	Ⓐ Ⓑ Ⓒ Ⓓ	174	Ⓐ Ⓑ Ⓒ Ⓓ	194	Ⓐ Ⓑ Ⓒ Ⓓ
115	Ⓐ Ⓑ Ⓒ Ⓓ	135	Ⓐ Ⓑ Ⓒ Ⓓ	155	Ⓐ Ⓑ Ⓒ Ⓓ	175	Ⓐ Ⓑ Ⓒ Ⓓ	195	Ⓐ Ⓑ Ⓒ Ⓓ
116	Ⓐ Ⓑ Ⓒ Ⓓ	136	Ⓐ Ⓑ Ⓒ Ⓓ	156	Ⓐ Ⓑ Ⓒ Ⓓ	176	Ⓐ Ⓑ Ⓒ Ⓓ	196	Ⓐ Ⓑ Ⓒ Ⓓ
117	Ⓐ Ⓑ Ⓒ Ⓓ	137	Ⓐ Ⓑ Ⓒ Ⓓ	157	Ⓐ Ⓑ Ⓒ Ⓓ	177	Ⓐ Ⓑ Ⓒ Ⓓ	197	Ⓐ Ⓑ Ⓒ Ⓓ
118	Ⓐ Ⓑ Ⓒ Ⓓ	138	Ⓐ Ⓑ Ⓒ Ⓓ	158	Ⓐ Ⓑ Ⓒ Ⓓ	178	Ⓐ Ⓑ Ⓒ Ⓓ	198	Ⓐ Ⓑ Ⓒ Ⓓ
119	Ⓐ Ⓑ Ⓒ Ⓓ	139	Ⓐ Ⓑ Ⓒ Ⓓ	159	Ⓐ Ⓑ Ⓒ Ⓓ	179	Ⓐ Ⓑ Ⓒ Ⓓ	199	Ⓐ Ⓑ Ⓒ Ⓓ
120	Ⓐ Ⓑ Ⓒ Ⓓ	140	Ⓐ Ⓑ Ⓒ Ⓓ	160	Ⓐ Ⓑ Ⓒ Ⓓ	180	Ⓐ Ⓑ Ⓒ Ⓓ	200	Ⓐ Ⓑ Ⓒ Ⓓ

新制多益
NEW
TOEIC

Michael A. Putlack ｜ Stephen Poirier ｜
Tony Covello ｜ 多樂院多益研究所 ｜ 著

★ ★ ★
解析本
★ ★ ★

聽力5回

全真模擬試題 ＋ 詳盡解析

LC

笛藤出版

NEW

TOEIC

聽力 5 回　解析本

全真模擬試題 ＋ 詳盡解析

LC

笛藤出版

PART 1
p.10

1. (C)   **2.** (A)   **3.** (B)   **4.** (C)   **5.** (D)
6. (B)

PART 2
p.14

7. (C)   **8.** (B)   **9.** (C)   **10.** (A)   **11.** (C)
12. (A)   **13.** (B)   **14.** (C)   **15.** (B)   **16.** (A)
17. (C)   **18.** (B)   **19.** (B)   **20.** (A)   **21.** (B)
22. (A)   **23.** (C)   **24.** (C)   **25.** (A)   **26.** (B)
27. (B)   **28.** (A)   **29.** (C)   **30.** (A)   **31.** (B)

PART 3
p.15

32. (C)   **33.** (A)   **34.** (C)   **35.** (A)   **36.** (B)
37. (C)   **38.** (D)   **39.** (B)   **40.** (C)   **41.** (C)
42. (A)   **43.** (A)   **44.** (C)   **45.** (B)   **46.** (D)
47. (C)   **48.** (A)   **49.** (C)   **50.** (C)   **51.** (B)
52. (A)   **53.** (B)   **54.** (C)   **55.** (A)   **56.** (A)
57. (B)   **58.** (C)   **59.** (A)   **60.** (A)   **61.** (D)
62. (C)   **63.** (D)   **64.** (A)   **65.** (C)   **66.** (D)
67. (C)   **68.** (B)   **69.** (D)   **70.** (B)

PART 4
p.19

71. (A)   **72.** (D)   **73.** (B)   **74.** (D)   **75.** (A)
76. (D)   **77.** (A)   **78.** (A)   **79.** (B)   **80.** (C)
81. (B)   **82.** (D)   **83.** (B)   **84.** (B)   **85.** (D)
86. (A)   **87.** (B)   **88.** (C)   **89.** (C)   **90.** (D)
91. (A)   **92.** (A)   **93.** (B)   **94.** (B)   **95.** (A)
96. (A)   **97.** (B)   **98.** (C)   **99.** (A)   **100.** (C)

PART 1

1.
(A) Clothes are being tried on in the dressing room.
(B) The woman is sewing some clothing.
(C) There are clothes hanging on a rack.
(D) She is speaking to someone in person.

(A) 更衣室裡衣服正被試穿。
(B) 那個女人正在縫衣服。
(C) 衣架上掛著衣服。
(D) 她正在和某人面對面地講話。

從照片右邊可以看到對衣架描寫的(C)是正確答案。在照片中因為女人正在講電話，所以不管是在穿衣服的(A)或是在縫衣服的(B)都不是正確答案。(D)的in person是表示「直接」、「親自」的意思，與正在通話的情況不符。

詞彙 try on （衣服等）試穿 dressing room 更衣室 sew 縫衣服
   rack 衣架 in person 直接，親自

2.
(A) The woman is standing behind the counter.
(B) The woman is giving the man his hotel key.
(C) The man is checking his luggage.
(D) The man is completing a registration form.

(A) 女人站在櫃檯後面。
(B) 女人正在給男人他的飯店鑰匙。
(C) 男人正在確認自己的行李。
(D) 男人正在填寫申請書。

正確描寫女人站立位置的(A)是正確答案。因為照片中出現的人物沒有交換鑰匙或是填寫申請書，所以(B)和(D)都不是正確答案。(C)的情況下，若是誤把checking聽成checking in(寄放行李)的話，有可能會出現誤把其當作是正確答案的失誤。

詞彙 check 確認，檢查 complete 完成 registration form 申請書

3.
(A) The traffic light has just changed.
(B) Some people are crossing the street.
(C) Everyone is moving in the same direction.
(D) Cars are moving through the crosswalk.

(A) 交通號誌燈變了。
(B) 人們正在過馬路。
(C) 所有人都朝著同一方向移動。
(D) 汽車正經過斑馬線。

僅憑照片是無法確認交通號誌燈有無改變，所以(A)不是正確答案。又因為可以看到在遠處的人是往不同方向走的，而右手邊的車輛則是停車的狀態，所以(D)和(C)是錯誤答案。正確答案是直接描寫正在過馬路的人們(B)。

詞彙 traffic light 交通號誌燈 cross 跨過，橫穿 crosswalk 斑馬線

4.
(A) Traffic is heavy going both ways.
(B) Someone is asking for directions.
(C) The cars are facing the same direction.
(D) The trees have all lost their leaves.

(A) 雙向道路交通繁忙。
(B) 有人在問路。
(C) 車輛都朝著同一方向行駛。
(D) 樹的葉子全都掉落了。

說明車輛全都朝著同一方向停的(C)是正確答案。因為無法得知人們的樣貌，所以(B)無法成為正確答案。(A)和(D)的描述都與照片中的情況無關。

詞彙 traffic 交通，車流量 ask for directions 問路 face 臉；朝向

5.
(A) She is sowing the ground with seeds.
(B) She is tying her shoes in a knot.
(C) She is using her sewing machine.
(D) She is sitting in an armchair.

(A) 她在土裡埋種子。
(B) 她在繫鞋帶。
(C) 她在用縫紉機。
(D) 她坐在扶手椅上。

照片中女人正坐在椅子上編織。(A)是利用和sew(縫紉)型態及發音相似的sow(播種)設下的陷阱，(B)是利用和knit(針織)型態及發音相似的knot(結)設下的陷阱。沒有看到縫紉機所以(C)並不是正確答案。正確答案是說明女人坐著的模樣(D)。

詞彙 sow 播，撒(種子) seed 種子 tie 綁 knot 結 sewing machine 縫紉機

6.

(A) Material is being checked out from the library.
(B) Books are being read by the students.
(C) The people are standing face to face.
(D) They are booking seats for an event.

(A) 圖書館的資料正被借閱。
(B) 書籍正在被學生們閱讀。
(C) 人們面對面站著。
(D) 他們正在預約活動的座位。

描寫兩個人正在閱讀書籍的(B)是正確答案。只有書架而不能借閱書，所以(A)是錯誤的，照片中兩個人是背對背的，與(C)所陳述的相反。(D)選項的book不是「書」的意思，而是指作為動詞使用的「預約」。

詞彙 material 材料，資料 check out 借(書) face to face 面對面 book 書；預約

PART 2

7.

Who do you prefer to promote?
(A) The promotion was a success.
(B) I prefer that new shampoo.
(C) Helen is doing great work.

你希望誰升職？
(A) 促銷活動很成功。
(B) 我更喜歡那個新出的洗髮精。
(C) Helen工作做得很好。

若有注意到疑問詞who的話，就可以很輕易地知道有指名Helen的(C)是正確答案。(A)的promotion是表示「促銷活動」的意思。

詞彙 prefer 偏好 promote 升職 promotion 升遷；促銷活動

8.

It would be better to follow Mr. Henderson's advice.
(A) Nobody is following her.
(B) Why do you think so?
(C) I advised her to wait.

最好聽從Henderson先生的建議。
(A) 沒有人跟隨她。
(B) 為什麼會這樣想？
(C) 我勸她等。

表示要根據Henderson先生的建議行事，詢問其理由的(B)是最

自然的回答。(A)和(C)是分別利用了在問題中出現過的follow及advice所設下的陷阱。

詞彙 follow 跟隨，追隨 advice 建議，忠告

9.

Didn't you remember to sign in?
(A) Yes, I can see the sign.
(B) No, I don't remember her name.
(C) It totally slipped my mind.

你忘記你要簽名了嗎？
(A) 是的，我可以看到簽名。
(B) 不，我不記得她的名字。
(C) 我完全忘記了。

若是知道(C)的slip one's mind(忘記)的意思的話，這是一題很輕易就能作答的問題。

詞彙 sign in 簽名，寫名字 totally 完全，全部 slip one's mind 忘記

10.

You can operate a forklift, can't you?
(A) I'm familiar with it.
(B) Yes, I can eat with a fork.
(C) No, he can't lift it.

你可以駕駛堆高機吧？
(A) 我很熟悉。
(B) 可以，我可以用叉子吃東西。
(C) 不，他拿不起來。

這一題是利用反問句的題目。詢問能否駕駛forklift(堆高機)，回答「我很熟悉」來表示肯定意義的(A)是正確答案。(B)和(C)是各自利用與forklift發音相似的fork及lift的錯誤答案。

詞彙 operate 操作 forklift 堆高機 be familiar with 熟悉，精通

11.

When did Mr. Harrison's plane take off?
(A) From Gate 21A.
(B) Headed to Barcelona.
(C) Two hours ago.

Harrison的飛機何時起飛？
(A) 從21A登機口。
(B) 前往巴塞隆納。
(C) 兩小時前。

利用疑問詞when詢問飛機的起飛時間，所以正確答案是(C)。(A)和(B)都是適用於在詢問場所時的回答。

詞彙 take off 起飛 head to 前往～

12.

Ms. Marston is waiting in her office.
(A) Tell her I'll be there in a moment.
(B) Yes, that's her by the office.
(C) Sorry, but I'm not in my office now.

Marston女士正在辦公室裡等候。
(A) 請幫我跟她說我稍後就到。

(B) 是的，在辦公室旁邊的人就是她。
(C) 抱歉，我現在不在辦公室。

因傳達了Marston女士正在等候的事實，以「請轉達我馬上就過去」回答的(A)是最為自然的答覆。

詞彙 in a moment 稍後

13.

How long will the road construction take?

(A) A stretch of road downtown.
(B) Two or three days.
(C) A work crew is there now.

道路施工需要多長時間？
(A) 通往市區的道路。
(B) 兩三天。
(C) 施工團隊現在在那裡。

利用how long在詢問道路施工的時間，因此表明具體期限為「兩三天」的(B)是正確答案。

詞彙 road construction 道路施工　a stretch of road 道路，路段　work crew 工人

14.

Do you like the oak table or the maple one?

(A) Yes, that's right.
(B) No, we don't have a table.
(C) Neither, to be honest.

你喜歡橡木桌子還是楓木桌子？
(A) 是的，沒錯。
(B) 不，我們沒有桌子。
(C) 老實說，兩個都不滿意。

以選擇疑問句來提問，所以兩者中選擇一個，兩個都選，或是兩個都不選的才會是正確答案。在選項中，用neither回答的(C)是最恰當的回答。

詞彙 oak 橡樹　maple 楓樹　neither 兩者都不是　to be honest 老實說

15.

Can the store give us a better price than that?

(A) Two dollars per gallon.
(B) I'll speak with the manager.
(C) Yes, that's the price.

那個賣場能夠給出比那價錢更低的價格嗎？
(A) 每加侖2美元。
(B) 我會和經理談談。
(C) 是的，是那價格。

利用助動詞can來詢問那些賣場可以報出更低的價格，因此包含著「不太清楚，要問問經理」的含義在的(B)才是正確答案。

詞彙 per 每　gallon 加侖(體積單位)

16.

Inspections are taking place during the night shift.

(A) Keep me informed on how they go.
(B) Working from midnight to eight A.M.

(C) She's investigating the matter.

視察會在晚上工作時間進行。
(A) 請持續告知我進展狀況。
(B) 從午夜工作到上午八點。
(C) 她正在調查此事。

已告知將要進行inspections(視察)，因此最自然的回覆是叮嚀要「告知視察的進行過程」的(A)選項。

詞彙 inspection 檢查，視察；調查　take place 出現，發生　night shift 夜間工作　keep ~ informed on 向～告知　investigate 調查

17.

Can't I make one last attempt?

(A) Nobody attempted it.
(B) No, it wasn't the last one.
(C) You had your chance.

我可以再試試看最後一次嗎？
(A) 沒有人嘗試過。
(B) 不，那不是最後一次。
(C) 你已經有過機會了。

表示出「再給我一次機會」的請求，因此選項要對此有接受或是拒絕的意思存在才是正確答案，所以要選擇有拒絕意味在的選項(C)。

詞彙 attempt 試圖；嘗試　chance 機會

18.

The contract will be delivered by tomorrow.

(A) Signed and approved.
(B) Thanks for the update.
(C) No, we're not in contact.

合同將於明天交付。
(A) 已經簽名並批准了。
(B) 謝謝你告訴我。
(C) 不，我們不聯繫。

已告知與合同有關的情報，因此對此做出「謝謝你告訴我」的回覆(B)是最合適的。(A)是以和contract意思相通的singed（簽名）及approved（批准），(C)是以和contract發音相似的contact（接觸，聯絡）造成混淆的陷阱。

詞彙 contract 契約，合同　deliver 投遞　approve 批准　update 最新情報；更新　in contact 聯繫，互相聯繫

19.

Is this the user's manual for the copier?

(A) No, I haven't used it all day.
(B) I think Mary's got it now.
(C) Ten double-sided copies.

這是影印機的使用手冊嗎？
(A) 不，我一整天都沒有使用過。
(B) Mary好像拿著使用手冊。
(C) 十份雙面複印件。

雖然是由be動詞起頭的疑問句，但這題要是單純地只在選項中找到yes或no的話，就會很難找到正確答案的題目。正確答案是(B)，但是需要把(B)選項前的"No, it isn't"當作是被省略掉的句子才行。作為參

考，這裡的it指的是使用手冊。

詞彙 manual 使用說明書，手冊 copier 影印機 all day 一整天 double-sided 兩面

20.

Why aren't you attending the conference in Las Vegas?

(A) Mr. Douglas sent Tina there instead.
(B) Yes, starting in a few minutes.
(C) I was in Las Vegas on vacation.

為什麼你沒有參加拉斯維加斯的會議？
(A) Douglas讓Tina代替我去了。
(B) 是的，幾分鐘之後開始。
(C) 我休假的時候在拉斯維加斯。

利用疑問詞why詢問為什麼不參加會議的理由，所以正確答案是表明不參加的理由(A)。

詞彙 attend 參加 conference 會議 on vacation 休假中

21.

Management just announced everyone's getting a bonus.

(A) He's not a manager.
(B) What a pleasant surprise.
(C) When is the announcement?

剛才管理層宣布大家都會得到獎金。
(A) 他不是經理。
(B) 這是個多麼令人驚訝又開心的消息。
(C) 什麼時候發表？

聽到獎金消息最自然的反應是(B)。已經發表過卻問「什麼時候發表」的(C)是錯誤的。

詞彙 management 經營，管理層 announce 告知，發表 bonus 獎金，分紅

22.

The sale isn't still going on, is it?

(A) Actually, it ends on Friday.
(B) Yes, that's where we're going.
(C) No, I didn't buy them on sale.

打折活動已經沒有了，對吧？
(A) 事實上，到星期五結束。
(B) 是的，那裡就是我們要去的地方。
(C) 不，我不在打折的時候買。

利用反問句詢問打折活動有沒有結束，因此用「到星期五結束」間接回答打折尚未結束的(A)是最合適的回答。

詞彙 sale 打折，促銷 still 還是，依舊 go on 進行，持續 on sale 促銷中

23.

That product is currently out of stock.

(A) Thanks. I'll take two then.
(B) He owns stock in that firm.
(C) I'm sorry to hear that.

那件商品現在缺貨。

(A) 謝謝，那我要買兩個。
(B) 他持有該公司的股票。
(C) 我很遺憾聽到這消息。

需要選擇對於缺貨這句話最合適的回應。對於缺貨這句話回答「謝謝」的(A)無法成為正確答案，而(B)的stock為股票的意思，因此正確答案是表現出遺憾的(C)。

詞彙 currently 現在 out of stock 缺貨 own 擁有 stock 股票 firm 公司

24.

Where should we set up the intern's desk?

(A) Yes, he's already at his desk.
(B) She's going to be here by nine.
(C) In the corner by Jack's cubicle.

我們應該要把實習生的桌子放到哪裡呢？
(A) 是的，他已經到他的位置了。
(B) 他會在9點以前到達這裡。
(C) 在Jack座位旁邊的角落。

利用疑問詞where詢問桌子要放在哪裡，因此正確答案是說出具體位置的(C)。

詞彙 set up 設置 intern 實習生 cubicle 小隔間，(以隔板分開的)辦公室

25.

Haven't they responded to our bid yet?

(A) Not to the best of my knowledge.
(B) I'll respond to you when I can.
(C) People keep making bids on the item.

他們還沒有回覆我們的出價嗎？
(A) 據我所知，還沒有。
(B) 有時間的話會答覆的。
(C) 人們持續對該項目進行投標。

利用否定疑問句詢問是否有回覆，因此表示「沒有」的否定意味的(A)才是正確答案。(B)和(C)都分別重複使用了問題中出現過的respond及bid來誘導回答錯誤的陷阱。

詞彙 respond 回應，答覆 bid 報價；投標 to the best of my knowledge 據我所知 make a bid 投標

26.

I suggest consulting on the matter with Ms. O'Leary first.

(A) I didn't pay the consultation fee.
(B) We'd better do that then.
(C) No, she's on vacation this week.

關於這個問題，我建議先和O'Leary女士商量一下。
(A) 我沒有付諮詢費用。
(B) 這樣比較好。
(C) 不，她這周休假。

利用動詞suggest提出建議，因此應該要有接受或拒絕意味在的句子來回答。正確答案是有接受意義的(B)。

詞彙 consult 諮詢，商量 consultation fee 諮詢費 had better 還是～好

27.

Should we go downtown by bus or in your car?

(A) I took the bus this morning.
(B) I prefer to drive there.
(C) His car is at the garage.

我們要搭公車去市區還是搭你的車去呢？
(A) 我今天早上搭了公車。
(B) 開車去比較好。
(C) 他的車在車庫裡。

藉由選擇疑問句來詢問要搭公車還是開車，因此明確地指明後者的(B)是正確答案。

詞彙　by bus 搭乘公車　garage 車庫

28.

What's the next item on the agenda?

(A) I need to check on that.
(B) No, I've got the agenda here.
(C) This item is on sale.

下一個提案是什麼？
(A) 我需要先確認一下。
(B) 不，這裡有提案。
(C) 這件產品正在促銷中。

詢問有沒有提案，對此最自然的回應是回答「不知道，需要確認」的(A)。對於以疑問詞what開頭的提問，用no回答的(B)不是正確答案。

詞彙　agenda 議題，提案　check on 確認，檢查

29.

How many hours of overtime did Mr. Collins work?

(A) The overtime rate is higher.
(B) Until seven thirty every day.
(C) Susan in Accounting can tell you.

Collins先生加班幾小時了？
(A) 加班費更多。
(B) 到每天七點三十分。
(C) 會計部門的Susan會告訴你的。

利用how many hours來詢問Collins先生的加班時長，對此指出「Susan應該知道」的(C)是正確答案。這裡不能把不是回答出「時間」而是回答「時刻」的(B)當成是正確答案。

詞彙　overtime 加班　overtime rate 加班費

30.

Shall we book seats on the train leaving in the morning?

(A) Okay, let's do that.
(B) No, it hasn't left yet.
(C) Yes, the books are on the seat.

要訂上午出發的火車座位嗎？
(A) 好，就那樣做。
(B) 不，還沒有離開。
(C) 是的，書在椅子上面。

以助動詞shall開頭的疑問句通常具有提案的意味，因此表示接受提案的(A)是最自然的回答。

詞彙　book 預訂；書　seat 座位，位子

31.

The electrician has arrived to look at the lighting.

(A) Yes, it's bright in here.
(B) Show him where the problem is.
(C) I already paid the electric bill.

電工來查看照明。
(A) 是的，這裡很明亮。
(B) 跟他說問題在哪裡。
(C) 我已經繳完電費了。

想一想電工到了之後要做什麼就能夠輕鬆地找到答案了。正確答案是「跟電工說明有什麼問題」的(B)。

詞彙　electrician 電工　lightning 照明　pay 支付　electric bill 電費帳單

PART 3

[32-34]

W　Hello. This is Stacia Peterson in the Accounting Department. My computer has stopped working, so I need someone to repair it at once.

M　Yes, Ms. Peterson. I sent a person to your office to fix it a couple of hours ago just as you requested. Hasn't he arrived yet?

W　Actually, he already fixed it and then left. But ten minutes after that happened, the computer stopped working again.

M　It sounds like you might need to get a new machine. Why don't you speak with your boss to see if the funding is available to purchase one?

W　你好，我是會計部門的Stacia Peterson。我的電腦當機了，我需要能馬上過來修理它的人。

M　好的，Peterson女士。按照妳的要求，在幾個小時以前我有派人到辦公室修理了，他還沒有到嗎？

W　其實他已經修好離開了，但是過了10分鐘之後電腦又當機了。

M　聽起來妳可能需要購買一台新機器了。要不要和你的上司談談，看看是否有預算再購買一台？

詞彙　request 要求　machine 機器　funding 資金　purchase 購買

32.

女人為什麼會打電話給男人？
(A) 為了尋求建議。
(B) 為了要求道歉。
(C) 為了請求修理。
(D) 為了提出提案。

在對話的開始部分，女人因為自己的電腦壞了，從「需要人來修理(so I need someone to repair it at once)」這點可以得知女人打電話的理由是(C)。

33.

根據女人說的話，暗示了什麼？

(A) **她之前打過電話給男人。**
(B) 她是客服人員。
(C) 她即將要離開辦公室。
(D) 她在對男人生氣。

當女人要求派人過來修理電腦的時候，男人說"I sent a person to your office to fix it a couple of hours ago just as you requested."詢問修理人員有沒有過去，透過這些可以推測出男人在那之前也收到女人要求修理電腦的請求，因此(A)是正確答案。

34.

男人對女人說什麼？

(A) 等他過去辦公室。
(B) 借用同事的設備。
(C) **考慮購買新的設備。**
(D) 要求更多的預算。

在對話的最後一部分，男人暗示女人的電腦處於無法修理的狀態同時還說"Why don't you speak with your boss to see if the funding is available to purchase one?"，這裡的one指的是電腦，最終男人的建議是買一台新電腦，因此正確答案是(C)。

詞彙　borrow 借用

[35-37]

M	Hello, Ms. Carter. This is Ken Stewart. I'd like you to know that the owner of the home you made a bid on has agreed to your offer. Congratulations.
W	That's wonderful news. My family will be so excited to hear that. When do you think we can complete the paperwork?
M	That should take a couple of days. Could you send me the name of the bank that will be financing your mortgage as well as the contact person? I need to speak with that person to arrange everything.
W	Of course. Hold on one second. I've got that information written down here.
M	Carter女士妳好，我是Ken Stewart。想通知妳，妳所投標的住宅屋主已接受妳的報價了。恭喜妳。
W	真是個好消息，我的家人聽到也會很高興的。您認為什麼時候能夠完成書面作業呢？
M	大約需要兩天左右，可以告訴我提供貸款的銀行及那裡的負責人名字嗎？要處理所有事情的話需要和那位商談。
W	當然，請稍等一下，這裡有寫相關內容。

詞彙　make a bid 投標　paperwork 書面作業，文件手續　finance 籌措資金　mortgage 貸款，融資　as well as 以及　contact person 聯絡人　arrange 排列；處理　write down 寫下

35.

男人是誰？

(A) **不動產仲介。**
(B) 銀行職員。
(C) 建築師。
(D) 財務顧問。

在對話的開始部分，男人告知女人「投標的住宅所有人已經接受妳的報價了(owner of the home you made a bid on has agreed to your offer)」，選項中可以轉達這類消息的人只有(A)選項的「不動產仲介」。

36.

女人問了什麼事情？

(A) 需要支付的金額。
(B) **簽約的時間。**
(C) 和男人見面的場所。
(D) 拒絕提案的理由。

透過"When do you think we can complete the paperwork?"可以知道女人好奇的地方是文件，即簽訂合同的時間，因此正確答案為(B)。

37.

女人接下來應該會做什麼？

(A) 和銀行約時間。
(B) 詢問價格。
(C) **給男人一些資訊。**
(D) 建議協商。

在對話的後半部分，當男人要求女人告知交易銀行及負責人時，女人請他稍等的同時還說了"I've got that information written down here."，即可知道女人會將相關資訊告知男人，因此正確答案為(C)。

[38-40]

M	Hello, Ms. Del Rio. This is Steven Carter calling from HR. I need to talk to you about your health insurance application.
W	Is there some kind of a problem? I filled out the forms and submitted them to your office this morning.
M	Yes, I have them here in front of me. However, you failed to sign two of the papers. And you didn't include another form. Without it, you cannot get any coverage.
W	Oh, I can't believe I did that. Why don't I visit your office to do everything? I need to complete a report, but I can be there twenty minutes from now.
M	妳好，Del Rio女士，我是人事部門的Steven Carter，我需要和妳談談關於申請健康保險的事情。
W	有什麼問題嗎？我今天早上填寫完表格後送到你的部門了。
M	是的，就在我面前，但是有兩張文件沒有簽名以及妳有尚未繳交的文件，如果沒有它的話，就會沒辦法申請到保險。
W	噢，我真不敢相信我會這樣。不然我直接過去你的部門一次解決所有事情如何？雖然我要寫報告但我20分鐘後可以過去。

詞彙 health insurance 健康保險 submit 提交 in front of 在～面前 fail to 未能做～；沒有做到 include 包括 coverage 範圍；(保險的)保障

38.

男人在哪一個部門工作？
(A) 會計。
(B) 儲運。
(C) 營業。
(D) 人事。

若是知道HR就是「人事部(Human Resources)」，處理健康保險(health insurance)等員工福利問題的部門一般都是人事部，了解的話就可以輕鬆地選擇正確答案(D)。

39.

問題是什麼？
(A) 男人拒絕了女人的要求。
(B) 女人沒有完成申請程序。
(C) 保險不包括女人的手術。
(D) 文件上有一些資訊不正確。

出問題的地方是「女人沒有簽名(you failed to sign two of the papers)」及「有遺漏的文件(you didn't include another form)」。因此包含這兩問題的(B)為正確答案。

40.

女人接下來會做什麼？
(A) 聯絡保險公司。
(B) 和男人約好見面時間。
(C) 完成負責的業務。
(D) 在文件上簽名。

從女人的最後一句話"I need to complete a report, but I can be there twenty minutes from now."可以得知女人在對話之後會做的事是(C)的「完成報告」。另外，(D)是在寫完報告之後女人將要做的事情。

[41-43]

M We've had discussions with the owner of the firm, and he's willing to sell to us.

W Do you think we should do it? Buying Deerfield Manufacturing would increase our market share considerably.

M That's true. But I'm not sure that we have enough money to make the purchase.

W Why don't we try to get some financing from the bank? If we request a reasonable amount, I'm sure we can acquire a loan.

M You're probably right about that. We could also consider attracting outside investment. I'll have our attorneys look into the matter in detail.

M 我們已經與公司老闆談過了，他很樂意賣給我們。

W 你認為我們應該要這麼做嗎？收購Deerfield Manufacturing的話，我們的市場佔有率將會大大地增加。

M 是的，但我不確定我們有足夠的資金去收購。

W 那接受銀行的資金支援怎麼樣？如果我們申請適當的金額的話，肯定能夠得到融資的。

M 或許妳說的是對的，我們也可以考慮吸引外部投資，我會讓律師們再仔細研究一下這件事。

詞彙 be willing to 願意 market share 市場占有率 considerably 相當地 financing 籌措資金；融資 loan 借出；貸款 attract 吸引，引誘 investment 投資 attorney 律師 look into 研究，調查 in detail 仔細地，詳細地

41.

談話者主要在討論什麼？
(A) 他們公司的投資。
(B) 他們市場佔有率的減少。
(C) 收購競爭公司的機會。
(D) 可以在市場購買的產品。

透過"We've had discussions with the owner of the firm, and he's willing to sell to us."這句話可以得知談話者在討論收購企業的問題，以及透過"Buying Deerfield Manufacturing would increase our market share considerably."這句話可以推測出收購對象是談話者們的競爭對手，因此討論的主題是(C)。

42.

女人建議如何籌措資金？
(A) 透過銀行接受融資。
(B) 透過自行籌措資金。
(C) 透過尋找投資人。
(D) 透過出售資產。

男人提出收購資金的問題時，女人說"Why don't we try to get some financing from the bank?"即女人提議透過銀行來籌措資金，正確答案為(A)。(C)是男人提議的方法。

詞彙 raise 提高；籌(款) investor 投資人 asset 資產

43.

男人說自己要做什麼？
(A) 和律師談話。
(B) 聯絡Deerfield Manufacturing的持有人。
(C) 投標一些產品。
(D) 私人投資。

對話的最後一部分，男人說"I'll have our attorneys look into the matter in detail."的同時也提到要讓律師們研究吸引外部投資相關問題，因此正確答案為將attorneys替換成 lawyers的(A)。

[44-46]

W Joseph, we've got a problem. Samantha submitted this report, but it's full of errors. I'm supposed to give a presentation on it in thirty minutes.

M What exactly is the matter with it? Did she use the wrong data?

W That's precisely what happened. She used sales information from the first quarter, but she was supposed to report on sales from the second quarter of the year.

M That shouldn't be too much of a problem. I've got the correct information on my computer. E-mail me the report, and I'll fix all of the incorrect data. It shouldn't take me too long.

W Joseph，我們遇到問題了。Samantha交了這份報告但卻是錯誤百出，而我30分鐘之後有個關於它的發表。

M 問題出在哪裡？她用了錯誤的數據嗎？

W 就是如此。她用了第一季度的銷售資料，但她應該是要寫一份關於第二季度銷售的報告。

M 這不是什麼太大的問題。我的電腦裡有正確的資訊，把報告用e-mail傳給我的話，我會把所有錯誤的數據都改掉，這不會花費太多時間。

詞彙 error 失誤，錯誤 precisely 明確地 incorrect 錯誤的，不正確的

44.

關於Samantha，女人說什麼？
(A) 業務未在規定時間內完成。
(B) 忘記要出席會議。
(C) 使用了錯誤的資料。
(D) 影印了不相干的資料。

女人在說了Samantha寫的報告錯誤百出後，指出「她應該要使用第二季度的數據，卻用了第一季度的(She used sales information from the first quarter, but she was supposed to report on sales from the second quarter of the year.)」，因此正確答案為(C)。

45.

女人為什麼會擔心？
(A) 會議遲到。
(B) 還沒準備好發表。
(C) 直到現在一次也沒有販售過。
(D) 無法登入電腦。

在對話的前半部分，若是清楚女人說的話"I'm supposed to give a presentation on it in thirty minutes."中的it是指「錯誤百出的報告」，就可以知道女人擔心的理由是(B)。

46.

男人建議要做什麼？
(A) 列印報告。
(B) 和銷售員交談。
(C) 演講。
(D) 重寫一份文件。

對話的最後，男人說"E-mail me the report, and I'll fix all of the incorrect data."，並說自己會把錯誤訂正過來，因此男人的提議是自己會修改報告，正確答案為(D)。

詞彙 sales representative 銷售人員，推銷人員

[47-49]

W I've got some great news. Last week, the final two salespeople in the office managed to exceed their annual quotas.

M That's never happened before, has it? It looks like we're all going to get bonuses next month. This is incredible news.

W You can say that again. It's been an outstanding year for everyone. The CEO wants to take everyone in the department out to dinner on Friday.

M I don't think I can make it because I'm meeting a customer then.

W You don't want to do that. When Mr. Patterson asks to meet people here, we need to be in attendance.

W 我有好消息。上週我們部門最後兩位業務人員超額完成了他們的年終目標。

M 這是從未發生過的事情，對吧？我們全部人都有可能拿到下個月的獎金。真是令人驚訝的消息。

W 你說得對。對每個人來說是很棒的一年，老闆希望星期五能和部門的全體員工一起吃晚餐。

M 我那時候得要跟顧客見面，應該是去不了了。

W 感覺你不能那樣做，若是Patterson先生要求和這裡的所有人見面的話，我們一定得要出席。

詞彙 salespeople 店員，業務人員 manage to 設法 exceed 超過 quota 配額 incredible 難以置信的，驚人的 outstanding 出色的 in attendance 參加，出席

47.

根據女人的說法，上周發生了什麼？
(A) 晚上有一場特別的聚餐。
(B) 錄取新進員工。
(C) 出現了創紀錄的銷售額。
(D) 被授予獎賞。

在對話一開始的部分，女人說上周最後兩位業務人員達到目標之後，男人問了"That's never happened before, has it?"，透過這些可以推測出這是史無前例的業績，因此正確答案為(C)。

詞彙 sales record 業績，創紀錄的銷售額 give out 分發，散發

48.

男人為什麼很高興？
(A) 會得到額外的獎金。
(B) 調職申請被批准了。
(C) 和新顧客簽約了。
(D) 和公司總裁見面了。

聽到達到目標時，男人說"It looks like we're all going to get

9

bonuses next month."的同時表現出對於獎金的期待感,正確答案是將bonuses替換成extra money的(A)。

49.

女人在說 "You don't want to do that" 的時候在暗示什麼?

(A) 男人必須要申請升職。

(B) 男人必須要完成報告。

(C) 男人必須要取消約會。

(D) 男人必須要立刻道歉。

後面的句子是表示「不可能」的意思,這裡的do that在文章脈絡上是指和顧客見面(meeting a customer),因此這句子間接表示出男人應該要取消和顧客的會面去見老闆,正確答案為(C)。

[50-52]

M	Mr. Lords gave us permission to attend next week's workshop on public speaking. Do you know how many people in the office intend to attend it? The company will pay for everybody to go.
W	That's a good question. I've heard quite a few people discussing it the past couple of days. Everyone seems rather excited about the event.
M	Well, the deadline for registration is tomorrow. I'd better make an announcement on the company Web page so that interested people can talk to me.
W	Good thinking. I'll spread the word as well. I know at least three people who want to go.
M	Lords先生允許我們參加下週有關公開演講的研討會,你知道辦公室裡有多少人想要參加嗎?公司會支付所有人的費用。
W	好問題。前兩天我聽到很多人都在討論,好像有很多人都很期待這次的活動。
M	嗯,明天就是申請截止日。為了能讓有興趣的人跟我說,感覺在公司網站上公告一下會比較好。
W	好主意,我也會把消息傳播出去的,至少我知道想要去的人就有3個了。

詞彙 permission 允許,准許 intend to 打算 quite a few 相當多 rather 相當,頗 make an announcement on 介紹,公布 spread the word 散佈消息

50.

對話主要在說什麼?

(A) 電影。

(B) 會議。

(C) 研討會

(D) 就業博覽會。

在對話的第一句話「關於下週公開演講的研討會(next week's workshop on public speaking)」就可以很容易預想到這會是對話的主題。正確答案為(C)。

51.

男人要在哪裡公告?

(A) 報紙。

(B) 網路。

(C) 公告欄。

(D) 員工休息室。

男人為了讓想要參加研討會的人能和自己說,他「要在公司網頁上公告(I'd better make an announcement on the company Web page)」,所以公告的地方是(B)。

詞彙 bulletin board 布告欄 employee lounge 員工休息室

52.

女人說自己要做什麼?

(A) 和其他職員說活動的事情。

(B) 要申請進行教育項目。

(C) 安排與她的主管見面。

(D) 明天休息一天。

如果知道對話最後部分的"I'll spread the word as well."中的spread the word是「傳播消息」的意思,就可以很容易地找到正確答案。也就是說,女人要做的事情是告訴同事關於申請研討會的內容,因此(A)是正確答案。作為參考,(A)選項的event是表示workshop的意思。

詞彙 supervisor 監督人,管理人 take a day off 休假一天

[53-55]

M	Lucy, I can't travel to Jenkins Consulting with you. Mr. Briggs needs me to do some work.
W1	Okay. I don't want to be late, so I'll just go ahead and leave now.
M	Great. I'll meet you there in an hour or so. Oh . . . I'll be driving. Do you know how to get there?
W1	Sorry, but I always take the bus since I don't own a car.
M	I wonder who knows where it is.
W2	You're going to Jenkins Consulting today? Why don't we go there together? I can give you directions.
M	Sounds good, Mary. I'll let you know as soon as I'm ready to leave.
M	Lucy,我不能和妳一起去Jenkins諮詢了。Briggs先生需要我先幫他做一些事。
W1	好,我不想遲到,所以現在要準備出發了。
M	好,大約一個小時後在那裡見吧。噢……我會開車去,妳知道要怎麼去嗎?
W1	抱歉,我沒有車所以都是搭公車去的。
M	我好奇有沒有知道那地方位置的人。
W1	你今天要去Jenkins諮詢嗎?那要一起去嗎?我可以幫你指路。
M	感覺不錯,Mary。我準備好了就會跟妳說的。

詞彙 give ~ directions 給~指路 as soon as 一~就~

53.

談話者主要在討論什麼？
(A) 即將來臨的面試。
(B) 公司的位置。
(C) 和Briggs先生的會議。
(D) 工作分配。

在討論一間叫作「Jenkins 諮詢」企業的位置，正確答案是將Jenkins Consulting稱為a business的(B)。

54.

男人要怎麼去Jenkins諮詢？
(A) 地鐵。
(B) 公車。
(C) 汽車。
(D) 計程車。

男人說"I'll be driving."之後問了Jenkins諮詢的位置，因此可以得知男人要開車去那地方，正確答案為(C)。做為參考，若是問到女人1是利用什麼交通手段的話，正確答案則會變成(B)。

55.

Mary提議要做什麼？
(A) 跟男人說位置。
(B) 寫男人的報告。
(C) 跟Briggs先生說。
(D) 聯絡Jenkins諮詢的某人。

在對話的最後部分，Mary提議要一起去Jenkins 諮詢的同時還說到"I can give you directions."，因為要指路所以提議一起走，正確答案為(A)。

[56-58]

W	Dave, did you happen to see the job posting on the internal message board? It's for a managerial position in the HR Department. I wonder if I should apply for it.
M	Why wouldn't you? You've got managerial experience, and I'm sure you're qualified. Would it be a better job than the one you've got now?
W	Definitely. The only thing is that it's not in this office. It's at the Montgomery branch, so I'd have a much longer commute.
M	If it's a good career opportunity, you might consider moving. Then you wouldn't have to worry about long driving times.

W	Dave你有看到公司公告欄上的招聘廣告嗎？是有關於人事部的管理職位，我不知道我該不該去應聘。
M	為什麼不去？妳不是有管理經驗也符合條件資格，會比現在的職位更好吧。
W	當然。只是問題是那職位並不在這裡的辦公室，因為是蒙哥馬利分公司的職位，所以通勤時間會更長。
M	如果在經歷上是個很好的機會的話，就考慮看看搬家吧。那樣的話也不用擔心會花很多時間在開車上了。

詞彙 job posting 招聘廣告　internal 內部的　message board 電子布告欄　managerial 經營上的，管理的　qualified 符合資格的　definitely 清楚地，確實地　the only thing is 只是　commute 通勤　opportunity 機會

56.

對話主要在講什麼？
(A) 調職。
(B) 搬新家。
(C) 累積主管經驗。
(D) 要求提高薪水。

對話的重點在於女人要不要去應聘「人事部的管理職位(a managerial position in the HR Department)」，因此正確答案為(A)。

57.

女人在說"Definitely"的時候是在指什麼？
(A) 她很期待在蒙哥馬利工作。
(B) 招聘的職位比現在的還高。
(C) 她申請要調去分公司。
(D) 她重視經歷。

雖然definitely是表示「確切地」或是「明確地」的意思，但在這種情況下，強烈地表示與對方有同感的時候也會經常使用到。在這裡，因為男人說「招聘的職位比現在的還高」，而女人表現出強烈的同感，由此可得知她所指的是(B)。

58.

男人建議女人做什麼？
(A) 在大學聽課。
(B) 購買更好的車。
(C) 搬去其他城市。
(D) 再積累更多經歷。

因為女人在擔心如果調職成功的話，通勤時間就會變長，所以男人在說"If it's a good career opportunity, you might consider moving."的同時還提議她要不要搬家，正確答案為(C)。

[59-61]

W1	Hello. I'd like to purchase these items, please. And I've got this coupon.
M	Hmm . . . It looks as if the coupon has expired. I'm afraid you can't use it.
W1	Expired? But I cut this coupon out of the *Scranton Times* this morning. How is that possible?
M	Hold on a moment, please. Denice, could you look at this coupon here?
W2	Ah, yeah. The newspaper made a printing mistake regarding the date. You can go ahead and process it, Luke. Do the same for any other customers as well.
M	Thank you very much. All right, ma'am, your total comes to $87.98. Will this be cash or charge?
W1	Cash.

W1	你好，我想要購買這些產品，還有我也帶了折價券。
M	恩……好像已經過了使用期限，很遺憾地這並不能使用。
W1	你說它過期了？但我是今天早上從Scranton Times剪下來的，怎麼可能會有這種事呢？
M	請稍等一下。Denice，能幫我看一下這張優惠券嗎？
W2	阿，好的。報社在日期上有印刷錯誤，直接處理就可以了，Luke，對其他顧客也是一樣的。
M	真的很謝謝妳。好的，客人這樣總共是87.98美元，請問要用現金還是刷卡呢？
W1	現金。

詞彙 coupon 優惠券 expire (時間)期滿 regarding 關於 process 處理 total 整體，全部 Will this be cash or charge? 現金還是刷卡呢？

59.

男人是做什麼的？

(A) 收銀員。
(B) 顧客。
(C) 主管。
(D) 賣場主人。

從整體對話的內容來看，因為對方是想要使用優惠券的顧客，那麼男人應該會是(A)選項的收銀員。

60.

問題出在哪裡？

(A) 日期印刷錯誤。
(B) 商品的保存期限已經過期了。
(C) 有幾個產品缺貨了。
(D) 顧客的信用卡遺失了。

從"The newspaper made a printing mistake regarding the date."中可以找到問題出在哪裡。也就是說，因為報社把日期印錯而導致在使用優惠券上造成混亂，因此正確答案為(A)。

61.

Denice對男人說要做什麼？

(A) 閱讀地方報紙。
(B) 向女人道歉。
(C) 退款。
(D) 給顧客優惠。

在對話的後半部分，女人2對男人下達「使用優惠券(You can go ahead and process it, Luke.)」及「對其他顧客也一樣(Do the same for any other customers as well.)」的指示，因此兩個選項中，指出前者的(D)為正確答案。

[62-64]

夏季特別講座

演講人	日期
Harold Grace	6月 11日
Angela Steele	6月 28日
Marcia White	7月 16日
Orlando Watson	8月 2日

W	We've got every speaker for this summer's lecture series at the library scheduled, right?
M	Unfortunately, one of them canceled on us. Marcia White e-mailed today to say that she can't make it.
W	Okay, we'll have to find a replacement for her. Do you have anyone in mind?
M	We could ask Derrick Stone to speak in her place. We wanted him to come here last year, but we couldn't accommodate his schedule. We could try again this year.
W	Let's do that. Were you the person that spoke with him last year?
M	That's right. I'll give him a call and see if he's interested.

W	這次在圖書館舉辦的夏季特別講座，所有演講人的日程都定好了，對吧？
M	遺憾的是，他們之中有一個人取消了。Marcia White今天傳了e-mail說她不能來。
W	這樣啊，那就得要找找代替她的人了。有考慮中的人嗎？
M	我們可以邀請Derrick Stone來演講以代替她。去年也希望他能過來的，但行程對不上，今年可以再邀請一次。
W	就那樣做，去年和他談的人是你嗎？
M	是的，我聯絡他看看他是否有興趣。

詞彙 lecture 講課，演講 cancel on 取消約定, 爽約 replacement 代替，替代物 in one's place 代替某人 accommodate 接受；滿足(要求)

62.

看圖，哪一天需要替代演講人？

(A) 6月11日。
(B) 6月28日。
(C) 7月16日。
(D) 8月2日。

在"Marcia White e-mailed today to say that she can't make it."這句子中可以得知講座中無法參加的演講人是Marcia White。如果在圖中找到她的名字的話，就可以知道要代替她的演講人要演講的日期是(C)的7月16日。

63.

關於Derrick Stone，男人說了什麼？

(A) 他是圖書館員工。
(B) 他這次的夏季行程排得滿滿的。
(C) 他不在這地方住了。
(D) 他去年曾作為演講人被考慮過。

男人在指定Derrick Stone為演講人候補之後，表示「去年也邀請過他，但行程對不上(We wanted him to come here last year, but we couldn't accommodate his schedule.)」，因此可以得知他在去年的活動當時曾作為演講人選被考慮過，正確答案為(D)。

詞彙 no longer 再也不

64.

男人接下來會做什麼？

(A) 聯絡Derrick Stone。
(B) 調整講座行程。
(C) 匯錢給演講人。
(D) 為了活動去印傳單。

從男人最後一句話"I'll give him a call and see if he's interested."可以知道他要打電話給演講人候選Derrick Stone，因此正確答案為(A)。

詞彙 flyer 傳單

[65-67]

部門	層數
營業部／儲運部	1樓
會計部／人事部	2樓
研發部	3樓
行銷部	4樓

M Pardon me, but I'm a new employee here, and I seem to be a bit lost. Can you tell me where Roger Potter's office is, please?

W Oh, it's your lucky day. His office is right across the hall from mine. We both work in the Marketing Department. I'll take you there now.

M Thanks a lot. By the way, my name's Doug Harper. I work in the Accounting Department.

W It's nice to meet you, Doug. I'm Amy Messier. I've heard about you. You'll be working with me on the Scofield project.

M Yes, that's right. My boss told me that it has been assigned to me.

M 不好意思，因為我是新進員工，好像迷路了，能告訴我Roger Potter的辦公室在哪裡嗎？

W 噢，你運氣很好呢，他的辦公室就在我辦公室的對面，我們兩個都在市場部工作，我現在就帶你去那裡。

M 謝謝妳，順帶一提，我的名字是Doug Harper，我在會計部工作。

W 很高興見到你，Doug。我叫Amy Messier。我有聽過關於你的事情。你將會在Scofield項目中和我一起工作。

M 是的，沒錯。我上司說，那項工作分配給我了。

詞彙 by the way 順帶一提　boss 上司，社長　assign 分配，交代

65.

男人的問題是什麼？
(A) 會議遲到。
(B) 忘記要帶文件。
(C) 找不到辦公室。
(D) 沒帶身分證。

在對話開始的部分，男人說自己好像迷路了之後，還說"Can you tell me where Roger Potter's office is, please?"，問了Roger Potter的辦公室位置，因此正確答案為(C)。

66.

看圖，談話者們應該會去幾樓？
(A) 1樓。
(B) 2樓。
(C) 3樓。
(D) 4樓。

男人要找的地方是Roger Potter的辦公室，女人說他的辦公室在自己的辦公室對面。另外，女人說Roger Potter和自己是同一部門，也就是市場部，最終他們要去的地方是市場部所在的(D)的4樓。

67.

可以知道關於談話者的什麼？
(A) 他們在其他公司一起工作。
(B) 他們都住在Scofield。
(C) 他們就快要在某個項目中一起工作。
(D) 他們今天有預定的會議。

在對話的後半部分女人說的話"You'll be working with me on the Scofield project."中可以得知談話者們將會一起投入到一個叫作Scofield的項目，因此正確答案為(C)。

詞彙 collaborate 合作，協助

[68-70]

	2	1	辦公室
電梯			
	3	員工休息室	4

M Hello, Jennifer. This is Dave. I just pulled into the parking lot, so I should be in your office in a moment.

W Don't go to my office this time. There are five people attending today's meeting, so you should drop by the conference room instead.

M I'm not sure where that is.

W Just take the elevator to the fourth floor. When you get out, it's the third room on the right. It's right beside the employee lounge.

M Okay. Does the room have a projector? I've got some slides to show you.

W No, but I'll have one of my assistants get one.

M	Jennifer，你好。我是Dave，剛才進停車場了，等一下就可以到妳的辦公室。
W	這次別來我辦公室，這次來開會的有五個人，所以要去會議室。
M	我不知道那地方在哪裡。
W	請搭電梯到四樓，出來後右手邊第三個房間，員工休息室就在旁邊。
M	知道了，會議室裡有投影機嗎？有幾張需要給妳看的投影片。
W	雖然沒有，但我會讓我助理帶過去的。

詞彙 pull into 到達　drop by 訪問　employee lounge 員工休息室　projector 放映機，投影機

68.
關於男人的暗示是什麼？
(A) 之前沒有見過女人。
(B) 他是開車去女人辦公室的。
(C) 希望女人作為客戶簽名。
(D) 只有要跟女人見面。

在對話的前半部分，男人一邊說「正在進入停車場 (I just pullled into the parking lot)」，一邊告訴對方自己的位置，因此可以知道男人開車，正確答案為(B)。從女人說的話"Don't go to my office this time." 可以知道(A)是錯誤的，以及在會有五個人參加會議這一點上也能夠知道(D)不是正確答案。

69.
看圖，會議室在哪裡？
(A) 1號房。
(B) 2號房。
(C) 3號房。
(D) 4號房。

女人對正在詢問會議室位置的男人說那地方在四樓右側的第三間房，就在員工休息室的旁邊。在地圖上找到符合這些條件的會議室地點是(D)。

70.
男人要求什麼？
(A) 茶點。
(B) 視聽設備。
(C) 影印。
(D) 筆跟便條紙。

在對話的後半部分，男人說"Does the room have a projector?"，詢問有沒有裝設投影機，因此正確答案為將projector替換成visual equipment的(B)選項。

詞彙 refreshment 零食，茶點　visual equipment 視聽設備，放映機器　photocopy 影印　notepad 便條紙

PART 4
[71-73]

M	The next item on the agenda concerns Blue Harvest Insurance. As you're aware, it's our major competitor in the auto insurance field. It appears we may be able to acquire the company. I spoke with Harvey Field, the president, and he told me the owner is looking to sell if the price is right. If we acquired it, we'd become the largest auto insurance provider in the country. We need to conduct a detailed examination of Blue Harvest and come up with a price we're willing to pay. Susan Phillips in Accounting is in charge of this project, so I'll let her tell you what we intend to do.
M	下一個是有關Blue Harvest保險的提案。大家應該都知道，在汽車保險領域中他們是我們的主要競爭對手。我們認為我們可以收購該公司，我和Harvey Field社長談過，他說如果價格合適的話，那裡的老闆也會考慮出售。如果我們收購的話，我們將會是全國最大的保險公司。我們必須要對Blue Harvest進行詳細的調查並計算出我們願意支付的收購價格。會計部的Susan Phillips會負責這次的項目，所以請聽她說明我們打算要做什麼。

詞彙 agenda 議題，提案　concern 關聯　competitor 競爭對手　insurance 保險　acquire 獲得，接受　provider 供應商　conduct 實施，實行　examination 調查，研究　come up with 想出(主意)　be willing to 樂意　in charge of 負責，承擔

71.
說話者主要在討論什麼？
(A) 收購競爭公司的計劃。
(B) 公司的年收入。
(C) 汽車保險業。
(D) 最近的保險費用計算問題。

談話的前半段，說話者提到收購Blue Harvest保險公司的可能性以及收購所需的工作等等，因此談話的主題為(A)。

詞彙 profit 收入，利潤　recent 最近的　price 價格，定價

72.
說話者想要做什麼？
(A) 排定會議。
(B) 改變位置。
(C) 保險。
(D) 分析競爭公司。

在談話的中間部分，說話者說到為了要收購競爭公司需要「對Blue Harvest詳細調查(a detailed examination of Blue Harvest)」以及「定下收購價格(come up with a price we're willing to pay) 」，因此正確答案是包含這兩者及有關連的(D)選項。

73.
接下來應該會發生什麼事？
(A) 說明預算方案。
(B) 其他人會講話。

(C) 實行問券調查。

(D) 會看到投影片。

在最後一句話介紹了名為Susan Phillips的負責人，並說到"I'll let her tell you what we intend to do"，也就是說，在談話之後預定將會由Susan Phillips來說話，正確答案為(B)。

[74-76]

> **W** Hello, David. This is Janice Holloway. I received your message and would love to meet to discuss your company's services. You mentioned Wednesday, but that's not ideal for me. Instead, I'm free on Thursday afternoon between two and four. Would you mind visiting my office? My firm is in the Jackson Building on Seventh Avenue. I recommend taking the subway here because traffic is always terrible that time of the day. Take Exit 4 at Seventh Avenue Station and walk straight ahead for two minutes. I'm on the ninth floor in room 902. Please call me back to confirm you'll be able to make it here.
>
> -
>
> **W** 你好,David. 我是Janice Holloway。我收到了你的訊息，希望能見面討論一下關於你公司的服務。雖然你提議星期三見面，但對我來說不是個好時間。我星期四下午2點到4點有空，您能來我的辦公室嗎？我們公司在第七大道Jackson大廈內。因為當天那個時段交通擁堵嚴重，建議你搭乘地鐵過來這裡。從Seventh Avenue站4號出口出來直走兩分鐘。我在9樓的902室。請再打電話告訴我你能不能過來。

詞彙 ideal 理想的 recommend 推薦 terrible 可怕的 confirm 確認 make it 做到；及時趕到

74.
說話者在講"That's not ideal for me"的時候在暗示什麼？

(A) 她不能夠接受接話採訪。

(B) 她不會離開自己的辦公室。

(C) 她覺得出價價格太低。

(D) 她沒辦法在星期三見面。

在文章脈絡上，that指的是對方要求見面的星期三，所以句子的意思可以看作是(D)。在接下來的句子中，說話者也有提議要在星期四見面，而不是星期三。

75.
說話者為什麼要建議搭地鐵？

(A) 預計交通堵塞會很嚴重。

(B) 大廈沒有停車場。

(C) 在市區開車很困難。

(D) 她的辦公室就在地鐵站旁邊。

說話者向對方推薦地鐵，並說明理由是"traffic is always terrible that time of the day."。也就是說，因為交通堵塞而提議利用地鐵的(A)選項為正確答案。辦公室距離地鐵站有兩分鐘路程，但距離很近這一點並不是推薦的直接原因。

詞彙 parking lot 停車場 next to ～的旁邊

76.
說話者要求聽者做什麼？

(A) 展示產品。

(B) 寄一封確認用e-mail。

(C) 帶文件過來。

(D) 打電話給自己。

在最後一句話"Please call me back to confirm you'll be able to make it here."中，說話者要求的是(D)的打電話。

詞彙 product demonstration 說明產品，展示產品 confirmation 確認 give ~ a phone call 給某人打電話

[77-79]

> **M** Let me congratulate everybody on your performance last quarter. You not only met your expected production targets but also exceeded them by 25%. That has never happened before. As a result, we'll be handing out bonuses to everyone. First of all, every employee at the company will receive a cash bonus of five hundred dollars. In addition, the top two performers in each department will receive an extra five days of paid vacation. Those winners will be announced next week after I consult with the department heads. Now, let's keep up the great work and outdo ourselves this quarter.
>
> -
>
> **M** 對於上一季度的成果，想要對大家說一聲恭喜。各位不僅僅是達成生產目標，而且還超額完成了目標量的25%。這是史無前例的事情，也因此，我們將給所有人發獎金。首先，公司所有職員將獲得獎金現金500美元。另外，各部門中成績最優秀的兩名職員將會有為期五天的特別休假。我和部門負責人商量過後，將於下周公佈獲獎者。好，繼續保持這氣氛，這一季度也好好做吧。

詞彙 performance 成果；表演 not only A but also B 不僅是A，B也 meet 見面；配合 production target 生產目標 exceed 超過 hand out 分給 bonus 獎金，分紅 first of all 優先，首先 extra 追加的，額外的 paid vacation 有薪假 announce 發表 consult 商量，討論 keep up 維持 outdo oneself 比之前好

77.
說話者在說"That has never happened before"的時候是指什麼事情？

(A) 公司不曾達成過生產目標量。

(B) 公司之前沒有收入。

(C) 公司之前沒有給過員工獎勵。

(D) 公司沒有在海外開過分公司。

若是直譯句子的話，意思是「以前沒有發生過那種事」，而在前面的句子中可以得知「那種事」就是指達成目標量，因此說話者所指的是(A)。

詞彙 match 配合，一致；達成(目標) make a profit 獲利，盈利 reward 獎勵 international 國際的

78.
全體員工會得到什麼？

(A) 現金。

(B) 認股權。

(C) 特別休假。

(D) 各式各樣的禮物。

說話者對於超額達成目標量所給予的獎勵是全體員工都會獲得獎金500美元(a cash bonus of five hundred dollars)，正確答案為(A)。

79.

說話者下週會做什麼？

(A) 訪問各部門。

(B) 提名獲獎者。

(C) 在新契約上簽名。

(D) 介紹這一季度的計劃。

next week是問題的核心語句，因此要仔細觀察next week提到的部分。說話者在談話後半部分說"Those winners will be announced next week after I consult with the depart"，因此下周會發生的事情是(B)。在這句話中，各部門負責人的會議是下週舉行還是本週舉行並沒有說明。

[80-82]

> W Castor is pleased to announce our newest perfume, Escape. Escape is a rich blend of aromas designed to make you feel fresh and smell wonderful. It will be available at retail outlets and on our online sales platforms on December 15, just in time for the holidays. Escape comes in a convenient pump spray bottle and is available in two sizes, 100 and 200 milliliters. Both are reasonably priced for people of all incomes. Complimentary samples are available wherever Castor products are sold, and customers can make advance orders now. Be one of the first to try Escape, which has a rich fragrance you'll never forget.
>
> W 很高興為您介紹Castor的最新香水Escape。Escape蘊含豐富的香味，可以感到清爽的心情以及美好的香氣。配合假期的到來，可於12月15日在零售店及線上購物網站購買。Escape可作為方便的按壓式噴霧瓶使用，有兩種尺寸，100毫升和200毫升。無關收入多少，為所有人準備的這兩款產品均都以合理的價格定價。所有銷售Castor產品的商家均可獲得免費樣品，客戶現在還可以預訂，搶先體驗一下擁有令人難忘的濃郁香氣Escape。

詞彙 perfume 香水 rich 富有的；豐富的 blend 混和；混和物 aroma 香氣 retail outlet 零售店 reasonably 合理地，理性地 income 收入，所得 complimentary sample 免費樣品 advance order 預約，預訂 fragrance 香氣

80.

Castor會是什麼類型的公司？

(A) 紡織公司。

(B) 電子產品公司。

(C) 化妝品製造公司。

(D) 美髮沙龍。

Castor的企業名稱在談話的後半部分中"Complimentary samples are

available wherever Castor products are sold, and customers can make advance orders now."聽得到，這裡的免費樣品是指Escape香水的樣品，因此Castor是(C)的化妝品公司。

81.

12月15日會發生什麼事？

(A) 開始打折。

(B) 可以購買新產品。

(C) 會有幾間零售店開門。

(D) 會有產品發佈會。

透過"It will be available at retail outlets and on our online sales platforms on December 15, just in time for the holidays."這個句子可以得知12月15日是新產品Escape的發售日，正確答案為(B)。

82.

為什麼人們會去販賣Castor產品的地方？

(A) 為了要抽獎品。

(B) 為了要應徵工作。

(C) 為了訂購。

(D) 為了拿到免費樣品。

在"Complimentary samples are available wherever Castor products are sold, and customers can make advance orders now."中可以得知如果要拿到免費樣品就得要去銷售Castor產品的地方。若是沒有錯過complimentary的話，這是一題很容易就可以找到正確答案的題目，正確答案為(D)。

[83-85]

> M Before I play the latest tune by the Dervishes, I should report on last night's city council meeting. A decision was made to construct a sports facility near Highland Park. Supporters claim the stadium will create many jobs for local residents both during construction and after it's done. However, many believe the city's existing facility is sufficient and another one isn't necessary. The final cost is estimated at fifteen million dollars. That likely won't remain the same though. It's not known how the stadium will be funded, but property taxes may need to be raised. Okay, that's enough news for now.
>
> M 在播放Dervishes最新歌曲之前，為您報導關於昨晚市議會的會議，決定在Highland公園附近建設體育設施。支持者主張在建設期間和建設期間以後，將會為當地居民創造更多的工作機會。但是大多數人認為現存的市內設施已經足夠了，不需要再增加設施。最終費用估計為1千5百萬美元。但是它不會一直保持同樣的價格。雖然還不知道將如何籌措體育場建設資金，但也是有可能需要提高財產稅。好的，就目前而言，這就是全部了。

詞彙 tune 歌曲 report on 將報導關於～ city council 市議會 claim 主張 existing 現存的 sufficient 充足的 final cost 最終費用 estimate 估算，推測 fund 資金；籌措資金 property tax 財產稅

83.

根據說話者所說的話，建設體育場的好處是？

(A) 職業運動可以在那裡比賽。

(B) 就業率會增加。

(C) 那裏可以開許多場演唱會。

(D) 會為了地方居民舉辦活動。

說話者借用支持者們的話來說「建設體育場的話，工作機會會變多(the stadium will create many jobs for local residents)」，因此可以得知建設體育場的好處是(B)。

詞彙 professional 專門的，專業的　employment 就業，招聘　entertainment 娛樂，宴會，餘興

84.

說話者為什麼會說" That likely won't remain the same though"？

(A) 為了聲稱修建體育場需要好幾年時間。

(B) 為了表示費用會改變。

(C) 為了預測稅金會上漲。

(D) 為了說體育場將會建得更大。

給的句子意思為「價格不會一直維持相同的狀態」，這裡所說的that就是指前面句子的final cost。因此，所給句子的含義是(B)。

85.

聽者接下來會聽到什麼？

(A) 廣告。

(B) 體育新聞。

(C) 天氣新聞。

(D) 音樂。

如果在談話的第一部分沒有錯過"before I play the latest tune by the Dervishes"這部分的話，聽者在聽完新聞之後會聽到的是Dervishes的最新歌曲。因此正確答案是(D)。

[86-88]

> W Thank you for attending this afternoon's workshop. We'll be discussing different methods small businesses can use to improve their marketing. As you know, the biggest difficulty small businesses face is that they have fewer resources than their larger competitors. So we'll learn how to minimize those disadvantages and how to maximize the benefits of being small. Our three goals over the next four hours are to understand selective audience targeting, how to utilize the image of being small, and how to benefit from local opportunities in ways larger firms cannot. Let's start by partnering up with one another and making a list of traditional concepts in targeting potential customers.
>
> W 感謝你們出席今天下午的研討會。我們將討論中小企業為了能夠更有效行銷的各種可行性方法。大家都知道中小企業面臨的最大困難是比起規模較大的競爭企業，我們只擁有少許的資源。因此我們必須找出將這種缺點最小化，將小的優點最大化的方法。在之後的4個小時裡，我們的三個目標將會是瞭解選擇性目標受眾，活用小的形象的方法，以及透過大公司無法獲得的本地機會中獲益。讓我們相互合作列出針對潛在客戶行銷的傳統概念。

詞彙 face 直面，面對　resource 資源　minimize 最小化　disadvantage 不利因素　maximize 最大化　benefit 優惠；獲利　goal 目的，目標　selective 選擇性的　audience targeting 目標受眾　utilize 活用　partner up with 和～成為合作夥伴，和～協力　potential customer 潛在顧客　make a list of 列表格

86.

聽者們會是誰？

(A) 企業老闆。

(B) 求職者。

(C) 新進員工。

(D) 營銷專業的學生。

透過談話的整體內容可以得知，該談話是為small businesses而進行的演講。因此聽者們應該是中小企業的社長，正確答案為(A)。

87.

根據說話者所說的話，中小企業的缺點是什麼？

(A) 資源的不足。

(B) 沒有地區影響力。

(C) 行銷能力的不足。

(D) 沒有出色的員工。

說話者指出中小企業面臨的最大問題是「資源比大企業不足(they have fewer resources than their larger competitors)」。因此在談話中提到的中小企業的缺點是(A)。

88.

說話者要聽者們做什麼？

(A) 進行角色扮演的活動。

(B) 記下自己說的話。

(C) 找一起做的人。

(D) 說明各自的情況。

說話者在最後一句中提出「夥伴們聚在一起(partnering up with one another)」和「列出現有概念(making a list of traditional concepts)」，選項中的正確答案是與他們中的前者含義有關的(C)。

[89-91]

> M I'm the first to admit that conditions are less than ideal for fast-food restaurants these days. We've seen a massive decline in spending by consumers concerned about the nutritional value of their meals. To improve our profitability, we must rebrand ourselves as a healthy establishment. We'll focus on our food selection, ingredients, and image. We'll be creating new menu options, such as sweet potato crisps to replace French fries. Several dessert selections will be eliminated since they're high in calories. Most importantly, our advertising will focus on items like salads and grilled chicken. Now, look at these slides, which show how we expect these moves to affect revenues.

M 我想先承認最近快餐店的情況並不理想，我們目睹了消費者對快餐店食譜營養學價值的擔心導致消費大幅減少。為了改善效益，我們的品牌形象必須要轉變為健康的餐廳才行。我們將專注於菜單、食材以及形象，將開發代替薯片等新菜單。因為熱量高的關係，有一些甜點則會消失。最重要的是，我們的廣告將聚焦於沙拉或是烤架上的炸雞之類的菜單。好的，看看這些投影片，你會知道透過這些措施將對收益會產生什麼樣的影響。

詞彙 admit 承認 ideal 理想的 massive 大量的 decline 減少，衰退 nutritional 營養學的 value 價值 profitability 效益 rebrand 改善品牌形象 ingredient 材料 eliminate 消失，去除 grilled 在烤架上烤的 move 動向 revenue 收入

89.
談話會發生在什麼地方？
(A) 協商會。
(B) 貿易博覽會。
(C) 員工會議。
(D) 頒獎典禮。

談話中處處可見we和fast-food restaurants的關係。也就是說，說話者的公司是管轄速食店的公司，可以推測出聽眾是那些公司的職員。因此談話進行的地方應該是(C)的員工會議。

90.
說話者期待公司會有什麼樣的盈利？
(A) 透過取消幾家加盟店。
(B) 透過購買更便宜的材料。
(C) 透過在行銷上投入更多資金。
(D) 透過改變公司形象。

為了提高收益，說話者強調「應該將品牌形象改變為健康的餐廳(we must rebrand ourselves as a hearthy establishment)」。因此正確答案為(D)。

91.
說話者對於甜點說什麼？
(A) 不再提供。
(B) 是低脂肪菜單。
(C) 降價了。
(D) 尺寸很大。

透過"Several dessert selections will be eliminated since they're high in calories."這句句子裡可以看出，部分熱量高的甜點將從菜單中消失。正確答案為(A)。

[92-94]

W You have reached Hudson Bank's credit services. Our offices are currently closed for the day. Our business hours are from Monday to Friday from 9 A.M. to 7 P.M. To report a lost or stolen card, press 1. To check your account balance, press 2. To transfer your account balance from another card to your Hudson Bank card, press 3. To apply for a new Hudson Bank credit card or to increase your credit limit, press 4. To leave a message to have us call you back, press 5. You may also check your account by going to www.hudsonbank.com. This message will automatically repeat in ten seconds.

W 您已連接到Hudson銀行的信用服務，我們分行的今日營業時間已經結束。我們的營業時間為週一到週五，上午九點至下午七點。欲申報卡片遺失或被盜取請按1號鍵，欲確認結帳金額請按2號鍵；如需其他張卡片的餘額轉帳至Hudson卡，請按3號鍵；若是要申請Hudson銀行信用卡或增加信用卡額度請按4號鍵；若是需要其他服務，請按5號鍵留下訊息，我們將會回電給您。帳戶查詢可在www.hudsonbank.com查詢。這則訊息將在10秒後自動重覆。

詞彙 account balance 帳戶餘額 transfer 轉帳 apply for 申請 credit limit 信用卡額度 automatically 自動地

92.
為什麼訊息會被撥放？
(A) 銀行現在關門了。
(B) 公休日。
(C) 客服都在忙線中。
(D) 有技術性問題。

從"Our offices are currently closed for the day."這句話中可以得知因為當日營業時間已經結束，所以會重覆撥放訊息。正確答案為(A)。

93.
要如何知道用信用卡的結帳金額是多少？
(A) 按1號鍵。
(B) 按2號鍵。
(C) 撥打另外一個電話。
(D) 留下語音訊息。

問題中的"how much money is owed on a credit card?"是指使用信用卡後負債的金額，也就是說，是「用信用卡結帳的金額(account balance)」。透過訊息可以得知能夠透過按下2號鍵進行確認，因此正確答案是(B)。

94.
關於銀行的服務提到了什麼？
(A) 正在更新。
(B) 可以透過網路使用。
(C) 無法透過網路使用。
(D) 為全世界的人們利用。

在談話的後半部分，說話者說"You may also check your account by going to www.hudsonbank.com."，並介紹帳戶查詢可以在網路上進行。因此在選項中提及的事項是(B)。

詞彙 no longer 不再，再也不

[95-97]

負責人	電話號碼
Robert Spartan	874-8547
Jessica Davis	874-9038
Marcia West	874-1294
Allen Barksdale	874-7594

W According to our sales predictions, we'll experience an excellent second quarter just about everywhere. Sales are up in Asia, Australia, and Europe. They're a bit down in the United States, but we'll still be profitable. The only place we're losing money is in Canada, but we just expanded there, so that's not very surprising. Now, one last thing before we finish. Some of you still haven't signed up for your medical insurance. That needs to be done no later than today at 6:00, so get in touch with Jessica Davis at once. This benefit is part of your employment package, so take advantage of it.

W 根據我們的銷售量預測，任何地方似乎都將會有出色的第二季度表現。亞洲、澳大利亞以及歐洲的銷售量都在增長。美國雖然稍微有點低迷，但還是會有盈利。唯一有赤字的地區是加拿大，因爲不久前在那裡進行了事業擴張，這並不會令人太過驚訝。好，在結束之前我再說一句話。在大家之中有一些人還沒有投保醫療保險。最晚必須在今天六點之前完成，請立即與Jessica Davies聯繫。這個福利是員工福利的一環所以請充分利用它。

詞彙 prediction 預測，預想 experience 經歷，體驗 profitable 盈利 medical insurance 醫療保險 not later than 最晚在～之前 get in touch with 和～聯絡 employment package 員工福利待遇 take advantage of 利用

95.

說話者對於加拿大提到了什麼？
(A) 最近在那裡開了新分店。
(B) 那裡是獲利最高的地區。
(C) 那裡的收入目前還沒有報告。
(D) 銷售量和亞洲的銷售量差不多。

加拿大提及的部分是"The only place we're lossing money is in Canada, but we just expanded there"。在這裡，說話者說，雖然加拿大蒙受損失，但其原因是事業擴張，因此從選項中找到與事業擴張有關的內容就會是正確答案(A)。

96.

根據說話者所說的話，聽眾應該要做什麼？
(A) 申請福利待遇。
(B) 加班。
(C) 提交資料報告。
(D) 報名參加研討會。

在談話的後半部分，說話者說"Some of you still haven't signed up for your medical insurance."，並催促聽眾加入醫療保險。因此正確答案為(A)。在上面的文章中，只有聽到signed up for的話並不能選擇選項(D)。

97.

看圖，聽眾應該要打哪一個電話號碼？
(A) 874-8547
(B) 874-9038
(C) 874-1294
(D) 874-7594

要求未投保的員工在六點前聯繫Jessica Davis，因此在圖表中找到Jessica Davis的電話號碼就能輕易知道正確答案是(B)。在聽問題之前，要事先知道圖表上寫著人名，特別要注意聽到人名的部分。

[98-100]

培訓計劃		
星期一	9:00 A.M. – 12:00 P.M.	行銷部
星期一	1:00 P.M. – 4:00 P.M.	人事部
星期二	9:00 A.M. – 12:00 P.M.	公關部
星期二	1:00 P.M. – 4:00 P.M.	會計部

W I'd like everyone to know that we finally received the schedule for the software training that we'll be getting from Rider Technology. It appears as though we'll have our session next Tuesday morning. It's supposed to last for three hours, and your attendance is mandatory. That means everyone has to cancel any meetings or appointments which you have scheduled during that time. If you don't attend, you'll receive an official reprimand and have to pay to get training on your own time. John, I know you're scheduled to fly to Hong Kong on that day, so you've been placed in the Monday afternoon class.

W 我想跟大家說我們將在Rider Technology進行的軟體培訓計劃終於到手了。我們的培訓時間在下星期二早上，預計進行3個小時並且每個人都要參加。這表示在相應時間要開會或有約的人都得取消，如果不參加的話會受到懲處而且得要另外抽出時間來付費接受培訓。John我知道你那天打算要去香港，所以你被安排在星期一下午上課。

詞彙 training 訓練，教育 as though 就像～一樣 last 持續，繼續 mandatory 義務性的，強制性的 official reprimand 懲罰 on one's own time 工作時間以外

98.

看圖，聽眾應該是在那個部門工作？
(A) 營業部。
(B) 人事部。
(C) 公關部。
(D) 會計部。

說話者說「我們的培訓時間是週二上午(we'll have our session next Tuesday morning)」，因此在圖表中找週二上午的培訓對象部門，可以知道是(C)的公關部。

99.

關於培訓，說話者說了什麼？

(A) 所有人都必須要參加。

(B) 會進行兩小時。

(C) 和新設備有關連。

(D) 聽眾會在實驗室裡上課。

透過提及到的「出席是強制性的(your attendance is mandatory)」部分以及「所有有會議或約會的人都應該要取消(everyone has to cancel any meetings or appointments which you have scheduled)」可以得知正確答案為(A)。作為參考，(B)的情況是培訓計劃預計進行3小時，在培訓時間內將會是進行與軟體相關的內容，因此(C)也是錯誤的。

100.

說話者對John說什麼？

(A) 要另外支付學費。

(B) 取消出差。

(C) 在其他天接受培訓。

(D) 預訂機票。

在最後一句話，說話者提到他事先知道一個叫John的人要去香港出差，然後說"you've been placed in the Monday afternoon class"。因此說話者指示John的事項為他不是星期二接受培訓而是在星期一，因此正確答案是(C)。

Actual Test 2

PART 1

1.

(A) Passengers are getting off the airplane.
(B) People are preparing to get on board.
(C) They are putting their bags under their seats.
(D) All of the people appear to be bored.

(A) 乘客們正在下飛機。
(B) 人們正在準備要搭乘。
(C) 他們正在往座位底下放包包。
(D) 每個人看起來都感覺很無聊。

照片中的人物不是下飛機，而是坐火車，所以(A)不是正確答案。人們只是提著行李，並沒有把行李放在座位上，所以(C)也是錯誤的。(D)利用與board(乘坐)發音相近的bored(無聊的)的陷阱。正確答案是說明人們準備要搭乘的(B)。

詞彙 get off (從搭乘的地方)下，下車 prepare 準備 get on board 搭乘 appear to 看起來

2.

(A) The laptop computer has been turned on.
(B) Papers are scattered on top of the desk.
(C) A monitor has been placed behind a keyboard.
(D) The printer is right beside the desktop computer.

(A) 筆記型電腦是開著的。
(B) 紙張散落在桌子上。
(C) 螢幕放在鍵盤的後面。
(D) 印表機就在桌上型電腦的旁邊。

因為看到的是無人的辦公室景象，所以要特別注意事物的佈置方式。因為看不到筆記本電腦及散落的文件，所以(A)和(B)不能成為正確答案，印表機與電腦是互相分開的，敘述他們相鄰的(D)也是錯誤的。正確答案是正確敘述螢幕和鍵盤位置的(C)。

詞彙 turn on 開 scatter 散開 on top of 在～的上面 place 放置，放下

3.

(A) Several people are sitting at a table.
(B) Everyone has taken a seat.
(C) Pictures are being drawn on the board.
(D) One person is standing by the window.

(A) 有幾個人坐在桌子上。
(B) 所有人都坐著。
(C) 黑板上正被畫畫。
(D) 有個人站在窗邊。

照片上的人各自有不同的動作，如果不留意每個人物的動作，就會很容易出錯。答案是描述人們坐在桌子上的(A)。 因為在中央的人站著，所以(B)不為正確答案，黑板上還沒有畫或寫著東西，所以(C)也是錯誤的。因為在左邊窗邊的人是坐著的，(D)也不是正確答案。

詞彙 take a seat 坐 draw 畫畫

4.

(A) Nobody saw the construction site.
(B) A tool is being used by a worker.
(C) The carpenter is nailing some wood.
(D) He is putting a brick on the wall.

(A) 沒有人看到施工現場。
(B) 工具正在被工人使用著。
(C) 木工在木頭上釘釘子。
(D) 他在牆上砌磚。

描述工人正在使用工具的(B)是正確答案。(A)的saw不是指意思為「鋸」的動詞，而是see(看)的過去式。(C)的情況是只有將nailing(釘釘子)改為cutting(截斷)等動詞，才能成為正確的描述。

詞彙 construction site 施工現場 tool 工具 carpenter 木工 nail 釘子；釘釘子 brick 磚頭

5.

(A) People have gathered together in groups.
(B) Bicycles are being ridden in the park.
(C) Some cars have been parked on the grounds.
(D) Someone is drinking from a water fountain.

21

(A) 人們成群結隊地聚在一起。

(B) 腳踏車正在公園裡被騎著。

(C) 車子正被停靠中。

(D) 有人在飲水台喝水。

正確描寫照片中人們聚在一起的樣子的(A)就是正確答案。照片裡的自行車上沒有人，所以(B)不是正確答案，因爲分開停放的不是「車(cars)」，而是「自行車(bicycles)」。雖然能看到噴水池，但找不到正在喝水的人，所以(D)也不是正確答案。

詞彙 gather together 聚集　water fountain 噴水池，飲水台

6.

(A) He is putting on some kitchen mitts.

(B) Bread has been baked in an oven.

(C) Food is being cooked on the stove.

(D) He is taking the bread out of the toaster.

(A) 他正戴著廚房用手套。

(B) 在烤箱中烤了麵包。

(C) 食物正在爐灶上被煮著。

(D) 他正從烤麵包機裡拿出麵包。

只有理解現在進行式和現在完成式的意義，才能找到正確答案的問題。(A)的情況只有將is putting(正戴著)換成has put(戴過)才能成爲正確的描述，(C)則需要將is being cooked(正在煮)換成has been cooked(煮熟了)才會是正確的描述。正確答案是描述烤完麵包的(B)。(D)的情況爲需要將toaster(烤麵包機)替換成oven(烤箱)等詞語取代才能成爲正確答案。

詞彙 mitt 手套　bake 烤　stove 暖爐，爐灶　take A out of B 從B拿出A

PART 2

7.

Can you contact the client this afternoon?

(A) Yes, he signed the contract.

(B) I don't think he has arrived yet.

(C) Sure. I'll get in touch with her.

可以請你在今天下午聯絡顧客嗎？

(A) 對，他在契約上簽名了。

(B) 他現在似乎還未到達。

(C) 當然的，我會去聯絡的。

利用助動詞can向對方請求，因此應要做出表示帶有接受或拒絕意味的答覆，選項中(C)表示出接受的意思。

詞彙 contact 聯絡　arrive 到達　get in touch with 和～聯絡

8.

Where should we meet before the conference?

(A) About two hours from now.

(B) In the hotel's lobby.

(C) On the sixteenth of March.

在會議之前我們要在哪裡見面？

(A) 大約兩小時後。

(B) 在飯店大廳。

(C) 3月16日。

如果考慮到疑問詞where，就能知道答案是指向場所的(B)。

詞彙 lobby 大廳

9.

Ms. Sullivan hasn't left the office for the day, has she?

(A) I just saw her step into the lounge.

(B) She works in the Accounting Department.

(C) For the past fifteen years or so.

Sullivan還沒有下班，對吧？

(A) 剛才看到她去休息室了。

(B) 她在會計部門工作。

(C) 大約十五年。

利用否定疑問句詢問Sullivan是否下班。答案是間接表達「還沒下班」意思的(A)。

詞彙 leave the office for the day 下班　step into 走進　lounge 休息室

10.

The bus should arrive in five minutes.

(A) The number 133 bus to the stadium.

(B) It's the second stop from now.

(C) Great. I'm getting tired of waiting.

五分鐘後公車就會抵達。

(A) 是去體育場的133號公車。

(B) 從現在開始兩站後。

(C) 真棒，我厭倦等待了。

告知公車即將抵達的訊息，因此表示對於這件事的喜怒哀樂之意的(C)是最自然的答覆。

詞彙 stadium 體育場　stop 車站　get tired of 對～感到厭煩

11.

Are you planning to go out for lunch?

(A) No, everyone went to the cafeteria.

(B) A turkey and cheese sandwich.

(C) I'll probably just eat at my desk.

要在外面吃午餐嗎？

(A) 不是，大家都要去自助餐廳。

(B) 是放了火雞肉和起司的三明治。

(C) 大概會在我位置上吃吧。

利用一般疑問句的方式，詢問對方是否在外面吃午飯。因此，間接表達「不」意思的(C)是正確答案。(B)在詢問午餐菜單時，可繼續作出此答覆。

詞彙 plan to 計劃　cafeteria 自助餐廳　turkey 火雞肉　probably 大概

12.

Why did Randolph, Inc. call off the deal?

(A) Its CEO refused to approve it.

(B) Nobody from there has called me.

(C) That's right. We have a deal.

Randolph 公司爲什麼取消交易？
(A) 那邊的總裁拒絕批准。
(B) 那裡沒有人打電話給我。
(C) 是的，我們簽約了。

利用疑問詞why詢問取消交易的理由，所以提出「總裁拒絕」理由的(A)是正確答案。(B)是重複使用問題中使用過的call，(C)是重複使用deal來誘導回答錯誤的陷阱。

詞彙 call off 取消　deal 交易　refuse 拒絕，否決　approve 批准

13.

We had better take the nonstop flight there.

(A) Two hours and twenty minutes.
(B) But it will cost a lot more.
(C) On our way to Moscow.

坐直達航班到那裡會比較好。
(A) 兩小時二十分。
(B) 但是費用會更高。
(C) 正往莫斯科去呢。

有提出利用直達航班的建議，因此，表明自己對他的看法(B)是最自然的答覆。

詞彙 had better ～比較好　nonstop flight 直達航班　on one's way to 正往～去

14.

Would you rather have an ocean view or a mountain one?

(A) Yes, that's the one I chose.
(B) I love looking out at the water.
(C) That's where we went today.

您想要海景房還是山景房？
(A) 對，那是我選的。
(B) 我喜歡看海。
(C) 那裡是我們今天去過的地方。

以選擇題提問，所以正確答案是間接選擇ocean view的(B)。

詞彙 ocean view 海景　mountain view 山景

15.

What kind of arrangement did the team negotiate?

(A) With a group from Farrow Manufacturing.
(B) The session lasted several hours.
(C) The details haven't been made public.

那個小組達成什麼協議了？
(A) 和從Farrow製造來的人一起。
(B) 會議持續了幾小時。
(C) 沒有公佈詳細內容。

當被問及達成何種協議時，提及談判對象的(A)或是提及會議時間的(B)無法成爲正確答案。正確答案是「還沒有發表，所以不知道」的(C)。

詞彙 arrangement 分配，排列；協商　negotiate 協商，促成　session 會議　detail 詳細的；詳細內容　make public 公佈

16.

The awards ceremony is taking place next Thursday.

(A) I'll be in Venice all next week.
(B) We had a wonderful time there.
(C) Congratulations on winning.

頒獎典禮會在下星期四舉辦。
(A) 我下週會一直待在威尼斯。
(B) 我們在那裡度過了美好的時光。
(C) 恭喜你得獎。

由於正在談論定於下週舉行的活動，所以正確答案是需要說出自己的行程，以間接地表明他不能參加頒獎典禮的(A)。這是一個非典型的以陳述句開頭較爲困難的題目，所以也可以採取逐一刪去的方式答題。

詞彙 awards ceremony 頒獎典禮　take place 出現，發生

17.

How much money will we make on the deal?

(A) I earned $50,000 last year.
(B) You've got yourself a deal.
(C) Close to a million dollars.

這筆交易我們能賺多少錢？
(A) 我去年賺了50,000美元。
(B) 那麼就那樣做吧。
(C) 將近一百萬美元。

因爲是以how much money詢問的，所以需要用具體的金額來回答，因此，正確答案爲(C)。(A)雖然也有提到具體金額，但由於使用了與問題無關的時態和主語，所以是錯誤的。

詞彙 make money 賺錢　deal 交易　You've got yourself a deal. 就那樣做吧.　million 百萬

18.

Isn't there someone who can sort these files?

(A) All sorts of different files.
(B) Tina is free right now.
(C) No, they haven't been sorted.

沒有人能幫我整理這些文件嗎？
(A) 各種類型的文件。
(B) Tina現在有空。
(C) 不，沒有分類。

因爲正在尋找整理文件的人，所以正確答案是指明具體人物的(B)。(A)和(C)是分別利用問題中使用的sort的發音及意思的錯誤答案。

詞彙 sort 分類；種類

19.

Have you made any plans for the weekend yet?

(A) I saw the exhibition at the gallery.
(B) That's what I'm planning to do.
(C) I'll probably spend time with my family.

周末有計劃了嗎？
(A) 我去看了美術館的展覽。
(B) 那就是我計劃要做的事情。

(C) 大概會跟家人們一起度過。

詢問是否制定了週末計劃。在被問及今後的計劃時，提及過去行動的(A)無法成為正確答案，(B)是利用題目中出現過的plan的陷阱。因此正確答案是表明「與家人一起度過」的計劃(C)。

詞彙 make plans 制定計劃 exhibition 展覽，展示會 gallery 美術館

20.

The supervisor hasn't made the schedule yet, has he?

(A) I worked the night shift last week.

(B) It's posted on the bulletin board.

(C) She's under constant supervision.

管理者還沒有安排好日程，對吧？
(A) 我上一周上了夜班。
(B) 已經張貼在公告欄上了。
(C) 她一直受到監督。

如果理解(B)的it指的是schedule的話，這是一題很容易解決的問題。對於日程是否確定的提問，用「已經公佈了」來回答的(B)就是正確答案。

詞彙 supervisor 監督官，管理者 night shift 夜班 post 黏貼；公佈 bulletin board 公告欄 constant 不變的 supervision 監督，管理

21.

A pipe in the bathroom is leaking water.

(A) Do you think you can fix it?

(B) On the third floor by the lounge.

(C) I'll check out the water fountain.

浴室管道正在漏水。
(A) 你覺得可以修好嗎？
(B) 在 3 樓休息室。
(C) 我會確認下飲水台的。

因為浴室正在漏水，所以詢問是否可以修理的(A)是最自然的回答。(C)的water fountain(飲水台)不是指浴室，而是廚房等設施。

詞彙 leak 漏(水) fix 修理 check out 確認 water fountain 飲水台

22.

Didn't you sign for the package when it arrived?

(A) It was just sitting on my desk.

(B) Yes, I put the sign in the window.

(C) She hasn't arrived here yet.

包裹來的時候你沒有領到嗎？
(A) 放在我書桌上了。
(B) 對，我在窗戶上貼了標誌。
(C) 她還沒有到這裡。

詢問對方是否有收到包裹(sign for the package)，因此間接表示yes意義同時回答「放在書桌上」的(A)為正確答案。

詞彙 sign for the package 收包裹，領包裹 sign 簽名；徵兆；標誌

23.

You could visit the factory in person tomorrow morning.

(A) Yes, that person is coming soon.

(B) We need to learn more facts.

(C) This afternoon would be better.

明天早上你可以直接拜訪工廠。
(A) 是的，那個人就快到了。
(B) 我們必須要知道更多事實才行。
(C) 今天下午的話更好。

表示明天上午可以親自訪問工廠。最自然的回答是(C)，(C)表示出「(比起明天上午)今天下午更好」的意思。

詞彙 in person 直接，親自 fact 事實

24.

Mr. Dennis is transferring to another department.

(A) Yes, the money was transferred.

(B) I wish him the best of luck.

(C) We can shop at the department store.

Dennis要調去別的部門了。
(A) 對，匯完那筆錢了。
(B) 希望他變得更好。
(C) 我們可以去百貨公司購物。

要注意問題的transfer和department的意思來解答問題。這裡的transfer意思為「調動」，而department意思為「部門」。但是(A)的transfer是表示「匯款」的意思，(C)的department store是「百貨公司」之意。因此正確答案是為部門調動的人祈求幸運的(B)。

詞彙 transfer 調動；匯款 department 部門 wish ~ the best of luck 祝～好運 department store 百貨公司

25.

How many days do you intend to stay here?

(A) A double room, please.

(B) Sometime this Friday.

(C) No more than three.

你會在這裡停留幾天？
(A) 請給我雙人房。
(B) 大概這週五。
(C) 三天之內。

如果著眼於"how many days"一詞，則正確答案中應該要提到天數。選項中只有(C)符合這些條件。

詞彙 intend to 想要 double room 雙人房

26.

Should I call Ms. Harper today or wait until tomorrow?

(A) You might as well do that now.

(B) No, she's not visiting today.

(C) I'm going there in a couple of days.

今天要打電話給Harper嗎？還是等到明天呢？
(A) 現在就打會比較好。
(B) 不，她今天不會來拜訪。

(C) 我兩天後會去那裡。

詢問應該要今天聯繫還是等明天。因此兩者中推薦前者的(A)是正確答案。

詞彙 might as well 做～比較好

27.

Did you determine how to solve the problem?

(A) No, he hasn't solved it yet.
(B) I think I know what to do.
(C) We're determined to win.

知道要怎麼解決問題了嗎？
(A) 沒有，他還沒有解決。
(B) 我好像知道要怎麼做了。
(C) 我們有要贏的覺悟。

只有瞭解determine的多種意思，才能夠回答問題。 determine是「決心」或「明白」的意思，在提問中被用作後者，在(C)選項中被用作前者的意思，而答案是間接表示知道的肯定含義(B)。

詞彙 determine 下決心，決定；研究出　solve 解決，解開

28.

Several documents have yet to be signed.

(A) No, I can't see the sign.
(B) It's a well-documented fact.
(C) I'd better get a pen then.

有幾份文件沒有簽名。
(A) 沒有，我沒看到招牌。
(B) 那是有被記錄下來的事實。
(C) 那我得要帶著筆過來才行。

利用have yet to(還沒有)指出文件中沒有簽名，所以說「為了簽名應該帶筆過來」的(C)是最自然的回答。(B)和(C)是利用各自問題中使用的sign和document所設下的陷阱。

詞彙 document 文件　have yet to 還沒做～　sign 簽名；標誌，招牌　well-documented 被記錄下的　had better 做～比較好

29.

Has anyone called the maintenance office yet?

(A) I think Todd may have.
(B) It doesn't need maintaining.
(C) I'll call you in an hour.

有人打電話給維修辦公室嗎？
(A) Todd好像打了。
(B) 那個沒有維修的必要。
(C) 我會在一小時後打電話給你。

詢問是否有人打電話給辦公室，所以回答「Todd做了」的(A)是正確答案。

詞彙 maintenance office 維修辦公室　maintain 維持；維修

30.

Shouldn't we reschedule the day's events?

(A) Her interview is scheduled next.
(B) No, it was pretty uneventful.
(C) I've already taken care of that.

不應該要調整一下那天活動的日程嗎？
(A) 她的採訪預定在下次進行。
(B) 不，那個很無聊。
(C) 我已經處理好了。

正在確認是否要調整活動日程。因此傳達「已經做了」意思的(C)才是正確答案。(A)和(B)是分別使用問題schedule和uneventful所設下的陷阱。

詞彙 reschedule 調整日程　uneventful 沒有什麼特別的，無聊的　take care of 照顧；處理

31.

Which detour do you think we should take?

(A) Yes, that's the one.
(B) Turn right at this intersection.
(C) I always take the train.

你覺得要怎麼繞路？
(A) 對，就是那個。
(B) 在這個十字路口右轉。
(C) 我常常搭火車。

在詢問應該要怎麼繞路，所以表示出「在這個十字路口右轉」的(B)是正確答案。

詞彙 detour 繞路　intersection 十字路口

PART 3

[32-34]

W	David, I looked over the report that you submitted. Overall, the writing is well done, and I like the analysis as well. However, you didn't include any visual information in it.
M	I was under the impression that you didn't want any. I guess I must have made a mistake. Shall I put some charts and graphs in it then? It shouldn't take me too long to make a few.
W	That would be perfect. Visuals like those let the reader get a clearer understanding of the information in the report. How about completing everything by the time lunch ends?
M	Sure, I can do that.
W	David，我仔細看了你交的報告。整體都寫得很好，分析的地方我也很滿意。但是裡面完全沒有視覺資料。
M	我以為你會不想要，看來我想錯了。那麼要放圖表和曲線圖嗎？做幾個的話不會花很多時間。
W	如果能那樣做就太好了。如果有這樣的視覺資料的話，讀者就能更明確地理解報告中的內容。能夠在中午結束之前完成嗎？
M	當然可以。

詞彙 look over 仔細查看 overall 整體的 analysis 分析 visual 視覺；視覺的 be under the impression that 我以為～ perfect 完美的

32.

說話者們主要在談論什麼？
(A) 寫作研討會。
(B) 女人的廣告企劃書。
(C) 男人的報告。
(D) 即將舉行的會議。

提到男人提交的報告(report that you submitted)中應該要包含視覺資料的內容。正確答案為(C)。

33.

女人對於男人沒有做什麼而感到不滿意？
(A) 文章內容並不明確。
(B) 沒有包含分析。
(C) 有幾個錯別字。
(D) 沒有圖表或曲線圖。

當女人指出報告中沒有視覺資料(you didn't include any visual information in it)這一點時，男子回答說會再加入圖表和曲線圖。因此，女人不滿意的地方可以看作是(D)選項。

詞彙 include 包含 contain 包括，包含 mistake 失誤；錯別字

34.

男人須什麼時候以前把事情做完才行？
(A) 女人會議結束以前。
(B) 午餐時間結束前。
(C) 工作時間結束以前。
(D) 這星期五以前。

在對話的後半部分，女人問說''How about completing everything by the time lunch ends?''男子回答說會那樣做的，因此男人是在(B)選項的「在中午結束之前」做好視覺資料。

[35-37]

M Ms. McDougal, I'm glad I ran into you. I'd like an update on the training session for the new employees. How's it going so far?

W Pretty well for the most part. This group is more advanced than most of the recent hires we've brought on. Only a couple of them are having trouble understanding the information.

M Make sure that those individuals get extra training. We need everyone up to speed because we've got much more work than normal these days.

W I'll be sure that everyone fully understands the material we cover. By tomorrow, they should be ready to start their jobs.

M McDougal小姐，見到你很高興。我想了解一下關於新進員工培訓的消息，目前為止進展得怎麼樣？

W 整體來說進展得很順利。這次的團體比我們最近教過的任何團體都還要優秀。只有兩三個人在理解培訓內容上遇到了困難。

M 請一定要讓那些人得到額外的教育。最近的工作比平時多了很多，所以大家都得要有一定水準的能力才行。

W 我會盡力讓所有人都完全理解相關內容的。明天就會做好事前工作的準備了。

詞彙 run into 偶然遇到 update 最新情報，最新消息 so far 到目前為止 for the most part 大概，一般 advanced 發展的；高級的 hire 雇用；新進員工 bring on 教育，指導 individual 個人 up to speed 表現出期待水準的 fully 完全地，全心全意地 material 材料，資料

35.

女人應該會是誰？
(A) 培訓負責人。
(B) 面試官。
(C) 顧客。
(D) 電腦軟體工程師。

通過對話開頭部分的內容可以看出女人是負責為新進員工培訓(training sessionfor the new employees)的(A)培訓負責人。

詞彙 trainer 指導者，培訓師

36.

女人對新進員工有什麼看法？
(A) 從全國各地來的。
(B) 無法理解內容。
(C) 比以前的新進員工知道的更多。
(D) 今天參觀了設施。

從''This group is more advanced than most of the recent hires we've brought on. ''中可以找到正確答案的線索。由於這次她說這次的新進員工比其他時候的新進員工更優秀，所以在選項中她提到對於新進員工的看法是(C)。

37.

女人暗示明天會發生什麼事？
(A) 為員工們準備的項目即將結束。
(B) 應聘者們將要面試。
(C) 會讓新進員工出差。
(D) 會開始培訓。

在對話的最後一句話''By tomorrow, they should be ready to start their jobs. ''中，女人說新進員工明天就會結束事前工作準備。因此，將新進員工培訓稱為''a program for employees''的(A)就是正確答案。

[38-40]

W	Hello. This is Gloria Randolph. I wonder if the work on my vehicle has been completed. I have to drive to Springfield for an urgent meeting, so I need it at once.
M	My mechanic just started working on it, Ms. Randolph. You requested a tune up, and that normally takes an hour and a half. Can you wait that long?
W	I don't believe so. Is it possible to shorten the wait to half an hour? That's when I'll be at your garage.
M	I tell Greg to do what he can in the next thirty minutes. But be sure to bring your car back here to complete the work when you return.

W 您好，我是Gloria Randolph。我想知道關於我的車子的相關作業是否結束了。因為有一場緊急會議，我得開車到春田，所以現在就需要車。

M 維修人員剛開始工作。Randolph小姐，您要求維修引擎，而這通常需要一個半小時，能請您稍等一下嗎？

W 感覺不太能。能夠把等待時間縮短為30分鐘嗎？我到維修廠大概需要那麼久。

M 我會跟Greg說30分鐘之內能做的都做。但是為了能夠順利結束工作，需要請您把車開回這裡。

詞彙 urgent 緊急的 mechanic 維修人員，修理工 tune up 引擎
shorten 縮短 garage 車庫，維修廠

38.

女人為什麼會打電話給男人？
(A) 為了要確認他所在的位置。
(B) 為了要請他修理引擎。
(C) 詢問有關自己車子的事情。
(D) 為了要知道要付多少維修費用。

在對話的前半部分，女人一邊說"I wonder if the work on my vehicle has been completed."一邊解釋自己打電話的原因。也就是說，為了確認汽車維修是否結束而打電話，因此(C)是正確答案。

39.

女人為什麼會說"I don't believe so"？
(A) 沒辦法等一個半小時。
(B) 不想要更換油。
(C) 明天早上沒辦法來。
(D) 覺得不需要服務。

給的句子是表示「不那麼認為」的意思，這是對''Can you wait that long?''這句的回答。當男人問及是否可以等待維修所需的一個半小時時，女人給出「不能」的否定答覆，也就是說，因此所給句子的含義可視為(A)。

40.

男人勸女人要做什麼？
(A) 之後兩天去租車。
(B) 考慮買一輛新車。
(C) 結束車子的相關作業。
(D) 離開之前和Greg說話。

在對話最後的部分，男人叮囑女人「請把車開回來讓我完成工作 (bring your car back here to complete the work)」，所以(C)為正確答案。

[41-43]

M	Wilma, I heard you managed to land a meeting with Mr. Sanders at PLL, Inc. Congratulations. How did it go?
W	Actually, the meeting got rescheduled since he had to go out of town. I was supposed to meet him this morning, but now he wants to get together on Friday.
M	Good luck. He'd make a great client for our firm.
W	Before I meet him, would you mind getting together for a bit? You've got more experience than I do.
M	That's not a problem at all. When do you have time?
W	How about discussing matters over lunch tomorrow?
M	I'm free then. Let's have lunch at noon.

M Wilma，聽說你已經跟PLL股份公司的Sanders先生約好要見面了。恭喜妳，後來怎麼樣了？

W 事實上，因為他要去郊區，所以就改約其他時間了。原本是要在今天早上見面的，但現在可能會在星期五見。

M 祝妳好運，那位會成為公司重要的顧客的。

W 在見那位之前我們先見下面如何？你的經驗應該比我還多。

M 當然沒問題。什麼時候有空？

W 明天邊吃中餐邊討論問題怎麼樣？

M 那時候我有空。那麼12點的時候一起吃午餐吧。

詞彙 land a meeting 約見面，召開會議 get together 見面，聚集
firm 公司 for a bit 一下子

41.

關於Sanders，女人說了些什麼？
(A) 現在在國外。
(B) 今天沒辦法和她見面。
(C) 來應徵她的公司。
(D) 恭喜她的成就。

關於與Sanders先生的見面，女人說本來預定要在今天見面的，但是行程變更，決定要改到星期五見面。因此正確答案是(B)。

42.

女人說"Would you mind getting together for a bit?"，她是在暗示什麼？
(A) 她需要男人的檔案。
(B) 她不確定她能不能夠確保新顧客。
(C) 她想要討論有關Sanders先生的話題。
(D) 她想要談論有關調動的事情。

對話中，女人向男人提議說要短暫見一面，並馬上說"You've got more experience than I do."表明理由。也就是說，女人為了聽取男人對潛在顧客Sanders見面的相關建議而提議見面，因此(C)是正確答案。

43.

說話者們明天要做什麼？

(A) 一起吃飯。
(B) 在女人的辦公室見面。
(C) 準備企劃書。
(D) 要去PLL股份公司。

在對話的後半部分，男人接受女人的提議「明天邊吃午飯邊討論問題(How about discussing matters over lunch tomorrow？)」，因此說話者們明天要做的事情為(A)。

[44-46]

> **M1** You're attending the farewell party for Justine Hamilton today, aren't you?
>
> **W** Yes, I should be able to make it back to the office by four o'clock. Did you purchase a gift for her?
>
> **M1** I had planned to do that, but I simply don't know what to buy. I have rarely interacted with her.
>
> **M2** Why don't you contribute to the office present, Sam? Several of us are pooling our money together to buy her something nice.
>
> **M1** Yeah, I think I'll do that. Who should I speak with, Richard?
>
> **M2** Talk to Darlene at the front desk. She's collecting money from everyone.
>
> -
>
> **M1** 你今天要參加Justine Hamilton的送別會對嗎？
>
> **W** 沒錯，我可以4點之前回到辦公室。你有買要送給她的禮物嗎？
>
> **M1** 本來打算要那樣做的，但不知道該買什麼。我幾乎沒有和她說過話。
>
> **M2** Sam，那麼一起買團體禮物如何?我們當中有幾個人想湊錢給她買件好禮物。
>
> **M1** 喔，這麼做似乎比較好。我應該要跟誰說，Richard嗎？
>
> **M2** 告訴前台的Darlene。她正在幫大家收錢。

詞彙 farewell party 歡送會 gift 禮物 interact with 和～交流，溝通 contribute to 貢獻，捐獻 pool 募集(資金)

44.

說話者們在討論什麼？
(A) 新進員工。
(B) 頒獎典禮。
(C) 為了同事的禮物。
(D) 為了慈善團體的捐獻。

在討論為了歡送會主角的禮物。正確答案為(C)。

45.

女人在暗示著什麼？
(A) 會和男人們一起在部門裡。
(B) 今天下午不會在位置上。
(C) 從員工那裡開始收錢。
(D) 是Justine Hamilton的好朋友。

對於是否會參加送別會的問題，女生回答是"Yes, I should be able to make it back to the office by four o'clock."。 通過這些可以知道女人在4點之前會外出工作，因此正確答案是(B)。

46.

Richard要男人做什麼？
(A) 幫忙準備活動。
(B) 提出提案。
(C) 買禮物。
(D) 給Darlene錢。

男子2對正在考慮禮物的男子1提議資助團購禮物之後，然後要他告訴Darlene。這裡的Darlene是「正在收錢(collecting money from everyone)」的員工，所以最終男子1說的話變成(D)。

[47-49]

> **W** It looks as if everything's ready for tomorrow's new product launch. Are you prepared to demonstrate how to use the products at tomorrow's press conference, Brad?
>
> **M** Yes, my presentation is complete, and I've been rehearsing all day. There's just one problem. You requested that we display items in different colors, but the only color I have so far is black.
>
> **W** We can't let that happen. We have to show everyone the wide variety of colors our products come in. Why don't you give Matthew a call?
>
> **M** I talked to him, and he said there's nothing he can do. Maybe we'll have better luck if you get in touch with him.
>
> -
>
> **W** 明天上市的新產品相關準備好像都結束了。Brad，明天的新聞發佈會上，你準備好要展示產品使用方法了嗎？
>
> **M** 是的，展示的準備都就緒了，我一整天都在彩排練習。只有一個問題，我覺得應該要展示不同顏色的產品，但我現在只有黑色。
>
> **W** 不能就這樣放任不管。我們需要向大家展示我們的產品有多樣的顏色。給Matthew打電話怎麼樣？
>
> **M** 我跟他聊了一下，他說自己幫不上什麼忙。也許你直接聯繫的話會有更好的結果。

詞彙 launch 開始，著手；上市 demonstrate 抗議；彩排 press conference 新聞發佈會 rehearse 預演，彩排 have good luck 好運氣 get in touch with 和～聯繫

47.

說話者們在說什麼？
(A) 營銷研討會。
(B) 產品展示。
(C) 股東大會。
(D) 總裁致辭。

透過對話的前半部分可以知道男人「在展示有關產品的使用方法 (demonstrate how to use the products)」，之後也一直在討論有關展示有關的問題，因此正確答案是(B)。

48.

根據男人說的話，他今天做了什麼？
(A) 和記者們見面。
(B) 在設計產品。
(C) 去了附近的賣場。
(D) 在練習發表。

當女人問及產品演示的準備情況時，男人回答稱已經做好演示準備，排練了一天(I've been rehearsing all day)。 因此，男人所做的是(D)。

49.

男人提議女人做什麼？
(A) 聯絡Matthew。
(B) 安裝產品。
(C) 修理產品。
(D) 準備企劃書。

女人說為了準備各種顏色的產品，請聯繫Matthew，男人說已經和他說過了，但是沒有結果，然後說"Maybe we'll have better luck if you get in touch with him."，即男人建議女人直接與Matthew通話，因此(A)是正確答案。

詞彙 set up 設置，安裝

[50-52]

M	Ms. Merriweather, I've been thinking about ways to entertain the clients from Munich. How about taking them to a local baseball game on Thursday night? They might enjoy that.
W	That's a great idea, but we've already booked tickets to see a classical music performance then. And they'll only be here for two nights.
M	Okay. You still need me to pick them up at the airport tomorrow, right? I'm planning to be there by two in case their plane arrives a bit early.
W	Cynthia will be accompanying you since she speaks fluent German. And be sure to drive the company van since there will be five people arriving.
M	Merriweather小姐，我正在考慮如何接待來自慕尼黑的顧客。妳覺得星期四晚上帶他們去附近的棒球場怎麼樣？他們應該會喜歡。
W	這是個好主意，但為了在那個時間觀賞古典音樂演出，已經訂好票了。而且他們只打算在這裡度過兩晚。
M	原來如此。我是明天要去機場接他們，對吧？我打算2點之前到那裡，以防飛機抵達得稍微早一點。
W	Cynthia能說一口流利的德語，她會陪你去的。另外，預計有5個人，別忘了開公司的休旅車。

詞彙 entertain 娛樂；使～開心 book 預訂 pick up 載，接 in case 萬一，預防 accompany 同行，陪同 fluent 流利的 van 休旅車，商務車

50.

顧客們打算要在星期四晚上做什麼？
(A) 觀看運動比賽。
(B) 看電影。
(C) 在餐廳吃晚餐。
(D) 參加音樂會。

聽到男人提議星期四晚上帶顧客們去棒球場時，女人說「已經預訂了古典音樂演出門票(we've already booked tickets to see a class)」。因此，顧客們週四晚上要做的是(D)。

51.

關於顧客們，暗示了什麼？
(A) 會於下午抵達。
(B) 會從辦公室開車過去。
(C) 會停留一週。
(D) 之前有拜訪過那地方。

從男人說的話''I'm planning to be there by two in case their plane arrives a bit early.''中可以得知，顧客們若是按照預定的話，會在下午2點抵達。因此正確答案是(A)。內容有提到顧客們預計要搭飛機過來且會停留兩晚，因此(B)和(C)是錯誤的。

52.

關於Cynthia，女人說了什麼？
(A) 她會開休旅車。
(B) 她會說外語。
(C) 她在柏林分公司工作。
(D) 她明天會搭飛機去那城市。

可以從''Cynthia will be accompanying you since she speaks fluent German.''這句話聽到，描述她是一個很會說德文的人，因此，正確答案是(B)。

[53-55]

M1	Janet, I've been looking at the flyers we made for next month's conference, and I'm not really happy with them.
W	How do you want to change them, Craig?
M1	Take a look at this. I had Jason in the Graphics Department design something new.
W	Wow, I definitely prefer this one to the one we have. Jeff, what's your opinion?
M2	Let me see . . . Yeah, let's go with this one instead. But we need to speak with the printer at once since our flyers are set to be printed this afternoon.
W	I had totally forgotten about that. I'll call right now and request that nothing get printed yet.
M2	Thanks, Janet.

M1	Janet，我在看為了下個月會議製作的傳單，但我一點也不滿意。
W	要怎麼更改才好呢，Craig？
M1	看看這個，我請設計部門的Jason重新設計了一個。
W	哇，確實比我們的還讓人滿意。Jeff，你覺得呢？
M2	稍等一下…那麼，就用這個吧。但是現在馬上就要聯絡印刷廠，因為傳單預計要在今天下午印刷。
W	我完全忘記這一點了。我現在就打電話跟他們說不要印任何東西。
M2	謝謝妳，Janet。

詞彙 flyer 傳單 take a look at 看 definitely 分明 printer 印刷業者，印刷所

53.

關於傳單，Craig說了什麼？
(A) 印刷費用過高。
(B) 他覺得設計得很好。
(C) 由設計部門製作。
(D) 他對它並不滿意。

在對話的開始部分，男人看了傳單說「不喜歡(I'm not really happy with them)」，然後把新設計的傳單給女人看。 因此，正確答案是把design換成相近詞appearance的(D)。

詞彙 approve 認同，贊成

54.

Jason做了什麼？
(A) 報名參加會議。
(B) 重新設計了一份。
(C) 拜訪印刷廠。
(D) 和女人談話。

Jason這個名字可以從男人的話中"I had Jason in the Graphics Department design something new." 聽到，從這句話可以得知Jason是重新設計的人。因此，Jason所做的是(B)。

55.

女人在說"I had totally forgotten about that."的時候，是在暗示什麼？
(A) 沒辦法調低價格。
(B) 沒辦法雇用新進員工。
(C) 最近的預算更動了。
(D) 要取消預訂。

文章脈絡上所賦予的句子that是指「傳單將於今天下午印刷(our flyers are set to be printed this afternoon)」。 接著女人立即說要打電話中斷印刷，因此通過文章可以知道的事項是(D)。

[56-58]

W	Mr. Hopkins, I'll be returning to the office from lunch a bit late. I have a dental appointment at 12:30.
M	That's fine, Melanie. I remember you told me about it last week. But try to return by 2:00.
W	Oh, that's right. We have a conference call with the clients in England then.
M	Right. They've been getting their products from us late, and they aren't pleased at all.
W	Don't worry. I'll make sure to get back here in plenty of time then.
M	Good. You're the person they really want to speak with, so we can't afford to be late with the call.

W	Hopkins先生，中午午休後我會晚一點回辦公室。我預約了12點30分的牙科。
M	好的，Melanie。我記得上星期你有跟我說過。但是請在2點之前回來。
W	噢，對了，有和英國顧客的電話會議。
M	是的。因為晚收到我們的產品，心情肯定會不好的。
W	請不要擔心，我一定會提早回來的。
M	好的，妳才是他們真正想要談話的對象，會議遲到的話是萬萬不可的。

詞彙 dental appointment 牙醫預約 conference call 電話會議，電話會談 plenty of 多 can't afford to 沒有做～的餘裕，無法承擔

56.

對話會是在哪裡進行的？
(A) 辦公室。
(B) 工廠。
(C) 會議中心。
(D) 牙醫。

在對話的開始部分，女人說「午飯後會稍微晚一點回到辦公室(I'll be returning to the office from lunch a bit late)」，因此，對話者們所在的地方應該是(A)。

詞彙 conference center 會議中心

57.

2點會發生什麼事？
(A) 會開始牙醫治療。
(B) 裝船貨物將會發送。
(C) 將會打電話。
(D) 將要開始和總裁的會議。

男人說2點之前回來，女人回答說會那樣做的，然後說"We have a conference call with the clients in England then."。透過這些可以知道2點將進行電話會議，因此(C)是正確答案。

58.

關於顧客，男人說了什麼？
(A) 他們是從英國來的。
(B) 他們訂購的商品沒有按時抵達。
(C) 他們需要產品展示

(D) 他們最近取消購買。

關於顧客，男人說的內容是"They've been getting their products from us late, and they aren't pleased at all."。 也就是說，由於顧客較晚收到貨，所以心情不會太好，因此正確答案是(B)。

[59-61]

M	We still don't have enough volunteers for the county fair. We require at least thirty more people.
W	We've already run advertisements in the newspaper and on the radio. What else can we do?
M	What about appealing to some of our sponsors? They can ask their employees to volunteer to assist us.
W	That should work. Should I only call a couple of big sponsors or speak with everyone?
M	Get in touch with all of them. That way, we'll be sure to have enough people. Remember what happened last year?
W	That's a good point. I'll start doing that as soon as lunch ends.
M	農畜產品博覽會的志工人數仍然不夠。我們至少還需要30個人。
W	已經在報紙和廣播上登了廣告，除此之外還能做些什麼呢？
M	向贊助企業請求協助如何？可以讓職員做志工幫助我們。
W	應該可以。我需要給兩個大的贊助公司打電話，還是詢問所有公司？
M	請聯絡所有地方，那樣的話肯定會有足夠的人。還記得去年發生了什麼事吧？
W	是個好指責。午餐時間一結束就馬上開始。

詞彙 country fair 農畜產品博覽會 run an advertisement 投放廣告 appeal to 呼籲 sponsor 志願者

59.

談話者們主要在談論什麼？
(A) 缺乏志工。
(B) 招聘廣告。
(C) 慈善活動。
(D) 博覽會的贊助企業。

在對話的整個過程中談到要如何增加博覽會的志工人數。因此，(A)是正確答案。

60.

關於去年的農畜博覽會，男人暗示了什麼？
(A) 在參加人數上締造新紀錄。
(B) 做事的人手不足。
(C) 因為天氣的緣故取消了。
(D) 持續進行了一週。

在對話後半部，男子指示要給所有贊助企業打電話，並說"Remember what happened last year?"，也就是說，他暗示著去年沒有給所有贊助企業打電話導致志願者人數不足，因此(B)才是正確答案。

61.

女人會在午餐時間之後做什麼？
(A) 面試應聘者們。
(B) 排定新的日程。
(C) 和贊助企業談話。
(D) 拜訪其他間公司。

當男人指示要給所有贊助企業打電話時，女人回答說"I'll start doing that as soon as lunch ends."。也就是說，午餐時間以後，女人將與贊助企業通電話，因此(C)才是正確答案。

[62-64]

M	Hello. I'd like to purchase this suit, please. And I have this coupon.
W	All right, sir. Let me see. Oh, do you know that if you wait until tomorrow to make this purchase, you can get a 20% discount?
M	Yes, I'm aware of that, but my friend is getting married tomorrow, so I need this suit today.
W	Ah, of course. Do you need to get it fitted?
M	Yes, that would be great. Do you know where I can get that done?
W	We can handle that here if you'd like. It will cost $10 and take about half an hour.
M	你好。我想購買這套西裝。另外我這裡有優惠券。
W	您好，客人，請讓我看一下。噢，您知道，等到明天再購買的話，可以享受8折優惠嗎？
M	是的，我知道，但是我的朋友明天要結婚，所以我需要這套西裝。
W	好的。需要依照您的體型進行修改嗎？
M	嗯，那應該會好一點。你知道在哪裡可以修改嗎？
W	如果您需要的話，可以在這裡進行。費用是10美元，大概需要半個小時。

詞彙 suit 正裝，西裝 fit 符合；合身的

62.

看圖，男人是在哪一天購買的？
(A) 星期三。
(B) 星期四。
(C) 星期五。
(D) 星期六。

在對話的前半部分，女人說明天購買的話可享八折優惠，在圖表中查看一週的折扣優惠，明天應該為星期五。因此，今天應該是(B)星期四。

63.

男人為什麼會需要西裝？

(A) 因為有頒獎典禮。
(B) 因為要面試。
(C) 因為有畢業典禮。
(D) 因為有結婚典禮。

從男人說的"my friend is getting married tomorrow"這句話中可以確認他想要購買西裝的理由。也就是說，為了要參加朋友的婚禮而購買，所以正確答案是(D)。

64.

關於男人，暗示了什麼？

(A) 要在賣場裡修改西裝。
(B) 會得到額外的10美元優惠。
(C) 會在其他天購買。
(D) 是賣場的常客。

在對話的後半部分，當男人詢問修改的地方在哪裡時，女人回答說可以在賣場進行修改。透過這些可以預想到男人會在賣場修改西裝，所以(A)才是正確答案。不要聽錯了修改費用10美元的內容，就以此選擇(B)作為正確答案。

詞彙 frequent shopper 常客

[65-67]

客房	最大容納人數
銀房	80
金房	100
鉑金房	120
鑽石房	150

M Hello. This is Peter Chin calling from the Hopewell Corporation. We're having a retirement ceremony next month on February 25, and we'd like to hold it at your hotel.

W That sounds great, Mr. Chin. We've hosted several awards ceremonies and other events from your firm in the past. How many people will be attending?

M We're expecting 100, but we'd like a room that can fit 120 in case more show up. We'll also be needing dinner and dessert for everyone.

W We can accommodate everything you said. However, I think it would be best if we discussed the arrangements in person.

- -

M 您好，我是Hopewell公司的Peter Chin。我們預定在下個月2月25日舉行退任典禮，希望能在那邊的酒店舉行。

W 好的，Chin先生，我們以前也曾多次主辦過貴公司的頒獎儀式及其他活動。這次計劃會有多少人參加呢？

M 我們預計會有100名，但是考慮到會有更多人參加，能夠容納120名的空間會比較好。另外也需要為所有人準備晚餐和甜點。

W 您說的所有事項都可以完成，但是還是親自見面討論準備事項會比較好。

詞彙 retirement 退休 host 舉辦，主辦 fit 符合，適用 in case 以防萬一 show up 展現出，出現 accommodate 接受；滿足(要

求) arrangement 準備，打交道；安排 in person 直接，親自

65.

男人的公司要舉辦什麼活動？

(A) 股東大會。
(B) 公司說明會。
(C) 頒獎典禮。
(D) 退任典禮。

在對話的前半部分，若沒錯過a retirement cremony(退任儀式)，就可以輕易知道(D)是正確答案。

詞彙 stockholders' meeting 股東大會

66.

看圖，最適合男人公司的場地是哪一個？

(A) 銀房。
(B) 金房。
(C) 鉑金房。
(D) 鑽石房。

對於女人詢問參加人數的提問，男生回答"We're expecting 100, but we'd like a room that can fit 120 in case more."。也就是說，雖然預計能容納100名左右，但表示希望能夠有充裕的空間足以容納120名，因此，如果在圖表中找能容納120名的空間的話，正確答案就是(C)。

67.

女人提議要做什麼？

(A) 這一週要繳交訂金。
(B) 直接見面開會。
(C) 在網路上確認預約。
(D) 選擇將要提供的飲食。

在女人的最後一句話"However, I think it would be best if we discussed the arrangements in person."中，可以得知女人對男人提議要直接見面後討論要準備的事物，因此，正確答案是(B)。

詞彙 deposit 定金，存款

[68-70]

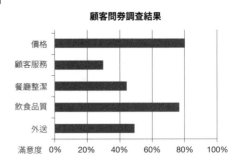

顧客問勞調查結果

32

W　Revenues at our restaurants in the Surrey area were up tremendously in the months of July and August.

M　That's great news. But I wonder why they aren't increasing in other cities.

W　Well, Devlin Research sent us the data concerning the customer survey we conducted last month. As you can see, our prices and the quality of our food got high marks.

M　It looks like our policy of using locally sourced food is paying off. Now, what about this category here? Only 45% of our customers rated it positively.

W　I was just about to get to it.

W　薩里地區的餐廳收益在7月和8月大幅增加。

M　這是個好消息。但是我想知道為什麼其他城市沒有增加。

W　嗯，上個月進行的顧客問卷調查相關資料是由Devlin Research發送的。正如您所看到的，在飲食的價格和品質方面得到了很高的評價。

M　我們使用當地出產的食材政策似乎取得了成功。那麼，這個類別是怎麼樣了呢？顧客中只有45%回答肯定。

W　我正要開始說。

詞彙　revenue 收入　tremendously 巨大地　concerning 與～有關　conduct 實施，實行　mark 痕跡；分數　policy 政策，方針　source 來源，根源；從～得到　pay off 成功，取得成果　category 範疇，類別　rate 評定等級，評價　positively 肯定地　be about to 正要　get to 抵達，接近；開始

68.

關於薩里的餐廳，女人說了什麼？
(A) 那之中的一部分因銷售不振而關門。
(B) 一週前實施了問券調查。
(C) 雇用了幾名新進員工。
(D) 比起以前賺了更多錢。

在對話的開始部分，女人說「薩里地區內的餐廳獲得了大幅收益 (revenues at our restaurants in the Surrey area were up tremendously)」，因此正確答案為(D)。

詞彙　lack 不足，缺乏

69.

關於餐廳，男人說了什麼？
(A) 時常提供特價。
(B) 最近更換了菜單。
(C) 使用鄰近地區生產的食品。
(D) 要求讓員工們接受親切教育。

從男人的話''It looks like our policy of using locally sourced food is paying off.''可以找到正確答案。男人將產生高額收益的原因歸為使用當地生產的食材，因此正確答案是(C)。

70.

看圖，女人接下來將會討論什麼？
(A) 顧客服務。

(B) **餐廳整潔。**
(C) 飲食品質。
(D) 外送。

在對話的最後部分，男人詢問關於只有45%的肯定反應的項目，女人回答''I was just about to get to it.''。也就是說，女人將會說只有45%肯定回覆的項目，因此，如果在圖表中找到這些數字的項目的話，(B)的餐廳整潔就是正確答案。

詞彙　cleanliness 清潔

PART 4

[71-73]

W　Attention, passengers with tickets for Flight 357 bound for Munich. Unfortunately, due to a computer error, today's flight is overbooked. If there are any passengers willing to give up their seats, please see the gate attendant at once. We need a total of five individuals. Passengers who choose not to fly now will receive two hundred euros in cash and be booked in a business-class seat on the next available flight. If that flight doesn't leave until tomorrow, a voucher for a hotel room and two free meals will be awarded. If not enough people volunteer, we will select individuals at random. We apologize for the inconvenience.

W　持有飛往慕尼黑357機票的乘客請注意。遺憾的，由於電腦出錯，今日航班出現了超賣情況。若有乘客願意放棄機位，請立即向登機口員工回報。總計需要五位，現在放棄的乘客將會得到200歐元以及下一班航班將會預約為商務艙座位。若直至明天為止都沒有航班，我們將會提供酒店住宿及2次免費用餐服務在內的抵用券。若自願者不足時，我們將會隨機挑選。非常抱歉給您帶來不便。

詞彙　bound for 前往　due to 因為　overbook 超賣　give up 放棄　attendant 工作人員，員工　book 預約　voucher 抵用券，商品券　award 授予，頒發　volunteer 自願　at random 隨意地，任意地

71.

廣播會在哪個地方播放呢？
(A) 在客運轉運站。
(B) 在火車站。
(C) 在地鐵站。
(D) 在機場。

因為航班的超賣問題正在尋找自願放棄的乘客。能夠聽到這種廣播的地方只有(D)的機場。

72.

為什麼會發生問題？
(A) 機器自行停止運轉。
(B) 有太多人預訂機位。
(C) 電腦系統自行中止。
(D) 有部分乘客遲到了。

說話者說「因為電腦出錯，機票超賣了(due to a computer error,

today's flight is overbooked)」，正在尋找放棄機位的乘客。因此，發生問題的理由可視爲(B)。(C)的意思為整個電腦系統的運作中止，不能將之與「電腦出錯」混淆了。

73.
說話者說自願者將會獲得什麼？
(A) 額外的里程數。
(B) 500歐元。
(C) 商務艙座位。
(D) 免費的頭等艙票券。

自願者可以得到的優惠有two hundred euros in cash(200歐元)，a business-class seat(商務艙座位)，以及a voucher for a hotel room and two free meals(住宿及用餐抵用券)。選項中屬於這些的是(C)。

[74-76]

> **M** The Shipping Department's budget has been increased so that it can hire new employees. Due to the popularity of our newest line of clothes, our sales have risen dramatically. As a result, we're falling behind on shipments. We promise customers three-day shipping, but their products have been arriving five or six days after being ordered. That's not good enough. So we're going to open a new shift from midnight to 8 A.M. We need twenty full-timers for this shift and ten more people to work part time on weekends. Larry, put an ad in the local newspapers at once. We need people to start by next Monday.
>
> -
>
> **M** 為了要在出貨部門聘用新職員，我們增加了預算。得益於新上市服裝的人氣，銷售量正在大幅增加，而其結果是配送工作正在落後。我們向顧客承諾會在三天內送達，但商品在訂購後五六天才到達。我們不能這樣下去，所以我們安排了新的工作時間，是從午夜12點至上午8點，需要20名正式員工和在週末工作的10名工讀生在這時間上班。Larry，立刻在當地報紙上刊登廣告，我們需要從下週一就開始工作的人。

詞彙 so that ~ can 為了要～ popularity 人氣 dramatically 急遽地 fall behind 落後 promise 約定 shift 輪班；轉移 from A to B 從A到B full-timer 正式員工 work part time 打工

74.
聽眾是在什麼類型的賣場裡工作？
(A) 家電產品賣場。
(B) 服裝賣場。
(C) 超市。
(D) 電子產品賣場。

在談話的前半部分，說話者說「因爲新上市的服裝產品(due to the popularity of our newest line of clothes)」銷售量增加，所以聽眾工作的地方為(B)的服裝賣場。

75.
說話者在說''That's not good enough''是指什麼？
(A) 應該要調降價格。
(B) 員工們應該要更努力工作。

(C) 公司應該要獲得更多收益。
(D) 應該要改善服務。

在文章脈絡上，that指的是配送服務延遲這一點，因此說話者指的是(D)。

76.
說話者讓Larry去做什麼？
(A) 刊登廣告。
(B) 聯絡顧客。
(C) 申請調職。
(D) 面試應聘者。

在談話最後的部分，說話者對Larry說「在當地報紙上刊登徵人廣告(put an ad in the local newspapers at once)」，因此說話者對Larry指示的事情為(A)。

[77-79]

> **W** From today until this Friday, Harrison Fruits and Vegetables is having a special clearance sale. We received a huge shipment from a supplier, and we've got to move everything in the next few days. Visit us to get fresh watermelons, mangoes, cherries, and strawberries. We're offering them at half price. Don't forget about our vegetables either. You can find just about anything you want at Harrison. During the sale period, vegetables are 30% off. If you can't find something, speak with one of our employees, who can order it for you. Harrison Fruits and Vegetables is located at 23 Mulberry Avenue. Free parking is available in the back.
>
> -
>
> **W** 從今天起至本週五，Harrison蔬果市場將進行特別促銷。我們從供應商那裡收到了大量商品，而所有商品必須在幾天以內處理完畢。請至賣場購買新鮮西瓜、芒果、櫻桃以及草莓，我們將會提供半價的優惠，另外也別忘了我們的蔬菜。在Harrison，您想要什麼都可以買到。促銷期間蔬菜打七折。找不到東西時，可以告訴我們的員工，我們將會為您訂購。Harrion蔬果市場位於Mulberry街23號，在賣場後面可以免費停車。

詞彙 from A until B 從A到B clearance sale 清倉大特價 shipment 運輸貨物

77.
賣場為什麼會進行特價優惠？
(A) 慶祝開店。
(B) 必須要處理商品。
(C) 即將歇業。
(D) 進行定期優惠。

如果知道清倉大特價(clearance sale)的概念，或是沒有漏聽"We received a huge shipment from a supplier, and we've got to move everything in the next few days."的話，就可以知道這次的特價是為了要清庫存。正確答案是(B)。

詞彙 celebrate 紀念，慶祝 get rid of 除去 go out of business 破產，歇業 annual 年度，每年的

78.

水果的折扣是多少？

(A) 八折。

(B) 七折。

(C) 六折。

(D) 五折。

說話者在宣傳西瓜、芒果、櫻桃、草莓的同時還說了它們都是打對折(at half price)販賣的。因此正確答案為(D)。

79.

關於停車，說話者說了什麼？

(A) 30分鐘免費。

(B) 停車位有限。

(C) 可以在賣場後面停車。

(D) 停車場在街道對面。

與停車有關的內容可以從最後一句"Free parking is available in the back."中聽到，這裡介紹可以停放在賣場後面，因此關於停車的相關事項是(C)。

[80-82]

> M Hello. My name is Cedric Davidson. Last week, I ordered a dozen table lamps from your company for my new restaurant. The items arrived today, but when I opened the boxes, I discovered that three of them had been damaged during shipping. Two lamps have dents while the other has several scratches on it. My restaurant opens three days from now, so I need those lamps replaced at once. Please send them to me by express shipping. It's imperative that you do this. My shipping number is 9048-93. Please call me at once to confirm you received this message.
>
> ⋯⋯⋯⋯⋯⋯⋯⋯⋯⋯⋯⋯⋯⋯⋯⋯⋯⋯⋯⋯⋯⋯⋯⋯⋯
>
> M 您好，我叫Cedric Davidson。上星期我為了新開的餐廳而從貴公司訂購了一打桌燈。產品於今天到貨，但當我打開箱子的時候，我發現其中三個在配送中途受損，兩盞燈有凹痕，另一盞燈則是有多處瑕疵。從現在開始算起，三天之後餐廳就要開始營業，所以必須立即更換那些燈。請用特級快遞寄給我。請一定要這樣做，我的郵件號碼是9048-93。如果您有收到這則訊息，請打一通確認電話給我。

詞彙 dozen 一打，12個的 dent 凹痕 scratch 瑕疵 replace 取代，代替 imperative 一定得要做的，緊急的

80.

說話者提及到什麼問題？

(A) 有一部分的產品損壞了。

(B) 訂購的產品送到錯誤的地址了。

(C) 送了錯誤的產品。

(D) 索賠金額過高。

在談話前半部分，說話者告知「自己訂購的商品有三個在配送過程中損壞(three of them had been damaged during shipping)」的問題，因此正確答案是(A)。

81.

三天之後會發生什麼事？

(A) 餐廳開業。

(B) 優惠活動結束。

(C) 簽訂合約。

(D) 訂購商品會出貨。

提問的核心語句「3天」被提及的地方是"My restaurant opens three days from now, so I need those is⋯⋯"。從這裡可以看出，三天之後，說話者的餐廳將要開業。因此，三天後發生的事是(A)。

82.

說話者為什麼會說"It's imperative that you do this"？

(A) 想要全額退款。

(B) 期望道歉。

(C) 急需替代品。

(D) 需要免費的安裝服務。

在文章脈絡上，this所指的是儘快寄出交換商品，因此所給的句子的意義可視為(C)。作為參考，"It is imperative that ~" 表示「做~是必須的」或「一定要做~」的意思。

詞彙 full refund 全額退款

[83-85]

> W Thank you for that introduction, Mr. Alberts. It's an honor to be standing here holding this special award. Writing books, especially works of fiction, isn't an individual task. First and foremost, I'd like to thank my editor, Janet Renton. She made countless suggestions which improved the quality of my work. Without her, I wouldn't be standing here today. In addition, I'd like to thank the proofreaders and designers at Twin Press. They did an amazing job. My agent Peter Welling encouraged me to keep working when I was struggling. Finally, I'd like to thank my fans. They were the ones that made *The Winding Road* such a success.
>
> ⋯⋯⋯⋯⋯⋯⋯⋯⋯⋯⋯⋯⋯⋯⋯⋯⋯⋯⋯⋯⋯⋯⋯⋯⋯
>
> W 謝謝你這樣介紹我，Alberts先生，我很榮幸能夠獲得如此特別的獎項並站在這裡。寫書，特別是寫小說並不是一個人的事情。首先是最重要的，我要感謝編輯Janet Renton小姐。她為了提高我作品的完成度提出了很多建議。如果沒有她，我今天是不會站在這裡的。另外，我也想感謝Twin出版社的校對人及設計師，你們做了一件很了不起的事情。以及我的代理人Peter Welling會在我感到困難時鼓勵我讓我得以繼續工作。最後，我想感謝我的粉絲們。*The Winding Road*之所以能夠如此成功，都是因為有他們。

詞彙 honor 名譽 fiction 虛構的事，小說 individual 個人的 first and foremost 首先；最重要的 editor 編輯 countless 數不清的 proofreader 校對人 agent 代理人 encourage 鼓勵，鼓舞 struggle 奮鬥，經歷困難

83.

這段演說應該會在什麼地方進行？

(A) 退休紀念派對。
(B) 送別會。
(C) 頒獎典禮。
(D) 簽字儀式。

在談話的開頭部分，說話者在說完 "It's an honor to be standing here holding this special award." 之後繼續講得獎感言。因此，談話進行的地方應該是(C)的頒獎典禮。

詞彙 retirement 隱退，退休 farewell party 送別會 signing ceremony 簽字儀式

84.
說話者是誰？
(A) 作家。
(B) 編輯。
(C) 校對。
(D) 代理人。

話者說「寫書不是一個人的事情(Writing books, especially works of fiction, isn't an individual)」之後並對編輯、校對、設計師以及代理人表達感謝。因此，說話者的職業應該是(A)。

85.
關於Peter Welling，說話者說了什麼？
(A) 他認識她多年。
(B) 他是她的家人之一。
(C) 他促成了她第一個合約。
(D) 他給了她繼續工作的動力。

在談話的後半部分，將代理人Peter Welling描述為「鼓勵我繼續工作(encouraged me to keep working when I was struggling)的人」。因此，正確答案是把encourage換成motivate的(D)。

[86-88]

W	Mr. Hancock, thank you very much for the work your firm did in promoting last Saturday's seminar. We set a record for attendance and doubled last year's number of international attendees. My team was highly impressed with your advertising and targeting methods. I'd like you to know that our next seminar will be held in early February, and I'd love to see a proposal from you regarding targeting first-time clientele for that event. If I like what I see, I can sign a new contract with your firm. My assistant will contact you with the date and details of the event by the end of the day.
W	Hancock先生，對於貴公司上週六舉行的研討會的宣傳活動深表感謝。我們達成了創紀錄的出席率，來自國外的參加者是去年的2倍。我們團隊對於你的廣告及戰略性目標推進技巧感到印象深刻。想通知您，我們下一次的研討會將於2月初舉行，希望能夠收到有關針對新參加者的提案。如若對內容感到滿意，將會與貴公司簽訂新合約。我的下屬會在工作日結束時與您聯繫，並告訴您活動的日期以及詳細事項。

詞彙 promote 宣傳；升職 set a record 創紀錄 attendee 參加者 be impressed with 對～有深刻印象，對～感動 target 當作目標；目標 method 方法 regarding 與～有關 first-time 初次的 clientele 顧客，委託人 assistant 助理

86.
說話者為什麼會對Hancock表達感謝？
(A) 他是在活動上很受歡迎的演講人。
(B) 他的公司成功地進行了研討會的宣傳。
(C) 他幫助公司達成創紀錄的利潤。
(D) 他和幾家企業簽訂了合約。

從談話的開頭部分可以得知話者之所以會感謝Hancock先生是因為「宣傳研討會(promoting last Saturday's seminar)」。正確答案是(B)。

87.
2月會發生什麼事？
(A) 會寄送提案。
(B) 將會有海外訪問。
(C) 將舉辦活動。
(D) 將會設立公司。

有提到2月的部分是"I'd like you to know that our next seminar will be held in early February."，透過這句可以得知2月將會舉辦研討會。正確答案是將seminar換成event的(C)。

88.
說話者的下屬會做什麼事？
(A) 將合約郵寄出去。
(B) 提供資訊。
(C) 從機場接顧客過來。
(D) 在文件上簽名。

談話的最後一句"My assistant will contact you with the date and details of the event by the end of the day."說明說話者的下屬將會打電話給Hancock告知活動日期及細節，因此下屬要做的是(B)。

[89-91]

M	Okay, everyone, the day's festivities are about to begin. We've got a huge crowd waiting to get inside the fairgrounds. Please do your best to provide assistance to anyone who asks for help. If you can't answer a question, direct the person to any of the three information booths set up here. Be sure to wear your red hats so that people can identify you more easily. It's going to be hot and sunny today, so don't forget to drink plenty of water. We don't want any medical emergencies. Thanks once again for volunteering to help out. It's people like you who make festivals like this successful.

M 好的，大家今天的活動馬上就要開始了。有無數的群眾們正等着要進入慶典活動，請盡力去幫助那些請求幫助的人。沒辦法回答問題時，請帶到任何一個設置在這裡的服務台。為了能讓人們能更容易認出來，請記住一定要戴著紅帽子。今天將是炎熱晴朗的日子，請不要忘記多喝水，我不希望發生緊急情況。再次感謝你們自願給予協助，讓我們能夠順利舉辦像這樣成功的慶典。

詞彙 festivity 慶典活動 be about to 正要 fairground 舉辦場地 ask for 請求 direct 指路，引導 identify 確認(身分) plenty of 許多 medical 醫學的，醫療的 emergency 緊急情況 volunteer 自願，志願服務

89.

聽的人會是誰？
(A) 售票員。
(B) 志願服務者。
(C) 攤販。
(D) 慶典參加者。

說話者在介紹慶典活動即將開始後，在說明為了進行慶典聽眾應該要做的事情。而且談話的後半部分說"Thanks once again for volunteering to help out."並對聽眾表示感謝，因此可以推測出聽眾是為了幫助慶典進行的(B)。

詞彙 ticket collector 售票員，檢票員 vendor 攤販，小販

90.

說話者說要聽眾戴上什麼？
(A) 太陽眼鏡。
(B) T恤。
(C) 手套。
(D) 帽子。

說話者在談話中間部分時說"Be sure to wear your red hats so that people can identify you more easily."指示聽眾要戴著帽子。正確答案是(D)。

91.

接下來會發生什麼事？
(A) 人們會去訪問醫院。
(B) 人們會進入慶典場地。
(C) 演出即將開始。
(D) 即將開始售票。

在談話的開始部分，話者說慶典即將開始之後提到了「等待入場的許多人們(a huge crowd waiting to get inside the fairgrounds)」。因此，談話之後人們將會入場，所以(B)才是正確答案。對於提問對話或談話之後的情況，正確答案的線索大多會出現在後半部分，但是也會有像這樣在開始部分就有線索的情況，所以得要注意。

[92-94]

M Hello. My name is David Harper. Last night, I purchased several vitamins on your Web site. I realized, however, that I only purchased a two-month supply of Vitamin B, so I'd like to increase my purchase in order to get six months of it. I tried making the change on your Web site, but I was unable to do so, which is why I'm calling you now. My order number is 9844-495KT. If you could call me back at 945-3847 sometime today to let me know how much I owe you, I'd really appreciate it. Thank you.

M 您好。我叫David Harper。昨天晚上我在您的網站上購買了幾份維生素，但是我發現我只購買了兩個月的維生素B，為了增加到6個月的分量，我想追加購買。我在您的網站上嘗試更改過，但是沒辦法更改，所以就打電話給您了。我的訂單編號是9844-495KT。今天之內請撥打945-3847，告訴我需要多付多少錢，真的很感謝您。謝謝。

詞彙 in order to 為了 owe 欠

92.

說話者需要多少維生素B？
(A) 2個月。
(B) 3個月。
(C) 6個月。
(D) 12個月。

話者說自己購買了兩個月的維生素B，希望把它增加到六個月份量(six months of it)。因此，說話者需要的數量是(C)。前面提到的a two-month supply是訂購錯誤的數量，不能選擇(A)為正確答案。

93.

說話者在說"I was unable to do so"是指什麼？
(A) 沒辦法追加訂購。
(B) 沒辦法結帳。
(C) 沒辦法告知地址。
(D) 沒辦法更改配送日期。

to do so 所指的事情就是前面的making the change on your Web site，這裡講到的變更是指「為了追加訂購(to increase my purchase)」的變更，因此依所給的句子可將說話者的意思看作是(A)。

94.

說話者要求什麼？
(A) 降價。
(B) 打電話。
(C) 確認用的e-mail。
(D) 贈品。

談話後半部分的"If you could call me back at 945-3847 sometime today to let me know how much I owe you, I'd really appreciate it."，從這句話可以看出，說話者拜託的是回電。正確答案是(B)。

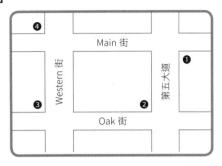

W The big story of the day is that the Fifth Avenue Bridge finally reopened this morning. It had been closed for the past three months after engineers noticed structural problems with it. Now that they've been repaired, traffic should move much more smoothly. However, there will still be some delays downtown as the construction work on Faraday Towers is still ongoing. So try to avoid the corner of Main Street and Western Avenue if you can. It's full of cement mixers and other construction vehicles today. Let's get a report on the weather right now. When we come back, I'll have the day's economic news for you.

W 今天的主要消息是今天早上 Fifth Avenue 橋終於重新開放了。過去三個月，因技術人員發現結構上的問題，一直處於關閉狀態。目前修理已經結束，交通會變得較為順暢。但是 Faraday Towers 的工程還在進行中，市區內的擁塞現象仍將持續，因此請盡量避開 Main 街及 Western 街的轉角，那裡今天擠滿了混凝土和其他建設重型機械。現在請先播報天氣預報，再次回來的時候，我將帶來今天的經濟新聞。

詞彙 notice 注意到，注目 structural 結構性的 smoothly 柔和的，順暢的 ongoing 進行中的 cement mixer 混凝土攪拌機 economic 經濟的

95.

橋為什麼會封閉？
(A) 和船撞上了。
(B) 道路上正在漆油漆。
(C) 正在修理。
(D) 幅度擴大。

話者在談話的前半部分告訴大家發現了橋上有結構性的缺陷，而「這件事解決了(they've been repaired)」，橋重新開放了。因此，橋被封閉的理由是爲了修理，所以正確答案是(C)。

96.

請看圖，Faraday Towers 在哪裡？
(A) 1號地點。
(B) 2號地點。
(C) 3號地點。
(D) 4號地點。

說話者說 Faraday Towers 工程將造成市區擁塞，同時叮嚀要避免「Main 街和 Western 街的轉角(the corner of Main Street and Western Aven)」。因此，在地圖上兩條公路的交匯處的(D) 4號地點應有 Faraday Towers。

97.

聽眾們接下來會聽到什麼？
(A) 廣告。
(B) 天氣新聞。
(C) 經濟新聞。
(D) 音樂。

從"Let's get a report on the weather right now."這句話可以知道聽眾們接下來會聽到(B)天氣新聞。作為參考，經濟新聞是再次開始廣播時會聽到的。

收件匣	
寄件人	**主旨**
Greg Towson	3月份銷售數據
Andrea Sparks	丹佛出差行程
Nicholas Wentz	其他分店開業相關
Melissa Martinez	員工的不滿事項

W I know several of you are interested in knowing about the positions available to transfer to at other branches. I was sent an e-mail listing them right before I came in here, so I'll post it when we're done. Now, we should get started with the meeting. First on the agenda is the marketing campaign which began on Monday. So far, it's quite a success as our advertisement has gone viral on the Internet. Sales are reportedly improving, but we won't have solid numbers until the end of next week. Overall, however, I'd say that we're going to be pleased by what we learn then.

W 我知道你們當中有一部分人對於其他分公司空缺的職位感興趣，因為我在來這裡之前收到了信件，所以會議結束後會公佈。好，讓我們開始開會吧。第一個議案是週一開始的營銷活動，我們的廣告在網上是很有口碑的，所以算是相當成功。根據報告，雖然銷售在增加，但下星期過後才會得到可靠的數據。總之，我想說的是，從整體上來說，我們將會對其結果感到滿意。

詞彙 marketing campaign 營銷活動，營銷戰略 go viral 口碑 reportedly 根據報告，根據傳聞 solid 結實的，穩固的；可靠的 not ~ until 直到 overall 整體上來說

98.

請看圖，說話者提到的 e-mail 是誰寄的？
(A) Greg Towson
(B) Andrea Sparks
(C) Nicholas Wentz
(D) Melissa Martinez

說話者收到的 e-mail 是寫有可以調到其他分公司職位的 e-mail，因此從電子郵箱中找到與此相關題目的 e-mail，就能知道正確答案是(C)。

99.

根據說話者說的話，星期一發生了什麼事？
(A) 推出了新的廣告。

(B) 提交銷售資料。

(C) 賣場有優惠活動。

(D) 僱用了新進員工。

第一個議案是「週一開始的營銷活動(the marketing campaign which began on Monday)」，因此週一開始有新的廣告。正確答案是(A)。

100.

聽者下一週為什麼會覺得高興？

(A) 所有人都會得到獎金。

(B) 銷售數據會是肯定的。

(C) 員工的上班時間會縮短。

(D) 會得獎。

說話者雖然不確定，但傳出銷售額正在增加的消息後說 "Overall,however, I'd say that we're going to be pleased by what we learn then."。也就是說，銷售增加的可能性非常高，因此高興的理由可以看作是(B)。

詞彙 positive 肯定的，確信的 reduce 縮減，減少

Actual Test 3

PART 1   p.38

1. (D)	**2.** (A)	**3.** (C)	**4.** (B)	**5.** (B)
6. (C)				

PART 2   p.42

7. (C)	**8.** (B)	**9.** (B)	**10.** (C)	**11.** (B)
12. (C)	**13.** (B)	**14.** (C)	**15.** (B)	**16.** (C)
17. (A)	**18.** (A)	**19.** (B)	**20.** (C)	**21.** (C)
22. (B)	**23.** (A)	**24.** (A)	**25.** (C)	**26.** (A)
27. (A)	**28.** (A)	**29.** (C)	**30.** (B)	**31.** (C)

PART 3   p.43

32. (A)	**33.** (A)	**34.** (B)	**35.** (B)	**36.** (D)
37. (B)	**38.** (B)	**39.** (A)	**40.** (D)	**41.** (C)
42. (A)	**43.** (D)	**44.** (B)	**45.** (A)	**46.** (C)
47. (B)	**48.** (A)	**49.** (C)	**50.** (A)	**51.** (B)
52. (A)	**53.** (B)	**54.** (B)	**55.** (A)	**56.** (C)
57. (D)	**58.** (D)	**59.** (B)	**60.** (D)	**61.** (D)
62. (A)	**63.** (B)	**64.** (B)	**65.** (A)	**66.** (C)
67. (A)	**68.** (D)	**69.** (B)	**70.** (A)	

PART 4   p.47

71. (C)	**72.** (D)	**73.** (B)	**74.** (B)	**75.** (A)
76. (D)	**77.** (C)	**78.** (B)	**79.** (C)	**80.** (B)
81. (D)	**82.** (A)	**83.** (C)	**84.** (D)	**85.** (B)
86. (C)	**87.** (A)	**88.** (B)	**89.** (B)	**90.** (D)
91. (B)	**92.** (D)	**93.** (B)	**94.** (A)	**95.** (D)
96. (B)	**97.** (C)	**98.** (B)	**99.** (A)	**100.** (C)

PART 1

1.

(A) The woman is packing her suitcase.
(B) The street is crowded with people.
(C) Trees are on both sides of the walkway.
(D) She is pulling her bag behind her.

(A) 女人正在收拾行李箱。
(B) 路上擠滿了人。
(C) 人行道兩側都有樹木。
(D) 她正拉著她的包包。

女人只是帶著行李箱走，所以(A)是錯誤的，(D)才是正確答案。而照片中的道路是空的，樹木只有在左邊才有，因此(B)和(C)各自都不能作為正確的解釋。

詞彙 suitcase 行李箱　be crowded with 擠滿　walkway 步道，人行道

2.

(A) Several containers are on the shelves.
(B) Various items are on display for sale.
(C) Dishes have been set out on the table.
(D) Bowls and plates are full of food.

(A) 架子上有些許容器。
(B) 有多種產品為了販賣而陳列。
(C) 餐桌上放着盤子。
(D) 碗盤上盛滿了食物。

正確答案是(A)。照片中的事物無法知道是不是販賣用的，因此(B)不能成爲正確答案，(C)和(D)是提到照片中沒有出現的桌子和食物的錯誤答案。

詞彙 container 容器，器皿　various 多樣的　on display 展示中的，陳列中的　set out 陳列，安排　sale 販賣　bowl 瓷碗，器皿　plate 盤子　be full of 充滿著

3.

(A) The audience is watching a play.
(B) Actors are rehearsing for a show.
(C) Musicians are performing on stage.
(D) The band is setting up their equipment.

(A) 觀眾們正在觀看戲劇。
(B) 演員們為了演出正在排練。
(C) 音樂家們正在舞台上演出。
(D) 樂團正在架設設備。

照片中的演出是音樂表演，所以提及戲劇(play)或演員(actors)的(A)和(B)都不能成爲正確答案，(C)才是正確答案。

詞彙 audience 聽眾　play 戲曲，戲劇　actor 演員　rehearse 排練，彩排　perform 表演　set up 設置　equipment 設備

4.

(A) The women are holding pens in their hands.
(B) They are looking at the same thing.
(C) The events are being documented.
(D) They are opening the book to the right page.

(A) 女人們手裡拿著筆。
(B) 她們正在看著同一個東西。
(C) 活動正被記錄下來。
(D) 他們正在打開正確的一頁。

要留意描述的對象是單數還是複數。也就是說，如果把(A)誤聽為 ''The woman is holding a pen in her hand. ''就可能會犯下將之選擇為正確答案的失誤。正確答案是說明兩個人在看書上同一個地方的(B)。

詞彙 document 文件；紀錄

5.

(A) He is adjusting the lens of the telescope.
(B) The researcher is using some equipment.
(C) The microscope is being repaired in his lab.
(D) They are looking at something with binoculars.

(A) 他正在調整望遠鏡的鏡頭。
(B) 研究人員正在使用著設備。

40

(C) 顯微鏡正在實驗室裡被修理著。

(D) 他們正在用雙筒望遠鏡看著什麼。

照片中的設備是顯微鏡(microscope)，因此分別提到telescope(望遠鏡)和binoculars(雙筒望遠鏡)的(A)和(D)是錯誤的。正確答案是把顯微鏡換成equipment(設備)的(B)。

詞彙 adjust 調整 telescope 望遠鏡 researcher 研究人員 microscope 顯微鏡 lab 實驗室 (= laboratory) binoculars 雙筒望遠鏡

6.

(A) A vehicle is parked in each of the driveways.

(B) All of the houses have a single story.

(C) The garage doors of the homes are shut.

(D) Traffic is moving in a single direction.

(A) 每條私有車道都停放着一輛車。

(B) 所有房子都只有一層。

(C) 住家的車庫門都是關著的。

(D) 車流是朝著同一個方向移動的。

照片中可以看到的車輛只有一輛停靠在右邊的車，所以(A)和(D)是錯誤的，大部分住宅都是兩層樓以上的，所以(B)同樣不是正確答案。正確答案是描述車庫門關著的(C)。

詞彙 driveway 私有車道，通道入口 story 層；故事

PART 2

7.

Why is the air conditioner making that noise?

(A) Sorry. I'll go ahead and turn it on.

(B) You're correct. It's a bit cold in here.

(C) There must be something wrong with it.

空調為什麼會發出那種噪音？

(A) 抱歉，我會過去開的。

(B) 你說得對，這裡有點冷。

(C) 分明就是有什麼問題。

利用疑問詞why來詢問空調發出的噪音原因為何，因此回答原因可能是故障的回覆(C)是最自然的。

詞彙 air conditioner 空調 make a noise 發出聲音，有噪音 go ahead 往前

8.

Fewer tourists than normal are visiting the city this summer.

(A) Revenues should be up then.

(B) I'm sorry to hear that.

(C) Summer is coming soon.

這個夏天來城市的遊客比平時少。

(A) 那樣的話收入會增加的吧。

(B) 聽到那種話真是遺憾。

(C) 夏天就快到了。

以對「遊客正在減少」的反應來尋找最合適的句子。正確答案是對那種事實表示遺憾的(B)。

詞彙 tourist 遊客 that normal 比起平時 revenue 收入

9.

Hasn't she already departed for the interview?

(A) Yes, she got the part she wanted.

(B) She's planning to take the next bus.

(C) She answered every question quite well.

她還沒面試完嗎？

(A) 是的，她拿到了自己想要的角色。

(B) 她正打算搭下一班公車。

(C) 她對所有的問題都回答得很好。

利用否定疑問句來詢問她是否離開了。因此，表示「將乘坐下一班車」並表達出尚未離開的(B)是恰當的回答。(A)是與題目的departed發音相似的''the part''，(C)是利用在題目的interview一詞中可以聯想到的answered every question所設下的陷阱。

詞彙 depart 離開，出發 interview 採訪，面試 part 部分，角色

10.

How often do you plan to send work updates?

(A) We haven't hired any workers yet.

(B) There are four updates so far.

(C) Every day for the next two weeks.

你打算多久做一次業務報告？

(A) 我們到現在都還沒僱用員工。

(B) 到目前為止更新四次了。

(C) 接下來的兩週每天都有。

以how often來詢問所以有提到「頻率」的回答才是正確答案。選項中提到頻率的回答只有(C)。

詞彙 work update 業務報告書，進展報告 hire 僱用 so far 目前為止

11.

You ought to reconsider accepting his offer.

(A) She took that into consideration.

(B) You think I need to reject it?

(C) I'm offering you a lead role on the project.

你應該要重新考慮一下要不要接受他的提議。

(A) 她有考慮到那一點。

(B) 你認為我應該要拒絕才行嗎？

(C) 希望你能在這個項目中扮演主導的角色。

有意見認爲「應該要重新考慮提案」，因此想要再次確認對方意見的(B)是最自然的答覆。

詞彙 reconsider 再考慮，重新考慮 take ~ into consideration 考慮 reject 拒絕 lead role 主導作用

12.

Thursday's weather is going to be pleasant.

(A) That's going to ruin the picnic.

(B) Yes, thank you for the present.

(C) We should dine outdoors then.

星期四的天氣會很晴朗。

(A) 郊遊應該會被取消。

(B) 是，謝謝你的禮物。

(C) 那我們就可以在戶外吃飯。

要尋找能夠與「星期四天氣會好」的陳述最自然地可以連結到一起的回覆。(A) 是在相反的情況下可能會做出的答覆，(B)是使用與pleasant發音相近的present的陷阱，因此，正確答案是(C)。

詞彙　pleasant 適宜的，心情好的　ruin 毀壞　picnic 遠足，郊遊　present 禮物；現在的　dine 吃飯　outdoors 在戶外

13.

Will you please speak with Mr. Taylor?

(A) He's waiting for you in his office.
(B) Hold on for about ten minutes.
(C) Mr. Taylor no longer works here.

你能夠和Taylor先生談談嗎？
(A) 他在自己的辦公室等你。
(B) 請等我大約10分鐘。
(C) Taylor先生不會繼續在這裡工作了。

注意please這個單字的話，就可以看出這是在拜託對方的句子。因此，表示「10分鐘後會那樣做」並願意接受請求的(B)才是正確答案。

詞彙　hold on 等待　no longer 再也不會

14.

Who's interested in flying to Tokyo with Mr. Randolph?

(A) It's a twelve-hour flight.
(B) The plane leaves tomorrow at midnight.
(C) I'd be delighted to go there.

誰有興趣和Randolph先生一起去東京？
(A) 12小時的飛行。
(B) 那班航班會在明天午夜出發。
(C) 若是我去的話，我會很開心的。

利用疑問詞who詢問誰想去東京。答案表達出「我想去」的(C)。

詞彙　be interested in 對～有興趣　midnight 午夜　delighted 高興

15.

Is the dental clinic on the third or fourth floor?

(A) That's correct.
(B) The higher one.
(C) To fill a cavity.

牙醫在三樓還是在四樓？
(A) 是的。
(B) 較高的那一層。
(C) 為了治療蛀牙。

正在詢問3樓和4樓中牙醫所在的樓層在哪裡，所以說「更高一層(higher one)」，迂迴地指出4樓的(B)就是正確答案。如果沒有聽清楚題目的後半部分，就有可能會出現選擇(A)為正確答案的失誤。

詞彙　dental clinic 牙醫　fill a cavity 治療蛀牙

16.

Will she agree to the suggested changes?

(A) No, I didn't change a thing.
(B) That's a great suggestion.
(C) That has yet to be determined.

她會同意更改的提議嗎？
(A) 不，我什麼也沒換。
(B) 真是個了不起的提案。
(C) 現在還不知道。

在詢問她是否同意。正確答案是推遲確切答案，「到目前為止還不知道」的(C)。

詞彙　agree to 同意　have yet to 還沒有　determine 決定；知道

17.

The local bank branch is right around the corner.

(A) I wasn't aware that it's so close.
(B) I've got to make a small deposit.
(C) Yes, it opens at ten every day.

拐彎就是地方銀行分行。
(A) 不知道離得那麼近。
(B) 我已經小額匯款了。
(C) 嗯，那裡每天10點開門。

因為告知了銀行的位置，所以回答「不知道離得那麼近」的(A)是最自然的回答。

詞彙　branch 分店，分公司；樹枝　aware 知道　make a deposit 存款，存錢

18.

When was the fax sent by the Boris Group?

(A) Approximately thirty minutes ago.
(B) It explains the terms of the agreement.
(C) Located in downtown Seattle.

來自Boris集團的傳真是什麼時候發送的？
(A) 大概30分鐘之前。
(B) 那裡解釋了合約條款。
(C) 位於西雅圖市中心。

因為這是以連接詞when開頭的疑問句，所以要選擇表現出時間的選項。答案是表示「30分鐘之前」的(A)。

詞彙　approximately 大約　terms of an agreement 合約條款　downtown 市內

19.

Who requested some time off this week?

(A) On Thursday and Friday.
(B) Catherine and Marie, I think.
(C) Just a couple of hours in the afternoon.

這週誰申請休假了？
(A) 在星期四和星期五。
(B) 我想是Catherine和Marie。
(C) 只有下午兩小時。

這是利用疑問詞who的疑問句，因此，直接指出請假的人的(B)是正確答案。

詞彙 request 請求，要求 time off 休息，休假

20.

You'd better pay the registration fee by Friday.

(A) Two installments of $100 each.
(B) You're right. I didn't register.
(C) Thank you for the reminder.

你最好在週五之前繳交註冊費。
(A) 每100美元兩期。
(B) 你說得對，我沒登記。
(C) 謝謝你讓我想起來。

利用had better向對方提出某種忠告。因此，對忠告表示感謝的(C)是最自然的回答。

詞彙 had better ~比較好 registration fee 註冊費 installment 分期付款

21.

Aren't the interns going through orientation today?

(A) It's hard to get oriented in this building.
(B) None of them was assigned to us.
(C) It's been rescheduled for tomorrow.

今天的實習員工不是都得去聽說明會嗎？
(A) 在這棟建築物裡很難找到方向。
(B) 他們之中沒有人被分配給我們。
(C) 日程改到了明天。

以一般的詢問方式提問，所以應該以yes/no的形式回答。 選項中稱「不是今天而是明天」間接傳達no意思的(C)是較恰當的答覆。

詞彙 intern 實習員工 orientation 說明會 get oriented 尋找方向，找路 assign 分配 reschedule 再調整日程

22.

Do you know where the local theater is?

(A) Ticket prices have increased too much.
(B) On the second floor of the West End Mall.
(C) The movie's scheduled to start at five.

你知道這附近哪裡有劇場嗎？
(A) 票券價格上漲太多了。
(B) West End Mall的2樓。
(C) 那部電影預定在5點開始。

以do you know開頭詢問之後，實際提問的內容就出現了。 在這個問題中，說話者真正要問的是劇場的位置，所以告知劇場位置的(B)是正確答案。

詞彙 local 當地的，附近的 theater 劇場 increase 增加 be scheduled to 預計

23.

Is that the fastest you can be here?

(A) I'll try to catch an earlier train.
(B) Monday morning at nine thirty.
(C) Yes, I'm standing here in my office.

那是你可以最快來到這裡的方法嗎？

(A) 我會努力趕上可以更快的火車。
(B) 星期一上午9點30分。
(C) 是的,我站在我的辦公室裡。

詢問對方那是不是能夠最快速的方法，正確答案是表達出「如果有更快的方法，我會選擇這個」的(A)。

詞彙 try to 努力 catch 抓住

24.

Employee evaluations are conducted every year.

(A) I wasn't aware of that.
(B) Let's evaluate the product.
(C) Her conduct was better than usual.

每年都會進行員工評價。
(A) 我不知道這一點。
(B) 我們來評價一下那個產品。
(C) 她的行動比平時還要好。

因為告知了進行員工評價的訊息，所以回答「不知道這一點」的(A)是最自然的回答。(B)是將evaluation(評價)換成動詞evaluate(評價)，(C)是將conduct(實施)換成名詞conduct(行為)所誘導的陷阱。

詞彙 evaluation 評價 conduct 實施，實行；行動 be aware of 知道，注意

25.

Which area are we opening the new branch in?

(A) The first week of next month.
(B) Because sales have been rising.
(C) The region down by the harbor.

我們要將新的分店開設在哪個地區？
(A) 下個月第一週。
(B) 因為銷售量在增加。
(C) 港口地區。

因為是用which area來詢問的，所以與場所相關的回答才是正確答案。只有(C)提到地點或地區。(A)是當問及時間點，(B)是當問及理由時才能繼續的回答。

詞彙 area 地區 sale 販售，販售量；折扣 rise 上升 region 地區 harbor 港口

26.

Enrollment is up more than twenty percent.

(A) That's the best news I've heard all day.
(B) I haven't registered for classes yet.
(C) The first day of class is tomorrow.

註冊率增加了20%以上。
(A) 這是今天聽到最好的消息。
(B) 我還沒有登記課程。
(C) 明天開始上課。

正在向對方傳達註冊率上升的消息。對此表示高興的(A)是恰當的答覆。(B)和(C)都是利用與「課程註冊登記(enrollment)」有關的錯誤答案。

詞彙 enrollment 註冊 all day 一整天 register for 登記

27.

The negotiations have been progressing, haven't they?

(A) Not as quickly as we'd hoped.

(B) I'm making progress on the sample.

(C) The next meeting is first thing tomorrow.

正在進行協商，不是嗎？

(A) 沒有期望中進行得那麼快。

(B) 我在改進樣品。

(C) 下次會議將優先在明天進行。

透過否定疑問句來詢問協商是否正在進行中，因此，間接表現出「雖然進展緩慢，但正在進行中」積極反應的(A)才是正確答案。

詞彙 negotiation 協商 progress 進行；進展，發展 as ~ as 像～一樣 make progress 發展，改善 first thing 最為優先，最初；最先要做的事

28.

There are no parking spaces available on this level.

(A) Let's go to the roof then.

(B) Right by the front door.

(C) Yeah, I see one over there.

這一層沒有停車位。

(A) 那麼就去上一層吧。

(B) 就在正門旁邊。

(C) 是的，那邊看見一個。

尋找對「沒有停車位」最自然的反應。正確答案是表示去別的地方的(A)。

詞彙 parking space 停車位 available 可利用的 level 樓 roof 屋頂，高層

29.

Why did Mr. Grogan already leave for the day?

(A) That's right. Today is Thursday.

(B) Mr. Grogan will see you in his office now.

(C) He's got a doctor's appointment.

為什麼Grogan先生已經下班了？

(A) 對的，今天是星期四。

(B) Grogan先生會在自己的辦公室見你。

(C) 他預約好醫院了。

利用疑問詞why詢問下班的理由。正確答案是提到「預約診療」的下班理由(C)。

詞彙 leave for the day 下班 doctor's appointment 預約醫院，預約診療

30.

Couldn't you check to make sure it's sealed properly?

(A) Yes, there are seals at the zoo.

(B) I already did that twice.

(C) That's not my property.

能不能幫我確認一下封口是否正常？

(A) 是的，動物園裡有海狗。

(B) 已經確認兩次了。

(C) 那不是我的。

用couldn't拜託對方確認封口是否正常，因此，回答「已經確認兩次」的(B)是最為恰當的答覆。

詞彙 seal 封印；海豹，海狗 properly 適當地 property 財產，持有物

31.

What time is the speech set to begin?

(A) In the room next to the auditorium.

(B) No, she doesn't have a speech problem.

(C) About fifteen minutes from now.

演講預定在幾點開始？

(A) 在禮堂旁邊的房間。

(B) 不，她沒有遇到語言問題。

(C) 大約15分之後。

因為是以what time來詢問，所以要表現出時刻才可以。正確答案是告知15分鐘後的(C)。

詞彙 next to 旁邊 auditorium 禮堂

PART 3

[32-34]

> M We think you'd be a great match for us here at Trinity Chemicals, so we'd like to offer you a job as a researcher. Would you be able to start on January 15?
>
> W The starting date is acceptable, but what about the salary? I believe that due to my experience, I should be paid more than what's mentioned in the advertisement.
>
> M I spoke about that with my boss, and he mentioned we can afford to pay you $85,000 a year plus performance bonuses. Is that acceptable?
>
> W I'd say we have a deal. I'll start making the arrangements to find a place here in Brownsville.
>
> -
>
> M 我們認為您是非常適合Trinity化學的人才，因此想向您提議擔任研究員一職。能從1月15日開始上班嗎？
>
> W 開始上班的時間不錯，但工資是多少？根據我的經驗，我覺得應該比招聘廣告中提到的還要多。
>
> M 我和老闆談到過這一點，他說可以支付年薪85,000美元加上獎金。那程度的話可以接受嗎？
>
> W 可以的。看來我得開始在Brownsville找個地方住。

詞彙 match 合適；適合的人/物品 researcher 研究員，調查員 acceptable 可以接受的 performance bonus 業績獎金，績效工資 have a deal 進行交易，簽約

32.

女人在做什麼？

(A) 招聘面試。

(B) 調職申請。

(C) 關於新項目的討論。

(D) 關於搬家的談話。

男子向女子提議研究員職務(a job as a researcher)後，女子開始嘗試協商年薪。因此，女人在做的是(A)面試。

33.

男人為什麼會提到自己的老闆？

(A) 為了傳達老闆的提案。

(B) 為了表明自己即將和老闆見面。

(C) 為了向女人提議跟老闆見一面。

(D) 為了要告知老闆的聯絡方式。

當女人要求更高的工資時，男人說「我和老闆談過(I spoke about that with my boss)」，之後告知老闆提出的工資上調方案，因此，他提到老闆的理由是(A)。

詞彙 repeat 反覆，重複 contact information 聯絡方式

34.

關於女人有什麼暗示？

(A) 她打算從二月份開始工作。

(B) 她接受Trinity化學的入職提議。

(C) 她現在住在Brownsville。

(D) 她資歷不多。

從對話最後部分，女人的話"I'd say we have a deal."中可以看出，女人最終接受了入職提議。因此，正確答案是(B)。因為女人將從一月份開始工作，所以(A)是錯誤的解釋。在對話最後的部分，女人說要找住的地方，(C)也與事實不符，同時，由於女人以自身經歷多為主張提高工資，所以(D)也是錯誤的。

[35-37]

M	Darlene, I saw you pulling into that parking garage at the corner of Winston Street and Eastern Avenue this morning. Don't you know we've got a parking lot here for employees? Part-timers are allowed to use it.
W	I tried to apply for a parking pass yesterday, but the office was closed when I went there. I didn't want there to be any problems today, so I parked in the pay lot.
M	Well, parking there for the entire day can be expensive. Let me take you to the office now to make the arrangements. Then, you can start parking here from now on.

M Darlene，我今天早上看到妳的車開進Winston街和 Eastern街拐角處的停車場。你不知道這裏有員工專用的停車場嗎？工讀生也可以使用的。

W 昨天想申請停車券的，但到了辦公室發現門關了。今天不想再出問題，所以就在收費停車場停車。

M 嗯，在那裡停一天的話，停車費會很多的。現在和我去辦公室把事情處理掉。那麼從現在開始就可以在這裡停車了。

詞彙 pull into 抵達 parking garage 停車場 part-timer 鐘點工，臨時工 parking pass 停車券 pay lot 收費停車場 take A to

B 把A帶去B arrangement 準備，安排；處理方式

35.

關於女人，男人在暗示什麼？

(A) 她馬上就要調職了。

(B) 她是鐘點工。

(C) 她搬到附近的城市了。

(D) 她住在離辦公室很遠的地方。

男子一邊告訴在外面停車場停車的女人有員工專用停車場，一邊說"Part-times are allowed to use it."，透過這些可以認定女人是工讀生，因此(B)是正確答案。

36.

女人昨天做了什麼？

(A) 買了新車。

(B) 面試了。

(C) 拒絕了要求。

(D) 訪問了辦公室。

問題的核心語句yesterday在''I tried to apply for a parking pass yesterday, but the office was closed when I went there. ''。 女人說要去辦公室申請停車券，但是辦公室門關了，所以女的昨天做的事情是(D)。

37.

男人提議什麼？

(A) 參觀設施。

(B) 幫助申請過程。

(C) 提交津貼申請表格。

(D) 告知去分公司的路。

聽到女人因為無法申請停車券而在外面停車場停車，男人說"Let me take you to the office now to make the arrangements. "，也就是說，男人向女人提出一起到辦公室解決停車券申請問題，因此(B)是正確答案。

詞彙 give a tour of 參觀 benefit 優惠；津貼 provide directions to 告知去～的路

[38-40]

W	This advertisement is impressive, James. How did you come up with it so quickly?
M	You should thank Roger.
W	Roger? I don't know who he is.
M	He's a freelance graphic designer who does work for us occasionally. The concept for the ad was ours, but he created it.
W	In that case, I'd love to have a talk with him. I've got another project to do, and it sounds like he could be of assistance. I hope he has some free time over the next couple of days.
M	I'll e-mail you his contact information as soon as I return to my office. Then, you can call him.

W	這次的廣告給我留下了深刻的印象，James，你是怎麼做得那麼快的？
M	這都要謝謝Roger。
W	Roger？我不知道他是誰。
M	偶爾會和我們一起工作的自由職業平面設計師。理念是我們想的，但廣告是他製作的。
W	那麼我想和他談談。有另一個項目需要進行，聽起來他能幫忙，希望他之後有時間。
M	我一回到辦公室就用e-mail把他的聯絡方式告訴你。那樣的話你就可以和他連繫了。

詞彙 impressive 印象深刻的 come up with 想出；生產
freelance 自由職業者 concept 概念，風格 create 創造，製造 in that case 在那種情況下，那樣的話

38.

當男人說"You should thank Roger"時，他在暗示什麼？
(A) Roger成功帶動了廣告活動。
(B) Roger製作了廣告。
(C) Roger解決了女人的問題。
(D) 上個月Roger銷售了大部分的產品。

給予的句子是聽到對廣告的稱讚後男人說的話。換句話說，它傳達了製作令人印象深刻廣告的功勞在於Roger手中的意思，因此，由此可以推測的事項是(B)。

詞彙 campaign 活動

39.

關於女人的話，暗示了什麼？
(A) 需要平面設計師的協作。
(B) 在營銷部工作。
(C) 是男人的上司。
(D) 和男人共用一個辦公室。

聽到一個叫Roger的人是自由職業平面設計師之後，女人說她"I've got another project to do, and it sounds like he could be of assistance."，由此可以看出她希望得到Roger關於平面設計的幫助，因此(A)是正確答案。

40.

男人會給女人什麼？
(A) 傳單。
(B) 請款書。
(C) 申請書。
(D) 電話號碼。

在對話最後的部分，男人對女人說了「我會用e-mail告訴妳Roger的聯絡方式(I'll e-mail you his contact information)」，所以男人會告知的是(D)。

[41-43]

W	Good morning. My name is Amanda Roth, and I've got a slight problem. I was issued this ID card yesterday, but it doesn't seem to be working properly. I can't get any doors to open with it.
M	Several new employees have mentioned the same problem. I think the most recent batch of IDs has a flaw. I need to reissue your ID card. Do you have time to fill out the paperwork?
W	I wish I did, but I have an orientation session that starts in five minutes. Should I return here once it's done?
M	Please do. It will take half an hour to complete the process, so make sure you have enough time when you come back.

W	您好，我叫Amanda Roth，有個小問題。昨天我辦了這張身分證，但好像感應不良。用一張開不了任何一扇門。
M	有幾位新進員工都提到了同一個問題。身份證的最新裝置似乎有缺陷，需要重發身份證，請問你有時間填寫文件嗎？
W	我希望我可以，但說明會在5分鐘後開始，結束之後再過來也可以嗎？
M	請那樣做吧。完成手續需要30分鐘左右，請確認時間是否充足之後再過來。

詞彙 issue 發給，發行 properly 正常地 recent 最近的 batch (電腦上的)配置，裝置 flaw 缺陷，瑕疵 reissue 重發 fill out 填寫

41.

女人為什麼要找男人？
(A) 請他開辦公室的門。
(B) 發現了文件上的問題。
(C) 公司身份證不能正常運作。
(D) 電腦無法正常登錄。

在對話的前半部分，女人找男人的原因是"I was issued this ID card yesterday, but it doesn't seem to be working properly."。也就是說，身分證的功能有問題而找來的，所以正確答案是(C)。

詞彙 unlock 開 function 功能；發揮作用 log in 登錄

42.

男人希望女人做什麼？
(A) 填寫表格。
(B) 參加說明會。
(C) 照相。
(D) 回答問卷。

男人說要重發身分證給女人，然後問有沒有「填寫文件的時間(time to fill out the paperwork)」，因此，男人想要的是(A)。

詞彙 questionnaire 問券，調查表

43.

男人說女人需要多少時間？
(A) 5分。
(B) 10分。
(C) 15分。
(D) 30分。

如果沒有漏聽男人最後一句話''it will take half an hour to complete the process.''的話，就可以輕鬆地知道正確答案是(D)。

[44-46]

M	Our revenues are down by thirty-two percent this year, and we're going to lose money for the fifth quarter in a row. I think we need to lay off some employees.
W	Unfortunately, I agree with you. How do you think we should go about this? Should we get rid of people according to seniority?
M	No. Some of our best workers started in the past year or two. Talk to the head of each department and find out who the poor performers are.
W	All right. I'll send out an e-mail today and make sure the list is on your desk first thing tomorrow morning.
M	今年收益減少了32%，將會連續虧損五個季度。我覺得應該把一些員工辭退。
W	很遺憾的，我也同意你說的話。你覺得我們應該怎麼做呢？是否該按照資歷順序解僱？
M	不，有幾個最優秀的員工是從一年或兩年前開始工作的。和各部門的負責人談一下，看看誰是績效最差的員工。
W	知道了。今天會發email，會優先爭取在明天上午前把名單放在你的桌子上。

詞彙 in a row 持續，連續　lay off 解僱　get rid of 除去　seniority 長輩；資歷　first thing 優先

44.

關於公司，提到了什麼？
(A) 是製造企業。
(B) 損失超過一年。
(C) 在幾個國家設有分公司。
(D) 最近僱用了好幾個新員工。

在對話的第一句中談到了今年公司收益減少和「連續五個季度虧損 (for the fifth quarter in a row)」，因此我們可以看到公司虧損持續一年以上，提的內容在選項中為(B)。

45.

女人建議採取什麼解僱方式？
(A) 根據工作資歷。
(B) 根據成果。
(C) 根據年薪。
(D) 按照距退休日期近的順序。

只有知道女人說的''Should we get rid of people according to seniority?''中的seniority意思為「資歷順序」或「工作年數」，所以女人提議的方式最終為(A)。

46.

男人希望女人做什麼？
(A) 分析最近的銷售資料。
(B) 決定解僱哪位職員。
(C) 和管理者說話。
(D) 將會議日程定在明天。

在對話的最後一部分，男人對女人說''Talk to the head of each department and find out who the poor performers are.''，也就是說要與各部門負責人談話，讓他們瞭解業績不佳的人，因此用supervisors來形容部門負責人的(C)才是正確答案。

[47-49]

W1	Kelly, I need you to deliver all of these items to 209 Westinghouse Road. They have to arrive by 2:30.
W2	I'd love to help you out, Ms. Morgan, but I've already got three other deliveries to make, and they're on the other side of town.
W1	Peter, how about you? What's your schedule like for today?
M	I've got a meeting with Mr. Andrews in Marketing in ten minutes. We're having lunch together, so I'm not sure when we'll return to the office.
W2	What about getting Jessica to do it? I heard her mention she's got a light schedule today.
W1	Thanks, Kelly. I think I'll do that.
W1	Kelly，請把這些物品全部送到Westinghouse路209號，2點半之前要送到。
W2	Morgan小姐，我很願意幫忙。但是已經有3件需要處理的配送，而且配送地址也是市區的另一邊。
W1	Peter，你怎麼樣？今天的行程如何？
M	我10分鐘後要和營銷部的Andrews先生開會，打算要一起吃午飯，不知道什麼時候會回辦公室。
W2	那件事交給Jessica如何？聽說她今天的行程很空閒。
W1	謝謝你，Kelly，我會這樣做的。

47.

問題是什麼？
(A) 會議取消了。
(B) 物品需要配送。
(C) 漲價了。
(D) 訂貨還沒到。

雖然女子1正在尋找送貨人，但是女子2和男人因為各自的行程無法送貨，因此，(B)是正確答案。

48.

男人說自己要做什麼？
(A) 和同事見面。
(B) 參加研討會。
(C) 登記參加營銷會議。
(D) 在辦公室吃午飯。

從男人說的話「和營銷部的Andrews先生開會 (I've got a meeting

with Mr.Andrews in Marketing)」可以得知男人將要做的事情是(A)。

49.

Kelly建議做什麼？
(A) 訪問Westinghouse路209號。
(B) 與Andrews先生進行商談。
(C) 和Jessica說話。
(D) 訪問營銷部。

對找人送貨的女子1說"What about getting Jessica to do it?"之後，告知Jessica有空閒，因此，女子2提議的是(C)。

[50-52]

M	Hello. This is Sid Davis calling from Global Parcels. Is this Ms. Carrie Woodruff?
W	This is she. How may I be of assistance?
M	I've got a package I'm going to be delivering to you within the next thirty minutes. Will you be in your office at that time?
W	Unfortunately, I'm away from my desk all day long. How about leaving it with my assistant, Deborah Sellers?
M	I'm really sorry, but I have instructions only to give it to you. You'll have to show me some ID to receive the item.
W	I see. Then you can visit anytime tomorrow between nine and noon.

M	您好，我是Global快遞的Sid Davis。請問是Carrie Woodruff小姐嗎？
W	我就是，有什麼事嗎？
M	30分鐘之內將會有妳的快遞。那時候在辦公室嗎？
W	很遺憾的是我今天一整天都不在。能夠轉交給我的部下Deborah Sellers嗎？
M	真的很抱歉，但是有指示只能給本人。收貨前需要您出示身份證。
W	這樣啊。那樣的話，明天9點到12點之間隨時都可以來找我。

詞彙 all day long 一整天　instruction 指示事項

50.

男人為什麼打電話給女人？
(A) 為了知道她所在的地方。
(B) 為了向她確認她最近的訂單。
(C) 為了詢問她的住址。
(D) 為了告知她能帶走她的快遞。

男人告訴女人預計會有快遞之後問"Will you be in your office at that time?"，也就是為了確認快遞到達的時候女人是否會在辦公室而打電話，所以打電話的理由為(A)。

51.

男人為什麼會說"I'm really sorry"？
(A) 為了失誤而道歉。
(B) 為了拒絕女人的要求。
(C) 為了拜託女人再說一遍。
(D) 為了要說找不到產品。

給予的句子是聽到將快遞付託給下屬以代替本人的要求後說的話，因此，應將其視爲「不能聽從委託」的意思。正確答案是(B)。

52.

女人應該要為男人做什麼？
(A) 出示帶有照片的身份證。
(B) 完成文件工作。
(C) 對一部分的商品以現金結帳。
(D) 和他的部下見面。

聽到女人要求將自己的快遞交給下屬，男人回答說不能那樣做，然後說"You'll have to show me some ID to receive the item."。也就是說，為了要領取快遞，需要用身份證確認本人身份，所以女人要做的是(A)。

[53-55]

W	James, do you happen to know anything about computers? Mine won't connect to the Internet for some reason.
M1	I think this is a company-wide problem because I just got logged off the system.
W	That's not good. One of my clients sent me an urgent e-mail, and I really need to read it.
M1	Matt, do you know anything about this? Is there some kind of a problem?
M2	Didn't you read the memo this morning? The entire system is down for maintenance and won't be back up until around 4:00.
W	Oh, no. I'd better call Mr. Rogers and explain the problem to him.

W	James，你對電腦很瞭解嗎？我的電腦不知道為什麼連不上網絡了。
M1	這次好像是整個公司的問題，因為我剛剛也被登出系統了。
W	糟糕，客戶中有一名要發緊急e-mail給我，我得要讀的。
M1	Matt，對此你知道些什麼嗎？有什麼問題嗎？
M2	今天早上沒有看備忘錄嗎？由於系統要檢修，整個系統都癱瘓了，大約四點以後才能重新運轉。
W	哦，這樣啊。看來我應該給Rogers先生打電話說明問題。

詞彙 urgent 緊急的　memo 備忘錄　maintenance 維持，維修

53.

說話者們主要在討論什麼？
(A) 電腦程序。
(B) 網絡問題。

(C) 女子的email。
(D) 員工會議。

在談話的整個過程中都在談論不能連接網絡的原因，因此對話的主題是(B)。

54.
關於備忘錄，Matt說了什麼？
(A) 他忘了要讀它。
(B) 它於今天早上發布。
(C) 他為了同事們把它寫好了。
(D) 它與預算會議有關。

提及memo(備忘錄)的句子是"Didn't you read the memo this morning？"，從這裡可以看出備忘錄是今早發佈的。因此，(B)是正確答案。

詞彙 refer to 指出；和～有關聯

55.
Rogers先生是誰？
(A) 女子的顧客。
(B) 說話者的管理者。
(C) 電腦工程師。
(D) 檢查員。

對女人來說，問題出在從顧客那收到了一封緊急郵件，但因為系統檢查讓她無法讀信。另外，在對話的後半部分，聽到「系統癱瘓的原因是因為檢查」的話，女人說"I'd better call Mr.Rogers and explain the problem to him."。綜合這兩點來看，估計Rogers先生是女人的客戶，所以正確答案是(A)。

[56-58]

M	We got reviewed in the *Mobile Times*, but the reviewer wasn't very positive about us. He liked neither the food nor the service.
W	That's going to affect our sales negatively. We should do something to avoid losing any customers. We also ought to write a letter to the editor disputing the reviewer's opinion.
M	How about if we offer entrées at half price for the rest of the week? And I'll work on the letter.
W	I like both ideas. In the meantime, I'll look into the complaints he made regarding the service and figure out who was on duty when he visited us.

M	*Mobile Times*刊登了我們的評論，但評論者對我們不太肯定。他對飲食不滿意，對服務也不滿意。
W	這會對銷售產生負面影響。為了留住顧客，我們得做些什麼。另外，還要給編輯寫信去回覆評論意見。
M	這週剩下的時間裡，主菜以半價提供如何？然後信由我來寫。
W	兩個主意都行。這段時間，我會調查一下關於服務的不滿事項，看看他來訪時是誰上班。

詞彙 review 檢討，批評；調查 positive 正面的 neither A nor B 不是A也不是B affect 產生影響 negatively 負面地 avoid 避開 dispute 爭論 entrée 主菜 in the meantime 途中，那段期間 look into 調查 regarding 關於 on duty 工作中的

56.
對話會在哪裡進行？
(A) 報社。
(B) 超市。
(C) 餐廳。
(D) 糕點店。

評論語是「對飲食和服務都不滿意(liked neither the food nor the service)」，從這一點可以看出說話者工作的地方是(C)餐廳。

57.
男人提議做什麼？
(A) 給編輯打抗議電話。
(B) 教育好員工。
(C) 取消訂購報紙。
(D) 以折扣價提供食物。

男人的提案可以在"How about if we offer entrées at half price for the rest of the week?"得知，男人建議主菜打五折。因此，(D)是正確答案。

詞彙 newspaper subscription 訂購報紙 at a discount 打折

58.
女人擔心什麼？
(A) 建築的租金。
(B) 可用空間。
(C) 定價。
(D) 服務品質。

在對話最後的部分，女人要調查「與服務相關的不滿事項(complants he made regarding the service)」，並要知道「當時是誰負責服務的(who was on duty when he visited us)」，因此，女人擔心的是(D)服務品質。

[59-61]

W	This concludes today's tour. We won't be closing for another two hours, so please feel free to look around the exhibits until then.
M	Pardon me, but is there a gift shop here? I'm interested in purchasing some posters of several of my favorite paintings because I think my children might enjoy them.
W	You can get everything you need on the first floor next to the east wing. If you have a membership here, you can get a fifteen-percent discount on all purchases.
M	I wasn't aware of that. I'll be sure to sign up for that first before I do any shopping.

W	會以這個來結束今天的旅遊。之後兩個小時內將不會關門，所以請盡情參觀展覽。
M	不好意思，這裡有紀念品店嗎？因為覺得孩子們會喜歡，所以想買幾張我喜歡的畫的海報。
W	你可以在東館旁邊的一樓購買所有需要的東西。如果有這裡的會員卡，所有購買的商品都可享有15%的優惠。
M	這一點我不知道。在購物前得要先註冊會員了。

詞彙 conclude 做結論；結束，完成　gift shop 紀念品商店　wing 翅膀；附屬建築　membership 會員資格，會員券　sign up for 註冊

59.

對話會在哪裡進行？
(A) 遊樂園。
(B) 博物館。
(C) 劇場。
(D) 紀念品店。

如果留意到tour(巡迴)，exhibits(展覽)和paintings(繪畫)等詞語，在選項中進行對話的地方只有(B)博物館。

60.

男人問了什麼？
(A) 是否乘坐公車。
(B) 票價。
(C) 巡迴時間。
(D) 賣場位置。

男人說"Pardon me, but is there a gift shop here?"正在詢問紀念品商店的位置，因此(D)是正確答案。

61.

根據女人的介紹，男子如何才能夠享受折扣？
(A) 至少消費15美元。
(B) 網上購買。
(C) 下載優惠券。
(D) 成為會員。

獲得折扣的資格是在句子"If you have a membership here, you can get a fifteen-percent discount on all pouchases,"說明會員可以得到15%的優惠，因此可以得到優惠的方法是(D)。

[62-64]

感謝您來到Marcy's購物

產品編號	產品	價格
KP895	螺絲起子	$5.99
RY564	電動鑽頭	$28.99
XJ292	鋸子	$12.99
MK646	鐵錘	$6.99

M	Excuse me. I purchased some items on sale on Saturday, but it appears as though the discount was not applied to one of them.
W	I'm sorry about that. Did you bring the receipt with you?
M	Yes, I've got it right here. It's item number RY564.
W	Hmm . . . It looks like you're right. You should have gotten twenty percent off.
M	Great. So what do I do to get the discount?
W	Please take the receipt over to the customer service booth. Show it to the lady working there, and she'll take care of everything for you.
M	Thank you for your help.

M	請問一下，我在週六的促銷中購買了幾件產品，但其中一種看起來似乎沒有折扣。
W	不好意思，你有帶發票嗎？
M	有的，在這裡。產品編號為RY564。
W	嗯……你說的似乎是對的。你可以得到八折優惠。
M	太好了。那要怎麼樣才能得到折扣呢？
W	請把收據帶到顧客服務中心。交給在那裡工作的女職員看的話，她會處理好一切的。
M	謝謝妳的幫助。

詞彙 as though 就像　apply to 適用於　booth 小空間，攤位　take care of 照顧；處理

62.

關於賣場，文章提到了什麼？
(A) 週末促銷了。
(B) 延長了營業時間。
(C) 位於購物中心。
(D) 上週開張了。

在對話開始的部分，從男子「在週六促銷期間購買了產品(I purchased some items on sale on Saturday)」這一點來看，週末賣場進行了促銷。正確答案是(A)。

詞彙 hours of operation 營業時間

63.

看收據，男人應該得到哪一個產品的折扣？
(A) 螺絲起子。
(B) 電動鑽頭。
(C) 鋸子。
(D) 鐵錘。

當女人問及是否有帶發票時，男人回答並告知該產品的編號為RY564。從圖表中尋找的話，便可看出男人需要折扣的物品是(B)的電動鑽頭。

64.

男人接下來會做什麼？
(A) 給女人一張自己的信用卡。
(B) 與顧客服務負責人交談。
(C) 從女人那得到優惠券。
(D) 給女人看自己買的商品。

在對話最後的部分，女人告訴男人要到顧客服務中心 (customer service booth)處理折扣問題，因此，男人要做的是(B)。

[65-67]

區域	票價
A區	$15
B區	$25
C區	$40
D區	$60

W　Hello. I'm calling to reserve two tickets for tonight's performance of *Swan Lake*. I'm really looking forward to seeing it.

M　I'm sorry to inform you there aren't any seats available for the show tonight. However, you can get seats for the Thursday night or Saturday night show. They both have tickets available in every section.

W　Okay, great. In that case, I guess we'll attend the Saturday night performance. And I'd like two seats in Section C, please.

M　You're going to enjoy sitting there. That's where I always prefer to sit when I attend performances. I need your name and credit card number, please.

- -

W　您好，我打電話是想要預訂今晚兩張天鵝湖的門票。我非常期待。

M　對不起，今晚演出的座位已經沒有了。但是週四晚上或者週六晚上的演出還有位置。兩場演出的所有區域都還有票。

W　這樣啊，我知道了。那我想參加星期六晚上的演出，然後我想預約C區的兩個位置。

M　妳會喜歡那個地方的，我去觀看演出時經常都會選這個區域。請告訴我您的姓名和信用卡號碼。

詞彙　look forward to -ing 苦苦等待；期待　inform 告知　prefer 偏好

65.

關於今晚的演出，男人說了什麼？
(A) 已售完。
(B) 延期了。
(C) 首演。
(D) 晚上7點開始。

對於想要今晚演出的門票電話，男子說"I'm sorry to inform you there aren't any seats available for the show tonight."，通過這些可以知道演出門票全部都已經售完，所以(A)才是正確答案。

66.

看圖，女人每張票要付多少錢？
(A) 15美元
(B) 25美元
(C) 40美元
(D) 60美元

因為已經預訂了C區(Section C)的座位，所以女人需要支付的門票價格在圖中尋找一下的話，答案就會是(C)的40美元。

67.

女人接下來會做什麼？
(A) 告知個人資訊。
(B) 選擇想要的座位。
(C) 確認地址。
(D) 把名字拼寫給男人聽。

在對話的最後部分，男人跟女人說「請說姓名和信用卡號碼(name and credit card number)」，因此，將其改為personal information的(A)就是正確答案。

[68-70]

說明會日程		
時間	講師	主題
9:00 A.M. – 9:15 A.M.	Tristan Roberts	歡迎問候
9:15 A.M. – 9:45 A.M.	Eric Mueller	工作內容和責任
9:45 A.M. – 10:00 A.M.	Marcus Wembley	個別保險業務
10:00 A.M. – 10:30 A.M.	Porter Stroman	公司內部設施

W　Do you have a minute to chat to me? I need to get your opinion on which computers we should purchase for the office.

M　I'd love to help you out, but it's 9:55, and I'm giving a talk to the new employees at the orientation session in five minutes. What about if we meet in the afternoon?

W　I've got to head to the airport at noon since I'm flying to Las Vegas for a conference tomorrow. I'll just e-mail you the information.

M　Thanks. I'll check it out as soon as I can and let you know what I think is best.

W　Great. I appreciate it.

- -

W　有時間和我說一下話嗎？辦公用電腦應該買哪一款，我想聽聽你的意見。

M　如果我能幫到忙就好了。但現在是9點55分，我得在5分鐘後在說明會上為新員工演講。下午見面怎麼樣？

W　我因為明天有一場會議，要去拉斯維加斯，所以12點得去機場。我用email告訴你相關內容吧。

M　謝謝。我會儘快確認一下之後告訴妳我覺得那種最好。

W　好的，謝謝。

詞彙　chat 閒聊，交談　head to 前往　check out 確認

68.

看圖，男人是誰？
(A) Tristan Roberts
(B) Eric Mueller
(C) Marcus Wembley
(D) Porter Stroman

從男人說的話"I'd love to help you out, but it's 9:55, and I'm giving a talk to the new employees at the orientation session in five minutes."

可以找到正確答案的線索。透過所給的句子可以看出男人是10點要演講的人，因此從圖表中尋找相關資訊的話，男人的名字應該是(D)的Forter Stroman。

69.

女人今天下午要做什麼？
(A) 擁有私人休息時間。
(B) 到別的城市去。
(C) 參加會議。
(D) 在說明會上講話。

從女人的話"I've got to head to the airport at noon since I'm flying to Las Vegas for a conference tomorrow."可以知道女人將在中午抵達機場前往拉斯維加斯。因此，(B)是正確答案。會議預定在明天舉行，因此(C)不為事實，(D)是男人上午要做的事情。

70.

女人要如何與男人討論問題？
(A) 透過email。
(B) 透過電話。
(C) 透過簡訊。
(D) 直接見面。

在對話的後半部分，女人在表明不能在下午見面的理由後說"I'll just e-mail you the information."。因此，預計說話者們會通過電子郵件交換意見，正確答案是(A)。

PART 4

[71-73]

> W Now that we know how to establish a small business, we ought to move on to the next topic at our workshop. For the next hour and a half, I'm going to tell you how to acquire a business license and inform you about what kinds of government loans are available for business owners. Now, getting a license requires dealing with the government. I know that can be hard at times. But there are a few simple steps you can take to make the process go smoothly. Please turn to page four of your booklets. Look at the chart there on the top of the page.
>
> W 目前我們已經知道了設立中小企業的方法，所以這會成為研討會的下一個主題。在接下來的一個半小時之內，我們會說明獲得事業許可的相關法律，並告知業主可以利用的政府貸款援助金的種類。好，為了得到許可我們必須得要與政府協商。我知道，這樣的事情有時會很吃力，但是透過採取一些簡單的措施可以使處理過程更加順暢。請翻開本子的第四頁。請看那一頁上端的圖表。

詞彙 now that 因為 establish 設立，制定 license 許可 inform 告知 loan 貸款，出借 deal with 面對，處理 government 政府 at times 有時 step 階段，措施 process 處理過程，程序 smoothly 柔和地 booklet 小冊子

71.

接下來的研討會將進行多久？

(A) 30分鐘。
(B) 60分鐘。
(C) 90分鐘。
(D) 120分鐘。

在談話的前半部分中，說話者表示之後的一個半小時(for the next hour and a half)會說事業許可及政府貸款支援金，因此演講時間是(C)。

72.

當說話者說"I know that can be hard at times"時，她指的是什麼？
(A) 銀行幾乎不給新企業貸款。
(B) 幾乎沒有人成功地開始事業。
(C) 也可以用稅金繳納很多金額。
(D) 得到事業許可並不容易。

通過文章脈絡掌握文章中的that意味著什麼才能找到正確答案。that指的是前面句子的與政府打交道的工作(dealing with the government)，意思是獲得事業許可和申請政府支援金，因此給予的句子可看作是(D)。

73.

聽眾接下來會做什麼？
(A) 回答問題。
(B) 看圖表。
(C) 填寫調查問卷。
(D) 休息。

最後一句"Look at the chart there on the top of the page."中可以得知聽眾們將會看第4頁圖表，答案是將chart換成graphic的(B)。

[74-76]

> W Coffee Time wants to prove we have the best coffee. Once you taste it, you'll never want to stop enjoying our coffee. We've decided to make this possible. Get unlimited coffee on Tuesdays. Each Tuesday, refill your cup as many times as you want all day. Coffee Time uses only the best beans from Kona, Hawaii, where they're cultivated on the slopes of Mauna Loa to ensure an amazing roast for the richest and smoothest taste. Come here and have a meeting, do your homework, or relax with your friends every Tuesday. All coffee drinks are eligible for this offer. We're located right across from the main entrance to Atlantic University.
>
> W Coffee Time想證明我們的咖啡是最好的咖啡，只要嚐一次，就永遠拒絕不了我們的咖啡。我們決定讓這樣的事情發生，因此星期二的時候可以無限暢飲咖啡。在每週二，你都可以隨心所欲地將你的咖啡杯裝滿。Coffee Time只使用夏威夷科納山最好的原豆，為了製造出味道豐富柔和的驚人碳焙咖啡而在毛納羅亞山的斜坡上栽培的。歡迎你每週二到這裡來聚會、做作業，又或者是和朋友來休息。所有咖啡在這次活動皆有販售。我們在Atlantic大學的正門對面。

詞彙 unlimited 無限制的 refill 重新裝滿 as～as 像～一樣 all day 一整天 bean 豆 cultivate 耕種 slope 傾斜，斜坡 roast 烤，炒；烘烤的 be eligible for 對於～有資格 entrance 入口

74.

在廣告什麼東西？
(A) 低價。
(B) 特別販賣。
(C) 新菜單。
(D) 實習機會。

廣告中介紹的是一家名為Coffee Time的賣場，這裡每星期二都會提供「無限的咖啡(unlimited coffee)」。因此答案為(B)。

75.

關於所使用的咖啡原豆提到的是什麼？
(A) 只出自於一個地區。
(B) 從印度尼西亞進口。
(C) 烘烤兩次。
(D) 由當地農民生產。

在談話中，Coffee Time提到「使用的只有夏威夷科納山的原豆(only the best beans from Kona, Hawaii)」，因此選項中提到關於原豆的是(A)。

詞彙 import 輸入，進口

76.

關於Coffee Time，給予的暗示是什麼？
(A) 馬上就要降價了。
(B) 需要更多的員工。
(C) 那裡的主人要開二號店。
(D) 多數顧客是學生。

在談話的後半部分，說話者說來咖啡廳「做作業吧(do your homework)」，最後一句話是說明位置在「Atlantic大學正門對面(right across from the main entrance to Atlantic University)」。因此，到那裡的大部分客人都有可能是大學生，正確答案為(D)。

[77-79]

M Hello. This is Earl Swan. I operate Swan's Computer Repairs downtown. This morning, I made an order for several computer parts. I wonder if I can modify it slightly. Part of it consisted of four hard drives with 5,900 RPM. I'd like to change it to seven hard drives with 7,200 RPM. Initially, I indicated I wasn't in a hurry to receive my items, but that's no longer the case. Instead, I must receive everything by Saturday. The timing is absolutely crucial. My customers are counting on me, so ship everything at once. Please contact me to let me know how much I owe for the items and for shipping.

M 您好，我是Earl Swan。我經營著位在市區的Swan's電腦維修店。今天早上我訂了幾個電腦零件，想知道能不能稍微更改一下訂單。訂購項目包括4個5,900 RPM硬碟，我想把這個換成7個7,200 RPM硬碟。最一開始跟您說我並不著急拿到產品，但情況有變，我週六之前必須要全部收到，這真的很重要，因為顧客們很期待，所以請立即發貨。請告訴我需要支付多少產品價格及運費。

詞彙 part 部分；零件 modify 修改 slightly 有點 consist of 由～組成 hard drive 硬碟 initially 最初 indicate 出現 in a hurry 緊急的 no longer 不再 timing 時期，時機 absolutely 絕對，非常 crucial 重要的 count on 相信；期望

77.

說話者為什麼打電話？
(A) 為了詢問產品是否有庫存。
(B) 為了確認價格。
(C) 為了更改訂單。
(D) 為了更改結帳日期。

談話的前半段，說話者說明自己訂了電腦零件，然後說''I wonder if I can modify it slightly.''之後，繼續提及欲更改訂單硬盤的種類，因此說話者打電話的理由(C)。

詞彙 alter 換，變更 payment date 支付日期，結帳日期

78.

當說話者說''The timing is absolutely crucial''時，他指的是什麼？
(A) 他馬上要給顧客打電話。
(B) 產品需要在星期六之前抵達。
(C) 他今天下午可以結帳。
(D) 他希望訂貨可以在今天配送。

給予的句子是「時機很重要」的意思，在前面的句子"Instead, I must receive everything by Saturday."中可以找到正確答案的線索。也就是說，說話者透過給定的句子再次強調到週六為止必須配送，因此說話者的意思可以看作是(B)。

79.

說話者有什麼要求？
(A) 安裝說明書。
(B) email回覆。
(C) 新請款單。
(D) 全額退款。

最後一句是"Please contact me to let me know how much I owe for the items and for shiping."，說話者正在要求對方告知更改訂單的費用，因此，他要求的是(C)新的請款單。

[80-82]

M Locally, the state is going against the national trend as it reported an increase of 1,200 manufacturing jobs during the past quarter. Economists attribute the job creation to the state budget expected to be passed next week. In addition, rumors that software conglomerate Macroshare is moving its headquarters to the city are heating up. Insiders say it's a done deal. These rumors have led to prices in the housing market shooting up. The average price of a three-bedroom home rose 12.6% last month alone. It's a seller's market, and things won't be changing for quite a while. Up next is Joe Stephenson with a traffic report.

M 地區新聞，有報導指出，我州的製造業就業崗位在上季度時增加了一千二百個，呈現與全國相反的趨勢，經濟學家們推測增加就業的原因可能是下週將會通過的州預算。另外，軟體領域的大企業Macroshare即將將總部遷至我市的謠言正在擴大，相關人士也已經證實這個消息。得益於這些傳聞，住宅市場的價格正在上升。含有三間臥室的住宅平均價格光上個月就增加了12.6%，呈現供不應求的狀況，而這情況在短期內不會改變。接下來是Joe Stephenson的交通資訊。

詞彙 locally 位置上，地區的　trend 趨勢　economist 經濟學家　attribute A to B 把A歸於B　creation 創造　rumor 傳聞　conglomerate 大企業　heat up 加熱；白熱化　insider 內部人士　done deal 既定事實　shoot up 遽增，暴漲　seller's market 對賣方有利的市場，供不應求（需求增多，供給減少的市場）

80.
新聞主要是關於什麼？
(A) 全國新聞。
(B) 經濟狀況。
(C) 技術發展。
(D) 州預算。

說話者轉達出該州就業機會增加及房屋價格上漲等經濟相關資訊，因此新聞的主題是(B)經濟狀況。

81.
對於房價，說話者提到了什麼？
(A) 很穩定。
(B) 正在急遽下降。
(C) 正在緩慢上升。
(D) 正在急遽上升。

說話者在提及某大企業的總部將搬遷的傳聞後說"These rumors have led to prices in the housing market shooting up."，之後也提到了具體的數值來談論住宅價格的急劇上漲幅度，因此(D)才是正確答案。

82.
聽眾接下來會聽到什麼？
(A) 交通資訊。
(B) 體育新聞。
(C) 音樂。
(D) 天氣新聞。

在說話者的最後一句話"Up next is Joe Stephenson with a traffic report."中可以確認下一個順序是(A)的交通資訊。

[83-85]

M Mark, this is Peter. During my visit to the South End store this morning, I noticed there were some long delays in the bag-packing process. I suggest reorganizing the counters to put the bags closer to the customers. The proximity of the bags to the cashiers creates the assumption that they'll do the bagging. Placing the bags near the customers indicates that they need to bag their own purchases. As a result, they'll initiate the process sooner and shorten the amount of time needed to complete each transaction. Let me know the results of the changes you make by next Monday.

M Mark，我是Peter。今天早上訪問South End賣場時，我發現在將商品裝進袋子的過程中，會出現長時間的拖延現象，因此我建議你調整櫃檯位置，讓袋子能夠離顧客更近一些。如果袋子距離收銀員很近的話，他們負責包裝的可能性就會很高，但若在顧客附近放一個袋子，顧客會覺得他們應該要把購買的產品放進袋子裡，因此顧客會更快地開始這樣的過程，結帳所需的時間也會減少。請在下週一之前告知我變更措施的結果。

詞彙 notice 注意，查覺　process 過程，程序　reorganize 重新組織，再調整　proximity 靠近，鄰近　assumption 假設，推測　initiate 開始　shorten 減少，縮減　transaction 交易

83.
說話者提到什麼問題？
(A) 收銀員們做不好運作。
(B) 顧客們抱怨價格。
(C) 交易需要很長時間。
(D) 收銀機不能正常運作。

在談話的前半部分中，說話者指出「將商品裝進袋子的過程需要很長時間(I noticed there were some long delays in the bag-packing process)」這一點後，在講可以減少時間的方案。因此，說話者提到的問題是(C)。

詞彙 cash register 收銀機

84.
男人提議什麼？
(A) 爲客戶樹立招牌。
(B) 請求收銀員幫助包裝。
(C) 向顧客收取袋子費用。
(D) 把袋子放在靠近顧客的位置。

男人的提案可以在"I suggest reorganizing the counters to put the bags closer to the customers."中確認。也就是說，將袋子放置在離顧客較近的地方，誘導顧客自行包裝是男子提議的事項，因此正確答案是(D)。

85.
男人要求下週前做什麼？
(A) 所有收銀員的照片。
(B) 關於變化的報告。
(C) 僱用新職員。
(D) 工作人員培訓。

在最後一句"Let me know the results of the changes you make by next Monday."中，男子要求下週一之前告知他變化的結果，因此，(B)是正確答案。

[86-88]

W	Several people have been asking how our newest branches are doing, and now it's time to let you know. I've finally been able to review the data from the country managers. Basically, the branches in Europe have been quite successful at attracting new clients. The office in Paris is looking like it may acquire more clients than any of our other branches around the world. I think Claire Putnam deserves some congratulations. We're flying her here this April to have her give a talk about what she's been doing. Obviously, there are quite a few things she can teach us.
W	有幾個人詢問我們新分行的情況如何，而我們現在即將對此進行報告。我終於可以審閱來自地區管理者的資料了。基本上，歐洲的分行都成功地吸引新客戶，但比起全球各地的分行，巴黎分行似乎吸引了更多的客戶，因此我認為Claire Putnam應該要受到祝賀。今年四月我們會請她來到這裡，並聽她講述她至今做了什麼，這分明會教給我們相當多的東西。

詞彙 branch 樹枝；分店，分公司 attract 吸引，引誘 deserve 足以，有～的資格 congratulation 祝賀 give a talk 說話，演說 obviously 分明地 quite a few 相當多的

86.
談話主要是關於什麼？
(A) 預計開店的歐洲分店。
(B) 公司從全球獲得的收益。
(C) 其他分店的情況。
(D) 最近僱用的經理。

通過談話的第一句可以預想到談話的主題將是新分店的情況(how our newest branches are doing)，此後也是持續在講關於海外分店成功的情況，所以談話的主題是將海外分店改寫為other company locations 的(C)。

87.
說話者在說''I think Claire Putnam deserves some congratulations''的時候，在暗示著什麼？
(A) Putnam小姐正在管理巴黎分行。
(B) Putnam小姐將成為卓越的老闆。
(C) Putnam小姐是年度員工。
(D) Putnam小姐使管理人員更加努力工作。

從邏輯上考慮，並不難找到正確答案。說話者讚賞巴黎分行吸引客

戶後，透過所給予的句子承認是Claire Putnam的功勞。因此，可以認爲Claire Putnam是引領巴黎分行的管理者，正確答案是(A)。

88.
4月會發生什麼事？
(A) 管理人員將出差。
(B) 有一個管理人員將發表演講。
(C) 公司將發表一份報告書。
(D) 歐洲會有新分店即將開業。

與4月有關的內容是在談話後半部分的"We're flying her here this April to have her give a talk about what she's been doing."可以聽到，這裡說話者說要在4月叫來Claire Putnam聽她講話，因此4月會發生的事情可以看作是(B)。

[89-91]

W	I know you've all received your schedules for this week, but I need to report a couple of changes. The reason is that Greg Sullivan just resigned effective immediately. We've got to take care of the work he was assigned in addition to working on our own projects. Carlos, I want you to handle Murphy International. I'll give you the files after lunch. Jessica, you have to fly to Spain tomorrow to speak with two clients in Madrid. And Peter, you'll be working closely with Mr. Stephenson at RWT International. Everyone whose name I mentioned needs to stay here, but the rest of you can go.
W	大家都已經知道這周的行程了，但我還是需要告訴大家幾項變動。原因是Greg Sullivan已經辭職了，所以我們除了要處理我們自己原有的項目外，還須處理他交接下來的工作。Carlos，我希望你來負責Murphy International，中午過後我會將檔案給你。Jessica，妳必須明天去趟西班牙，並接見馬德里的兩名客戶，然後Peter，請你與RWT International的Stephenson先生密切合作。我提到名字的人都得留在這裡，其餘的人可以先行離開。

詞彙 resign 辭職 effective immediately 立即生效的 have got to 必須 assign 分擔，分配 handle 辦理，處理 work closely with 和～密切合作 rest 剩下的

89.
Greg Sullivan做了什麼？
(A) 簽了新的合約。
(B) 辭職。
(C) 遷往其他州。
(D) 要求提高工資。

Greg Sullivan這個名字在"The reason is that Greg Sullivan just resigned effective immediately."中就能聽到。從這裡可以看出他是辭職的人，因此，將resign換成quit one's job的(B)就是正確答案。

90.

說話者說Jessica應該去哪裡？

(A) 午餐會議。

(B) Murphy International公司。

(C) 自己的辦公室。

(D) 其他國家。

說話者對Jessica說「去西班牙的馬德里和兩位客戶見面吧(you have to fly to Spain tomorrow to speak with two clients in Madrid)」。因此，Jessica應該去的地方是(D)國外。

91.

關於Greg Sullivan，說話者暗示什麼？

(A) 他能講外語。

(B) 他讓RWT International公司成為他的客戶。

(C) 他寫了一份關於自己工作的詳細報告。

(D) 他與同事相處融洽。

說話者在離職的Greg Sullivan所負責的業務中，Murphy International的工作交給Carlos，出差到西班牙的工作交給Jessica，還有將RWT International的工作分配給Peter。因此，上述三項工作都可推斷爲Greg Sullivan的工作，(B)是正確的解釋。

[92-94]

> M Good morning, everyone. My name is Larry Wilkins, and I'm here from Briggs Consulting. I understand that you've been having difficulty understanding the government regulations which went into effect a bit more than two weeks ago. That's completely understandable as they are rather confusing. However, for the next hour and a half, I shall explain them to you so that you can be sure to comply with the law in the future. Now, when you came into this room, you were all given a booklet by my assistant. Would you please open it to the first page so that we can get started?
>
> -
>
> M 大家好，我叫Larry Wilkins，我來自Briggs諮詢公司。我理解要弄懂兩周前政府開始施行的規定會有些困難，因爲有點混淆，所以完全會有可能那樣的。但是，在之後一個半小時裡，我會進行說明，並保證各位今後將會確實遵守法律。好的，剛才進來的時候，應該都有拿到我助理分發的冊子，現在打開第一頁開始看吧？

詞彙 have difficulty –ing 有困難 regulation 規定，規則 go into effect 發揮效力 understandable 可以理解的 confusing 混亂的 comply with 遵照，遵守 in the future 未來，之後 booklet 小冊子，說明書

92.

說話者是什麼人？

(A) 公務員。

(B) 律師。

(C) 會計師。

(D) 顧問。

說話者說他本人隸屬於「Briggs諮詢公司」，並將說明「政府規定(government regulations)」，考慮到這些所屬和負責的業務，可以認

爲說話者的職業是(D)顧問。

詞彙 government employee 公務員

93.

關於自己的演講，說話者提到什麼？

(A) 它會持續至少一個小時。

(B) 將說明如何遵守法律。

(C) 可能需要聽眾回答問題。

(D) 將包括觀看影片。

透過說話者說的「進行說明讓聽者可以遵守複雜的法律(I shall explain them to you so that you can be sure to comply with law in the future)」可以知道正確答案是(B)。作爲參考，演講時間是一個半小時，因此(A)是錯誤資訊，(C)和(D)是未提及的事項。

94.

說話者請聽眾做什麼？

(A) 看印刷品。

(B) 有問題就舉手。

(C) 在文件上簽字。

(D) 向下屬提交表格。

在談話的最後一句"Would you please open it to the first page so that we can get started?"由此可知，說話者要求的是翻開冊子看。因此，將booklet換成printed material的(A)就是正確答案。

[95-97]

出發時間	目的地
11:00 A.M.	格倫代爾
11:30 A.M.	樸茨茅夫
12:45 P.M.	哈佛
1:00 P.M.	格倫代爾
2:15 P.M.	史普林菲爾德
3:30 P.M.	樸茨茅夫

> M Hello, Christina. It's George. Mr. Chang called me to confirm he'd like us to visit him this Thursday. Please be sure to bring all of the cloth samples as I don't have any. We need to show him everything we can produce because he wants to make a big order for some shirts he plans to make. The meeting has been scheduled for three thirty. We could take the train departing at one, but that wouldn't give us much time in case there's a delay. I suggest leaving at eleven thirty instead. We'll be a couple of hours early, but we can grab something to eat while we wait.
>
> -
>
> M 您好Christina，我是George。張先生打電話說希望能確認我們是否能在本週四見他。我並沒有任何樣品，因此請你別忘了要把所有的布料樣品帶來。他希望能大量訂購他想要製作的襯衫，所以我們得向他展示所有我們可以生產的東西。見面時間預定爲3點30分。我們可以坐一點出發的火車，當然，如果延遲的話，時間會很趕，所以我建議11點30分出發，雖然會提前兩個小時到達，但是也可以一邊等一邊吃東西。

詞彙 cloth 布，布料 depart 出發 in case 在～的情況下，為了應付 ～ grab 緊抓住，掌握

95.

說話者應該在哪個行業工作？
(A) 製造業。
(B) 航運業。
(C) 電腦行業。
(D) 紡織業。

從話者要求對方不要忘記帶衣服樣品(cloth samples)來看，可以推測出說話者是在(D)紡織業工作。

詞彙 shipping industry 航運業，運輸業 textile 紡織物

96.

看圖，他們會在哪裡見面？
(A) 格倫代爾。
(B) 樸茨茅夫。
(C) 哈佛。
(D) 史普林菲爾德。

在談話的後半段，說話者建議11時30分坐火車，因此在時間表上如果找到11時30分列車的目的地，就可以知道(B)樸茨茅夫是與客戶見面的場所。

97.

說話者提議到達後做什麼？
(A) 採購物品。
(B) 尋找住宿設施。
(C) 飲食。
(D) 租用車輛。

在最後一句中，說話者說如果早到的話，「邊等邊吃東西(we can grab something to eat while we wait)」，因此，說話者提議的是(C)。

詞彙 accommodations 住宿，住處 rent 租用，出租

[98-100]

層數	展示
1樓	美術與建築
2樓	美國原住民遺蹟
3樓	美國歷史
4樓	大眾文化

W May I have your attention, please? The Native American exhibit will be closing in the next five minutes. We ask everyone in that section to please move toward the nearest exit. The rest of the museum will not be closing for another hour, so you can feel free to look around the other displays. Before departing, we request that you return any audio guide equipment which you may have borrowed. You can take it to the help desk on the first floor. And don't forget to visit the souvenir shop, where you can purchase a variety of items to remind you of your visit here.

W 請注意一下這裡！北美原住民展館預計在5分鐘後關閉，請所有人移動至附近的出口。其餘展館在一小時內不會閉館，可以盡情參觀。離開這裡之前，如有借來的語音導覽設備的話請歸還，拿至一樓服務檯就可以了。還有也請不要忘記紀念品店，在那裡可以購買讓您回憶起訪問這裡的各種商品。

詞彙 exhibit 展示 move toward 朝～移動 feel free to 盡情地，隨心所欲地 borrow 借 souvenir shop 紀念品店 a variety of 多樣的 remind A of B 可藉由A想起B

98.

看圖，幾樓的展館即將閉館？
(A) 一樓。
(B) 二樓。
(C) 三樓。
(D) 四樓。

因為說美國原住民展覽(Native American exhibit)五分鐘後關門，因此在圖表中尋找的話，就可輕鬆地知道(B)二樓展館馬上就會關門。

99.

聽眾為何要去一樓？
(A) 為了歸還租借設備。
(B) 為了申請巡迴。
(C) 為了看電影。
(D) 為了購買紀念品。

提問的first floor可以在''You can take it to the help desk on the first floor.''一句中聽到。這裡的it指的是從博物館租借的音響設備，所以如果去一樓的話可以看作是(A)。

100.

說話者對聽眾說要到哪裡去？
(A) 售票處。
(B) 特別展館。
(C) 紀念品店。
(D) 咖啡館。

在最後的句子，說話者勸告聽眾們去紀念品店 (soubenir shop)。因此(C)是正確答案。

詞彙 temporary 臨時的，一時的

PART 1

1.

(A) She is reaching down into her bag.
(B) She is checking the size of her feet.
(C) She is putting on one of her shoes.
(D) She is buying some tickets at the zoo.

(A) 她正伸手拿包包。
(B) 她正測量著自己腳的大小。
(C) 她正在穿鞋。
(D) 她正在動物園買票。

正確描述了在鞋店穿鞋的樣子的(C)是正確答案。(A)和(B)分別利用照片裡可以看到的bag(包)和feet(腳)這種單詞設下的陷阱。

詞彙 reach down 身體向下伸展，伸手

2.

(A) The doctor is examining a patient.

(B) The items are being monitored.
(C) The man is submitting a form.
(D) A paper is being filled out.

(A) 醫生在為病人看病。
(B) 產品正在被檢查。
(C) 男子正在提交表格。
(D) 文件正在被填寫。

照片中的男子只是單純地在寫文件，所以正確答案是(D)。 (A)的情況是，不能因為男人穿著白大褂就斷定他是醫生，(B)的monitor不是名詞，而是被用作「檢查」的動詞。

3.

(A) Bicycles are being ridden on the street.
(B) Helmets are being worn by the riders.
(C) Vehicles are being parked by the road.
(D) Traffic is being directed by the police.

(A) 自行車在街上被騎著。
(B) 安全帽被摩托車上騎士戴著。
(C) 車輛被停放在道路上。
(D) 警方正在管制交通。

因為騎摩托車的人都有戴著安全帽，所以(B)是正確答案。照片中使用的交通手段不是自行車，而是有摩托車意思motorcycle或bike等，因此(A)不能成爲正確答案。無法知道車輛是停車的狀態，還是警察正在管制交通，所以(C)和(D)都不是正確答案。

詞彙 direct 監督，指揮，指示

4.

(A) Tables have been set with silverware.
(B) Chairs have been placed around the tables.
(C) Customers are being seated by the server.
(D) The talks are being tabled for the day.

(A) 桌上放著餐具。
(B) 桌子周圍放著椅子。
(C) 服務員在接待客人。
(D) 會談將延遲到以後舉行。

提及照片中沒出現的餐具(silverware)和顧客(cutomers)以及服務員(server)的(A)和(C)不是正確答案。正確答案是正確描述桌椅擺放方式的(B)。(D)是利用table的陷阱，這裡table被用作動詞，意思是「延遲、推遲」。

詞彙 silverware 餐具類 server 服務員 talk 講話，會談 table 桌子，餐桌；推遲

5.

(A) A man is putting up a telephone pole.
(B) Electric wires are being repaired.
(C) He is working on a traffic light.
(D) People are using the crosswalk.

(A) 一名男子正在豎起電線杆。
(B) 電線正被修理。
(C) 他正在做與交通信號燈有關的工作。
(D) 人們正在穿越斑馬線。

照片中，男人工作的對象是號誌燈(traffic light)，因此(A)和(B)是錯誤

的，(C)是正確答案。在斑馬線前的人停下來了，因此(D)的陳述與照片上的情況相反。

詞彙 put up 建造 telephone pole 電線杆 electric wire 電線 traffic light 交通號誌燈 use the crosswalk 穿越斑馬線

6.

(A) She is looking at the monitor.
(B) A movie is being screened.
(C) They are having a discussion.
(D) She is typing on her phone.

(A) 她正看著螢幕。
(B) 電影正在上映中。
(C) 他們在討論。
(D) 她正用手機打字。

正確描述了女人凝視著螢幕的模樣(A)是正確答案。(B)是利用screen的陷阱，在這裡screen被用作動詞，意思是「上映」，而不是「畫面」。正在打字的女子使用的不是電話，而是鍵盤，因此(D)也不能成爲正確的陳述。

詞彙 screen 畫面；上映 have a discussion 討論 type 打字

PART 2

7.

Is this the most energy-efficient method?

(A) Yes, I've tried several methods.
(B) That's what Terry told me.
(C) We use lots of energy here.

這是最具成本效益的方法嗎？
(A) 是的，我嘗試了幾種方法。
(B) Terry是這樣對我說的。
(C) 我們在這裡使用大量的能源。

利用一般疑問句來詢問特定的方法是否有效。答案是「(我也)聽說這是最具成本效益的」，委婉表達了肯定之意的(B)。(A)是重複使用method，(C)是重複使用energy誘導回答錯誤的陷阱。

詞彙 energy-efficient 具成本效益的 method 方法

8.

I'd better sweep the floor before Ms. Burns returns.

(A) And I'll organize the desks.
(B) Sometime around three.
(C) It's on the fifth floor.

在Burns小姐回來之前我應該先把地板打掃一下。
(A) 那我整理一下桌子。
(B) 3點左右。
(C) 是五樓。

因爲表明要清掃的意志，所以「我也要整理書桌」響應對方計劃的(A)是最自然的回答。(B)和(C)是分別就時間和地點提問時可能延續的答覆。

詞彙 sweep 清掃，打掃 organize 組織；整理

9.

How much did we spend on the business trip?

(A) I need to review my receipts.
(B) More than ten days.
(C) Both Vienna and Copenhagen.

我們出差花了多少錢？
(A) 我要確認一下發票。
(B) 超過10天。
(C) 維也納和哥本哈根。

利用how much詢問出差費用是多少。答案是「得要確認收據才能知道」，迴避正面回答的(A)。

詞彙 review 研究 receipt 收據 both A and B A和B兩個都

10.

Would you like to take the stairs or the elevator?

(A) Down to the basement.
(B) I don't mind walking.
(C) Straight ahead to the right.

您是要走樓梯，還是要坐電梯？
(A) 地下室。
(B) 走路也沒關係。
(C) 直行右轉。

要求對方在樓梯和電梯中選擇一個。因此，表示「走路也沒關係」間接選擇階梯的(B)是最自然的回答。

詞彙 basement 地下室 mind 顧慮 straight 直的；挺直地

11.

The car is running out of gas.

(A) I jog thirty minutes each day.
(B) Great. We can keep driving then.
(C) Let's fill it up at the next stop.

汽油快用完了。
(A) 我每天慢跑半小時。
(B) 好啊。那麼可以繼續開車。
(C) 在下一次停下來的地方加油吧。

只有知道run out of gas(用完油)和fill up(加油)的表現，才能找到正確答案的問題。正確答案是「下次停車時加油」的(C)。

詞彙 run out of 用完，耗盡 gas 汽油，石油 (= gasoline) fill up 裝滿

12.

The awards ceremony was postponed, wasn't it?

(A) No, she's not on the phone.
(B) Last weekend, I believe.
(C) I haven't heard anything like that.

頒獎典禮延期了，不是嗎？
(A) 不，她不是在通話。
(B) 我覺得是上週末。
(C) 我沒聽過那樣的話。

利用否定疑問句詢問是否延期舉行頒獎典禮，所以回答「還沒聽到

那樣的話」的(C)是最自然的回答。

詞彙 postpone 延遲，推遲　on the phone 通話中的

13.
When will the new recruits sign their contracts?
(A) For $45,000 a year.
(B) Either today or tomorrow.
(C) Several more interviews to go.

新員工什麼時候會在合約上簽字？
(A) 一年45,000美元。
(B) 今天或明天。
(C) 還有幾次面試。

利用疑問詞when詢問簽約時間，直接提到預定日期的(B)是正確答案。

詞彙 recruit 新兵，新進員工　either A or B A和B其中之一

14.
Didn't you spend any time sightseeing?
(A) Yes, I have excellent vision.
(B) I wasn't interested in that.
(C) On the twentieth of next month.

你沒有安排時間觀光嗎？
(A) 是的，我視力很好。
(B) 我對旅遊不感興趣。
(C) 下個月20號。

利用否定疑問句詢問對方是否旅遊了，因此，(B)表示他「沒有興趣」，從而間接表明他沒有旅遊，這是最恰當的答覆。

詞彙 sightseeing 觀光　vision 勢力; 幻想

15.
Have you received the medical test results yet?
(A) They'll be faxed in an hour.
(B) That was the end result.
(C) The hospital is five minutes away.

拿到健康檢查結果了嗎？
(A) 一小時之內會傳真過來。
(B) 那是最後的結果。
(C) 距離那間醫院5分鐘。

詢問是否收到健康檢查的結果。正確答案是「一小時內通過傳真到達」告知尚未收到結果的(A)。(B)是重複使用result，(C)是從medical test(健康檢查)中可以聯想到的hospital(醫院)一詞所設下的陷阱。

詞彙 medical test 健康檢查　fax 傳真；用傳真傳送　end result 最終結果

16.
Mr. Logan said he's expecting a return call.
(A) I'd better contact him now.
(B) Yes, he returned my call.
(C) I'll go back home late tonight.

Logan先生說他希望你能回覆他電話。

(A) 那我現在聯繫一下。
(B) 是的，他回覆了我的電話。
(C) 我今天晚一點要回家。

傳達了希望對方回電的第三者的訊息。選項中看起來最自然的回答是表明會「馬上打電話」的(C)。

詞彙 return call 回覆電話

17.
What was your impression of Mr. Salisbury?
(A) No, I didn't meet him.
(B) I think we can trust him.
(C) This art isn't very impressive.

你對Salisbury先生印象如何？
(A) 沒有，我沒有見到他。
(B) 我覺得他是一個值得信賴的人。
(C) 這件藝術品並不怎麼讓人印象深刻。

利用疑問詞what詢問對Salisbury先生的印象，(B)的回答是最恰當的答覆。對於以疑問詞開頭的提問，用no回答的(A)不能成為正確答案，(C)是利用了impression(印象)的形容詞型態impressive(印象深刻的)所設下的陷阱。

詞彙 impression 印象　trust 信任，信賴　impressive 印象深刻的

18.
How about attending the workshop with Mr. Wright?
(A) I'm going out of town this weekend.
(B) We've worked together for years.
(C) No, this isn't the right answer.

和Wright先生一起參加研討會怎麼樣？
(A) 我這個週末要去郊區。
(B) 我們在一起工作了很多年。
(C) 不，這不是正確的答案。

how about具有提案的意義，所以接下來應該有接受或拒絕的答覆。答案是「本週末不會在市區」間接表達拒絕之意的(A)。

19.
What did you think of the offer they made?
(A) Yes, you should turn off the lights.
(B) We'll make it there in ten minutes.
(C) We should insist on more money.

你對他們的提案是怎麼想的？
(A) 是的，你必須要關燈。
(B) 我們10分鐘後會到達那裡。
(C) 我們應該要主張更多的金額。

what do you think of是徵求對方意見或見解時使用的表達方式。因此，通過「應進一步要求資金」，直接闡述自己意見的(C)是最自然的答覆。

詞彙 make it 達成；到達　insist on 主張，堅持

20.
Who is leading the orientation session tomorrow?

(A) In Room 233 at ten thirty.

(B) Let me check the schedule.

(C) Only new employees should attend.

明天的說明會由誰來進行？

(A) 在233號房間10點30分開始。

(B) 我確認一下日程表。

(C) 只有新員工才能參加。

利用疑問詞who詢問主持人是誰，應該直接表明主持人的名字或不清楚的回答。因此答案是「確認一下」，推遲了確切答覆的(B)。(A)是關於地點及時間的問題，(C)應是對於詢問參加對象的問題給予的答覆。

21.

Did you remember to transfer the funds?

(A) No, it wasn't very fun for me.

(B) I'm visiting the bank after lunch.

(C) She transferred from London.

你還記得要轉帳嗎？

(A) 不,我不覺得它有趣。

(B) 我午餐後會去銀行。

(C) 她是從倫敦調來的。

詢問對方是否知道需要轉帳。因此,在午餐時間後去銀行轉帳,間接表示知道的(B)才是正確答案。(A)是利用與funds(資金)發音相似的fun(有趣)的陷阱,(C)是重複使用transfer誘導回答錯誤,這裡的transfer「調職」的意思。

詞彙 transfer 移動,搬,轉帳,調職 fund 資金

22.

Employee manuals are available in Mr. Kelly's room.

(A) I'm engaged in manual labor.

(B) At least 500 workers at headquarters.

(C) Thanks. I'll get one for you, too.

職員守則可以從Kelly的房間裡拿到。

(A) 我從事體力勞動。

(B) 總部至少有500名工作人員。

(C) 謝謝。我也會給你一份的。

正確答案是告知了可以找到職員守則的場所,因此對此表示感謝的(C)。

詞彙 manual 說明書,手冊；手做的 be engaged in 專注於 manual labor 體力勞動 headquarters 總部,總公司

23.

Why didn't you make the payment yet?

(A) She likes to pay with cash.

(B) Actually, I did that this morning.

(C) I made this with my bare hands.

爲什麼還沒有結帳呢？

(A) 她喜歡用現金結帳。

(B) 其實今天早上結過了。

(C) 我空手完成這個工作。

詢問爲何沒有使用疑問詞why進行結帳。答案是「事實上已經結帳

了」,指出對方誤解了的(B)。

詞彙 make the payment 支付,結帳 bare hands 空手

24.

Susan didn't turn down the job offer, did she?

(A) No, she's going upstairs now.

(B) This is my final offer to you.

(C) I'm afraid that's what she did.

Susan沒有拒絕工作提議,是吧？

(A) 不,她正在上樓呢。

(B) 這是我最後的提案。

(C)我很怕她已經拒絕了。

利用否定疑問句詢問是否拒絕入職提議。因此,(C)才是正確答案。

詞彙 turn down 拒絕,否決

25.

Won't there be a problem with your manager?

(A) Don't worry. I have permission.

(B) Her name is Georgia Sanders.

(C) No, they know the solution.

會不會對你的管理者造成問題？

(A) 不要擔心。我得到了許可。

(B) 她的名字叫Georgia Sanders。

(C) 不,他們知道解決方案。

利用否定疑問句詢問上司有沒有問題。答案是表明「已經得到了上司的許可,不用擔心」的(A)。

26.

There's an empty cab coming this way.

(A) Then let's take it to the theater.

(B) Okay. Let me put on my cap.

(C) I can fill your cup with water.

空的計程車正往這邊開來。

(A) 那就搭它去電影院吧。

(B) 好啊。讓我戴個帽子。

(C) 我可以幫你倒水。

聽到計程車正在來的路上,讓我們找到最能延續下去的答案。答案是表示出「那麼坐計程車去吧」的(A)。(B)和(C)分別是分別利用與cab(計程車)發音及形態相似的cap(帽子)和cup(杯)所設下的陷阱。

詞彙 empty 空著的 cab 計程車 put on 穿,穿戴

27.

Is. Mr. Willis or Ms. Carter interested in supervising the project?

(A) That's exactly who is working on it.

(B) I'll be meeting with them both later today.

(C) Yes, the project doesn't have a manager.

那個項目是想要由Willis先生負責,還是由Carter小姐負責呢？

(A) 那位就是負責該工作的人。

(B) 晚一點我會和兩個人見面。

(C) 是的，這個項目沒有經理。

正在詢問Willis先生和Carter小姐中打算要誰負責該項目。正確答案是說出兩個人(both)都要見面才能知道，迴避正面回答的(B)。

詞彙 supervise 監督

28.

What time is the concert scheduled to begin?

(A) At the local concert hall.
(B) This Friday afternoon.
(C) A bit after seven o'clock.

演奏會幾點開始？
(A) 在附近的音樂廳。
(B) 這週五下午。
(C) 七點過後。

利用what time詢問演奏會的開始時間，因此親自表明開始時間的(C)是最自然的回答。(A)是問地點，(B)是問星期幾的問題才可能延續的答覆。

29.

Couldn't we drive instead of taking the train?

(A) Okay. We can take the train if you want.
(B) But I already purchased tickets.
(C) Yeah, let's go to the airport then.

我們不能開車去，反而要搭火車嗎？
(A) 好吧，你想要的話可以坐火車。
(B) 但是已經買票了。
(C) 是的，那就去機場吧。

正在以委婉的方式向對方提出乘車去的建議。因此，通過提及「已經買票了」來表明不能接受提案的(B)是正確答案。

30.

It's about time for the store to close.

(A) I'd better go to the cash register.
(B) You're right. It's really close by.
(C) Sure. You can tell us a story.

現在是賣場關門的時間了。
(A) 我應該要去收銀台。
(B) 你說得對，真的很近。
(C) 當然，可以跟我們說。

想一想在賣場營業時間結束的時候採取什麼樣的行動是最自然的，就可以很輕鬆地發現答案是(A)。

詞彙 it's about time 要～的時間 cash register 收銀機 close by 附近

31.

What caused the equipment to break down?

(A) Okay. Come back here in ten minutes.
(B) We're still trying to determine that.
(C) Because they are in mint condition.

爲什麼設備故障了？

(A) 好吧，請10分鐘後再過來這裡。
(B) 我們一直在努力去瞭解這一點。
(C) 因爲狀態非常好。

What之後是caused延續下去的，所以這個問題是在詢問理由。因此，以「尚未掌握理由」爲由，推遲正面回答的(B)是最自然的回答。

詞彙 break down 發生故障 determine 了解；決定 in mint condition 狀態非常好的，和新品沒有兩樣

PART 3

[32-34]

> W Hello. I don't believe I've met you before. I'm Susan Groves, and I live in the unit at the end of the hall.
>
> M It's a pleasure to meet you, Susan. I'm Daniel West. I recently moved here from San Diego, so I'm kind of unfamiliar with this area.
>
> W Well, there's a get-together downstairs in the recreation room every Friday night. We have some food and talk with one another. It's a great way to meet your neighbors.
>
> M Thanks for informing me about it. I've got a company event to attend this Friday night, but I'll be sure to make it to the one next week.
>
> -
>
> W 你好，之前好像沒有見過，我是Susan Groves，住在走廊盡頭的公寓裡。
>
> M 很高興見到你，Susan，我是Daniel West。最近從聖地亞哥搬過來的，對這個地方還不熟悉。
>
> W 嗯，星期五晚上會在樓下的娛樂室舉行聚會，邊吃邊聊天，是個可以和鄰居見面的好方法。
>
> M 謝謝你告訴我。這週五晚上我必須得要參加公司活動，但下星期我一定會參加聚會的。

詞彙 unit 組成單位；單元 be unfamiliar with 對～不熟悉 get-together 聚會 recreation room 娛樂室 one another 互相 neighbor 鄰居

32.

對話在那裡進行？
(A) 購物中心。
(B) 辦公室。
(C) 餐廳。
(D) 公寓建築。

從整個內容來看，可以知道這個對話是現有公寓居民和新搬來的居民之間的對話。因此，能夠進行對話的地方應該是(D)的公寓建築。

33.

女人對男人提出什麼建議？
(A) 提供其他工作崗位。
(B) 在他家晚上開派對。
(C) 了解鄰居。
(D) 維修房屋。

聽到男人說他是新搬來的，女人說他們每星期五會舉行的聚會(get-together)，一邊說"It's a great way to meet your nighbor"。也就是說，女人在委婉地表示說要參加聚會與鄰居們交往的意思，因此女人提出的提議可以看作是(C)。

34.

男人星期五晚上要做什麼？
(A) 參加與工作有關的活動。
(B) 待在家裡。
(C) 觀看體育比賽。
(D) 參加戶外派對。

在對話的最後，男人說這週五有公司活動要參加(I've got a company event to attend this Friday night)，因此男人星期五會做的事情是(A)。

詞彙 cookout (在戶外的) 餐會，派對

[35-37]

W	Hello. My name is Amy Erickson, and I'm calling regarding my electricity bill. I'm pretty sure there has been a mistake since it's much higher than what I normally pay.
M	If you would let me know your address, Ms. Erickson, I can check out the matter.
W	Of course. I live at 220 Patterson Drive. This month, I received a bill for $850, but I usually only pay about a couple of hundred dollars.
M	Okay, I've got your information on the screen here. It appears as though a mistake was made. You only owe $150 this month. I'm going to mail you a new bill today, and you can disregard the old one.

- -

W	您好，我叫Amy Erickson，我打電話給你是因為有關的電費帳單的事情。因為要交的費用比平時還要多很多，這份很明顯是錯的。
M	Erickson小姐，如果告訴我妳的地址，我可以幫你確認問題。
W	好的。我住在Patterson路220號。這個月收到了850美元的帳單，但我平時只交200美元左右。
M	這樣啊，畫面顯示訊息了，看起來似乎有失誤。 這個月只要交150美元就可以。今天會寄出新的帳單，你可以忽略掉現有的。

詞彙 electricity bill 電費帳單　normally 一般，平時　owe 欠債 disregard 無視

35.

女人為什麼會給男人打電話？
(A) 被徵收的金額過多。
(B) 不通電。
(C) 應停止供應瓦斯。
(D) 房屋損壞。

在對話的開始部分，女人說因為電費帳單而打電話，然後說"I'm pretty sure there has been a mistake since it's much high."，也就是說，因為電費比平時多而打電話，所以(A)才是正確答案。

詞彙 charge 徵收(費用)　disconnect 斷開

36.

男人向女人要什麼？
(A) 電話號碼。
(B) 姓名。
(C) 地址。
(D) 帳號。

男人說"If you would let me know your address, Ms. Erickson, I can check out the matter."，由此可知他要求女人的(C)地址。

37.

男人要送什麼給女人？
(A) 退款。
(B) 帳單。
(C) 致歉信。
(D) 優惠券。

在對話的最後部分，男子正在叮囑女子今天會寄出新的請款書(I'm going to mail you a new bill today)並要作廢原本既有的。因此男人要送的是(B)請款單。

[38-40]

W	Hello. I need to close my account, please.
M	Of course. If you don't mind my asking, what's the reason? Are you displeased with the service we provide?
W	Not at all. However, I'm moving to another city, so I guess I'll have to do my banking there.
M	If you're simply moving away, you might be interested in our newest free app. It allows you to conduct online banking from anywhere in the world.
W	Really? So I wouldn't have to close my account?
M	That's right. Why don't I have my manager speak with you? She can explain exactly how to use the service.
W	Sure. That's fine with me.

- -

W	你好，我需要註銷帳戶。
M	這樣啊，可以請問一下理由是什麼嗎？您不滿意我們的服務嗎？
W	不是那樣的，是因為我搬到其他城市了，所以好像得要利用那裡的銀行才行。
M	如果只是搬家的話，您可能會對我們最新的免費應用程式感興趣。通過應用程式，您可以在全世界任何地方使用網路銀行業務。
W	是真的嗎？那就不用註銷帳戶了吧？
M	沒錯。要讓您跟我們經理談嗎？她應該能準確地說明如何使用。
W	當然。這樣比較好。

詞彙 close an account 註銷帳戶　reason 理由　app 應用程式 conduct 實行，實施

38.

對話會在哪裡進行？
(A) 報社。
(B) 銀行。
(C) 工程。

(D) 郵局。

考慮到close my account(註銷帳戶)，do my banking(辦理銀行業務)，conduct online banking(網路銀行)等描述的話，對話進行的地方會是(B)銀行。

詞彙 utility company 公共企業

39.

當女人說"Not at all"時，她在指什麼？

(A) 對自己所接受的服務感到滿意。

(B) 她不想回答問題。

(C) 能夠交談的時間不多。

(D) 她對男人說的話感興趣。

給予的句子是對於"Are you displeased with the service we provide?"帶有否定意味的答覆。也就是說，女人對銀行服務表示滿意，因此，所給予句子的含義可認為答案為(A)。

40.

男人建議女人做什麼？

(A) 購買應用程式。

(B) 訪問其他店。

(C) 與管理人員交談。

(D) 支付新服務的費用。

男人向女人介紹新銀行應用程式後說"Why don't I have my manager speak with you?"，因此男人提議的是通過經理聽取有關應用程式的說明，正確答案是(C)。

[41-43]

M	Excuse me. I wonder if you have any shirts like this one in a size large. I just got a new job, so I have to improve my wardrobe.
W	You've come to the right place, sir. We've got a special sale on all items made by Crayton. You can get thirty percent of your purchase.
M	Wow, that's an outstanding deal. I was only planning to purchase four shirts, but that deal can't be beat. I might have to get more. Is it okay if I try on a shirt to see if it fits though?
W	Of course. The fitting rooms are right over there in the corner.
M	不好意思，我想知道跟這個類似的襯衫有沒有L碼的。我剛剛找到新工作了，得買些衣服。
W	您找對地方了，客人。Crayton製作的所有產品現正進行特別優惠。購買的話可以得到三折的優惠。
M	哇，這個折扣真多。我只打算要買四件襯衫的，如果有那麼多折扣的話，還要多買一些才行。我要確認衣服是否合適，可以試穿嗎？
W	當然了，試衣間就在那邊的角落裡。

詞彙 wardrobe 衣櫃 outstanding 出色的，顯著的 deal 交易 beat 贏；超越 try on 試穿 fit 適合 fitting room 更衣室，更衣間

41.

女人是誰？

(A) 銷售人員。

(B) 收銀員。

(C) 銀行員工。

(D) 賣場主人。

女人向想要購買襯衫的男人說明打折活動，並告知更衣室的位置等。因此女人應是在服裝賣場工作的(A)銷售人員。

42.

男人提到關於自己的什麼事情？

(A) 以前曾與女人講過話。

(B) 上星期搬到了該地區。

(C) 最近大學畢業。

(D) 最近找到工作。

在對話的前半部分，男人一邊說"I just got a new job, and I have to improve my wardrobe."，一邊解釋著自己為什麼買衣服。也就是說，因為找到了新工作，所以要買衣服，選項中提到的關於男人的事項是(D)。

43.

男人問了什麼？

(A) 更衣室。

(B) 退款政策。

(C) 顧客服務諮詢台。

(D) 可購買的風格。

在對話後半部，當男人問到「可以試穿襯衫嗎(if I try on a shirt to see if it fits though)」時，女人告訴他更衣室(fitting rooms)的位置。因此，正確答案是將fitting rooms改為changing rooms來表現的(A)。

[44-46]

W	Mr. Archer, we have a huge problem at the factory in Midland. The foreman called to inform me that two of the four assembly lines have broken down.
M	That's where we make the products we sell in Europe and Asia, right? We can't afford to have any more delays in exporting our items. How long will it take to fix the problems?
W	He's positive that the first one will be running by midnight, but the second one looks more serious. He wouldn't give me a time estimate regarding it.
M	I want you to head there and supervise the repairs. Give me hourly updates until everything is running normally again.

詞彙 huge 巨大的 foreman 工頭，廠長 assembly line 裝配線 break down 發生故障 afford to 承擔；提供，給予 export 輸出 positive 肯定的；確信的 serious 嚴重的，真摯的 estimate 推測，推斷 supervise 監督，指揮 hourly 每個小時

44.

問題是什麼？
(A) 訂單生產的延遲。
(B) 一些機器不能運作。
(C) 有一個客戶沒有轉帳。
(D) 有一些設備的零件遺失。

在對話的前半部分，女人正告訴男人「兩條裝配線發生故障(two of the four assembly lines have brocken down)」的消息。因此，正確答案是(B)。

45.

當女人說"The second one looks more serious"時，她在暗示什麼？
(A) 修理不會在今天之內結束。
(B) 更換費用可能非常昂貴。
(C) 需要僱用更多的工作人員。
(D) 應該要跟代表聯繫。

從給予句子的前面內容可以找到正確答案的線索。女人曾說「第一個裝配線將在子夜前後啓動(the first one will be running by midnight)」，所以第二裝配線在子夜以後也不會啓動。因此，女人的暗示可以視爲(A)。

46.

男人對女人說要她去哪裡？
(A) 歐洲分公司。
(B) 中部地區。
(C) 她的辦公室。
(D) 負責維修工作的公司。

在對話最後的部分，男人說的話"I want you to head there and supervise the repairs."中，there指的是工廠所在的地方，即(B)中部地區。

[47-49]

詞彙 out of ～都沒有了 extra 多加的，另外的 storage closet 收納櫃 document 文件 at once 現在馬上，立刻 secretary 秘書 borrow 借用

47.

Bob在找什麼？
(A) 墨水盒。
(B) 工作人員。
(C) 迴紋針。
(D) 複印紙。

在對話的開始部分，男子說「影印機的碳粉沒了(the printer is out of toner)」，然後在詢問剩下的墨水匣(extra cartridges)在的地方。因此，男人尋求的是(A)。

48.

依照女人說的話，週四會發生什麼事？
(A) 修理技師會來。
(B) 將在文件上簽字。
(C) 物品即將要發貨。
(D) 文件將會寄出。

女人一邊說"The new shipment isn't scheduled to arrive until Thursday."一邊說訂貨要到星期四才會送到。因此，星期四要完成的工作是(C)。

49.

George對Bob說什麼？
(A) 請求賠償。
(B) 到其他部門。
(C) 與上司交談。
(D) 去對面的賣場。

從"If I were you, I'd go up to the Marketing Department, Bob. "中可以找到正確答案的線索。男子2對男子1說去營銷部詢問能否使用那裡的印表機，所以(B)是正確的答案。

詞彙 reimburse 賠償，還債

[50-52]

> **W** David, you're visiting the Forest Shopping Center at lunch today, right? Do you mind if I go with you? I have to get my phone fixed.
>
> **M** You're welcome to go along with me, but I was at the mall yesterday, and the repair center isn't there anymore. You're referring to the place located on the third floor, right?
>
> **W** Yes, that's the one I mean. I wonder what happened to it. I guess I'll have to figure out where it moved.
>
> **M** Well, let me know the address, and if it's near the mall, I don't mind dropping you off there while I do some shopping.
>
> ----
>
> **W** David，你今天中午會去Forest購物中心，對吧？你介意我跟你一起去嗎？我需要修理電話。
>
> **M** 雖然歡迎妳一起去，但是我昨天去了購物中心，那裡沒有維修中心了。你指的是在三樓的維修中心對嗎？
>
> **W** 是的，那就是我說的地方。我想那裡應該發生了什麼事，應該要打聽一下要搬遷到哪裡去了。
>
> **M** 嗯，你告訴我地址，如果是在購物中心附近的話，我可以讓妳在那下車，我去購物就可以了。

詞彙 refer to 指出，指稱 drop off (從車上)下來 figure out 打聽到，計算，理解

50.
女人要求男人做什麼？
(A) 把她送到什麼地方。
(B) 協助她的工作。
(C) 告訴她住址。
(D) 向她提出建議。

從對話的前半部分可以看出，女人向男人提議一起去購物中心，而在對話的最後部分，男人說「讓女人下車，我去購物(I don't mind dropping you off there while I do some shopping)」。綜合上面所述，最後女人要求的是把車開到購物中心，正確答案是(A)。

51.
女人要修理什麼？
(A) 文件包。
(B) 電話。
(C) 筆記本電腦。
(D) 影印機。

如果在對話開始部分能夠聽到女人說的"I have to get my phone fixed."，就能輕鬆知道答案是(B)。

52.
女人接下來會做什麼？
(A) 瞭解可利用的公車。
(B) 尋找賣場的位置。

(C) 向其他同事尋求幫助。
(D) 給朋友打電話。

從"I guess I'll have to figure out where it moved."這句話中可以看出，女人要做的就是找到維修中心的位置。因此，(B)是正確答案。

[53-55]

> **W** Jack, you've been to Duncan Associates before, haven't you? How would you suggest going there?
>
> **M** Take the subway. You'll have to walk about five minutes when you arrive at the station though.
>
> **W** Shouldn't I take the bus? According to this map, there's a bus stop directly in front of the Hoover Building.
>
> **M** I made that mistake as well. I wound up being half an hour late for my meeting.
>
> **W** Oh, thanks for the tip. I'll be meeting Ms. Voss. Do you know her?
>
> **M** I've spoken with her a couple of times. She tends to ask lots of questions, so be sure you know your presentation material thoroughly.
>
> ----
>
> **W** Jack，你以前去過Duncan協會是嗎？要到那裡該怎麼走比較好呢？
>
> **M** 請搭地鐵。但是從車站出發還需要走5分鐘左右。
>
> **W** 坐公車不行嗎？根據這張地圖的話，公車站就在Hoover大樓前面。
>
> **M** 我也犯了那樣的失誤，結果會議上我遲到了30分鐘。
>
> **W** 噢，謝謝你告訴我。我要跟Voss小姐見面，你知道她嗎？
>
> **M** 我與她見過兩遍。她會問很多問題，所以一定要熟悉說明內容。

詞彙 directly 直接地；筆直地 wind up -ing 最後以～結束 tend to 傾向於～ thoroughly 澈底地

53.
女人為何要去Duncan協會？
(A) 為了進行說明。
(B) 為了訂立合約。
(C) 為了就業面試。
(D) 為了討論提議的事項。

女人想訪問Duncan協會的理由可以從對話後半部分的內容中找到。聽到女人說她要見Voss小姐時，男人說她經常會問問題，忠告說應該熟悉說明內容(be sure you know your presentation material thoroughly)。由此可以看出，女人拜訪Duncan協會的理由為(A)。

54.
男人對女人說要怎麼去Duncan協會？
(A) 搭車。
(B) 搭乘公車。
(C) 搭計程車。
(D) 搭乘地鐵。

當問到去Duncan協會的方法時，男人直接說"Take the subway."。正確答案是(D)。

55.

男人為什麼會說"I made that mistake as well"？

(A) 為了要說他曾經因為坐公車而遲到。

(B) 為了要說他寫錯地址。

(C) 為了要告訴女人注意Voss小姐。

(D) 為了要說會議曾沒有做好準備。

給予的句子是對於女人提出乘坐公車如何的問題的反應。男人和他說話的理由可以直接在下面的文章中找到，男人自己也曾坐過公車，但結果是遲到了30分鐘(being half an hour late for my meeting)，說了自己選擇公車卻出錯的經驗。因此，(A)是正確答案。

詞彙 incorrectly 不正確地，錯誤的 cautious 小心的，注意的

[56-58]

M	Did you just read your e-mail? I wonder what this emergency meeting is being called for. Do you have any ideas?
W	I heard Mr. Miller saying we might be landing a couple of big contracts soon. If they go through, everyone will probably be working plenty of overtime.
M	The company should hire more workers instead of making us stay late every night. I'm tired of constantly having to come in on the weekend.
W	I know how you feel, but there are budget issues to consider. Anyway, we've got five minutes until the meeting starts, so we'd better head to the conference room now.

M 讀過電子郵件了嗎？我很想知道召開緊急會議的原因，妳知道什麼嗎？

W 我從Miller先生那裡聽到不久之後將簽署兩份重要的合約。如果成功的話，可能全員都會有相當程度的加班。

M 比起每天都留我們到很晚，公司應該要僱用更多的員工。我厭倦了週末也總要來公司這一點。

W 雖然知道是什麼樣的心情，但也要考慮預算問題。不管怎樣，五分鐘後會議就要開始，所以現在最好就去會議室。

詞彙 emergency meeting 緊急會議 call for 召開(會議等) land a contract 簽訂合約 go through 通過，促成 plenty of 許多的 be tired of 對～感到厭倦，對～感到厭煩 constantly 不變地，經常 head to 前往

56.

說話者主要在討論什麼？

(A) 簽署的合約。

(B) 晉升機會。

(C) 通知的會議。

(D) 需要解決的緊急情況。

在對話的開始部分，可以預想到該對話是「召開緊急會議的理由(what this emergency meeting is being called for)」。正確答案是(C)。

57.

男人對加班有什麼看法？

(A) 因為能多賺錢所以喜歡。

(B) 對加班不感興趣。

(C) 更願意經常加班。

(D) 不喜歡在下班後一直待到很晚。

男人主張公司應該多招聘員工以取代讓他們加班，所以正確答案是(B)。(D)的情況，男人不喜歡的是「週末工作(having to come in on the weekend)」，而不是「夜班(staying late after work)」，所以不能將(D)選作答案。

58.

女人勸說要做什麼？

(A) 完成預算報告的編寫工作。

(B) 前往會議室。

(C) 申請調動。

(D) 與Miller先生交談。

在對話最後的部分，女人說距離會議開始的時間只剩下5分鐘，然後說「去會議室吧(we'd better head to the conference room now)」。因此，將conference room改寫為meeting room的(B)就是正確答案。

[59-61]

W1	Tina, I noticed you're scheduled for the morning shift tomorrow. Would you mind trading shifts with me?
W2	That depends. When do you want me to work, Lucy?
W1	Tomorrow night. My sister is arriving in town, so I should be at the train station to pick her up.
W2	I'd love to help, but I have tickets to see a movie. I've been waiting weeks for it to come out.
M	I can help you out, Lucy, but I'm not interested in giving up one of my shifts. I need as much work as I can get.
W1	That's fine. Let's talk to Ms. Kelly and let her know what we're planning to do.

W1 Tina, 我發現妳被安排明天早班，你可以跟我換班嗎？

W2 我得看情況。希望我什麼時候上班呢Lucy？

W1 明天晚上。我妹妹要來市區，我要去火車站接她。

W2 雖然我想幫忙，但是我有預購好的電影票。我等了幾個星期才上映的。

M Lucy, 我可以幫你。但我不想放棄我的工作時間，想要盡可能地多做一些事情。

W1 好的。我會跟Kelly小姐談談，讓他知道我們的計劃。

詞彙 notice 注意，察覺 shift 上班時間 trade 交易，交換 give up 放棄

59.

Lucy為何想改上班時間？

(A) 預約了醫院。

(B) 想回故鄉。

(C) 為了要進行面試。

(D) 應該要與家人團聚。

想要更改上班時間的理由可以從"My sister is arriving in town, so I should be at the train station to pick her up"這一句中找到。女子為了要接妹妹而希望換班，所以(D)是正確答案。

60.

Tina明天會做什麼？

(A) 看電影。

(B) 參加就業博覽會。

(C) 與客戶見面。

(D) 外出就餐。

聽到女1拜託明天換班，女2表示"I'd love to help, but I have tickets to see a movie. "並說明拒絕的理由。由此可以看出，她明天要做的是(A)看電影。

61.

男人為何提議要幫助Lucy？

(A) 不希望明天工作。

(B) 希望有更多的時間工作。

(C) 想進一步積累經驗。

(D) 沒有週末計劃。

男人表示，雖然自己想幫忙，但他想要維持自己的工作時間並說"I need as much work as I can get. "，也就是說，男人可能是為了有更多的時間工作，因此(B)是正確答案。

[62-64]

城市	剩餘距離
水城	5公里
新威斯頓市	19公里
普羅維登斯	46公里
貝爾蒙特	83公里

W I'm getting pretty hungry. How about stopping and getting some lunch soon?

M All right, we can do that. Oh, there's a sign for Watertown. We should be able to get there in just a few minutes.

W That sounds good. I'll go online and try to find a restaurant we can eat at there.

M Make sure it's a place that cooks food quickly. We need to be in Providence for our meeting by 1:30 P.M., so we can't afford to spend too much time eating.

W No problem. Give me a couple of minutes, and then I can give you directions.

W 肚子好餓啊。停車吃午餐怎麼樣？

M 好吧，也行。喔，有水城的路牌。幾分鐘後就會到那裡。

W 太好了。我上網找一家可以吃飯的餐廳。

M 一定要是速食料理的餐廳才行。因為我們要在下午1點半前參加在普羅維登斯舉行的會議，所以吃飯不能花很多時間。

W 沒問題。給我幾分鐘，我就能指路。

詞彙 sign 預兆，跡象；招牌 spend time -ing 花時間做～ give directions 指路

62.

看圖，到說話者們第一次停車需要多遠的距離？

(A) 5公里。

(B) 19公里。

(C) 46公里。

(D) 83公里。

由於預計會在一個叫Watertown的地方停車，因此從圖表中找到此處的剩餘距離，正確答案是(A)。

63.

女人說要做什麼？

(A) 尋找停車地點。

(B) 打給主管。

(C) 指路到最終目的地。

(D) 在網路上尋找吃飯地點。

從"I'll go online and try to find a restaurant we can eat at there."這句話中可以看出，女人要做的就是搜尋餐廳。正確答案是(D)。(C)不是正確答案，因為他們不是到最終目的地(final destination)，而是到餐廳的路。

64.

說話者們說今天下午要做什麼？

(A) 參加會議。

(B) 進行產品演示。

(C) 參加研討會。

(D) 主管教學。

男人一邊叮嚀女人儘快找到準備吃飯的地方，一邊說「下午1點30分時要參加會議 (for our meeting by 1:30 P.M.)」，表明了必須要儘快的理由。由此可以看出，說話者們要做的事情是(A)。

[65-67]

黑白打印（宣傳冊）	每頁2美元
彩色印刷（宣傳冊）	每頁4美元
黑白打印（海報）	每頁3美元
彩色印刷（海報）	每頁5美元

M Hello. I'm calling from Freeport Manufacturing. We'd like to have some brochures printed in a hurry. Can you do that?

W It depends. How many do you need, and how fast do you need them?

M The brochures are ten pages long, and we'd like them in color. We need 500 by 10:00 tomorrow morning to distribute at a sales conference we're attending.

W We can do it, but you must give me the file before 3:00 in order to receive them by that time.

M That's fine. Should I visit the store to give you the information?

W E-mailing the file would be easier. That would also allow us to start immediately.

- -

M 早上好。我是Freeport Manufacturing，我們需要盡快印製這本小冊子，可以嗎？

W 這取決於具體情況。你需要多少，什麼時候要？

M 這本小冊子有10頁，我希望它是彩色的，要在明天早上10點前完成500份，以便在即將舉行的展覽會上分發。

W 雖然是有可能的，但你想要在那時間拿到的話，就必須在3點之前把它交給我。

M 好的，我需要到店裡交資料嗎？

W 用電子郵件提供檔案會更方便。那樣的話，我們馬上就能開始作業。

詞彙 in a hurry 急切地　distribute 分配　in order to 為了要～
immediately 立刻

65.

男人為什麼著急？

(A) 將在明天的會議上分發資料。
(B) 活動日程提前。
(C) 在最後關頭，因為變更的事項而導致工作嚴重延誤。
(D) 他的上司今天之內需要資料。

男人一邊告知印刷品的份數和時間一邊說必須在明天的展覽會上分發(to distribute at a sales conference we're attending)。因此，男人匆忙的理由可視為(A)。

詞彙 hand out 分配　last-minute 最後關頭，最後時刻

66.

看圖，男人要支付的基本費用是多少？
(A) 每頁2美元
(B) 每頁3美元
(C) 每頁4美元
(D) 每頁5美元

由於男子說他想將小冊子印製成彩色，因此在圖表中找到滿足這兩種條件的費用，男子所要支付的費用是(C)每頁4美元。

67.

女人要如何從男人那裡得到資料？
(A) 直接見面。

(B) 傳真。
(C) 電話。
(D) 電子郵件。

從對話最後部分"E-mailing the file would be easier."中可以看出，女人偏好的方式是通過電子郵件接收檔案。因此正確答案是(D)。

[68-70]

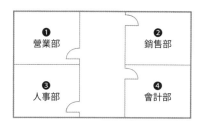

W Bruce, there aren't any snacks in the lounge. Do you know what happened to them?

M Someone must have forgotten to purchase more. I haven't seen any there for a couple of days.

W A couple of clients are coming soon, and I'd like to have some refreshments for them while we talk.

M I could run out to the store and buy a few things if you'd like. It shouldn't take too long to go across the street.

W I'd appreciate your doing that. Ask Ms. Dresden in Accounting for a company card so that you don't have to pay out of pocket. We'll be in meeting room 3 when you return.

- -

W Bruce，休息室裡沒有零食了。你知道發生了什麼事嗎？

M 肯定是有人忘了要多買一點放那了，我也有兩三天沒看到了。

W 顧客們馬上就要到了，我希望能在和他們聊天的時候可以提供一些茶點給他們。

M 如果你要的話，我可以到店裡買。走到馬路對面不會花很多時間。

W 如果能那樣的話就太謝謝你了。如果你不想花錢，請向會計部的Dressden拿公司信用卡，等你回來的時候，我們會在3號會議室。

詞彙 lounge 休息廳，休息室　refreshment 茶點，零食

68.

女人在找什麼？
(A) 公司卡。
(B) 報告資料夾。
(C) 零食。
(D) 客戶。

對話中，女人需要的是refreshments(茶點)，snacks(餅乾、零食)等。所以正確答案是(C)的零食。

69.

男人提議做什麼？

(A) 指路。

(B) 採購。

(C) 用自己的錢。

(D) 倒咖啡。

從"I could run out to the store and buy a few things if you'd like. "男人說的話中可以得知他提議的是去商店裡買零食回來。因此，(B)是正確答案。

70.

看圖，男人接下來會去哪裡？

(A) 1號辦公室。

(B) 2號辦公室。

(C) 3號辦公室。

(D) 4號辦公室。

女人讓男人去找「會計部的Dressden(Ms. Dressden in Accounting)」領取公司卡，所以在圖表中男人要去的地方是(D)4號辦公室。不能和對話的最後一句"We'll be in meeting room 3 when you return."搞混，選擇(C)作為答案。

PART 4

[71-73]

> **M** Hello, Ms. Hardy. This is Peter Croft. I know I called a couple of hours ago to postpone this afternoon's meeting, but there's been a sudden change in plans. The staff meeting my boss wanted me to attend was just called off, so I'm now free to meet you at four. If you don't have something else scheduled, would you mind getting together then as we had originally planned? It will take me about an hour to drive to your office, so as long as you get back to me before three, I can be there on time. I'm looking forward to hearing from you soon.
>
> - - - - - - - - - - - - - - -
>
> **M** 您好，Hardy小姐，我是Peter Croft。我在兩個多小時前打了電話給你推遲了今天的見面。但計劃突然變更了，我們老闆叫我參加的員工會議剛才被取消了，因此我可以跟你約在四點見面了。若沒有別的預定事項的話，我們按原計劃在那個時間見面怎麼樣？我開車去你的辦公室大概需要一個小時左右，3點前回覆我的話，我可以準時抵達那裡。等待你的消息。

詞彙 postpone 推遲，延遲 staff meeting 員工會議 call off 取消 originally 原來，本來 as long as 只要

71.

說話者為什麼打電話給Hardy小姐？

(A) 為了請求今天見面。

(B) 為了推遲會議。

(C) 為了邀請她參加研討會。

(D) 為了要求用電子郵件發送檔案。

說話者不需要改變約定的時間了，然後詢問Hardy「在原來約定的時間見面怎麼樣(would you mind getting together then as we hador)」。因此，說話者打電話的理由是為了提出按照原定計畫說今天見面的要求，所以正確答案是(A)。

72.

關於自己的老闆，說話者說了什麼？

(A) 要求說話者出差。

(B) 取消預定的會議。

(C) 目前不在辦公室。

(D) 打算與說話者一起去。

說話者表示有空的原因是「老闆要求參加的員工會議被取消(The staff meeting my boss wanted me to attend was just caled off)」。透過這些可以推測出取消員工會議的人就是老闆，因此正確答案是(B)。

73.

說話者對Hardy小姐暗示了什麼？

(A) 她的辦公室在他的辦公室旁邊。

(B) 她準備在合同上簽字。

(C) 她的經紀人想見她。

(D) 他希望她能聯絡他。

在談話後半的部分，說話者請Hardy小姐在3點前回覆，然後說"I'm looking forward to hearing from you soon."。透過這些可以確認說話者希望得到Hardy小姐的回覆，因此(D)是正確答案。

[74-76]

> **W** This morning, the mayor's office finally gave its approval for the construction of the Willard Tunnel. The tunnel, which was first proposed five years ago, will connect people living on both sides of Desmond Mountain. Currently, drivers must either go over or around the mountain, which results in lengthy travel times. When completed, the tunnel will go through the mountain, saving at least thirty minutes of driving time. This should help alleviate complaints about the city's infrastructure. In a recent survey, residents cited poor traffic conditions as the biggest inconvenience of living in the city. Once the tunnel is done, this should no longer be the case.
>
> - - - - - - - - - - - - - - -
>
> **W** 今天早上市政府終於批准了Willard隧道的工程。這條隧道，在五年前首次計劃施工，將連接居住在Desmond山兩側的人們。原先司機們得翻山或繞山行駛，導致移動時間變長。但當工程完成，隧道將會貫穿山體，開車時間可節省至少半個小時，人們對於城市基礎設施的不滿也會減少。在最近的問卷調查中，居民們認為惡劣的交通狀況是居住在市區最不方便的地方，在隧道完工後就不會再有這種事了。

詞彙 approval 准許 propose 提議 connect 連結 lengthy 長的 go through 通過，貫通 alleviate 減少，緩和 infrastructure 基礎設施 cite 引用，提及

74.

五年前發生了什麼事？

(A) 批准。
(B) 要求資金。
(C) 擬訂計劃。
(D) 建立城市。

在談話的前半部分，Willard隧道工程是「5年前首次提議(was first proposed five years ago)」，因此5年前發生的事情是(C)。

詞彙 grand 給，授予　found 搭建，建立

75.

隧道打算建在哪裡？
(A) 河下。
(B) 海灣下。
(C) 通過山。
(D) 通過山坡。

在談話的中間部分，隧道工程完工後說「隧道會貫通山(the tunnel will go through the mountain)」，因此隧道將建成的地方是(C)。

詞彙 bay 海灣

76.

說話者說"This should no longer be the case"時，她在暗示什麼？
(A) 人口不會再減少。
(B) 將會有更多的企業進駐。
(C) 失業率將下降。
(D) 交通狀況將會得到改善。

給予的句子意思為「不會再有那種事情了」，這裡的this就是指前面的句子。也就是說，說話者傳達了人們不會再認為交通擁堵的問題很嚴重的意思，因此說話者所暗示的是(D)。

[77-79]

> **W** Two weeks ago, another stationery store opened down the street. Since then, we've been losing business, so sales are down. I've spoken with our owner, and he authorized us to come up with some special promotions to get our customers back. The first thing we'll do is have a contest. Anyone who makes a purchase will be entered into a raffle which will offer some great prizes. We'll be advertising the raffle on our Web site as well as on posters we put up in the neighborhood. The promotion is starting tomorrow, and the drawing for prizes will be held on the last day of the month.
>
> **W** 兩週前，市區又開了一家文具店。從那時起，我們的市場就開始萎縮，銷售額也在減少。我和老闆談過，他同意我們所提出的特別促銷活動，好讓顧客回流。我們要做的第一件事就是主辦活動，讓所有購買者都可以參與到的活動。我們會在我們的網站上為抽獎活動打廣告，在附近地區也會張貼廣告海報。促銷活動將於明天開始，而抽獎將在本月最後一天進行。

詞彙 stationery store 辦公用品店，文具店　lose business 錯失生意，生意不好　authorize 給予權限　come up with 想到；生產，提出　promotion 宣傳，促銷活動　contest 比賽，競爭　enter into 參加　raffle 彩券，抽獎　draw for a prize 抽籤

77.

說話者提到什麼問題？
(A) 銷售量下降。
(B) 顧客抱怨。
(C) 價格上漲。
(D) 品質下降。

說話者在討論因競爭對手辦公用品店的開業而「銷量減少、銷售額下降(we've been losing business, so sales are down)」的問題後，在討論他的解決方案，因此說話者提到的問題是(A)。

78.

將舉辦什麼類型的活動？
(A) 打折銷售。
(B) 贈送免費樣品的活動。
(C) 募款活動。
(D) 抽獎活動。

多次出現raffle(彩券，抽獎)這個單字，而且通過類似drawing for prizes(抽籤)的描述也會知道是(D)的抽獎活動。

79.

活動在何時結束？
(A) 明天。
(B) 本週末。
(C) 這個月。
(D) 下個月。

活動時間在談話的最後一句"The promotion is starting tomorrow, and the drawing for prizes will be held on the last day of the month. "中可以確認，活動的開始日期為明天，結束日期為本月最後一天，因此(C)是正確答案。

[80-82]

> **M** Everyone, please listen carefully. You're here today because you applied for various positions at Westminster Consulting. Please remain seated in this area until your name is called. At that time, you'll be taken to the person you're interviewing with. You'll be with that person for at least an hour. When you're finished, you'll be asked to take a short test to determine your skills. Be sure to bring all the official documents required for the position as you'll be asked to hand them over at that time. If you have any questions, my assistant, Mr. Kenmore, will be more than happy to answer them.

M 請大家注意，今天大家來到這裡是因為你們應徵了Westminster諮詢公司的各種職位。在你們名字被叫到之前請先留在原位。叫到名字的話，會帶大家到面試官面前，至少都會和面試官待上一個小時。面試結束後，為了要確認大家的能力，會進行一個簡單的測試。面試時將會要求提交文件，所以請不要忘記帶應聘部門所需的正式文件。如果您有疑問，我的下屬Kenmore會很樂意回答。

詞彙 various 多樣的 take a test 考試，測試 determine 決定；了解 skill 技術，能力 official 正式的 hand 繳交

80.

聽眾是誰？
(A) 實習員工。
(B) 應聘者。
(C) 研究員。
(D) 下屬員工。

透過「應聘Westminster諮詢公司的各職位(you applied for various positions at Westminster Consulting)」，「將會為要面試的人帶路(you'll be taken to the person you're interviewing with)」等描述，可以認為談話的對象應該是(B)的應聘者。

81.

說話者要聽眾做什麼？
(A) 帶文件。
(B) 填寫表格。
(C) 回覆電子郵件。
(D) 簡單地參觀學習。

在談話的後半部分，說話者對聽眾們叮嚀說「請帶應聘領域需要的文件去面試場所(be sure to bring all the official documents required for the position)」，所以將 official documents改寫為 some papers的(A)就是正確答案。

82.

聽眾將會如何得到幫助？
(A) 透過聯繫話者。
(B) 透過請求協助話者的人。
(C) 透過查閱手冊。
(D) 透過瀏覽網站。

在最後一句"If you have any questions, my assistant, Mr. Kenmore, will be more than happy to answer them. "可以知道需要幫助的人可以向說話者的下屬Kenmore提出請求。正確答案是(B)。

[83-85]

M As you can see, the frame of the building is complete. Now, we need to work on finishing the rest of it. This process is going to take around three more months. We were scheduled to be done building it this December, but we'll likely be done in October. We're quite pleased about that. We'll also be around half a million dollars under budget. Let me take you on a brief walk through the construction site. This is an active site, so there's work going on. Let's all be careful because accidents sometimes happen. Would everyone please take a hardhat from this pile and then follow me?

M 如您所見，建築結構已經完成了，現在必須要完成剩下的部分，而這個過程大約需要3個月左右的時間。原計劃是到今年12月完工，但很有可能10月就可以完工，對於這一點我們都覺得很高興，而且我們目前還有約50萬美金的預算。現在將會帶大家參觀一下建設工地，因為是施工現場，所以正在進行施工，有時會發生事故，請大家小心。從擺放安全帽的地方各自拿一頂之後跟著我走好嗎？

詞彙 frame 結構，架子 be likely to 可能 under budget 預算內 brief 短的，簡略的 construction site 工地現場 active 有活力的，活潑的 hardhat 安全帽 pile 堆，一疊

83.

說話者在那個領域工作？
(A) 建築業。
(B) 紡織業。
(C) 製造業。
(D) 旅遊業。

說話者正試圖向聽眾說明即將完工的建築物，並展示施工現場。因此，說話者所在的領域應該是(A)建築行業。

84.

說話者為什麼會說"We're quite pleased about that"？
(A) 客戶認可其想法。
(B) 工程將比預期更快結束。
(C) 最近沒有發生任何事故。
(D) 預算上還有資金。

從前文的內容來看，所指句子的that是指原計劃在12月份完成的工程預計在10月份完成。因此，給予的句子所指的可看作為(B)。如果知道ahead of schedule(比預定時間早)的意義的話，就能夠輕易地找到正確答案。

85.

說話者要聽眾做什麼？
(A) 與工作人員交談。
(B) 相互介紹。
(C) 查看圖紙。
(D) 佩戴安全裝備。

最後一句"Would everyone please take a hardhat from this pile and then follow me?"中，說話者正在勸導聽眾們要戴安全帽。正確答案是把hardhat改寫為some safety gear的(D)。

詞彙 plans 設計圖，圖紙　put on 穿上(衣服等)，穿戴　gear 裝備

[86-88]

W　I'd like to welcome everyone on today's Western Express train bound for Kent. We are scheduled to arrive at our final destination at 4:47 this afternoon. We will be stopping at stations in Millwood, Haven, and Cypress Creek along the way. An attendant will be coming by to check your tickets shortly. Please have them available if they are requested. If you would like something to eat or drink, you can visit the café car, which is located in car number seven. We thank you for riding with us, and we hope you have a pleasant journey.

W　歡迎各位乘坐今天開往肯特的Western特快列車。我們預計於今天下午四點四十七分到達最終目的地，途中將會停靠Millwood、Haven以及Cypress Creek車站。為了要確認各位所持車票，乘務員等等將會經過，若收到請求的話請出示您的車票。想要用餐或喝飲料時，可以前往餐車，餐車位於7號車廂。感謝各位乘坐我們的列車，祝你們旅途愉快。

詞彙 bound for 前往　final destination 最終目的地　attendant 乘務員，服務員　café car (火車裡的)餐車　journey 旅行

86.

這段介紹會在哪裡聽見？
(A) 在飛機上。
(B) 在公車上。
(C) 在地鐵上。
(D) 在火車上。

透過談話前半部分的"welcome everyone on today's western Express train"跟歡迎致詞、驗票說明以及介紹餐車的句子就可以很輕鬆地知道這段廣播會在(D)火車內聽到。

87.

說話者說''Please have them available if they are requested''時，她是指什麼？
(A) 聽眾將被要求提供護照。
(B) 聽眾可能需要出示車票。
(C) 聽眾可能需要換座位。
(D) 聽眾應該要拿到收據。

只有知道them和they指的是什麼，才能找到正確答案。透過上一個句子可以確認兩個代名詞所指的是tickets，因此應將所給予的句子其意思視為(B)。

88.

說話者說能夠使用什麼？
(A) 食物。
(B) 讀物。
(C) 無線網路。

(D) 毯子和枕頭。

在談話後半部，說話者為了乘客們想要吃東西或喝飲料的情況(if you would like something to eat or drink)正在介紹餐車。因此，可以使用的是(A)用餐。

詞彙 refreshment 茶點　wireless Internet 無線網路　blanket 毯子
pillow 枕頭

[89-91]

M　Before we conclude today's staff meeting, here's an update on the planned renovations of our office. They're scheduled for next Monday and Tuesday. As a result, none of us can work at our desks on those two days. Half of us will be moved to the large conference room while the other half will work from home. HR will give me the list of which employees will be allowed to work offsite tomorrow morning. During the renovations, you won't be permitted access to your computers, so make sure you upload any files you think you'll need to a portable hard drive. Do you have any questions regarding what I've just mentioned?

M　在今天的員工會議結束之前，想先告訴大家關於原訂的辦公室工程。工程將於下週一和週二進行，因此，在那兩天內，任何人都無法在座位上工作。我們之中將會有一半的人前往大會議室，而另外一半將會在家工作。在家工作的職員名單預計將於明天上午從人事那裡收到。施工期間不能使用電腦，請勿忘記將檔案放進外接硬碟。對於我現在說的話有什麼問題嗎？

詞彙 update 更新；最新情報　renovation 維修，修理　allow 准許　offsite 異地　access 接近權　upload 上傳　portable 可攜帶的　regarding 關於　mention 提及

89.

說話者主要在討論什麼？
(A) 夏季休假。
(B) 員工福利。
(C) 辦公室工程。
(D) 出差。

在談話的前半部分中，說話者表示會告知關於辦公室維修工程(an update on the planned renovations of our office)的事情，並說明施工期間及其他相關事項。因此，談話的主題是(C)的辦公室工程。

90.

明天會發生什麼事？
(A) 新電腦將送達。
(B) 將會收到名單。
(C) 將購買辦公桌。
(D) 將會僱用員工。

明天要發生的事情在"HR will give me the list of which employees will be allowed to work offsite tomorrow morning"這一句中可以確認。也就是說，明天將會收到在家工作的員工名單，因此(B)是正確答案。

91.

說話者要聽眾做什麼？
(A) 將所需要的設備放進箱子。
(B) 清理本人的位置。
(C) 登記參加公司活動。
(D) 轉移電腦檔案。

在談話的後半部分，說話者叮嚀在施工當天無法使用電腦，所以需要的檔案要放在外接式硬碟裡(so make sure you upload any files you think you'll need to a portable hard drive)。因此，(D)是正確答案。

詞彙 box up 打包 **workspace** 工作空間

[92-94]

M	Now that winter is rapidly approaching, the Delmont Ski Resort is set to reopen for the skiing season. Our doors are opening this weekend on Friday, November 14. There's already snow on the slopes, so be one of the first to ski down Mount Trinity. We've created two more courses, so there will be new challenges for even the most experienced skiers. If you make a reservation for our opening weekend, you'll get fifty percent off our regular rates as well as a free dinner at Montross, our restaurant. Sample world-renowned chef Isaac Campbell's delicious meals at Montross. Call 980-9495 to make your booking today.
M	冬天很快就要到了，Delmont滑雪渡假村為迎接滑雪季做好了準備，我們預定於本週五11月14日開始營業。滑坡上已有積雪，請成為第一個從Trinity山滑雪下來的主人公吧。我們新增加了兩種路線，經驗豐富的滑雪愛好者們可以嘗試新的挑戰。另外，若是預約開幕週的週末，可享受定價的五折優惠，且可在本店Montross免費用餐，品嚐在Montross中享譽世界的Isaac Campbell主廚的美味佳餚。今天就撥打980-9495來預約吧。

詞彙 rapidly 快速地 **approach** 接近，靠近 **slope** 傾斜面，斜坡 **challenge** 挑戰 **experienced** 經驗豐富的，老練的 **as well as** 不只是～也有～ **world-renowned** 全世界知名的 **booking** 預約

92.

Delmont 滑雪度假村發生了什麼變化？
(A) 為滑雪愛好者提供了新的空間。
(B) 客房變得更大。
(C) 進行了維修工程。
(D) 僱用了新的主廚。

滑雪度假村的變化部分在"We've created two more courses, so there will be new challenges for even the most experienced skiers."中可以得知增加了兩個新路線這一個變化，所以將滑雪道改寫為new places for skiers的(A)就是正確答案。

93.

對遊客有什麼特別優惠？
(A) 客房費用優惠。
(B) 免費滑雪教學。

(C) 以半價使用設施。
(D) 每天提供免費早餐。

在談話後半部分，可以得知會對預約的人提供「渡假村費用50%折扣(fifty percent off our regular rates)」以及「免費晚餐(a free dinner at Montross, our restaurant)」因此兩種優惠中意指為前者的(A)是正確答案。

94.

Montross是什麼？
(A) 鄰近城市。
(B) 山。
(C) 餐廳。
(D) 咖啡廳。

透過談話後半部分的內容可以得知Montross是世界著名的主廚在渡假村內的餐廳。正確答案是(C)。

[95-97]

講師	時間	主題
Leslie Davidson	10:00 A.M.–11:00 A.M.	進口及出口
Marcus Wild	11:10 A.M.–12:00 P.M.	國際法
Jeremy Sparks	1:00 P.M.–1:50 P.M.	有效率的後勤部門
Allison Booth	2:00 P.M.–3:20 P.M.	電腦科技

W	Hello. My name is Wendy Hamilton. I'm the purchasing manager at Paulson Manufacturing. I saw an advertisement for the upcoming conference that's being held in St. Paul next weekend. It looks fascinating. I'd like to reserve two tickets for the conference as one of my colleagues will be attending with me. I hope there are still tickets available as I'm really looking forward to listening to the talk about international law. It sounds like it's going to be very informative. Would you please contact me at 480-9038 so that I can make the necessary arrangements? Thank you.
W	您好，我叫Wendy Hamilton。我是Paulson Manufacturing的採購部長。我看到了下周末即將在聖保羅舉行討論會的廣告，它看起來很有趣。因為我要和我的同事一起參加，所以我想要預訂兩張會議的門票。我想聽有關的國際法的演講，它看起來是對我非常有幫助的。希望還有票。可以請你撥打480-9038讓我能夠做好準備嗎？謝謝。

詞彙 upcoming 即將到來的，不久 **fascinating** 夢幻的，帥氣的 **colleague** 同事 **look forward to** 期待，期盼 **international law** 國際法 **informative** 提供資訊的，有益的 **arrangement** 準備

95.

說話者為什麼會打電話？
(A) 為了要研討會的宣傳冊子。
(B) 為了要詢問價格。

(C) 為了要確認演講時間。

(D) 為了要預訂討論會的門票。

在"I'd like to reserve two tickets for the conference as one of my colleagues will be attending with me. "這句話中可以得知說話者打電話的理由是為了(D)的預購門票。

96.

活動將會在什麼時候舉行？

(A) 本週末。

(B) 下週末。

(C) 本月。

(D) 下個月。

在談話的前半部分中，說話者說看到關於下週末在聖保羅舉行的討論會的廣告而聯絡(an advertisement for the upcoming conference that's being held in St. Paul next weekend)。透過這些可以確定討論會舉行的日子是(B)下週末。

97.

請看圖表，說話者想要聽那一位講師的演講？

(A) Leslie Davidson

(B) Marcus Wild

(C) Jeremy Sparks

(D) Allison Booth

說話者說他非常期待國際法(international law)的演講，所以在圖表中找到國際法的講師，就不難看出答案是(B)。

[98-100]

日期	活動
6月 27日	募款活動
7月 15日	仲夏夜之夢
7月 25日	募款活動
8月 3日	羅密歐與茱麗葉
8月 11日	募款活動

W   Once again, we have had a successful event today. I'd like to thank all of you for coming here to assist us. Without your help, none of this would have been possible. I especially appreciate your effort since you're not getting paid. You're just doing this work because you're interested in helping us here at the Grandison Theater. Well, I'd like to let you know that as my way of thanking you, I'm giving each of you two free tickets to next week's performance of *Romeo and Juliet*. Before you leave, see me about tickets. And thanks for helping us raise so much money here in July.

W   我想再說一遍，今天的活動很成功。我想要感謝來這裡幫忙的所有人，如果沒有大家的幫助，什麼事情都做不到。因為這是無償的工作，所以我更要感謝大家的辛苦付出。大家只因為對Grandison劇場感興趣就做了這些事情。嗯，為表達我的感謝之意，我會贈與大家兩張下週演出的羅密歐及朱麗葉的免費門票。門票的相關事項，請在離開之前來找我。謝謝你們幫助我在7月份募集到這麼多款項。

詞彙 effort 努力 get paid 有償 raise 提高；籌(款)

98.

聽眾是誰？

(A) 聽眾。

(B) 表演者。

(C) 志願者。

(D) 戲劇評論家。

通過前半部分的談話內容可以知道聽眾們是不收報酬(you're not getting paid)幫忙劇場募捐活動的人。因此，聽眾應該是(C)志願者。

99.

說話者會給聽眾什麼東西？

(A) 獎金。

(B) 帶薪休假。

(C) 免費門票。

(D) 戲劇中的角色。

在談話後半部分，說話者為了感謝志願者們，說「會給你們各兩張下周演出的門票(I'm giving each of you two free tickets to next week's performance)」，所以說話者將要給的是(C)的免費門票。

100.

看圖。談話是在什麼時候進行的？

(A) 6月27日。

(B) 7月25日。

(C) 8月3日。

(D) 8月11日。

在談話的最後一句"And thanks for helping us raise so much money here in July." 中可以得知該談話的對象是參加7月基金募款活動的志願者們。因此，在圖表上找到7月的Fundraiser(基金籌備活動)的日期，就可以確定談話進行的日期是(B)的7月25日。或者是可以透過"next week's performance of *Romeo and Juliet*."的語句來推測出該談話會在羅密歐和朱麗葉演出前的7月25日進行。

PART 1

1.

(A) A tourist is taking some photographs.
(B) Shoppers are making some purchases.
(C) Pictures have been put on display.
(D) One person is speaking with the shopkeeper.

(A) 有一位遊客正在拍照。
(B) 購物者正在購物。
(C) 畫作被陳列著。
(D) 有一個人正在和店主講話。

正確描述商店懸掛畫作的情景(C)是正確答案。照片中並沒有看到拍照或是和店主交談的人，還有正在購買商品的人，所以其餘選項都是錯誤答案。

詞彙 tourist 遊客 take a photograph 拍照 put ~ on display 展示，陳列

2.

(A) The speaker is pointing at the screen.
(B) The chairs are arranged in rows.
(C) Some people are watching a movie.
(D) One audience member's hand is raised.

(A) 演講者正指著螢幕。
(B) 椅子被整齊地排列著。
(C) 有些人正在看電影。
(D) 聽眾中有一個人舉著手。

適當說明座椅擺放方式的(B)是正確答案。錯誤說明演講者動作的(A)不是正確答案，提及畫面中看不到的電影 (movie)的(C)也不是正確答案。因為沒有舉著手的聽眾，所以(D)也是錯誤的。

詞彙 point at 指著 arrange 排列，佈置 in rows 成排

3.

(A) Students are buying textbooks at a store.
(B) The librarian is checking in a book.
(C) One woman is showing her library card.
(D) Several people are waiting in line.

(A) 學生們正在賣場購買教材。
(B) 圖書館管理員正在還書。
(C) 有一個女人正在展示自己的借閱證。
(D) 有幾個人正排著隊。

可以看到人們在圖書館排隊等待借書的情景，因此(D)是正確答案。(B)的check in意思為「返還(書)」，但如果(B)要成為正確答案，則主語必須改為student或woman等。女人遞給男人的不是借閱證(library card)而是書，所以(C)也不能成為正確答案。

詞彙 textbook 教科書，教材 check in 返還(書) wait in line 排隊等待

4.

(A) The man is pushing a shopping cart.
(B) The man is cooking some food.
(C) The man is shopping for groceries.
(D) The man is standing at the checkout counter.

(A) 男人正推著購物車。
(B) 男人在做飯。
(C) 男子在購買食品。
(D) 男子站在收銀台。

男人不是在推購物車(shopping cart)，而是提著籃子，所以(A)是錯誤的解釋，男人站的地方也不是收銀台(checkout counter)，而是在貨架前，因此(D)也不是正確答案。正確答案是適當說明正在挑選食品的男子行為(C)。

詞彙 shopping cart 購物車 shop for 選購，打探 grocery 食品 checkout counter 收銀台

5.

(A) Customers are entering the store.
(B) There is a beach next to the building.
(C) The doors to the establishment are closed.
(D) The signboard shows the day's specials.

(A) 客人正走進店裡。
(B) 建築物旁邊有海灘。
(C) 店家的門是關著的。
(D) 告示牌寫著今日特餐。

因為看不到客人的樣子所以(A)不是正確答案，(B)是如果把beach(海邊)誤聽成bench(長椅)則可以會誤造成答案的陷阱。另外，由於在門旁的上告示牌沒有寫任何東西，所以(D)也是錯誤的解釋。正確答案是將餐廳改寫為establishment(機關，設施，營業場所)的(C)。

詞彙 enter 進去　next to ~的旁邊　establishment 機關，設施，營業場所　signboard 招牌，匾額　the day's special 今日精選料理

6.

(A) She is using the dishwasher.
(B) The mechanic is fixing the vehicle.
(C) He is looking at the appliance.
(D) A kitchen item has been installed.

(A) 她正在使用洗碗機。
(B) 維修人員正在修理車輛。
(C) 他在看家電。
(D) 廚房用品已經被裝好了。

可以看到男人正在修理洗碗機。正確答案是將洗碗機換成appliance(家電產品)敘述的(C)。(A)和(B)是分別利用照片中可以看到的dishwasher(洗碗機)和mechanic(技師，維修人員)的陷阱，即使是承認照片中的男子正在安裝什麼，但也看不出已經修理完畢的事實，因此用現在完成式來描述照片的(D)並不是正確答案。

詞彙 dishwasher 洗碗機　mechanic 技師，維修人員　fix 修理　appliance 家電產品

PART 2

7.

Who designed the signboard for the store?
(A) It'll be installed later today.
(B) A new firm down the street.
(C) We paid $1,000 for it.

是誰設計了商場的招牌？
(A) 今天晚點將會安裝它。
(B) 街上一家新出現的公司。
(C) 我們為它支付了1,000美元。

利用疑問詞who詢問設計招牌的人是誰。正確答案是指廣告公司的(B)。像這樣即使是用who提問，也可以用組織或團體等來回答。

詞彙 signboard 招牌，匾額　install 安裝　firm 公司

8.

The parade will be held along First Avenue.
(A) Let's go early to get a good spot.
(B) Okay. I'd like some lemonade, please.
(C) My address is 904 First Avenue.

遊行將會沿著1號街進行。
(A) 要早一點去佔個好位置。
(B) 好啊，我要檸檬水。

(C) 我的地址是1號街904號。

聽完遊行將要舉行的消息，則要找到能夠最自然延續下去的正確答案。答案是「要早點去找到好位置」的(A)。(B)是與parade(行進)發音相近的lemonade(檸檬水)，(C)是重複使用問題中出現的First Avenue來誘導回答錯誤的陷阱。

詞彙 parade 行進，遊行　spot 位置，場所　lemonade 檸檬水

9.

How many applications have we received?
(A) Seven as of this morning.
(B) Simply apply it like this.
(C) I haven't submitted mine yet.

我們收到了多少份申請書？
(A) 到今早為止有7份。
(B) 請像這樣塗抹。
(C) 我還沒有提交。

利用how many詢問收到了多少份申請書。因此直接告知申請書個數的(A)是正確答案。(B)是利用application(申請)的動詞型apply(申請；擦，塗抹)，(C) 利用與application意思連接的submit(提交)誘導誤答的陷阱。

詞彙 application 申請　as of 到~為止　apply 志願，申請；塗抹，擦拭(油漆等)　submit 提交

10.

Isn't the keynote address scheduled for nine thirty?
(A) That's all right. I'll reschedule everything.
(B) Be sure to address the CEO politely.
(C) Not anymore. It starts at ten now.

演講不是預定在9點30分開始嗎？
(A) 沒關係，我會調整一下全部的行程。
(B) 請一定要嚴謹地對待代表。
(C) 不是，是10點開始。

利用否定疑問句確認演講的時間。因此最自然的回答是告知演講時間改變了的(C)。

詞彙 keynote address 演講　reschedule 調整行程　address 地址；演說　politely 鄭重地，謙遜地　not anymore 再也不

11.

What is your opinion of the demonstration?
(A) I wasn't very impressed.
(B) She didn't state her opinion.
(C) No, I haven't demonstrated it.

你對演示有什麼意見？
(A) 沒什麼印象。
(B) 她沒有說出自己的意見。
(C) 沒有，我沒辦法證明。

「What is your opinion of ~?」是在詢問對方意見時經常使用的句子。選項中直接闡述自己意見的(A)是最為恰當的答覆。

詞彙 opinion 意見　demonstration 演示；示威　state 說；陳述　demonstrate 展示；證明

12.

Was there an invoice in the package you just opened?

(A) Yes, he has a loud voice.

(B) The box is sitting on the desk.

(C) I think I threw it in the trash.

你剛才開封的包裹裡有發貨單嗎？
(A) 是的，他聲音很大。
(B) 那個箱子在桌子上。
(C) 我好像扔進了垃圾桶。

正在詢問包裹內是否有貨單。(A)是與invoice(貨單)發音相似的voice(聲音)，(B)是利用能夠從package(包裹)中聯想到的box(箱子)進行回答。正確答案是說明「裡面有貨單但好像扔了」的(C)。

詞彙 invoice 發貨單，發票 voice 聲音 trash 垃圾

13.

TML, Inc. is hiring hundreds of assembly line workers.

(A) The factory located by the harbor.

(B) I should tell Carl since he needs a job.

(C) She works daily from nine to five.

TML股份公司將聘用數百名裝配線員工。
(A) 工廠位於港口附近。
(B) Carl正在找工作，應該要告訴他。
(C) 她每天從9點工作到5點。

聽到招聘消息並從中找到最自然的反應。答案是回答應將招聘消息告知正在找工作的人的(B)。

詞彙 assembly line 裝配線 factory 工廠 harbor 港口 daily 每天 from A to B 從A到B

14.

Mr. Richards didn't make any mistakes, did he?

(A) Not as far as I can tell.

(B) I like my steak medium rare.

(C) No, that's not Mr. Richards.

Richards先生沒有出錯，是嗎？
(A) 據我所知他沒有。
(B) 請把我的牛排做成半熟的。
(C) 不，那不是Richards先生。

通過附加問句詢問Richards先生是否有失誤，因此暗示他沒有犯錯的(A)是正確答案。如果知道as far as(就~)一詞就可以很容易地找到正確答案。

詞彙 as far as I can tell 據我所知，我所知道的

15.

Should I work on the survey or the sales report now?

(A) I'm not in sales. I do marketing.

(B) Yes, that's what you ought to do.

(C) The deadline for the survey is tomorrow.

我現在要做問卷調查，還是要做業績報告的工作？
(A) 我不是業務，我是負責銷售的。
(B) 是的，那是你該做的事。

(C) 問卷調查工作的截止日期是明天。

如果沒有聽清楚連接詞or的話就會很容易錯選(B)作為正確答案。提出的問題包括在兩個業務中要做什麼，並徵求對方的意見，因此指出更緊迫的業務且告知他們應該做的事情(C)是正確答案。

詞彙 survey 問卷調查 ought to 應該 deadline 截止，期限

16.

You'd better renew your driver's license soon.

(A) Right. It expires next month.

(B) I learned to drive when I was a teen.

(C) She's not licensed to do that.

你的駕照最好近期更新一下比較好。
(A) 也是，下個月就要到期了。
(B) 我十幾歲時學開車的。
(C) 她沒有資格做那件事。

因為給出了駕照要更新的忠告，而表明了接受忠告立場的(A)是正確答案。(B)是利用driver's license(駕駛執照)中可以聯想到的drive(駕駛)的錯誤答案，(C)是重複使用license的陷阱，這裡使用license作為動詞的意思為「許可、賦予資格」。

詞彙 renew 更新 driver's license 駕照 expire 到期，消失 license 許可，賦予資格

17.

Can you explain the process a second time?

(A) The restaurant doesn't use processed foods.

(B) What exactly don't you understand?

(C) Yes, I just explained it a moment ago.

能夠再說明一遍程序嗎？
(A) 餐廳不使用加工食品。
(B) 你哪裡不懂？
(C) 是的，我剛才已經解釋它了。

利用助動詞can請求對方說明。因此，反問「說明哪些部分」的(B)是最自然的回答。

詞彙 process 過程；處理，加工 a second time 重新，再次 processed food 加工食品

18.

How do you feel about eating out for lunch?

(A) Sorry, but I can't feel anything.

(B) He's planning to order a pizza.

(C) I brought some food from home.

午飯在外面吃怎麼樣？
(A) 對不起，我什麼都感受不到。
(B) 他正打算訂披薩。
(C) 我從家裡帶了食物過來的。

「How do you feel about ~？」是徵求對方意見時常用的表達方式，但在這個問題中它還具有建議在外面吃午飯的意思。正確答案是從家裡帶了食物過來以委婉的方式拒絕提案的(C)。

19.

Were the clients impressed with the tour of the facility?

(A) A three-hour guided tour.

(B) That's how they looked to me.

(C) All the way from India.

顧客們在參觀設施時印象深刻嗎？

(A) 與導遊一起進行的3小時旅行。

(B) 對我來說是的。

(C) 從印度開始一直。

詢問顧客們參觀設施是否滿意。因此，透過「對我來說是」來傳達肯定意義的(B)是最自然的回答。

詞彙 client 顧客 be impressed with 對~印象深刻 tour 觀光，參觀 all the way from 從~一直

20.

I can upgrade you to a double room.

(A) I'd really appreciate that.

(B) No, I'm staying in a single.

(C) She hasn't received her grade yet.

可以為您升級成雙人間。

(A) 如果可以的話，我很感激。

(B) 不，我住單人房。

(C) 她還沒有拿到成績單。

問題主要是在飯店裡能聽到的句子，這是飯店員工想給客人升級客房時使用的表述。因此對於好意表示感謝的(A)是最適當的回答。

詞彙 upgrade 改進；升級 double room 雙人房 appreciate 感謝 grade 等級，成績

21.

Let's buy our tickets before we get something to eat.

(A) Great. I'm ready to order now.

(B) All right. Which movie shall we watch?

(C) I think we're sitting in the front row.

吃東西之前先買票吧。

(A) 太好了，我準備好點餐了。

(B) 好啊，要看什麼電影？

(C) 我想我們可能會坐在第一排。

透過以"Let's"開頭的間接祈使句來提出先買票的提議。在選項中最能夠呼應提案的(B)是最自然的回答。

22.

Which exit should we take?

(A) On the highway.

(B) The one coming up.

(C) Yes, that's the exit.

應該要走哪個出口？

(A) 在高速公路上。

(B) 接下來的出口。

(C) 是的，那是出口。

這是在詢問從高速公路上離開的路時會聽到的句子。因此如果找到有指定出口的選項的話，就能輕易知道正確答案是(B)。作為參考，(B)中的one指的是exit(出口)的不定代名詞。

詞彙 exit 出口 highway 高速公路

23.

Who should we assign to Ms. Jacob's team?

(A) Laurel Carter would be a great match.

(B) Yes, I can see the sign over there.

(C) They won the game in the last minute.

Jacob小姐的團隊應該要指派誰？

(A) Laurel Carter應該會很適合。

(B) 是的，我可以看那邊的標誌。

(C) 他們在最後一刻贏得了比賽。

如果知道提問的who是帶有目的性的話，就會更容易找到正確答案。提問應該要指派誰給團隊，所以有提及具體人名的(A)就是正確答案。

詞彙 assign 分配 match 適合；合得來的人 sign 徵兆；標誌 in the last minute 最後一刻

24.

Expect a slight delay due to the weather.

(A) Lots of rain and heavy winds.

(B) We ought to leave early then.

(C) Somewhere around half an hour.

因為天氣的關係，預計會稍微延遲一點。

(A) 有暴雨和強風。

(B) 那麼應該要早點離開。

(C) 30分鐘左右。

選項中對於因為天氣的原因可能會延遲的說法，最自然的反應只有意指「那樣的話，應該要早點出發」的(B)。

詞彙 expect 期待，預計 slight 瑣碎的，小的 due to 因為 heavy wind 強風

25.

Didn't Stevenson's close down last week?

(A) It sells men's and women's clothes.

(B) Four or five days from now.

(C) I went shopping there yesterday.

Stevenson's上週沒有停止營業嗎？

(A) 那裡有出售男性服裝和女性服裝。

(B) 從現在起4-5天後。

(C) 我昨天還在那裡購物。

正在詢問一家名為Stevenson's的商店是否關閉。正確答案是透過「昨天也去購物了」間接告知沒有停業事實的(C)。(A)是在詢問銷售物品時，(B)則是在詢問日期時應會給予延續的答覆。

詞彙 close down 關門，停業

26.

Does the vehicle run well, or is it still experiencing problems?

(A) Yes, that's what's bothering me about it.

(B) I run for an hour every day of the week.

(C) I haven't noticed anything wrong.

車子開得還好嗎？還是出問題了？

(A) 是的，就是那一點在折磨我。

(B) 我整個星期每天都會跑步一小時。

(C) 我沒發現奇怪的地方。

利用連接詞or詢問車況好不好。因此「到目前為止沒有問題」委婉的表示車況良好的(C)是最自然的回答。

詞彙 experience 經歷，遭受 notice 注意到，意識到

27.

We should arrive half an hour early, shouldn't we?

(A) I don't believe that's necessary.

(B) It's a quarter to six now.

(C) Several people are already here.

我們要提前半個小時到達，不是嗎？

(A) 我不認為一定要這樣。

(B) 現在是5點45分。

(C) 已經有幾個人抵達這裡了。

如果知道提問的should帶有義務或責任的意義的話，就可以很容易地找到正確答案。正確答案是提出不一定要那樣，表示出異議的(A)。

詞彙 necessary 需要的

28.

This manuscript has a few mistakes in it.

(A) At the printer's to be copied now.

(B) Yes, the editor is looking at it.

(C) Would you mind pointing them out?

這篇稿子有幾個錯別字。

(A) 正要在印刷廠印刷。

(B) 是的，編輯在看。

(C) 能指出來給我看嗎？

告訴對方有錯字。因此請求告知錯字在哪裡的(C)是最自然的回答。(A)和(B)都是從manuscript(原稿)中可以聯想到的單字printer's(印刷廠)和editor(編輯)來誘導選出錯誤答案的陷阱。

詞彙 manuscript 原稿 mistake 失誤，錯誤；錯字 printer's 印刷企業，印刷廠 editor 編輯 point out 指出，指責

29.

Will you trade shifts with me on Friday?

(A) Sorry, but that's my day off.

(B) That sounds like a fair trade.

(C) No, they didn't change anything.

星期五能和我換一下班嗎？

(A) 對不起，但那天我休息。

(B) 看起來像是公平交易。

(C) 不，他們什麼都沒換。

利用助動詞will請求對方交換上班時間。因此以那天休息來表示拒絕的(A)是最恰當的答覆。

詞彙 trade 交易，交換；貿易 day off 休息日 fair 公平的

30.

Where does Mr. Livingstone keep the files on clients?

(A) More than five hundred of them.

(B) In the cabinet behind his desk.

(C) He's in the storage room now.

Livingstone把顧客的文件放在哪裡保管？

(A) 500個以上。

(B) 桌子後面的櫃子。

(C) 他現在在倉庫。

利用疑問詞where詢問文件保管的場所。正確答案是直接提及保管位置的(B)。

詞彙 storage room 倉庫，儲藏室

31.

When should we stop to get gas?

(A) We're okay for a couple of hours.

(B) The gas station back there was closed.

(C) This car doesn't get good gas mileage.

我們應該什麼時候停車加油？

(A) 再兩三個小時應該沒問題。

(B) 那裡的加油站已經關閉了。

(C) 這台車的油耗量不好。

需要知道gas意味著gasoline(汽油)才能找到正確答案。因為詢問什麼時候要加油，所以回答「兩三個小時沒關係」的(A)是最自然的回答。作為參考，(C)的gas mileage意指「油耗」。

詞彙 gas 汽油 (= gasoline) a couple of 一兩個的 gas station 加油站 gas mileage 油耗

PART 3

[32-34]

W	Good afternoon, sir, and welcome to Derringer's. Is there anything in particular that you're interested in acquiring today?
M	Yes, there is. My anniversary is coming up, so I'd like to buy my wife something nice. I was thinking of getting her some kind of jewelry, but I'm not particularly good at picking anything out.
W	These pearl earrings look classy, and they're currently thirty percent off their regular price. How do you think they look?
M	They're quite nice, and the price can't be beat. Do you happen to have a bracelet that matches the earrings?

W	您好，歡迎來到Derringer's。您有什麼特別想購買的嗎？
M	是的，沒錯。結婚紀念日快到了，我想給妻子買個好看的。我打算要買珠寶，可我不怎麼會挑。
W	這款珍珠耳環蠻高檔的，且現在定價優惠七折。您覺得如何？
M	相當漂亮，價格也非常滿意。有跟這耳環相配的手鍊嗎？

詞彙 in particular 尤其，特別地　acquire 得到，獲得　anniversary 紀念日，結婚紀念日　jewelry 珠寶　be good at 擅長　pick out 挑選，選擇　classy 簡練的，高檔的　bracelet 手鍊　match 相配

32.

男人為什麼會到商場？
(A) **為了要送禮物給妻子。**
(B) 為了修理產品。
(C) 為了瞭解有什麼在打折。
(D) 為了找他訂購的產品。

男人來到商場的理由可以在"My anniversary is coming up, so I'd like to buy my wife something nice."中確認。　男人是為了要在結婚紀念日送禮物給妻子而來到商場的，所以(A)才是正確答案。

33.

關於耳環，女人說了什麼？
(A) 由黃金製成。
(B) **正在打折。**
(C) 手工製作。
(D) 她最喜歡的風格。

女人在推薦珍珠耳環的同時說道「現正折扣30%」這一點(they're currently thirty percent off their regular price)。因此，在選項中提及珍珠耳環的事項是(B)。

34.

男人向女人要求什麼？
(A) 項鍊。
(B) 戒指。
(C) **手鍊。**
(D) 手錶。

在對話最後的部分，男人詢問"Do you happen to have a bracelet that matches the earrings?"的同時還請求推薦一下可以和耳環搭配的(C)手鐲。

[35-37]

M	Excuse me. I'm looking for last month's issue of *Cycling Monthly*. I noticed you have the July issue but not the August one.
W	Did you look through all the copies of *Cycling Monthly* we have? Last month's magazine might be at the very back.
M	Yeah, I checked out all ten.
W	We might have a copy or two in the backroom.
M	That's great. Would you mind looking there for me? I'd rather not go to another place since my lunch break is almost over.
W	I'd love to, but I'm the only one here now. My boss should be back in about five minutes though.

M	不好意思。我在找上個月的*Cycling Monthly*。這裡有7月號的但沒有8月號。
W	請問有看過我們擁有的所有*Cycling Monthly*了嗎？上個月的雜誌大概會在很後面。
M	是的，10本全都確認過了。
W	倉庫裡可能有一兩本。
M	太好了。能幫我看看嗎？午休時間快結束了，所以我不想去別的地方看看。
W	雖然我想這麼做，但現在這裡只有我在。大約5分鐘後老闆會回來的。

詞彙 look for 尋找　check out 確認　backroom 後屋，密室　would rather 寧願　lunch break 午休時間

35.

說話者們主要在討論什麼？
(A) 女人的工作時間。
(B) **男人想要的產品。**
(C) 男人正在閱讀的雜誌。
(D) 書店的營業時間。

男子正在書店裡尋找「上個月的Cycling Mothly(last month's issue of Cycling Monthly)」。正確答案是(B)。

36.

女人為什麼提到倉庫？
(A) 為了告訴男子她將前往那裡。
(B) 為了告知主管的位子。
(C) **為了說出產品可能在的地方。**
(D) 為了告知她不久前才從那裡過來。

聽到男人查看了賣場內所有的書籍後，女人說"We might have a copy or two in the backroom."並提到倉庫裡也許還有上個月的。因此，女人提到倉庫的理由是(C)。

37.

關於男人，暗示了什麼事情？
(A) **馬上就要回到工作場所。**
(B) 想買輛新的自行車。
(C) 之前從未去過該賣場。
(D) 正在訂閱幾本雜誌。

在對話的後半部分，男人說午休時間快結束了(since my lunch break is almost over)沒辦法去別的地方看看。由此可以看出，男人應該馬上就要回公司，因此(A)才是正確答案。

詞彙 workplace 工作場所，工作崗位

M It looks like you're done with your meal, so why don't I clear the table off for you? Would you care to look over our dessert menu?

W I'd love to try a piece of that raspberry cheesecake, but I have to be leaving soon. I'm scheduled to meet a client twenty minutes from now. I'll just take a cup of coffee, please.

M Okay. I'll be right back with it. I'll bring you the check, too, so that you can be on your way once you're finished.

W I'd really appreciate your doing that. Thanks for your consideration.

M 看起來您已經用完餐了，需要幫您整理桌子嗎？有需要看一下甜點菜單嗎？

W 我很想吃一塊覆盆子奶酪蛋糕，但馬上就得離開了，20分鐘後得去見客戶，請給我一杯咖啡就好。

M 好的，等會為您送上咖啡。為了讓您吃完後馬上就能離開，我會把帳單一起拿過來的。

W 如果能那樣做的話，真的非常感謝。謝謝你的關心。

詞彙 Would you care to ~? 你可以~嗎？ check 帳單 be on one's way 離開 consideration 考慮，關心

38.
對話是在哪裡進行的？
(A) 咖啡廳。
(B) 餐廳。
(C) 餐飲業公司。
(D) 食品店。

從男人說的話「用完餐了，我會幫你整理桌子」中可以看出他們正在談話的地方是(B)餐廳。如果沒有聽清楚對話的開頭部分，就會出現只聽到raspberry cheesecake、coffee等單字進而選擇(A)為答案的失誤。

詞彙 catering company 餐飲業公司(為活動提供食物的公司企業) deli 食品店

39.
女人為什麼要馬上離開？
(A) 上班遲到了。
(B) 需要完成項目。
(C) 要去搭乘火車。
(D) 需要出席會議。

從女子的話"I'm scheduled to meet a client twenty minutes from now."中可以知道要走的理由就是要見客戶。因此(D)是正確答案。

40.
男人會拿什麼給女人？
(A) 菜單。
(B) 飲料。
(C) 奶酪蛋糕。
(D) 餐巾紙。

通過對話的後半部分內容可以得知男人會拿給女人的有a cup of

---

coffee(咖啡)和check(帳單)兩樣東西。正確答案是這兩種中的(B)。

M Ms. Winters, I'm afraid that I won't be able to submit my report this afternoon. I requested some data from the Sales Department, but nobody there has sent me anything yet. May I give it to you tomorrow?

W When did you ask for it?

M This morning as soon as I arrived here.

W Doug, you should have handled that a long time ago. I asked you to prepare the report last week.

M I'm really sorry, Ms. Winters. I'll go up to the third floor and request the information I need in person. And I'll turn in the report by five.

W I'm looking forward to reading it.

M Winters小姐，很遺憾，我可能無法在今天下午時提交報告。我向營業部要求資料，但到現在還沒有任何東西發過來。明天給你可以嗎？

W 什麼時候提出要求的？

M 今天早上一到這裡。

W Doug，那件事情應該在很久以前就要處理。我不是上週要求你準備報告嗎。

M 真的很對不起，Winters小姐，我會直接到三樓去要資料，然後在五點之前提交報告的。

W 我想要盡快看到。

詞彙 submit 提交 handle 辦理，處理 turn in 提交

41.
男人的問題是什麼？
(A) 收到有誤的資料。
(B) 忘記需要列印文件交給女人。
(C) 這週沒有任何業績。
(D) 沒有完成所給予的工作。

在對話的開始部分，男人告訴女人「今天下午沒辦法提交報告(I won't be able to submit my report this afternoon)」。因此，正確答案是將"submit report"寫作assigned work的(D)。

42.
女人為什麼會說"You should have handled that a long time ago"？
(A) 為了要求道歉。
(B) 為了主張應要拿到預算報告。
(C) 為了拒絕男人的請求。
(D) 為了建議男人使用其他解決辦法。

should have＋p.p.意指為「本應~但未做到」，給定的句子表達了「那件事之前就應該要處理，但沒做到」的遺憾。另一方面，該句是對男人要求延長提交報告的期限的答覆，因此最後所給的句子其含義可視為(C)。

43.
關於營業部，暗示了什麼？
(A) 那裡的員工正在休假。

(B) 目前沒有可以進行通話的電話。

(C) 辦公室所在位置比男人的辦公室樓層還高。

(D) 接受了女人的指示。

對話的後半部分，男人說「（為了要得到營業部的資料）我會上去三樓(I'll go up to the third floor)」，從這一點來看，營業部所在的層數比男人在的辦公室層數還高。因此(C)是正確答案。

詞彙　supervise 監督，指揮

[44-46]

W	Two new employees are starting in our department tomorrow. I'm positive that you'll get along with them. I interviewed both and like them a lot.
M	That's great. Maybe we should all go out to lunch together so that everyone can meet them. Do you have time tomorrow?
W	I'll be at the branch office in Louisville until three. And I think Henry and Frank will be attending an orientation event then anyway.
M	Okay, I suppose we can do it another time. I'll let everyone know what's going on and make sure the new people receive a warm welcome.
W	明天開始將會有兩個新進員工在我們部門工作。我確信你會和他們相處得很好。兩個人都是我面試的，我很滿意。
M	太好了。為了能讓大家見個面，我們可以一起去吃午餐。明天有時間嗎？
W	我會在路易維爾的分公司待到3點。另外我知道Henry和Frank到時也會參加說明會活動。
M	這樣啊，看來得要利用其他時間了。我會告訴大家這件事，並確保新進員工會得到熱烈歡迎。

詞彙　get along with 與~和睦相處　so that ~ can 為了要　anyway 無論如何；況且　go on 發生，進行

44.
說話者們主要在討論什麼？
(A) 路易維爾的分公司。
(B) 實施面試的必要性。
(C) 即將開始的項目。
(D) 新僱用的員工。

通過對話的第一句可以推測出對話的主題是從明天開始工作的兩名新進員工(two new employees)，因此正確答案是(D)。

45.
男人提議要做什麼？
(A) 一起吃飯。
(B) 將其他項目交給自己。
(C) 把自己介紹給Henry認識。
(D) 面試更多的人。

聽到關於新進員工的消息，男人提議說「一起吃午餐吧(we should all go out to lunch together)」。因此男人提議的是(A)。

46.
女人明天要做什麼？
(A) 參加說明會。
(B) 與客戶共進午餐。
(C) 會待在其他分公司。
(D) 帶訪客參觀。

對於男人說大家明天一起吃午餐的提議，女人說"I'll be at the branch office in Louisville until three."間接表達了不參加的意思，因此女人明天要做的事是(C)。另外，如果是問Henry和Frank明天要做的事情的話，則答案將是(A)。

詞彙　take part in 參加，參與　spend 花費(時間／金錢)，消費

[47-49]

M	Excuse me. I'm planning to paint my house, so could you recommend a paint that is good enough to last for several years?
W1	Whitman makes excellent paint which is guaranteed to last for at least ten years. As you can see, it comes in a variety of colors.
M	I'm aware of the quality, but the prices are too much for me. Do you have anything a bit cheaper?
W2	Actually, sir, starting tomorrow, we're having a special promotion on Whitman paint. Buy ten or more cans, and you'll get twenty percent off.
M	Thanks for the information. I'll come back here tomorrow after work.
M	不好意思，我打算粉刷我的房子，能推薦一個能夠維持多年的好油漆嗎？
W1	Whitman是保證至少持續10年的優秀油漆。 如您所見，它還有多樣的顏色。
M	雖然知道它的品質，但是價格太高了。有稍微便宜一點的嗎？
W2	老實說，客人，從明天開始Whitman油漆會進行特別促銷。購買10桶以上的話可以打8折。
M	謝謝你告訴我。我明天下班後再過來。

詞彙　recommend 勸誘，推薦　last 持續　guarantee 保障，保證　a variety of 多樣的

47.
對話會在哪裡進行？
(A) 傢俱賣場。
(B) 建築公司。
(C) 建築材料和裝修用品賣場。
(D) 電子產品賣場。

銷售員正在向想要購買油漆的顧客推薦特定品牌的油漆。 因此對話進行的地方應該是(C)建築材料及裝修用品賣場。

詞彙　home improvement store 販賣建築材料及裝修用品的賣場

48.

關於Whitman產品，男人說了什麼？

(A) 非常昂貴。

(B) 品質不佳。

(C) 顏色不多。

(D) 不持久。

男人被推薦使用Whitman油漆後說"I'm aware of the quality, but the prices are too much for me."，因此選項中它提到有關於Whitman油漆的事項是(A)。

49.

關於男人，暗示了什麼？

(A) 請女人提出建議。

(B) 想要獲得免費樣本。

(C) 打算要去其他賣場。

(D) 明天將會採購。

聽到女子2說油漆的優惠將從明天開始，男人說"I'll come back here tomorrow after work."。也就是說，男人為了要享有折扣，預計明天將會再次到賣場購買油漆，所以(D)才是正確答案。

[50-52]

> M Hello. This is Keith Hampton. I scheduled an appointment with Dr. Murphy tomorrow, but I wonder if it's possible to see him today. My tooth is in a lot of pain.
>
> W I'm terribly sorry to hear that, Mr. Hampton. How close to our location are you? There's an open slot at 2:30, but that's only fifteen minutes from now. Do you think you can make it here by then?
>
> M I'm in the Wakefield Shopping Center right now, so I'll head over there at once. Is it okay if I'm about five minutes late?
>
> W That's fine. I'll go ahead and pencil you in for that time. See you in a few minutes.
>
> -
>
> M 您好，我是Keith Hampton。我預約了明天Murphy醫生的門診，但我想知道今天能否進行診療，因為我牙齒太痛了。
>
> W 我很遺憾聽到這樣的話，Hampton先生您現在離我們醫院有多遠？雖然2點30分有個空檔，但是距離現在只有15分鐘。那時候之前能來到這裡嗎？
>
> M 我現在在Wakefield購物中心，所以可以馬上過去。可能會晚5分鐘左右沒關係嗎？
>
> W 沒關係的，我會先幫你預約。待會見。

詞彙 schedule an appointment with 和～約好見面 pain 疼痛 location 位置 slot 洞口，位置 pencil in 預先安排

50.

女人在哪裡工作？

(A) 服飾賣場。

(B) 牙科。

(C) 體育館。

(D) 托兒所。

這是因為牙齒疼痛而要提前預約時間的患者和醫院職員的對話。因此女人工作的地方應該是(B)。

詞彙 childcare 育兒

51.

男人想做什麼？

(A) 聽取其他醫生的看法。

(B) 與他人交談。

(C) 以現金結帳。

(D) 更改預約時間。

對話開始部分的"I scheduled an appointment with Dr. Murphy tomorrow, but I wonder if it's possible to see him today."這句話中可以看出男人想要什麼。男人詢問明日的預約掛號能否更改為今天，因此男人想要的是(D)。

詞彙 second opinion 他人的意見

52.

關於Wakefield購物中心，暗示了什麼？

(A) 由多層數組成。

(B) 在離女人較近的地方。

(C) 最近剛開業。

(D) 在那裡的所有店家正在進行促銷。

女人問15分鐘內能不能過來，男人的回答是"I'm in the Wakefield Shopping Center right now, so I'll head over there at once."。通過這句話可以推測出Wakefield購物中心離醫院不遠，因此(B)是正確的答案。

[53-55]

> M Stephanie, you still drive to work every day, don't you? Would you mind picking me up tomorrow morning? My car broke down, and I won't be able to drive it until next Monday.
>
> W Don't you live in the Silver Springs neighborhood? It would take me a while to go there to pick you up.
>
> M Actually, I moved right down the street from you three days ago. I live at 487 Baker Street, so I can be at your house when you're ready to leave.
>
> W I had no idea. That won't be a problem then. Just be outside my house no later than half past seven tomorrow.
>
> -
>
> M Stephanie，你現在還是每天開車上班，對吧？你介意明天早上載我一趟嗎？我的車壞了，到下個星期一為止都不能用。
>
> W 你不是住在Silver Springs社區嗎？我如果要去接你的話，得花上很長一段時間。
>
> M 其實三天前我就搬到你家的下一條街。我現在住在Baker街487號，只要你準備要出發我就可以立刻去你家。
>
> W 我不知道呢，但應該沒問題吧。明天7點30分之前到我家門前來。

詞彙 neighborhood 附近，鄰近；地區 no later than 不遲於，早於

53.

男人的問題是什麼？

(A) 忘記要買公車的定期票。

(B) 幾天不能開車。

(C) 在上班途中迷路。

(D) 早上常常塞車。

在對話的開始部分，男人拜託女人載他，並說"My car broke down, and I won't be able to drive it until next Monday."表明理由。也就是說，車子故障了會有幾天不能用車，所以男人的問題就出在(B)上。

詞彙 bus pass 公車定期票　get caught in traffic 塞車

54.

當女人說"Don't you live in the Silver Springs neighborhood?"時，她在暗示什麼？

(A) 她不瞭解那個城市。

(B) 她不能載著男人去他家。

(C) 她認為她不能幫助男人。

(D) 她記不清準確的位置。

給予的句子是關於男人請求載他一程的回答，具體意思可通過下面的句子"It would take me a while to go there to pick you up."知道。也就是說，因為要到男人居住的地方需要花費很長一段時間，所以間接地表示自己很難接受請求，(C)才是正確答案。

詞彙 be unfamiliar with 對…不熟悉，對…不習慣

55.

女人對男人說什麼？

(A) 早上在自己家門口前等待。

(B) 準備出發時給自己打電話。

(C) 告訴自己他的住址。

(D) 在下班前提醒她。

在對話的最後部分，女人說"Just be outside my house no later than half past seven tomorrow."，囑咐男人說他要在7點半之前到她家門前。因此正確答案是(A)。

詞彙 reminder 提醒；催函

[56-58]

M　Have you looked over your copy of the marketing report yet? I'm somewhat alarmed by everything that I've been reading so far.

W　The report is sitting on my desk, but I've been in meetings nearly the entire afternoon. What exactly are you referring to, Mr. Henderson?

M　Our newest marketing campaign is not remotely successful. In fact, sales of our products started declining virtually as soon as the new ads were released.

W　It sounds like there's a connection, but we need to confirm that before we end the campaign. How about organizing a focus group to get some other opinions?

M　您是否有查看過市場行銷報告的副本了？到現在為止，我讀到的內容中多少讓我有些受到衝擊。

W　報告放在我的桌上，但我整個下午都在開會。確切內容是什麼？Henderson先生。

M　我們最近的行銷策略不太成功。實際上，新廣告一開始，產品銷售量就開始減少了。

W　雖然看似有關係，但在廣告活動結束之前，還是需要確認一下。成立焦點小組以便聽取不同意見如何？

詞彙 alarmed 害怕的，震驚的　so far 現在為止　remotely 遠遠地；一點點　decline 減少，衰退　virtually 實際上　release 解放；上市　connection 連接　organize 組織，計畫　focus group 焦點小組(由代表各階層的少數人組成的小組)

56.

問題是什麼？

(A) 與諮詢公司斷絕交易。

(B) 活動推遲。

(C) 廣告尚未結束。

(D) 銷售量減少。

男人以報告內容為基礎向女人指出行銷策略不成功，並說「事實上銷售量開始減少(sales of our products started declining virtually)」。透過這些可知道問題出在行銷失敗而導致的銷售額下降，因此正確答案是(D)。

57.

根據女人說的話，女人在做什麼？

(A) 正在參加會議。

(B) 正在閱讀報告。

(C) 從事關於焦點小組的工作。

(D) 正在撰寫廣告詞。

女人說沒有讀報告的原因是「整個下午都在參加會議(I've been in meetings nearly the entire afternoon)」。因此女人所做的事是(A)參加會議。

58.

女人對男人說什麼？

(A) 更專注於工作。

(B) 與行銷部門的人交談。

(C) 瞭解別人的想法。

(D) 整理銷售數據。

在對話的最後部分，女人為了確認廣告的效果提議組成焦點小組聽取意見(organizing a focus group to get some other opinions)。因此(C)是正確答案。

詞彙 focus on 集中在~上　compile 編輯，編撰

[59-61]

W	Excuse me. I acquired several blouses here last night, but I wonder if I can return them to get something else.
M1	Sure, we permit exchanges if you made the purchase within ten days. Did you bring them with you?
W	Yes, they're right here. I thought I liked the color, but I'd prefer to have something darker.
M1	Oh, I'm sorry, but we can't accept this one since the plastic has been opened. We can take the other seven items though.
M2	Don't worry about that, Andrew. Ms. Cormack is a long-term customer here, so we can let her exchange everything.
W	Thanks, Mr. Davenport. I appreciate that.

W 不好意思，昨晚我在這裡買了幾件女式襯衫，想知道我能不能換成其他件。

M1 當然，購買的產品在10天以內都可以換貨。帶過來了嗎？

W 是的，在這裡。我挺喜歡這個顏色的，但我覺得比較暗的顏色會比較好。

M1 噢，對不起，因為塑膠袋已經開封了，所以這個不能退貨。但是其他7件商品都可以退貨。

M2 別擔心那一點，Andrew。Cormack小姐從很久以前就是這裡的顧客了，所以可以幫她交換所有商品。

W 謝謝你，Davenport先生，非常感謝。

詞彙 plastic 塑膠製品，塑膠 long-term 長期的

59.
對話是在哪裡進行的？
(A) 服飾賣場。
(B) 食品賣場。
(C) 家電賣場。
(D) 文具店。

這是想要換女式襯衫(blouses)的顧客和賣場職員之間的對話。因此，對話進行的場所應該是(A)。

60.
女人想要什麼？
(A) 用信用卡結帳。
(B) 在網路上訂購。
(C) 交換產品。
(D) 退款。

在對話的開頭部分，從"I wonder if I can return them to get something else"女人說的話中可以看出，女人想要換貨。正確答案是(C)。

61.
關於Cormack小姐，Davenport先生提到了什麼？
(A) 她擁有賣場。
(B) 她以前見過他。
(C) 她屬於購物者俱樂部。
(D) 她昨晚從他那邊購買了商品。

男子2對男子1表示即使原則上不能退款，但因為女人從很久以前就是賣場的顧客(long-term customer)，所以可以進行退款。因此可以推測出男子2和女人是以前就認識的關係，所以正確答案是(B)。

詞彙 belong to 屬於 shopper's club 購物者俱樂部

[62-64]

產品	數量	價格
複印紙(5,000張)	4	$12.99
圓珠筆 (20個)	2	$10.99
釘書機	2	$5.99
迴紋針(1,000個)	1	$8.99

M	Hello. My name is Jarvis Sanders. I made an order over the phone last night, but I'd like to alter it.
W	Of course. I'm looking at your order form right now, Mr. Sanders. What do you need?
M	I didn't order enough writing utensils, so could you increase my order to five boxes?
W	That won't be a problem. I'll pack your order now and have Lewis deliver it after lunch.
M	If he's coming then, please tell him to drop off the items with Ms. Muller on the third floor, please. She'll also pay him for everything.
W	I'll be sure to inform him of that. Thank you.

M 您好，我叫Jarvis Sanders。昨晚通過電話訂購，但是我想要更改訂單。

W 原來如此，我現在正在查看您的訂單，Sanders先生，您需要什麼呢？

M 我沒有訂到足夠的用筆，能幫我把訂貨量增加到5箱嗎？

W 沒問題。我現在會把訂購商品包裝好，中午以後會讓Lewis送貨的。

M 請跟他說他到達時把物品交給三樓的Muller小姐。全部物品的費用也是會由她付清的。

W 我會轉告他的，謝謝。

詞彙 alter 改變，變更 writing utensil 筆記用品，文具類 drop off 交給，放下 inform A of B 告知B給A

62.
男人什麼時候訂購的？
(A) 上星期。
(B) 兩天前。
(C) 昨天。
(D) 今天早上。

如果在對話開始部分的"I made an order over the phone last night"中沒有錯過last night(昨晚)的話，就可以很容易地找到正確答案。正確答案是(C)。

63.
請看圖。男人想要更多的產品，單價是多少？
(A) 5.99美元
(B) 8.99美元
(C) 10.99美元

(D) 12.99美元

如果知道writing utensils指的是筆記用具，那麼只要在選項中找到符合書記用具的價格即可。正確答案是20支入的圓珠筆的單價(C)的10.99美元。

64.

Muller小姐將會做什麼？
(A) 以後再打電話給賣場。
(B) 收到訂購商品。
(C) 網路匯款。
(D) 準備配送。

通過對話後半部分男人的話中"please tell him to drop off the items with Ms. Muller"這個部分可以看出Muller小姐是會收到訂購商品的人。正確答案是(B)。

詞彙 submit an online payment 透過網路匯款

[65-67]

6月19日	6月20日	6月21日	6月22日	6月23日
		遊行		

M　When do you feel we should have the product demonstration here? I was thinking of Wednesday. How does that sound?

W　I believe that's the day of the annual parade. Traffic here will be terrible then, so let's schedule it for the day afterward.

M　Okay, I'll write up a press release and give it to you to check over. I should have it done within a couple of hours.

W　Thanks. I'll e-mail you a list of the journalists whom we need to invite. This will be a big event, so we need as much publicity as possible.

- -

M　你覺得應該要什麼時候在這裡開產品演示會？我覺得星期三。你覺得怎麼樣？

W　據我所知那天是每年會舉行遊行的日子。那時這裡的交通堵塞會很嚴重，所以就安排在後一天吧。

M　好的，我會寫一份報導資料交給你審閱，會在兩小時內完成的。

W　謝謝，我把我們需要邀請的記者名單用電子郵件傳給你。因為這次是大型活動，所以要盡可能地多吸引媒體的關注。

詞彙 product demonstration 產品演示會 annual 年度的 press release 報導資料 check over 審閱 journalist 新聞工作者，記者 publicity 媒體的關注，大眾知名度

65.

關於遊行，女人說了什麼？
(A) 預計將首次舉行。
(B) 將在週末進行。
(C) 在市內是很受歡迎的活動。
(D) 會造成交通堵塞。

女人說星期三是遊行活動日，「那天交通堵塞會很嚴重(traffic here will be terrible then)」，並提議安排其他日期。因此女人提到關於遊行的是(D)。

詞彙 for the first time 首次，最初

66.

請看圖，產品演示會將在何時舉辦？
(A) 6月19日。
(B) 6月20日。
(C) 6月22日。
(D) 6月23日。

當男人說星期三舉行活動時，女人說當天有遊行，把日程定在隔天(the day afterward)。因此，在圖表中找到星期三後一天的日期的話，正確答案就會是(C)的6月22日。

67.

女人將會給男人什麼？
(A) 記者們的名字。
(B) 報導資料。
(C) 校對的劇本。
(D) 為遊行做的廣告。

女人將會給男人的是a list of the journalists(記者名單)。 如果在選項中找到符合具有這些意義的東西，將journalists改寫為reporters的(A)就是正確答案。

詞彙 script 腳本，劇本 proofread 校對

[68-70]

Davis Clothes
★ 特價促銷 ★

時間 8月15日-25日
對象 賣場內所有服裝產品
折扣 折抵20%
理由 夏季大甩賣

W　Did you see the advertisement for our sale which was printed in the *Greenville Gazette* this morning?

M　I haven't had the opportunity to read the paper yet. Is there some sort of a problem?

W　Yeah, check this out. It's supposed to read 30 here, not 20. I just noticed that.

M　All right, please inform the sales staff to let our customers know about the mistake. In addition, I'll call the paper about the misprint.

W　Okay. After talking to the staff, I'll print some posters to hang up throughout the store.

M　Good thinking. That might help attract a few more people here.

W	有看到今天早上*Greenville Gazette*上刊登的我們的促銷廣告了嗎?
M	我到現在還沒有機會看報紙。有什麼問題嗎?
W	好吧,看看這個。不是20而是30,我也才剛發現。
M	好的,請告知員工讓顧客知道這些失誤,關於誤打的事情我也會打電話給報社的。
W	知道了。跟員工們說完之後,我會印幾張海報掛在賣場的各個地方。
M	是個好主意。那樣做的話,我覺得會有助於引起更多人的關注。

詞彙 inform 告知 misprint 誤打 hang up 拖延;懸掛 attract 吸引,引誘

68.

看圖,哪些部分有誤打?
(A) 期間
(B) 對象
(C) 折扣
(D) 理由

從女人說的"It's supposed to read 30 here, not 20."這句話中可以找到正確答案的線索。找到一個以20替代30的數字項目,就可以知道發生誤打的部分是(C)的折扣。

69.

男人要求女人做什麼?
(A) 向工作人員說明。
(B) 給報社打電話。
(C) 重新發佈廣告。
(D) 向顧客道歉。

男人對女人囑咐「告訴銷售員工,讓顧客們知道失誤(inform the sales staff to let our customers know about the mistake)」。因此男人要求的是(A)。作為參考,(B)是男人要做的。

70.

關於海報,男人說了什麼?
(A) 要是彩色的。
(B) 女人需要手工製作。
(C) 也許會有效果。
(D) 女人應該要貼在窗戶上。

聽到女人說要貼海報,男人說"That might help attract a few more people here.",表示出對海報的效果有所期待。 因此正確答案是(C)。

詞彙 effective 具效果的

PART 4
[71-73]

W	We've already got a big crowd waiting outside the building, and there's still half an hour before we open our doors for the first time. It'll be a busy day for all of us. Expect to be on your feet the entire time we're open. Now, I know some of you are a bit nervous since you've never done this kind of work before. Don't worry if a customer asks a question but you don't know the answer. Just inform your manager that you need assistance. That's all there is to it. All right, why don't we head to our workspaces and get ready to sell lots of items?
W	建築外面已經有很多人在等著了,距離開門還有30分鐘。今天對於我們所有人都將會是忙碌的一天,你們要想成你們在營業時間之內將會一直站著。好的,我想各位當中有幾個人會因為沒有做這種工作而相當緊張。當顧客提問時,即使不知道答案也不要擔心,跟經理說你需要幫助就好。好的,我們去負責區域準備販售吧?

詞彙 crowd 人群 for the first time 第一次,最初 on one's feet 站著 a bit 一點點 nervous 匆匆的,緊張的 That's all there is to it. 那就是全部

71.

今天將會發生什麼事?
(A) 新店將會開業。
(B) 將實施培訓。
(C) 將會解決顧客的不滿。
(D) 將會實施促銷。

通過談話的第一句"We've already got a big crowd waiting outside the building, and there's still half an hour before we open our doors for the first time."可以知道新店即將開業。因此今天要發生的事情是(A)。

72.

聽眾中為什麼會有幾個在緊張?
(A) 對遲到感到擔憂。
(B) 不喜歡生氣的顧客。
(C) 必須要在人們面前講話。
(D) 沒有相關經驗。

"Now, I know some of you are a bit nervous since you've never done this kind of work before."從這句話中可以得知,聽眾中有一部分人感到緊張是因為沒有具有跟賣場開業相關的經驗。因此(D)是正確答案。

詞彙 speak in public 公開演講 relevant 關聯的

73.

說話者要聽者做什麼?
(A) 恭敬地對顧客。
(B) 加班。
(C) 編寫表格。
(D) 向上司求助。

在談話後半部分，說話者向聽眾囑咐無法回答顧客的問題時，向經理求助(Just inform your manager that you need assistance)。因此，在選項中，說話者對聽眾說的話是(D)。

[74-76]

> M Thank you for arriving here at Denton, Inc. to see our newest product in action. I'm sure everyone is excited to see how well the Fleer 2000 works. I've been informed that Dr. Bates, who will be giving the demonstration, is tied up in his lab at the moment, but he should be here soon. His assistant told me that he'll arrive ten minutes from now. In the meantime, I'd like to share a few features of the Fleer 2000 with you so that you can understand exactly what it's capable of doing. So let me turn the podium over to Dr. Lisa Schnell, who can fill you in on everything.
>
> M 感謝你們來到Denton公司觀賞我們最新產品的性能，相信大家都對Fleer 2000出色的功能寄予厚望。即將進行演示的Bates博士現在仍忙在實驗室的工作，但很快就會來到這裡的。研究員們告訴我大約再10分鐘之後就會來的。在這段時間，為了讓大家正確理解Fleer 2000的功能，我想先分享產品的幾個特點。將麥克風交給能詳細說明一切的Lisa Schnell博士。

詞彙 in action 運轉中，活動中 tie up 繫 at the moment 現在，此時 in the meantime 這段期間 share 分享 feature 特徵，特性 be capable of 可以做到 podium 講台 fill in on 告知關於~的資訊

74.

問題是什麼？
(A) 一些軟體中有病毒。
(B) 機器故障。
(C) 有一人還沒到。
(D) 缺少一些零件。

說話者向參加產品演示的人表示感謝後表示「負責產品演示的人還沒有到(Dr. Bates, who will be giving the demonstration, is tied up in his lab at the moment)」。也就是說，成為問題的是將進行演示的Bates博士沒有來，因此將博士換成a person的(C)就是正確答案。

75.

產品演示什麼時候開始？
(A) 幾分鐘後。
(B) 一小時後。
(C) 明天。
(D) 下週。

在談話的中半部分，因為說了「將進行演示的人10分鐘後會抵達(he'll arrive ten minutes from now)」，所以(A)是正確答案。

76.

接下來會發生什麼事？
(A) 將作出道歉。

(B) 將由其他人來演講。
(C) 產品將會進行維修。
(D) 實驗室的門即將打開。

在談話的最後部分，說話者說將要講述產品的特點，會把麥克風交給一位叫Lisa Schnell的人(let me turn the podium over to Dr. Lisa Schnell)，因此談話之後會發生的事情是Lisa Schnell的演講，所以正確答案是(B)。

[77-79]

> M Good morning. My name is Sam Richards. One of my colleagues at Darwin Construction ordered some supplies yesterday evening, but I believe she made a mistake. She ordered two boxes of copy paper for the office in addition to some other supplies. But we actually need twenty-two boxes. She's new here, so she didn't realize how little she was ordering. In case you need the order number, it's PTR9049. You can go ahead and charge everything to our account. We'd also like everything delivered by tomorrow morning, so feel free to charge us extra for delivery if that's necessary.
>
> M 你好。我是Sam Richards。我一個Darwin建設同事昨晚下了訂單，但我認為她訂錯了。她和其他辦公品一起訂購了兩箱影印紙。但實際上是需要22箱。因為她是新進員工，所以沒有意識到自己少訂到了。如果需要訂單編號的話，訂單編號為PTR9049。請繼續進行訂單，並請向我們收取費用。希望在明天上午之前所有物品都能寄出，若有需要的話，請再額外收取費用。

詞彙 in addition to 除~以外 realize 醒悟，意識到 in case 如果，假如 extra 另外的，追加的

77.

關於說話者，可以推測出什麼？
(A) 他親眼見過聽眾。
(B) 他是Darwin建設的員工。
(C) 他明天會去找聽眾。
(D) 他在研發部門工作。

談話前半部分的「Darwin建設的同事昨晚下了訂單(one of my colleagues at Darwin Construction ordered some supplies yesterday evening)」中可以知道說話者是Darwin建設的員工。正確答案是(B)。

78.

說話者是怎麼更改訂單的？
(A) 取消。
(B) 大量訂購各種物品。
(C) 特快快遞。
(D) 購買價格更低的產品。

說話者要變更兩樣，其中一樣是與影印紙的訂單數量有關，另一樣是與配送方法有關。特別是最後一句"We'd also like everything delivered by tomorrow morning, so feel free to charge us extra for delivery if that's necessary."中，說話者說即使有追加費用也想要在明天早上之前收到物品，因此正確答案是(C)。

詞彙 cancel 取消　expedite 迅速地處理

79.

說話者為何說"She's new here."？

(A) 為了說明某人犯錯誤的理由。

(B) 為了介紹某個人。

(C) 為了要給某人參觀機會。

(D) 為了要說明文件提交的方式。

給出的句子是「她是新進員工」，這是說話者為了說明訂貨失誤的原因而說出的話。因此正確答案是(A)。

詞彙 insist 主張，堅持　paperwork 文件，文書工作

[80-82]

> **W** Thank you for coming to the Lemon Tree. My name is Glenda, and I'll be serving you this evening. I know there are lots of great options on the menu, but let me tell you about tonight's special. It's a pork chop stuffed with herbs and served with your choice of a baked potato or sautéed vegetables. It's available for only $19.99 tonight. You should give it some serious thought. Why don't I come back in a couple of minutes to give you time to think over your selections? I'll bring back some rolls and water for you as well.
>
> -
>
> **W** 歡迎您來到Lemon Tree。我的名字是Glenda，今晚會由我來服務大家。儘管我知道菜單上有很多好菜，但我還是想提一下今晚的精選餐點，正是香草豬排，還可以選擇搭配烤馬鈴薯或者炒蔬菜。今晚可以用19.99美元的價格品嘗。請認真考慮一下，為了能讓你們有更多時間思考，我待會再過來。我會帶著麵包捲和水過來的。

詞彙 option 選擇　pork chop 豬排　stuff 塞　herb 香草，藥草　sautéed 炒的　serious 真摯的，嚴肅的　roll 麵包捲　as well 同樣地

80.

談話應該是在哪裡進行的？

(A) 糕點店。

(B) 自助餐廳。

(C) 餐廳。

(D) 咖啡廳。

透過"I'll be serving you this evening, lots of great options on the menu"、"tonight's special"這些相似的表現可以推斷出說話者的職業是服務生，而說話者工作的地方就會是(C)餐廳。

81.

說話者說"You should give it some serious thought."的時候，她在暗示什麼？

(A) 聽眾之後會回來。

(B) 豬排好吃。

(C) 沒有可以坐的位置。

(D) 推薦甜點。

文句的意思是「應該認真思考這個」，這裡it指的是精選餐點豬排。也就是說，說話者以迂迴的方式推薦這道豬排餐點，因此這裏暗示

的是指(B)。

82.

說話者要聽者做什麼？

(A) 看菜單。

(B) 結帳。

(C) 點餐。

(D) 換位置。

在談話的後半部分，話者說"Why don't I come back in a couple of minutes to give you time to think over your selections?"邊要聽者考慮要選擇什麼樣的餐點，因此(A)是正確答案。

[83-85]

> **W** I've got some great news. I'm sure everyone remembers that we talked about the increase in complaints at our stores at last month's last meeting. Well, we decided to attempt the solution which Henry made at that meeting. I must say his idea was absolutely perfect. In the three weeks that have passed since we implemented his suggestion, complaints about customer service have declined by nearly 45%. In addition, sales at our stores have risen by approximately 27%. Henry, I'd like to thank you very much for that suggestion. My guess is that you'll be getting promoted for that pretty soon.
>
> -
>
> **W** 有好消息。相信大家都記得在上次會議中我們曾討論過關於上個月我們店的不滿事項增加的事情。嗯，在那次會議中我們決定嘗試一下Henry提出的解決辦法。我要說他的點子實在是很完美，在實行他的提議三週後，有關顧客服務的不滿事項減少了近45%。另外，我們店的銷售額增加了27%左右，Henry，非常感謝你提出這樣的建議，也因此我想你很快就會升職的。

詞彙 complaint 不滿　solution 解決，解決方案　implement 移植　decline 衰退，減少　nearly 幾乎　approximately 大約　promote 晉升；宣傳

83.

根據說話者說的話，上個月的會議發生了什麼事？

(A) 討論了銷售數據。

(B) 提議點子。

(C) 新產品介紹。

(D) 宣佈晉升者。

通過談話的前半部分內容可以知道上個月有個與不滿事項增加有關的會議，並決定嘗試Henry的解決方案(we decided to attempt the solution which Henry made at that meeting)。因此，上個月在會議上發生的事情是(B)。

84.

說話者對顧客服務的不滿事項說了什麼？

(A) 最近減少了。

(B) 銷售下降。

(C) 增加了45%。

(D) 不再出現。

說話者表示為了解決不滿的措施實施後，「有關顧客服務的不滿減少了將近45%(complaints about customer service have declined by nearly 45%)」，因此(A)為正確答案。

85.

關於Henry，暗示了什麼？
(A) 他是部門主管。
(B) 他在行銷部門工作。
(C) 他是新進員工。
(D) 正在參加會議。

Henry是提出解決問題方案的人，在談話後半部分說話者說"Henry, I'd like to thank you very much for that suggestion."並表達感謝。從直呼名稱的情況來看，可以推測出Henry正在談話進行的地方，所以(D)是正確的答案。

[86-88]

M Thank you for waiting patiently for me to arrive. I'm so sorry I didn't make it here by two, but I got lost while driving here. This is my first time visiting Langford. Anyway, today, I'd like to talk about the paintings here on display at the Holloway Gallery. While some are mine, there are many others created by other highly talented individuals. So I'll explain a few of the ideas that went into our work, and then I'll give everyone a tour of the works on display. I hope you find the next couple of hours to be both educational and entertaining.

M 感謝你們耐心地等候我到達。我很抱歉沒來得及在兩點前抵達，因為我開車時迷路了。這是我第一次來到Langford。總之，今天，我要談談在Holloway美術館這裡展出的繪畫作品。有一部分是我的，也有許多才華橫溢的人畫的作品。因此在對作品中的一些創意進行說明後，將給大家一起參觀展示中作品的時間。希望以後的兩個小時能夠成為既有益又有趣的時間。

詞彙 patiently 耐心地，堅韌地 make it 抵達 on display 展示中的 highly talented 才華洋溢的 educational 有教育意義的 entertaining 有趣的

86.

說話者為什麼要道歉？
(A) 忘記時間了。
(B) 錯過航班。
(C) 出現失誤。
(D) 遲到。

道歉的理由可以從"I'm so sorry I didn't make it here by two"的敘述中找到。也就是說，因為遲到而道歉，所以(D)才是正確答案。

詞彙 lose track of time 沒有意識到時間

87.

演講者是誰？
(A) 館長。
(B) 雕刻家。

(C) 畫家。
(D) 設計師。

說話者說要談論展覽中的美術作品之後說了"While some are mine, there are many others crated by other highly talented individuals. "，由此可以看出美術作品的一部分是說話者所畫的，因此職業應該是(C)畫家。

88.

說話者之後會做什麼？
(A) 銷售產品。
(B) 安排參觀。
(C) 進行演示。
(D) 簽名。

在談話的後半部分，說話者說在解釋作品中的創意後一起參觀展示中的作品(I'll give everyone a tour of the works on display)，因此說話者會做的事情是(B)。

[89-91]

M Hello. This is Greg Anderson. I'm sorry that I cannot answer your call at this time. Currently, I'm on a business trip in Asia and won't be back in the country until next Tuesday, April 11. If you have an urgent need to speak with me, please contact me online. I'll be checking my e-mail at least three times a day, so I'll be able to get back to you fairly quickly. If you require the services of someone in the office, please dial extension 77 right now. You'll be connected to Ruth Duncan, who can assist you with whatever you want.

M 您好，我是Greg Anderson。很遺憾我現在無法接電話。我現在正在亞洲出差，下週二4月11日以後會回到國內。若有事需要緊急聯絡我的話，請在線上與我聯繫。我每天至少會確認三次電子郵件，所以能夠在短時間內回覆。如果辦公室內有人需要幫助，請立即撥打內線號碼77，與Ruth Duncan連接後，想要什麼她都會幫助你。

詞彙 at this time 現在，此時 urgent 緊急的 at least 至少，最少的 fairly 相當地，頗為 extension 內線號碼 right now 現在馬上 connect 連接

89.

信息的目的是什麼？
(A) 為了告知電子郵件地址。
(B) 為了說明。
(C) 為了請求聽者再打一次電話。
(D) 為了重新確認約定時間。

這是告知不在的語音信箱留言。說話者說明了自己的出差日程、可以聯繫自己的方法，以及在辦公室內可以獲得幫助的方法等，因此信息的目的可以看作是(B)。

90.

Greg Anderson在哪裡？
(A) 度假地。
(B) 海外。
(C) 預約看診的醫院。
(D) 親戚家。

Greg Anderson是此則留言的當事人，從"I'm on a business trip in Asia and won't be back in the country until next Tuesday, April 11. " 所說的話來看，他現在可能在國外的亞洲，因此(B)是正確答案。

91.

關於Ruth Duncan，話者暗示了什麼？
(A) 她是同事。
(B) 她是實習員工。
(C) 她在工廠裡。
(D) 她會處理他的私人事務。

在談話的最後一句中，Ruth Duncan被介紹在辦公室內需要幫助時「能夠給予幫助的人(who can assist you with whatever you want)」。因此可以推測出她是說話者的同事，所以(A)是正確答案。

[92-94]

M	Good evening, everyone. This is Frank Allen with tonight's weather report. I'm sure most of you were expecting to hear Leslie Haynes, but she caught a cold so won't be with us for the next couple of days. Today's weather was pleasant with sunny skies and a high of twenty-eight degrees Celsius. We've got great news for the parade tomorrow as we can expect continued sunny weather with a high of twenty-seven degrees. The day after the parade, we'll be getting cloudy skies, and you should expect rain to fall on Friday. That's all for now. Let's go to Scott Schultz with local sports.
M	大家好。我是播報今天天氣的Frank Allen。相信大多數人都在期待著Leslie Haynes的新聞，但是她感冒了，所以接下來的兩天不能和我們一起了。今天我們會看到晴朗的天空，且氣溫會上升到28°C，感覺非常舒適。而晴朗天氣將會持續下去，因此對於明天的遊行來說是個好消息，預計最高氣溫為27度。到了遊行後一天可能會看到陰天，並且星期五會下雨。就目前而言，這就是全部了。接下來將會是告訴您當地體育的Scott Schultz。

詞彙 catch a cold 感冒 parade 行進，遊行 cloudy 多雲的，陰天

92.

關於Leslie Haynes，說話者說了什麼？
(A) 她辭掉了工作。
(B) 她現在生病了。
(C) 她即將傳達消息。
(D) 她將會參加遊行。

在談話的前半段，說明了有一位叫Leslie Haynes的人「因為感冒，大概會有兩天左右不能播報新聞了(she caught a cold so won't be with us for the next couple of days)」，所以正確答案是(B)。

詞彙 resign 辭職 give a report 報告，報導

93.

遊行當天天氣會怎麼樣？
(A) 會是陰天。
(B) 會是晴天。
(C) 會下雨。
(D) 將會起風。

說話者告知說「有一個為了明天遊行帶來的好消息(great news for the parade tomorrow)」後，表示預計會是「持續晴朗的天氣(continued sunny weather)」。因此，預計遊行的天氣會是晴朗的，所以正確答案是(B)。

94.

當說話者說"That's all for now"時，表示什麼？
(A) 接下來將會出現廣告。
(B) 將會播放音樂。
(C) 自己的報導結束了。
(D) 新聞廣播將要結束。

給定的句子意思為「到目前為止，那是全部了」，是某件事情在作結尾時經常能聽到的表達。如果預料到說話者是主播或是記者的話，那麼就可以知道最後給出的句子其意思就是(C)。

[95-97]

講師	主題	時間
Glenn Harper	業務規程	1:00 – 1:50 P.M.
Tanya Radcliffe	角色扮演活動	2:00 – 2:50 P.M.
Maria Wills	國際法	3:00 – 3:50 P.M.
Jessica Dane	Q&A 時間	4:00 – 4:50 P.M.
Teresa Jones	小組活動	5:00 – 5:50 P.M.

W	I hope everyone found the activity with Mr. Harper you just had to be informative. As you are aware, he's got more than three decades of business experience, so he really knows what he's talking about. Now, it's time for me to work with you for the next fifty minutes. We're going to take the knowledge you learned and practice using it in various situations. So we'll do some role-playing activities for the first half hour. Then, we'll discuss what happened during those activities and provide feedback. So let's get started by dividing into groups of four. Would everyone please look at page one of the handout I gave you?
W	希望剛才和Harper先生進行的活動能對大家有益。大家應該都知道，他擁有30年以上的經歷，所以他對於他說的內容是真的很了解。好的，接下來的50分鐘我會和大家在一起，讓大家在各種情況下練習活用剛才學習到的知識。因此在最初30分鐘裡將會開始角色扮演活動。接下來我們將會討論在這些活動中發生了什麼事情，並對此交換意見。那就分成四個小組開始吧。請大家看一下我發下去的印刷品第1頁好嗎？

詞彙 informative 給予情報的，有益的 decade 10年 knowledge 知識 practice 練習 various 多樣的 role-playing 角色扮演 feedback 反應，回饋 divide 分開 handout 印刷品

95.

請看圖，演講人是誰？

(A) Tanya Radcliffe

(B) Maria Willa

(C) Jessica Dane

(D) Teresa Jones

說話者是在Harper先生之後擔任演講的演說者，從圖表中的Speaker 項目可以看出(A)的Tanya Radcliffe是說話者的名字。考慮到說話者將進行角色扮演活動這一點的話，也可以通過主題確認說話者的名字。

96.

演講期間聽眾們將會做什麼？

(A) 閱讀書籍。

(B) 相互反饋。

(C) 口頭發表。

(D) 收看簡短的影片。

在談話的後半部分，說話者在自己演講的時間裡進行角色扮演活動之後會「討論其結果，並交換反饋意見(we'll discuss what happened during those activities and provide feedback)」，因此聽眾要做的事情是(B)。

詞彙 one another 相互 oral 口頭的，口述的

97.

說話者要聽者做什麼？

(A) 擅長筆記。

(B) 填寫文件。

(C) 自我介紹。

(D) 分組。

在談話後半部分，說話者說"So let's get started by dividing into groups of four."提議組成4組。因此(D)是正確答案。

詞彙 take notes 摘記，記筆記 fill out 填寫(表格)

[98-100]

Martindale先生的下午配送業務	
顧客	**地址**
Henry Voss	Cleverdale 路 584 號
Judith Smith	Anderson 路 90 號
Karen Winkler	State 街 291 號
Peter Duncan	Washington 路 73 號

M Hello, Karen. This is Jake Martindale. I've got a delivery for Ms. Winkler, but there's a bit of a problem. I'm standing outside her house right now, but there's nobody home. According to the instructions I was given, I'm supposed to deliver her new couch at 1:30. I'm not sure what I should do. I can't leave it outside, and I can't stay here for too long because I have some other deliveries to make. I tried dialing the number she left, but the phone has been turned off. Would you please call me back at once to tell me what to do?

M 你好，Karen，我是Jake Martindale。我有快遞要給Winkler 小姐，但出了點問題，我現在在她家外面，但家裡沒人。根據我收到的指示，我要在一點半配送新沙發，但我不知道我該怎麼辦。我不能放在外面，也不能待在這裡那麼久，因為我還得配送其他物品。我嘗試撥打她留下的號碼，但電話卻關機了。現在可以回電給我，告訴我該怎麼辦嗎？

詞彙 delivery 投遞，配送 couch 沙發，長椅 turn off 關掉(電源) at once 立刻，馬上

98.

請看圖，說話者現在在在哪裡？

(A) Cloverdale路584號。

(B) Anderson路90號。

(C) State街291號。

(D) Washington街73號。

透過談話的前半部分內容可以看出說話者在Winkler小姐的家門口。從圖表中找到她的地址，就知道現在說話者所在的位置是(C)。

99.

說話者是如何聯絡顧客的？

(A) 電話。

(B) 用簡訊。

(C) 用傳真。

(D) 透過電子郵件。

"I tried dialing the number she left, but the phone has been turned off."這句話中有正確答案的線索。因為說話者曾試圖打電話，所以(A) 是正確答案。

100.

說話者要求什麼？

(A) 發票。

(B) 現金結帳。

(C) 有關安裝的幫助。

(D) 口頭指示。

談話的最後一句是"Would you please call me back at once to tell me what to do?"，說話者正在拜託對方用電話下達指示，因此(D)是正確答案。

詞彙 verbal 口頭的，言語的

ANSWER SHEET

TOEIC TOEIC 實戰測試

裁切線

確認

准考證號碼

姓名

LISTENING COMPREHENSION (Part 1-4)

No.	ANSWER	No.	ANSWER	No.	ANSWER	No.	ANSWER	No.	ANSWER
1	Ⓐ Ⓑ Ⓒ Ⓓ	21	Ⓐ Ⓑ Ⓒ	41	Ⓐ Ⓑ Ⓒ Ⓓ	61	Ⓐ Ⓑ Ⓒ Ⓓ	81	Ⓐ Ⓑ Ⓒ Ⓓ
2	Ⓐ Ⓑ Ⓒ Ⓓ	22	Ⓐ Ⓑ Ⓒ	42	Ⓐ Ⓑ Ⓒ Ⓓ	62	Ⓐ Ⓑ Ⓒ Ⓓ	82	Ⓐ Ⓑ Ⓒ Ⓓ
3	Ⓐ Ⓑ Ⓒ Ⓓ	23	Ⓐ Ⓑ Ⓒ	43	Ⓐ Ⓑ Ⓒ Ⓓ	63	Ⓐ Ⓑ Ⓒ Ⓓ	83	Ⓐ Ⓑ Ⓒ Ⓓ
4	Ⓐ Ⓑ Ⓒ Ⓓ	24	Ⓐ Ⓑ Ⓒ	44	Ⓐ Ⓑ Ⓒ Ⓓ	64	Ⓐ Ⓑ Ⓒ Ⓓ	84	Ⓐ Ⓑ Ⓒ Ⓓ
5	Ⓐ Ⓑ Ⓒ Ⓓ	25	Ⓐ Ⓑ Ⓒ	45	Ⓐ Ⓑ Ⓒ Ⓓ	65	Ⓐ Ⓑ Ⓒ Ⓓ	85	Ⓐ Ⓑ Ⓒ Ⓓ
6	Ⓐ Ⓑ Ⓒ Ⓓ	26	Ⓐ Ⓑ Ⓒ	46	Ⓐ Ⓑ Ⓒ Ⓓ	66	Ⓐ Ⓑ Ⓒ Ⓓ	86	Ⓐ Ⓑ Ⓒ Ⓓ
7	Ⓐ Ⓑ Ⓒ	27	Ⓐ Ⓑ Ⓒ	47	Ⓐ Ⓑ Ⓒ Ⓓ	67	Ⓐ Ⓑ Ⓒ Ⓓ	87	Ⓐ Ⓑ Ⓒ Ⓓ
8	Ⓐ Ⓑ Ⓒ	28	Ⓐ Ⓑ Ⓒ	48	Ⓐ Ⓑ Ⓒ Ⓓ	68	Ⓐ Ⓑ Ⓒ Ⓓ	88	Ⓐ Ⓑ Ⓒ Ⓓ
9	Ⓐ Ⓑ Ⓒ	29	Ⓐ Ⓑ Ⓒ	49	Ⓐ Ⓑ Ⓒ Ⓓ	69	Ⓐ Ⓑ Ⓒ Ⓓ	89	Ⓐ Ⓑ Ⓒ Ⓓ
10	Ⓐ Ⓑ Ⓒ	30	Ⓐ Ⓑ Ⓒ	50	Ⓐ Ⓑ Ⓒ Ⓓ	70	Ⓐ Ⓑ Ⓒ Ⓓ	90	Ⓐ Ⓑ Ⓒ Ⓓ
11	Ⓐ Ⓑ Ⓒ	31	Ⓐ Ⓑ Ⓒ	51	Ⓐ Ⓑ Ⓒ Ⓓ	71	Ⓐ Ⓑ Ⓒ Ⓓ	91	Ⓐ Ⓑ Ⓒ Ⓓ
12	Ⓐ Ⓑ Ⓒ	32	Ⓐ Ⓑ Ⓒ	52	Ⓐ Ⓑ Ⓒ Ⓓ	72	Ⓐ Ⓑ Ⓒ Ⓓ	92	Ⓐ Ⓑ Ⓒ Ⓓ
13	Ⓐ Ⓑ Ⓒ	33	Ⓐ Ⓑ Ⓒ	53	Ⓐ Ⓑ Ⓒ Ⓓ	73	Ⓐ Ⓑ Ⓒ Ⓓ	93	Ⓐ Ⓑ Ⓒ Ⓓ
14	Ⓐ Ⓑ Ⓒ	34	Ⓐ Ⓑ Ⓒ	54	Ⓐ Ⓑ Ⓒ Ⓓ	74	Ⓐ Ⓑ Ⓒ Ⓓ	94	Ⓐ Ⓑ Ⓒ Ⓓ
15	Ⓐ Ⓑ Ⓒ	35	Ⓐ Ⓑ Ⓒ	55	Ⓐ Ⓑ Ⓒ Ⓓ	75	Ⓐ Ⓑ Ⓒ Ⓓ	95	Ⓐ Ⓑ Ⓒ Ⓓ
16	Ⓐ Ⓑ Ⓒ	36	Ⓐ Ⓑ Ⓒ	56	Ⓐ Ⓑ Ⓒ Ⓓ	76	Ⓐ Ⓑ Ⓒ Ⓓ	96	Ⓐ Ⓑ Ⓒ Ⓓ
17	Ⓐ Ⓑ Ⓒ	37	Ⓐ Ⓑ Ⓒ	57	Ⓐ Ⓑ Ⓒ Ⓓ	77	Ⓐ Ⓑ Ⓒ Ⓓ	97	Ⓐ Ⓑ Ⓒ Ⓓ
18	Ⓐ Ⓑ Ⓒ	38	Ⓐ Ⓑ Ⓒ	58	Ⓐ Ⓑ Ⓒ Ⓓ	78	Ⓐ Ⓑ Ⓒ Ⓓ	98	Ⓐ Ⓑ Ⓒ Ⓓ
19	Ⓐ Ⓑ Ⓒ	39	Ⓐ Ⓑ Ⓒ	59	Ⓐ Ⓑ Ⓒ Ⓓ	79	Ⓐ Ⓑ Ⓒ Ⓓ	99	Ⓐ Ⓑ Ⓒ Ⓓ
20	Ⓐ Ⓑ Ⓒ	40	Ⓐ Ⓑ Ⓒ	60	Ⓐ Ⓑ Ⓒ Ⓓ	80	Ⓐ Ⓑ Ⓒ Ⓓ	100	Ⓐ Ⓑ Ⓒ Ⓓ

READING COMPREHENSION (Part 5-7)

No.	ANSWER	No.	ANSWER	No.	ANSWER	No.	ANSWER	No.	ANSWER
101	Ⓐ Ⓑ Ⓒ Ⓓ	121	Ⓐ Ⓑ Ⓒ Ⓓ	141	Ⓐ Ⓑ Ⓒ Ⓓ	161	Ⓐ Ⓑ Ⓒ Ⓓ	181	Ⓐ Ⓑ Ⓒ Ⓓ
102	Ⓐ Ⓑ Ⓒ Ⓓ	122	Ⓐ Ⓑ Ⓒ Ⓓ	142	Ⓐ Ⓑ Ⓒ Ⓓ	162	Ⓐ Ⓑ Ⓒ Ⓓ	182	Ⓐ Ⓑ Ⓒ Ⓓ
103	Ⓐ Ⓑ Ⓒ Ⓓ	123	Ⓐ Ⓑ Ⓒ Ⓓ	143	Ⓐ Ⓑ Ⓒ Ⓓ	163	Ⓐ Ⓑ Ⓒ Ⓓ	183	Ⓐ Ⓑ Ⓒ Ⓓ
104	Ⓐ Ⓑ Ⓒ Ⓓ	124	Ⓐ Ⓑ Ⓒ Ⓓ	144	Ⓐ Ⓑ Ⓒ Ⓓ	164	Ⓐ Ⓑ Ⓒ Ⓓ	184	Ⓐ Ⓑ Ⓒ Ⓓ
105	Ⓐ Ⓑ Ⓒ Ⓓ	125	Ⓐ Ⓑ Ⓒ Ⓓ	145	Ⓐ Ⓑ Ⓒ Ⓓ	165	Ⓐ Ⓑ Ⓒ Ⓓ	185	Ⓐ Ⓑ Ⓒ Ⓓ
106	Ⓐ Ⓑ Ⓒ Ⓓ	126	Ⓐ Ⓑ Ⓒ Ⓓ	146	Ⓐ Ⓑ Ⓒ Ⓓ	166	Ⓐ Ⓑ Ⓒ Ⓓ	186	Ⓐ Ⓑ Ⓒ Ⓓ
107	Ⓐ Ⓑ Ⓒ Ⓓ	127	Ⓐ Ⓑ Ⓒ Ⓓ	147	Ⓐ Ⓑ Ⓒ Ⓓ	167	Ⓐ Ⓑ Ⓒ Ⓓ	187	Ⓐ Ⓑ Ⓒ Ⓓ
108	Ⓐ Ⓑ Ⓒ Ⓓ	128	Ⓐ Ⓑ Ⓒ Ⓓ	148	Ⓐ Ⓑ Ⓒ Ⓓ	168	Ⓐ Ⓑ Ⓒ Ⓓ	188	Ⓐ Ⓑ Ⓒ Ⓓ
109	Ⓐ Ⓑ Ⓒ Ⓓ	129	Ⓐ Ⓑ Ⓒ Ⓓ	149	Ⓐ Ⓑ Ⓒ Ⓓ	169	Ⓐ Ⓑ Ⓒ Ⓓ	189	Ⓐ Ⓑ Ⓒ Ⓓ
110	Ⓐ Ⓑ Ⓒ Ⓓ	130	Ⓐ Ⓑ Ⓒ Ⓓ	150	Ⓐ Ⓑ Ⓒ Ⓓ	170	Ⓐ Ⓑ Ⓒ Ⓓ	190	Ⓐ Ⓑ Ⓒ Ⓓ
111	Ⓐ Ⓑ Ⓒ Ⓓ	131	Ⓐ Ⓑ Ⓒ Ⓓ	151	Ⓐ Ⓑ Ⓒ Ⓓ	171	Ⓐ Ⓑ Ⓒ Ⓓ	191	Ⓐ Ⓑ Ⓒ Ⓓ
112	Ⓐ Ⓑ Ⓒ Ⓓ	132	Ⓐ Ⓑ Ⓒ Ⓓ	152	Ⓐ Ⓑ Ⓒ Ⓓ	172	Ⓐ Ⓑ Ⓒ Ⓓ	192	Ⓐ Ⓑ Ⓒ Ⓓ
113	Ⓐ Ⓑ Ⓒ Ⓓ	133	Ⓐ Ⓑ Ⓒ Ⓓ	153	Ⓐ Ⓑ Ⓒ Ⓓ	173	Ⓐ Ⓑ Ⓒ Ⓓ	193	Ⓐ Ⓑ Ⓒ Ⓓ
114	Ⓐ Ⓑ Ⓒ Ⓓ	134	Ⓐ Ⓑ Ⓒ Ⓓ	154	Ⓐ Ⓑ Ⓒ Ⓓ	174	Ⓐ Ⓑ Ⓒ Ⓓ	194	Ⓐ Ⓑ Ⓒ Ⓓ
115	Ⓐ Ⓑ Ⓒ Ⓓ	135	Ⓐ Ⓑ Ⓒ Ⓓ	155	Ⓐ Ⓑ Ⓒ Ⓓ	175	Ⓐ Ⓑ Ⓒ Ⓓ	195	Ⓐ Ⓑ Ⓒ Ⓓ
116	Ⓐ Ⓑ Ⓒ Ⓓ	136	Ⓐ Ⓑ Ⓒ Ⓓ	156	Ⓐ Ⓑ Ⓒ Ⓓ	176	Ⓐ Ⓑ Ⓒ Ⓓ	196	Ⓐ Ⓑ Ⓒ Ⓓ
117	Ⓐ Ⓑ Ⓒ Ⓓ	137	Ⓐ Ⓑ Ⓒ Ⓓ	157	Ⓐ Ⓑ Ⓒ Ⓓ	177	Ⓐ Ⓑ Ⓒ Ⓓ	197	Ⓐ Ⓑ Ⓒ Ⓓ
118	Ⓐ Ⓑ Ⓒ Ⓓ	138	Ⓐ Ⓑ Ⓒ Ⓓ	158	Ⓐ Ⓑ Ⓒ Ⓓ	178	Ⓐ Ⓑ Ⓒ Ⓓ	198	Ⓐ Ⓑ Ⓒ Ⓓ
119	Ⓐ Ⓑ Ⓒ Ⓓ	139	Ⓐ Ⓑ Ⓒ Ⓓ	159	Ⓐ Ⓑ Ⓒ Ⓓ	179	Ⓐ Ⓑ Ⓒ Ⓓ	199	Ⓐ Ⓑ Ⓒ Ⓓ
120	Ⓐ Ⓑ Ⓒ Ⓓ	140	Ⓐ Ⓑ Ⓒ Ⓓ	160	Ⓐ Ⓑ Ⓒ Ⓓ	180	Ⓐ Ⓑ Ⓒ Ⓓ	200	Ⓐ Ⓑ Ⓒ Ⓓ

ANSWER SHEET

TOEIC TOEIC實戰測試

准考證號碼

姓名

確認

LISTENING COMPREHENSION (Part 1-4)

No.	ANSWER	No.	ANSWER	No.	ANSWER	No.	ANSWER	No.	ANSWER
1	Ⓐ Ⓑ Ⓒ Ⓓ	21	Ⓐ Ⓑ Ⓒ	41	Ⓐ Ⓑ Ⓒ Ⓓ	61	Ⓐ Ⓑ Ⓒ Ⓓ	81	Ⓐ Ⓑ Ⓒ Ⓓ
2	Ⓐ Ⓑ Ⓒ Ⓓ	22	Ⓐ Ⓑ Ⓒ	42	Ⓐ Ⓑ Ⓒ Ⓓ	62	Ⓐ Ⓑ Ⓒ Ⓓ	82	Ⓐ Ⓑ Ⓒ Ⓓ
3	Ⓐ Ⓑ Ⓒ Ⓓ	23	Ⓐ Ⓑ Ⓒ	43	Ⓐ Ⓑ Ⓒ Ⓓ	63	Ⓐ Ⓑ Ⓒ Ⓓ	83	Ⓐ Ⓑ Ⓒ Ⓓ
4	Ⓐ Ⓑ Ⓒ Ⓓ	24	Ⓐ Ⓑ Ⓒ	44	Ⓐ Ⓑ Ⓒ Ⓓ	64	Ⓐ Ⓑ Ⓒ Ⓓ	84	Ⓐ Ⓑ Ⓒ Ⓓ
5	Ⓐ Ⓑ Ⓒ Ⓓ	25	Ⓐ Ⓑ Ⓒ	45	Ⓐ Ⓑ Ⓒ Ⓓ	65	Ⓐ Ⓑ Ⓒ Ⓓ	85	Ⓐ Ⓑ Ⓒ Ⓓ
6	Ⓐ Ⓑ Ⓒ Ⓓ	26	Ⓐ Ⓑ Ⓒ	46	Ⓐ Ⓑ Ⓒ Ⓓ	66	Ⓐ Ⓑ Ⓒ Ⓓ	86	Ⓐ Ⓑ Ⓒ Ⓓ
7	Ⓐ Ⓑ Ⓒ Ⓓ	27	Ⓐ Ⓑ Ⓒ	47	Ⓐ Ⓑ Ⓒ Ⓓ	67	Ⓐ Ⓑ Ⓒ Ⓓ	87	Ⓐ Ⓑ Ⓒ Ⓓ
8	Ⓐ Ⓑ Ⓒ Ⓓ	28	Ⓐ Ⓑ Ⓒ	48	Ⓐ Ⓑ Ⓒ Ⓓ	68	Ⓐ Ⓑ Ⓒ Ⓓ	88	Ⓐ Ⓑ Ⓒ Ⓓ
9	Ⓐ Ⓑ Ⓒ	29	Ⓐ Ⓑ Ⓒ	49	Ⓐ Ⓑ Ⓒ Ⓓ	69	Ⓐ Ⓑ Ⓒ Ⓓ	89	Ⓐ Ⓑ Ⓒ Ⓓ
10	Ⓐ Ⓑ Ⓒ	30	Ⓐ Ⓑ Ⓒ Ⓓ	50	Ⓐ Ⓑ Ⓒ Ⓓ	70	Ⓐ Ⓑ Ⓒ Ⓓ	90	Ⓐ Ⓑ Ⓒ Ⓓ
11	Ⓐ Ⓑ Ⓒ	31	Ⓐ Ⓑ Ⓒ Ⓓ	51	Ⓐ Ⓑ Ⓒ Ⓓ	71	Ⓐ Ⓑ Ⓒ Ⓓ	91	Ⓐ Ⓑ Ⓒ Ⓓ
12	Ⓐ Ⓑ Ⓒ	32	Ⓐ Ⓑ Ⓒ Ⓓ	52	Ⓐ Ⓑ Ⓒ Ⓓ	72	Ⓐ Ⓑ Ⓒ Ⓓ	92	Ⓐ Ⓑ Ⓒ Ⓓ
13	Ⓐ Ⓑ Ⓒ	33	Ⓐ Ⓑ Ⓒ Ⓓ	53	Ⓐ Ⓑ Ⓒ Ⓓ	73	Ⓐ Ⓑ Ⓒ Ⓓ	93	Ⓐ Ⓑ Ⓒ Ⓓ
14	Ⓐ Ⓑ Ⓒ	34	Ⓐ Ⓑ Ⓒ Ⓓ	54	Ⓐ Ⓑ Ⓒ Ⓓ	74	Ⓐ Ⓑ Ⓒ Ⓓ	94	Ⓐ Ⓑ Ⓒ Ⓓ
15	Ⓐ Ⓑ Ⓒ	35	Ⓐ Ⓑ Ⓒ Ⓓ	55	Ⓐ Ⓑ Ⓒ Ⓓ	75	Ⓐ Ⓑ Ⓒ Ⓓ	95	Ⓐ Ⓑ Ⓒ Ⓓ
16	Ⓐ Ⓑ Ⓒ	36	Ⓐ Ⓑ Ⓒ Ⓓ	56	Ⓐ Ⓑ Ⓒ Ⓓ	76	Ⓐ Ⓑ Ⓒ Ⓓ	96	Ⓐ Ⓑ Ⓒ Ⓓ
17	Ⓐ Ⓑ Ⓒ	37	Ⓐ Ⓑ Ⓒ Ⓓ	57	Ⓐ Ⓑ Ⓒ Ⓓ	77	Ⓐ Ⓑ Ⓒ Ⓓ	97	Ⓐ Ⓑ Ⓒ Ⓓ
18	Ⓐ Ⓑ Ⓒ	38	Ⓐ Ⓑ Ⓒ Ⓓ	58	Ⓐ Ⓑ Ⓒ Ⓓ	78	Ⓐ Ⓑ Ⓒ Ⓓ	98	Ⓐ Ⓑ Ⓒ Ⓓ
19	Ⓐ Ⓑ Ⓒ	39	Ⓐ Ⓑ Ⓒ Ⓓ	59	Ⓐ Ⓑ Ⓒ Ⓓ	79	Ⓐ Ⓑ Ⓒ Ⓓ	99	Ⓐ Ⓑ Ⓒ Ⓓ
20	Ⓐ Ⓑ Ⓒ	40	Ⓐ Ⓑ Ⓒ Ⓓ	60	Ⓐ Ⓑ Ⓒ Ⓓ	80	Ⓐ Ⓑ Ⓒ Ⓓ	100	Ⓐ Ⓑ Ⓒ Ⓓ

READING COMPREHENSION (Part 5-7)

No.	ANSWER	No.	ANSWER	No.	ANSWER	No.	ANSWER	No.	ANSWER
101	Ⓐ Ⓑ Ⓒ Ⓓ	121	Ⓐ Ⓑ Ⓒ Ⓓ	141	Ⓐ Ⓑ Ⓒ Ⓓ	161	Ⓐ Ⓑ Ⓒ Ⓓ	181	Ⓐ Ⓑ Ⓒ Ⓓ
102	Ⓐ Ⓑ Ⓒ Ⓓ	122	Ⓐ Ⓑ Ⓒ Ⓓ	142	Ⓐ Ⓑ Ⓒ Ⓓ	162	Ⓐ Ⓑ Ⓒ Ⓓ	182	Ⓐ Ⓑ Ⓒ Ⓓ
103	Ⓐ Ⓑ Ⓒ Ⓓ	123	Ⓐ Ⓑ Ⓒ Ⓓ	143	Ⓐ Ⓑ Ⓒ Ⓓ	163	Ⓐ Ⓑ Ⓒ Ⓓ	183	Ⓐ Ⓑ Ⓒ Ⓓ
104	Ⓐ Ⓑ Ⓒ Ⓓ	124	Ⓐ Ⓑ Ⓒ Ⓓ	144	Ⓐ Ⓑ Ⓒ Ⓓ	164	Ⓐ Ⓑ Ⓒ Ⓓ	184	Ⓐ Ⓑ Ⓒ Ⓓ
105	Ⓐ Ⓑ Ⓒ Ⓓ	125	Ⓐ Ⓑ Ⓒ Ⓓ	145	Ⓐ Ⓑ Ⓒ Ⓓ	165	Ⓐ Ⓑ Ⓒ Ⓓ	185	Ⓐ Ⓑ Ⓒ Ⓓ
106	Ⓐ Ⓑ Ⓒ Ⓓ	126	Ⓐ Ⓑ Ⓒ Ⓓ	146	Ⓐ Ⓑ Ⓒ Ⓓ	166	Ⓐ Ⓑ Ⓒ Ⓓ	186	Ⓐ Ⓑ Ⓒ Ⓓ
107	Ⓐ Ⓑ Ⓒ Ⓓ	127	Ⓐ Ⓑ Ⓒ Ⓓ	147	Ⓐ Ⓑ Ⓒ Ⓓ	167	Ⓐ Ⓑ Ⓒ Ⓓ	187	Ⓐ Ⓑ Ⓒ Ⓓ
108	Ⓐ Ⓑ Ⓒ Ⓓ	128	Ⓐ Ⓑ Ⓒ Ⓓ	148	Ⓐ Ⓑ Ⓒ Ⓓ	168	Ⓐ Ⓑ Ⓒ Ⓓ	188	Ⓐ Ⓑ Ⓒ Ⓓ
109	Ⓐ Ⓑ Ⓒ Ⓓ	129	Ⓐ Ⓑ Ⓒ Ⓓ	149	Ⓐ Ⓑ Ⓒ Ⓓ	169	Ⓐ Ⓑ Ⓒ Ⓓ	189	Ⓐ Ⓑ Ⓒ Ⓓ
110	Ⓐ Ⓑ Ⓒ Ⓓ	130	Ⓐ Ⓑ Ⓒ Ⓓ	150	Ⓐ Ⓑ Ⓒ Ⓓ	170	Ⓐ Ⓑ Ⓒ Ⓓ	190	Ⓐ Ⓑ Ⓒ Ⓓ
111	Ⓐ Ⓑ Ⓒ Ⓓ	131	Ⓐ Ⓑ Ⓒ Ⓓ	151	Ⓐ Ⓑ Ⓒ Ⓓ	171	Ⓐ Ⓑ Ⓒ Ⓓ	191	Ⓐ Ⓑ Ⓒ Ⓓ
112	Ⓐ Ⓑ Ⓒ Ⓓ	132	Ⓐ Ⓑ Ⓒ Ⓓ	152	Ⓐ Ⓑ Ⓒ Ⓓ	172	Ⓐ Ⓑ Ⓒ Ⓓ	192	Ⓐ Ⓑ Ⓒ Ⓓ
113	Ⓐ Ⓑ Ⓒ Ⓓ	133	Ⓐ Ⓑ Ⓒ Ⓓ	153	Ⓐ Ⓑ Ⓒ Ⓓ	173	Ⓐ Ⓑ Ⓒ Ⓓ	193	Ⓐ Ⓑ Ⓒ Ⓓ
114	Ⓐ Ⓑ Ⓒ Ⓓ	134	Ⓐ Ⓑ Ⓒ Ⓓ	154	Ⓐ Ⓑ Ⓒ Ⓓ	174	Ⓐ Ⓑ Ⓒ Ⓓ	194	Ⓐ Ⓑ Ⓒ Ⓓ
115	Ⓐ Ⓑ Ⓒ Ⓓ	135	Ⓐ Ⓑ Ⓒ Ⓓ	155	Ⓐ Ⓑ Ⓒ Ⓓ	175	Ⓐ Ⓑ Ⓒ Ⓓ	195	Ⓐ Ⓑ Ⓒ Ⓓ
116	Ⓐ Ⓑ Ⓒ Ⓓ	136	Ⓐ Ⓑ Ⓒ Ⓓ	156	Ⓐ Ⓑ Ⓒ Ⓓ	176	Ⓐ Ⓑ Ⓒ Ⓓ	196	Ⓐ Ⓑ Ⓒ Ⓓ
117	Ⓐ Ⓑ Ⓒ Ⓓ	137	Ⓐ Ⓑ Ⓒ Ⓓ	157	Ⓐ Ⓑ Ⓒ Ⓓ	177	Ⓐ Ⓑ Ⓒ Ⓓ	197	Ⓐ Ⓑ Ⓒ Ⓓ
118	Ⓐ Ⓑ Ⓒ Ⓓ	138	Ⓐ Ⓑ Ⓒ Ⓓ	158	Ⓐ Ⓑ Ⓒ Ⓓ	178	Ⓐ Ⓑ Ⓒ Ⓓ	198	Ⓐ Ⓑ Ⓒ Ⓓ
119	Ⓐ Ⓑ Ⓒ Ⓓ	139	Ⓐ Ⓑ Ⓒ Ⓓ	159	Ⓐ Ⓑ Ⓒ Ⓓ	179	Ⓐ Ⓑ Ⓒ Ⓓ	199	Ⓐ Ⓑ Ⓒ Ⓓ
120	Ⓐ Ⓑ Ⓒ Ⓓ	140	Ⓐ Ⓑ Ⓒ Ⓓ	160	Ⓐ Ⓑ Ⓒ Ⓓ	180	Ⓐ Ⓑ Ⓒ Ⓓ	200	Ⓐ Ⓑ Ⓒ Ⓓ

NEW TOEIC 新制多益

TOEIC

聽力 **5** 回

全真模擬試題 ＋ 詳盡解析

★★★ 解析本 ★★★